RAINY LAKE

RAINY LAKE

Mary François Rockcastle

A Novel

To Charmagne —
For the power of
memory, water, and the
patient stars.

Mary F. Rockcastle

GRAYWOLF PRESS, SAINT PAUL

Publication of this volume is made possible in part by a grant provided by the
Minnesota State Arts Board through an appropriation by the Minnesota State
Legislature, and by a grant from the National Endowment for the Arts.
Significant additional support has been provided by the Andrew W. Mellon
Foundation, the Lila Wallace-Reader's Digest Fund, the McKnight
Foundation, and other generous contributions from foundations, corporations,
and individuals. Graywolf Press is a member agency of United Arts, Saint Paul.
To these organizations and individuals who make our work possible,
we offer heartfelt thanks.

Published by Graywolf Press
2402 University Avenue, Suite 203
Saint Paul, Minnesota 55114

9 8 7 6 5 4 3 2
First Graywolf Printing, 1994

Library of Congress Cataloguing-in-Publication Data
Rockcastle, Mary François, 1952–
Rainy Lake : a novel / Mary François Rockcastle.
p.   cm.
ISBN 1-55597-218-7 : $22.50
1. Summer resorts—New Jersey—Fiction. 2. Family—New Jersey—
Fiction. 3. Girls—New Jersey—Fiction. I. Title.
PS3568.0333R35   1994
813'.54–dc20   94-29928
                                                                      CIP

ACKNOWLEDGMENTS

I WOULD NOT BE A WRITER TODAY, NOR WOULD THIS book have been published, without the support and encouragement of numerous individuals and organizations. My gratitude to them is boundless.

Heartfelt thanks to the following people, whose invaluable feedback, friendship, and example have encouraged and nurtured me: Deborah Keenan, Alexs Pate, Patricia Weaver Francisco, Sandra Benitez, Judith Katz, Jill Breckenridge, Julie Landsman, and Randy Garber. Thanks also to Susan Sencer, Mary Lu Schmiedlin, Janice Post-White, Robert Blum, Gary Schalge, and David Mura, who helped me in my research for the novel. Thanks to Alan Burns, my first mentor and teacher, for all his early lessons.

My gratitude to The Loft, an organization that has supported my efforts as a writer for over fifteen years. Thanks also to the Ragdale Foundation, where I wrote the first chapters of this novel, to the McKnight Foundation and the Bush Foundation for their generous financial support and for their recognition of my worth as a writer.

Thanks to Anne Czarniecki, for her belief in my novel and for her careful editing of the manuscript. To Scott Walker, my gratitude for sending this book out into the world. Thanks to the board and staff of Graywolf Press, particularly to Gordon Thomas and Janna Rademacher, who have stood steadfastly behind this book. My warmest thanks to Diane Katsiaficas for her inspired artwork that graces the cover.

My love and gratitude to my husband, Garth Rockcastle, who provided not only the financial means for me to continue writing, but a standard of excellence for me to follow. I give thanks to and for my daughters, Maura and Siobhan, for giving me a reason to persevere.

This novel is dedicated to the memory of my parents, Mary and Eugene François, who taught me to dream and to believe in the wonder of all that is known and unknown.

Every year
everything
I have ever learned

in my lifetime
leads back to this: the fires
and the black river of loss
whose other side

is salvation,
whose meaning
none of us will ever know.
To live in this world

you must be able
to do three things:
to love what is mortal;
to hold it

against your bones knowing
your own life depends on it,
and, when the time comes to let it go,
to let it go.

from "In Blackwater Woods"
Mary Oliver

. . . so in love the heart surrenders itself entirely to
the one being that has known how to touch it.

The Life of Reason
George Santayana

For Mary and Eugene François

RAINY LAKE

For each of us there is a memory, a flash so bright that it erases everything but this: water, and the passage of a small boat beneath a bridge. It has taken fifteen years for me to put words to this. Words are, in the end, what I have. They are the invisible gift my brother saw in me, long before I saw it myself.

This isn't just about us—my brother and me and our parents—how we started out with such grace and steered right into the eye of the hurricane. It's about Billy Dove as well, who taught me the important things: fly-fishing on the Virgin River, being a white girl, and trusting my naked self. Carline's here, and Terese, and the men who drifted in and out of the Pink Elephant on Saturday afternoons. Behind everything is the lake, its presence more than music, its smell as sweet as a brown boy's skin. And the house, of course, that lopsided day-dream my father poured his best self into until he ran dry.

I was eleven years old, Bryan thirteen, the year my parents bought the property at Rainy Lake. They paid six thousand dollars for it, believing with all their hearts that they were buying not only a summer home but a piece of the American dream.

THE HOUSE (1963)

I DON'T REMEMBER EVER SEEING THE LOG CABIN before that day. What I do remember is my *father's* house, the white one on the point, that tiny knob of land that lay like a man's thumb at the mouth of Catfish Cove. You could see it if you stood in the middle of the suspension bridge, which was the artery that linked one side of Rainy Lake to another. *That* was the house my father wanted, the only one on Rainy we thought was worthy of him.

My father, Charlie Fillian, is an architect. In those years he was still trying to realize the picture he carried in his head, a picture shiny with promise and audacious dreams. It didn't matter that the house on the point wasn't for sale, that we couldn't have afforded it if it were. My father had his fantasies, same as any other man. So each year we followed him across the bridge, tentative and respectful, as if we were making the discovery for the first time. He always stopped in the dead center of the bridge, where the loss of equilibrium was the greatest.

"See, May," he'd say to my mother as he rested his arms on the taupe-colored wood of the railing. "Now, *that's* a house. See how well-proportioned it is, how true the lines are, what a view you'd get from those windows. You wouldn't hear all the noise from the beach. And just look how the trees screen the traffic from the highway."

I'd look up, drawn by the sparkle in his voice, the way his gray eyes shone like the new agate I'd found underneath the clubhouse steps. His hands fluttered in that funny way they did whenever he was most excited. I loved seeing him like that, all charged up and hopeful.

1

My brother Bryan would swing himself up onto the railing, one arm looped around a black cable, and study the blue water. "They say there's a catfish in the Cove that weighs over five pounds. We could catch it if we lived there, couldn't we, Dad?"

My mother would flash a placating smile and close her small hand around Bryan's ankle.

This day, however, as we swayed clumsily in the center of the bridge, my mother pointed to a FOR SALE sign tacked onto a large oak tree. I followed the rickety wooden steps to a tall, narrow log cabin, its sloping front porch held aloft with stilts.

"You've got to be kidding, May." My father's head swiveled around to her. "That house is going to end up in the lake someday."

"Look at the windows, Mom," Bryan said. "They're all crooked."

"That's because the house has settled. Not good, May. Those logs are probably riddled with termites, too."

I shook my head, knowing what would happen when my father or brother took that condescending tone with my mother. She lifted her head high on her neck and elbowed past them.

"Come on, Danny, let's have a look."

I followed her round body across the bridge and through the swinging gate attached to a green boathouse. The next property, the second house in from the gate, was the one for sale. May stood on a flagstone in the overgrown lot and surveyed the undeveloped patio by the water and the half-submerged dock. Directly across the lake stood the Pink Elephant Bar and Grill and next to that, Sal and Joey's General Store. Through the arch of the suspension bridge we could see the main beach and clubhouse. Whoever lived here would be smack in the middle of Rainy Lake.

"Let's go up," she said.

The railings swayed beneath my hand as we climbed the rotting steps to the porch. May reached through a jagged tear in the screen door and unhooked it. The bottom of the door scraped along the floor.

"Needs to be planed," she said.

"Mom, what if someone *lives* here?"

"I asked. A woman at the beach said it's been vacant for several years."

The door into the kitchen was locked. Undeterred, May sailed out the door on the other side of the porch and walked slowly along a shuddery catwalk that ran along the south side of the house.

"Aha!" She pointed triumphantly to a broken pane in one of the windows.

"Climb on the railing, Danny, and reach inside. See if you can unlock it. Don't cut yourself."

I was smaller than most eleven-year-old girls, but I could climb anything. In fact, shimmying up the parts of trees without branches was my specialty. I grabbed onto the end of a log for support, stood on the railing, and slipped my arm through the opening. The latch was as wobbly as the rest of the house and came undone easily. I ducked as the window creaked open.

"Now climb inside and open the back door."

With my mother's two hands on my backside pushing up, I hoisted myself onto the sill and dropped to the floor. It was hot and musty and deadly quiet. I blinked, thinking of the house on the Thousand Islands, the big one the rich man had built for his new bride, except that she died right after they were married and he abandoned it, leaving the house huge and unfinished, filled with his grief and their broken dreams. Who had owned this house? Had they been happy, or had something awful happened, causing them to flee, leaving behind their furniture and all these books, shelf upon shelf rambling across one wall in an endless chain?

When I stepped forward I heard over my head a loud scratching and a high-pitched squeak. I brushed one hand over my hair and shuddered when I touched something hard, flakes of brown paint from the window casing.

"Danny!" Behind the black pot-bellied stove was my mother's face peering in from the window next to the door.

The door stuck and it took my pulling and her pushing to get it opened. When it lunged forward, my mother spilled inside with it.

"What's the matter?" she asked.

I pointed to the top of the stone fireplace. "Listen."

She tilted her head toward the noise. "It must be an animal that's nested up there. Or maybe there's something caught in the chimney."

My mother circled the room, fingering the spines of books, a white porcelain pitcher on the mantelpiece, the black knobby andirons in front of the fireplace that left a sooty smudge on her fingertips. I turned the tiny key in the lock of an antique secretary and swung the door down. The compartments were full: pads of white notepaper, a fountain pen and bottle of black ink, paper clips and a paper knife, sheets of music.

"Oh, Danny," my mother whispered from the middle of the room. "It reminds me of the fireplace in that cottage in the Adirondacks your grandfather used to take us to."

As I remember her face, her perfect skin and inky blue eyes, I can see it all: May sweeping through the house like a tornado, cleaning and polishing, putting new slipcovers on the homey couches, red-checked curtains on the windows, a fresh coat of sunshine yellow on the walls of the sleeping porch, and white chenille bedspreads on the iron beds. I can see my own reflection in the gleaming brass pipes and fittings on the pot-bellied stove. It didn't matter that the floor tilted downhill, that the windows had to be pried open from their lopsided casings, that the roof probably leaked, and that who-knew-what was living behind the walls of the house.

"It has a feeling to it, Danny, as if we already belong. And just *think* what your father will be able to do with it."

The screen door banged open, and there in a square of sunshine stood my father and brother. As I watched Charlie's blinking, unsuspecting face, I felt a flutter of tenderness for him. I knew he didn't want this crooked, deteriorating house and that the fight yet to be fought was probably futile. He walked across the room and stopped. At first I thought it was the noise from behind the fireplace, but then I realized it was my mother's face that had caught him. He looked from her to me, his eyes searching for steady ground.

"Imagine, Charlie," May said, walking forward and winding her arm around his. "This place all cleaned up, a fire, the children in bed on the sleeping porch. It's like starting over, isn't it?"

"What's that noise?" Bryan peered up at the dark rafters.

"Bats." The lines in Charlie's face drooped.

"Bats, Dad? You're not kidding, real bats?" Bryan whirled around, hoping to see one.

"I bet you could get this place cheap," I said.

"Did you see the slope that runs alongside the house, all the way down to the lake?" my mother asked.

"Yeah?"

"We could do a terraced garden, Charlie, like the ones at the Alhambra. Do you remember, the gardens at the Generalife, all those lovely cypress trees? And there's a patio out back —did you see it? It must be fate because it's unfinished, as if it's been waiting for you."

"That slope is covered with poison ivy, May, and the people who owned this place probably realized too late that it was ridiculous trying to build a patio out back where nobody's going to sit when the lake and all the best views are in front."

"You could dig it up, Charlie. How long would it take?"

I followed my mother down the stairs, saw her sweep the primitive kitchen with forgiving eyes and push open the glass door onto the front porch.

"I've always wanted a house on the water. You couldn't ask for a better location, Charlie. Next to the bridge, across from the main beach. The kids could fall out of bed and be at swim-team practice. You can even see the tennis courts across the highway."

"But May, think how *noisy* it would be here. And the view isn't good at all. You'll see that Ballantine sign from the Pink Elephant blinking on and off all night. You can see Route 206 for God's sake. Why buy a vacation home where you can see the highway from your front porch?"

Bryan had climbed down the stairs and was poking around under the house. "Hey Dad," he called up. "There's a boat under here. Looks like a Chris-Craft."

May smiled at the first sign of interest in my father's eyes as he led us down to the water.

"I'll be damned, Bry, it does look like a Chris-Craft."

"It sure is a beautiful boat, Dad."

"It's in rough shape."

"What kind of wood is it, Charlie?" May asked.

"Solid mahogany."

"There isn't much rot, Dad. Just these few planks on the bottom. We could replace those, strip and refinish the rest. Geez, Dad, we could do some real fishing in a boat like this. And waterskiing—we could buy our own skis."

"Hold your horses, Bry. What're you going to use for an engine?"

Bryan shook his head, clearing away all obstacles. "We'll have to find a used inboard somewhere."

"The ski equipment and engine aside," my father said, "do you know how much it would cost just to repair this boat? We'd need new mahogany planks to replace the old—they'd have to be custom cut—materials for refinishing, new hardware, cushions, lights, steering wheel . . . "

"I'll get a job."

"Bryan, we're talking over five hundred dollars here. And then a motor, even used . . . "

"Look, Dad, all I'm saying is this is one incredible boat. I could refinish it, you know I could. If I come up with the money, what's the problem?"

Charlie's shoulders slumped as he peered up under the house. When he'd finished his examination there, he circled the perimeter of the house. His eyes were squinted nearly shut, his mouth half-open. Finally, he sat down on the wooden steps where we were waiting.

"That front porch is going to have to come off right away. The roof looks bad and God knows how many bats are nesting under the soffits. The front of the house has settled—I'm not sure how bad it really is. These stilts should go pretty soon; you can see they're rotting away like the rest of the place. Logs are loaded with powder post beetles and carpenter ants. Hardly a kitchen to speak of, May. Dock needs to be rebuilt." He sighed.

"I bet you could get this place for a song, Charlie." My mother smiled up at him, resting her curly head on his shoulder.

*

My parents spent the next few days of that summer's vacation talking to the realtor and arguing about the house. We were renting in Strawberry Point on the other end of Rainy Lake; we'd chosen the tall green house with the floating dock in the middle of the lake we all liked so much. Me because I'd just learned how to swim well enough to dive under the barrels and resurface in the green darkness beneath the dock; Bryan because he caught endless bass between the dock and Gull Island.

My mother was right about the house being cheap. Even Charlie was surprised at the price. The house, the realtor said, had been empty for six years. The last owners were two old-maid music teachers. They'd called it the G-Clef, which they had imprinted in the wet concrete of the unfinished patio.

"We can afford it," May said.

"But it needs so much money just to keep it from collapsing," Charlie argued.

"You're exaggerating."

7

"I wish I were. I'm an architect, I should know."

After our nightly game of Monopoly, Bryan and I went to bed in the bunkroom off the kitchen. Normally, since Bryan was thirteen and I eleven, he was allowed to stay up later. But during summer vacation Charlie said he and May needed time alone, which meant that Bryan came to bed when I did.

Most nights Bryan glued together the little wood pieces of his model Yankee schooner while I sat on the top bunk with my box of paper dolls. Really I had six boxes but on vacation I only brought one. This year I'd chosen my Gidget paper dolls—Mom and Dad, Moon Doggie and the surfer boys, and five of the beach girls: Doris, Tammy, Annette, Noreen, and Penny. Penny was from my Sky King set, but she didn't have anyone her age in that one so I'd made her one of the beach girls. I laid out the cardboard surfboards on the bed and slipped the boys' feet inside the slots so they could stand up and ride the waves, which I made with my knees under the covers. Then I unfolded one piece of blue tissue paper for the water and one piece of light brown for the sand. The bikinis wouldn't stay on very well so I'd glued them; that way the beach girls could leap up and catch their beach balls without any accidents.

When I tired of the game, I took out a pair of scissors and one of the sheets I kept folded on the bottom of the box. I enjoyed cutting out the doll equipment almost as much as playing—opening up the sheet and seeing all the clothes and accessories, making sure my scissors stayed on the lines and didn't miss any of the little fold-over flaps. This one was an Annie Oakley set, complete with horses, saddles, and bridles. Bryan clicked off the lamp beneath me, and I listened to the familiar swish swish of his feet on the sheet. It was a Fillian family habit—we all did it—and meant he was ready to go to sleep.

The walls in the cabin only went partway up to the ceiling, and since I had the top bunk, I could kneel on my pillow and peer over the wall at my parents. After ten o'clock my father made their favorite cocktails. He lined up the ingredients on the red counter: gin, grenadine, eggs, cream, and ice. He measured everything carefully into a silver cocktail shaker. I loved to watch him screw the little silver cap onto the spout. Once during the day I tried to screw it and unscrew it myself, but the cap slipped through my fingers and bounced onto the rug.

While my father was shaking vigorously, May filled one bowl with potato chips and another one with her homemade onion dip. Then she shuffled the cards and placed them on top of the blue-checked tablecloth. My father poured two glasses full of the Pink Lady cocktails and carried them on a silver tray to the table. He looked just like a waiter, brandishing the tray in smooth arcs over his head. My mother licked the filmy white wing the drink made on her upper lip.

Charlie shuffled and dealt the cards, and they started to play. When my mother mentioned the garden alongside the house, I slid down onto my pillow and guided Gidget over the waves. Through the din of laughing beach girls I heard Charlie's patient voice talking about how the house lacked integrity, how much money it would cost to fix it up, how noisy it would be. My mother hung on like a bull terrier. Carefully I gathered the dolls and placed them inside the box, which I tucked between my pillow and the wall. Then I snapped off the light.

As I look back on this time I'm aware of how much I can't explain. I understood why my father wanted that perfect white house on the point. My mother's motivations, on the other hand, were indecipherable to me. Maybe it was as simple as a stone fireplace, a terraced garden, the main beach pulsing before her eyes. Maybe it was something hunkered so deep inside her that even she couldn't articulate it.

*

Memory is a little like the rosary beads I keep wrapped up in the back of my bureau drawer. Occasionally I take them out and finger them one by one, the way I used to, each bead another prayer, one bead leading to another, creating a whole constellation with its own order, its own litany of indulgences. What happened next that summer was like one of those perfect round beads, coloring everything connected to it, before and after.

It was a Saturday afternoon and Bryan and I were squatting on the railroad tracks, ears against metal, listening to the vibrations of an oncoming train. Behind us, the screened front door of the Pink Elephant Bar and Grill opened into a black funnel studded with the reflection of glasses suspended over a wooden bar. I could hear men's voices, laughter, glass clinking against glass. Now and then a man appeared in the doorway, one hand shielding his vision from the sunlight, and shuffled off toward the bridge, beyond which my parents sat on a red plaid blanket under the elm tree on the west end of the beach. My mother stood up and tucked her brown hair under a white bathing cap. Charlie cupped her elbow in his right hand as they walked to the end of the dock and dove side by side into the water. The sun moved across the jeweled surface of the lake.

The track hummed and I felt a perceptible shiver when I lay my cheek against it.

"Put down your pennies," Bryan commanded.

The first sound was a glass shattering inside the bar. Then the train whistle keened loudly in the distance, followed by a man's startled cry. Bryan raised his head from the track and gazed into the dim interior of the bar. One shout followed another, the words indistinguishable, merging into a loud, angry swell. A flurry of motion appeared in the darkness: a white shirt, the gleam of a watch, a hand upraised, the thump of bodies on wood. I looked toward the water, where my parents had been. When Bryan yanked me backwards I stumbled, pulled up immediately by a jerk of his wrist. His fist was wrapped around the collar of my shirt.

"It's coming!" he yelled, his chin pointed toward the black, belching nose of the train.

A split second before the train hurtled past us, blocking my view of the Pink Elephant, I heard the second cry, a sound that raised goose bumps on my sunburned arms. Bryan had heard it also, for his hand tightened on my shirt.

"What do you think . . . ?"

The question died on my tongue as the caboose whistled past, and there in the doorway of the Pink Elephant stood a tall, burly man locked neck, arms, and hands in the grip of four other men. I recognized Paddy Doonan and Ed Casey from church. The taller man they were holding tossed his head from side to side, like a horse trying to rid itself of a painful bit.

"Somebody get Doc Malone!" A man pushed past them and ran toward the beach.

"You had to do it, didn't you, Raymond? Couldn't let it slide . . . "

"Why'd you have to bring a knife in there?"

"*You* married her," Paddy Doonan said. "You've gotta have a couple of screws loose to put your hands on a black woman in the first place, but *marrying* her," he shook his head. "A man who'd do that is no better than an animal."

My brother put his hand on my shoulder.

"Hush up, Paddy," Ed Casey said.

Raymond, the man they were holding, lunged toward Paddy Doonan. His lips were bared and quivering.

"Whoa, boy, without a knife you're not so scary. They're gonna lock you up, Dove. You won't have any trouble holding your liquor then. You just better hope you haven't killed him."

Puffing slightly, Doc Malone ran around the end of the bridge to reach the knot of men in front of the Pink Elephant. He looked so odd, caught in bewildered relief against the dark passageway into the bar, with his sunburned face, plaid Bermuda shorts, and emerald green shirt.

"It's Lloyd Sloane," Ed Casey said, motioning over his shoulder. "Ray Dove went and stabbed him."

"Jesus," Doc Malone muttered, venturing reluctantly through the door.

My brother steered me away from the fracas until we stood a few feet from the bridge, still on the far side of the tracks. People were hurrying over from the beach, children in front, swimsuits dripping, adults milling behind in sunglasses and pastel-colored beach jackets. Cigarettes showered the air with tiny orange sparks. My parents appeared on either side of us. May had unsnapped the strap of her bathing cap and hastily folded back the sides, which jiggled like two wings above her ears.

"Somebody said a man was *stabbed* in there," she said.

"How long have you been here?" my father asked.

"We didn't see anything, " Bryan said. "It happened inside the Pink Elephant."

"Who is that man?" Charlie asked.

"Raymond Dove," I said. "He's the one who did it."

"He's a brawler," said a plump woman standing in front of us. Her short hair was dyed corn yellow with a quarter inch of brown, graying roots. "So is Lloyd. They've been going at each other ever since Lloyd got his hand mangled at the tool and dye in Neptune. Nobody really believes Ray was responsible, not unless he'd been drinking, which my Joe says Ray doesn't do on the job . . . "

"It's 'cause of his wife," another woman said.

"What do you mean?" my mother asked.

"See for yourself." The woman cocked her head toward the parking lot where a dusty red Chevy had just pulled in.

A light-skinned black woman got out of the car first, then a boy who looked about sixteen and a younger boy around my brother's age. The woman wasn't very tall, about my mother's height, and she had brown hair pulled into a tight coil at the nape of her neck. I remember thinking how pretty she was, her skin a rich mocha color. Her lips were taut, as if she were chewing on them from within. She was wearing a white uniform, like a nurse or a waitress, with white-seamed stockings and white, rubber-soled shoes.

The older boy darted through the crowd and leaped into the cluster of men, where he pulled at the hands pinning Raymond Dove. He was tall like his father, only handsomer, with long, muscular arms. If I hadn't seen his mother I wouldn't have thought of him as black, or even mixed . . . Italian maybe or Mexican, like the boys whose parents ran the corner grocery store near St. Andrew's, our parish church in Westfield, New Jersey.

A police car arrived, its siren blaring, and a blonde-haired policeman strode toward the Pink Elephant. "Ease up there, come on now, back off." The policeman forced the boy back from the circle of men holding Raymond Dove, who was bucking violently now in an attempt to break free.

"You're gonna strangle him—make them let him go!" the boy cried out.

The woman stood a few feet away, her arms at her sides, not making a sound. When he saw her, Raymond Dove grew suddenly still and dropped his eyes. Following a command from the policeman, the men twisted Ray's arms behind his back, and the officer snapped on a pair of handcuffs.

"What has he done?" the woman asked, her voice carrying through the crowd.

"He stabbed Lloyd Sloane." Paddy eyed her coldly. "Your name comes up and Ray here goes hog wild."

As the older boy lunged toward Paddy, the woman stepped forward and blocked her son with her outstretched arm.

"That's enough, Douglass. Go find your brother."

I searched for the other boy in the crowd, finding him before Douglass did. He was standing where Bryan and I had been only minutes before. Our flattened pennies winked in the sunshine alongside his gray sneakers. He was indistinguishable at first glance from the other boys his age: he was tall, wearing blue jeans and a white T-shirt rolled up on his biceps, and he had short curly hair and skin like a lifeguard. It was the way he carried himself that set him apart, the quiet, watchful coil of his body, eyes that smouldered even at a distance.

An ambulance screamed to a stop behind us, and two attendants rushed in dizzying white into the black interior of the bar. Raymond Dove's wife turned as the policeman led him toward the parking lot. The crowd parted to let them through, voices descending like hail onto his rigid back.

"You're gonna pay for this."

"Shame on you, Raymond Dove, shame."

"Your woman and those boys better not set foot over here. They should stay on Disappointment where they belong."

"Lots of niggers where you're going, you oughtta do just fine."

At the word nigger I looked up at my father, registering his disapproval in the tight band of his lips.

"What's her name?" my mother asked the woman with the corn-yellow hair.

"Marcella Dove. She works in the Happy Day Diner in Neptune. The family lives over on Disappointment Lake. You know, through the channel in Strawberry Point."

My mother nodded.

"Douglass is the older boy; the younger one's Billy. There's another colored family over there—*her* folks. We don't get too many around here."

Just as the door to the police car slammed shut, the ambulance attendants appeared in the Pink Elephant doorway carrying a stretcher. There was a slow whistling sound at the sight of the sheet pulled over Lloyd Sloane's face. I'll never forget that moment: the dead man, the red flower blooming on the white, and just a few yards away the crumbling face of Marcella Dove as she followed the path of the stretcher to the back of the ambulance.

Turning away from it, I saw the boy rooted on the tracks. His skin was stretched like muslin across the bones in his face. I shuddered in sympathy for him. I couldn't imagine such a tragedy ever happening in my own family, which had closed in around me like a solid wall. As we left the beach I glanced back once, but the boy on the tracks was gone.

*

On our last day of vacation that summer, Bryan and I left at dawn with Charlie in the rented motorboat for our final morning of fishing in the old lake. I'd packed breakfast already: cream cheese and jelly for Bryan, peanut butter and jelly with bologna in the middle for me, a cold corned-beef-hash sandwich for my father, and three wedges of the Sara Lee pound cake my mother loved so much. It was my favorite time on the lake—the houses dim and sleepy, the water the color of gunmetal, and the smells: fish and mud and bark and gasoline.

Charlie steered the boat effortlessly through the tall weeds that rimmed the approach into the old lake. I still don't know why they called it that, maybe because that's where Rainy Lake started, in this small, deep pool surrounded by reeds, and then nature added to it by stretching and twisting the lake into its current shape. The old lake was the place I loved best. The Spanish have a name for it, *querencia*, the place where peace is, where you return in your memory. Partly I loved it because the fishing there was so good, but also because of its history, the fact that it had existed before anything else—before Rainy's big blue middle, the coves and channels, the beaches and clubhouse, the bridge, the club itself. And because it was the place where the waters of the two lakes, Rainy and Disappointment, mingled. In the thicket of weeds there was a sudden parting, and you could drift in total secluded silence into the channel joining Rainy to Disappointment Lake.

As he guided the boat, my father studied the surface of the water. He was wearing his red-and-black-plaid Pendleton shirt and the usual khakis. His dark blue beret was pulled forward at a jaunty angle on his forehead. He always wore it fishing, not only because it protected the skin under his thinning blonde hair, but because it was his signature. Lots of men had them, little mannerisms or details about their clothing that

15

said to the world, *This is who I am.* For my father it was the blue beret and the khakis. No matter how many swanky clients he had to meet with in a day, he never wore a business suit, always his khakis and one of the sports coats my mother selected for him at Bamberger's department store.

My father liked to set himself apart from other men, even the men in the architectural office where he worked. He thought they capitulated too easily to the demands of clients and developers. He believed that his responsibility as an architect was to educate as well as serve. His domestic politics, for the most part, were liberal. He liked to talk *big,* working himself up to transcendental pronouncements. My brother and I believed everything Charlie said about art and style, about civil rights, about a federal government that was big enough to offer an opportunity for everybody.

Bryan was sitting in the bow of the boat. One long, blue-jeaned leg was curled under him, the other stretched out. The black canvas of his Converse sneaker darkened as the water in the boat's bottom lapped against it. His hands were bunched inside the pockets of his red Sanford Junior High football jacket. The light wind lifted a stroke of flaxen hair and laid it across his sunburned cheek.

He is beautiful, I thought, *and it isn't fair.* Bryan had inherited Charlie's platinum blonde hair and strong build and my mother's face. I don't know whose features I got—May's freckles and brown curly hair, except that her hair hair curled gently around her face while mine zigzagged off in all directions. And who gave me that gangly body that was all arms and legs, with bones so prominent Bryan said I could pose for one of those African starvation posters?

Charlie cut the motor and motioned me to take the oars. The wood creaked, breaking with tiny splashes the hushed silence of the old lake. Bryan opened his tackle box and started rigging his line.

"What're you using, Bry?" Once we'd neared the area where we were going to fish, my father insisted we speak in whispers. He didn't want to scare the fish, but also he said it was important that we respect the quiet and peacefulness we found at such times on the lake.

"Leeches. The minnows are all gone."

"What about you, Danny?" Charlie asked.

"I got some night crawlers first thing this morning." I took my right hand off the oar and pulled out a wad of dirt and worms I'd stuck in my pocket.

Bryan flipped me a small white container. "Put 'em in here. God, Danny, you'll ruin your clothes."

"Fishing for sunnies?" my father asked.

I nodded. Sunfish were my favorite, despite the fact that they were little and I always threw them back. I loved their tawny color, big eyes, and round bodies.

" 'Cause if you are, I'd use one of these jig spinners. I have a chartreuse twister tail here that's just the thing."

I shook my head. "I don't think fish are fooled by those things, Dad. If I were a fish I'd go for real food, not one of those shiners with a tail."

My father smiled. "What I spend on these lures is almost sinful."

"We should keep more fish, Dad," Bryan said. "If we ate them, you could consider the money as going for food."

"We *do* eat them, Bryan. I keep as many as I think we can eat in a few meals. Any more than that, your mother won't cook 'em. Each fish I take from the water means something— it's part of a balance between us and the lake."

My father believed that *we* were the guests, and nature was inviting us in for a visit. I'm grateful for those early lessons, when my father's actions set a standard my brother and I were proud to follow.

Bryan cast his line toward a bed of slender green reeds. There was always that moment of silence when you waited . . . and then you heard the plink of broken water, the creak of wood as the oar drifted in its metal bracket. I shifted my gaze from the delicate lines ringing the fat part of the worm to

17

Bryan's line, and watched how he let the bait fall to the bottom, then reeled it in slowly.

"Now I know *you* know what you're doing, Bry, but you might want to try bouncing the rod a little, gently up and down, kind of like a yo-yo, like this."

Having rigged his line with a jig and a bit of pork rind, Charlie flicked the rod smoothly over his head, aiming for the weeds just along the shoreline. His arm went up and down in a series of rhythmical hops. When the muscles along his jaw tightened and he narrowed his eyes like that, I knew he'd had a hit. He let the line flow freely for a second, pointed the rod tip down, reeled in the slack, and pulled up hard.

"Got him!" His eyes leaped as he turned the reel.

"How big, Dad?" I grabbed the net and leaned forward over the water.

"Can't tell yet. Not too big."

When the fish came into view, my father dipped his hand into the lake to wet it, grabbed the fish just inside his open mouth, and pulled him out of the water.

"I could have got him, Dad."

"I know, Danny, but he's not that big. The less he touches anything, the better off he'll be. This slime is his only protection. That's why you always wet your hand before you touch a fish."

"He's a good-sized bass. Whaddya think, about a pound and a half?" Bryan asked.

"Two pounds more likely. Hand me those needle-nose pliers, Danny."

After my father released the fish, we moved slowly around the edge of the pool. I caught two sunnies and a perch, and Bryan and Charlie each caught a few keeper-sized bass. As the sun rose higher, I took off my jacket and lounged against one of the cushions. I sniffed long and hard, letting the water and gasoline smells trickle through my head.

"You gonna buy the house, Dad?" Bryan sat back against the bow and unwrapped his cream-cheese-and-jelly sandwich.

My father's shoulders sagged. "I don't know. What do you think?"

Bryan scrunched up his lip and I tried to think what the best thing would be. "Mom'd be pretty upset if you said no, wouldn't she?"

Charlie nodded.

"But you don't want it, do you, Dad?"

"No, I don't. It's not that I wouldn't love to buy. We've been renting now for six years. But *that* house . . . it's nothing like what I had in mind. Even if the white house *were* for sale . . . well, no use thinking about it."

"So whaddya do? You don't want to buy, Mom does."

"That's marriage for you, Bry. Your mother has no idea what kind of work we're looking at if we buy that house."

"You could design one neat patio for the front, Dad." I crumpled up my waxed paper and pitched it into the lunch bag.

That spring my father had had the first article, ever, published about his work in the May issue of *Better Homes and Gardens* featuring suburban patios in New Jersey. Of course, he would have preferred it if they'd chosen a house he'd designed, but he was happy nonetheless, and hung the framed cover photograph in his office. Even the other architects in the firm, who never liked to give compliments, said the patios were remarkable.

No less remarkable were my mother's flower arrangements. She was doing more business out of our kitchen than the local florist. The judge who awarded her first prize at the annual Westfield Garden Club floral-arranging contest said her entry was more than just beautiful. May Fillian's flowers were strange and idiosyncratic, he wrote on her scorecard, they cast a spell on the viewer. It was the same with my father's patios: they were a way of showing us that he was, after all, the kind of architect he'd set out to be.

"It would be a challenge, Danny. There's not much space by the water. Even if we rebuilt the porch and put in some concrete columns, it's still an unattractive sight when you look up at the house from the water. I'd want to put up some kind of screen or latticework. I was thinking about designing a deck where we could entertain, and that would serve as a middle ground between the house and patio. It would break that long vertical plane where the stilts are."

"Have you ever built a deck before?" I tried to picture what it would look like.

"Not really. I've seen a few, though. With these new split-level houses they're building, you'll see all kinds of decks. Bet there isn't a single deck on Rainy Lake."

"Yours will be the first, Dad." Bryan rerigged his line with his favorite Red Devil and cast out behind him.

"Maybe we shouldn't buy here," I said, peering through the channel toward Disappointment.

"Why not?" Charlie asked.

"I don't know, maybe this isn't the place for us." I couldn't help thinking of Lloyd Sloane, who'd been buried a few days ago, and Raymond Dove, who was facing years in prison for manslaughter.

"What's wrong with it?" Bryan asked.

"I can tell you one thing, if we buy that house, you kids and your mother will have the whole summer away from the city. How many kids do you know who own a summer house on a lake like this? My parents lived in an *apartment;* they never even had a car." My father stood up and aimed toward the channel. "A couple of times each summer they'd take me and my friend Eddie Tompko on a bus to Coney Island."

I bent over my tackle box and perused the contents. They were like jewelry, these lures and flies, tiny explosions of color entombed in their plastic boxes. Charlie kept a whole carton of lure and fly-tying equipment beneath the bottom bookshelf in the living room. I hadn't yet learned how to fly-fish like my father and brother, but Charlie had taught me how to make my own lures and proclaimed my flies every bit as good as

Bryan's. Quite a feat for a girl, he'd said, surprised at the discovery.

I selected my latest Sneaky Pete lure, the green and yellow head with the orange tail that reminded me of the girls who sat on the end of the bridge at night smoking cigarettes.

"The first thing I'd have to do, you know, would be to jack up the house, make sure it was level. It wouldn't be a vacation, not for me. I'd have to work on the place every minute just to make sure it didn't cave in underneath us."

I wondered how long he'd hold out before they made an offer. The surface of the lake had changed. The blue lacquer of the previous hour was dimpled now with restless, charcoal waves. Charlie moved into the back of the boat and started the motor. We trolled out of the old lake and around the perimeter of Strawberry Point. My mother would have risen by now and started packing. She preferred it that way—no one blocking her path as she cycloned through the cabin, cleaning and folding.

There was nothing so sad as seeing the suitcases and boxes waiting by our white Dodge station wagon when we returned from fishing on our last day at Rainy Lake. Something changed in my parents during these summer vacations; a skin seemed to shed, leaving them happier and younger. I hoped that if they bought the house, if two weeks of being happy stretched into two months, they'd get used to it, so that when we left the lake they'd carry their happiness with them.

I couldn't see that when my parents made the purchase offer on the house, forces were set in motion that would propel us toward that summer afternoon in 1969, six years later, when the world went spinning off its axis. I don't believe things happen without a reason. I think that what is random and accidental converges with the shape of our own characters, the time we live in, and the relationships that guide us.

"It's clouding up. Look, Dad, over the island—gonna rain for sure. I wish we could stay. There's nothing better than a good old lightning storm out on the lake."

Bryan gazed at the ashen swirl over Gull Island. How he loved the volatility of weather, the snapping white limbs of lightning and the sudden gusts that took your breath away. I look back at him now and see it all ahead of us. Even the trees seemed to know, their green fading with the receding light, the regretful whisper of wind.

BATS (1964)

I HAD NO PROBLEM SHARING THE HOUSE WITH THE bats, but my mother saw it differently. They were here first, I said, all those years when the house was deserted. She thought they were disgusting. They got in your hair and gave you rabies. That's not true, I told her. They're too smart to get mixed up in somebody's hair. All they want is to be left alone or to flee into the darkness.

I don't know what it was that drew me to them. Maybe it was the book, *A Concise History of Bats*, which belonged to Hildy Rue, one of the old-maid music teachers. The book tried to dispel the nightmare notions of bats. It described them as innocent creatures who pollinated tropical fruits like cloves, figs, and avocados; who gobbled up pounds of insects every night; who did not bite unless provoked; who were not blind; who squeaked like real animals and who could, in total darkness, make sounds higher than the human ear could hear; and who rarely gave anybody rabies. Even the vampire bats did not actually suck blood; they made a painless little stab and tranquilly lapped up the drops, and they lived in places like Mexico and Brazil, nowhere near Rainy Lake.

The most important fact for me was that the bats living in houses, the little brown myotis bats, were most likely pregnant females. The nest was a maternity colony where each would deliver one baby. These baby bats, who *were* blind in the beginning, would cling to their mother's breast, feed on her milk, and be ready to fly at the age of three weeks.

*

My mother's optimism about the house was dampened the first night we saw a bat. Dumbfounded, I stood at one end of the living room as my mother galloped toward the bathroom, emerging a few minutes later with a towel wrapped turban-style around her head. My father pulled his hand out of the bowl of warm water and epsom salts he'd been soaking his hammered thumb in and grabbed a tennis racket. When the bat disappeared into the dark rafters, Charlie shone his flash-light into every seam and corner of the ceiling.

"Maybe it went out the same way it came in," May said.

"No." My father aimed the beam at the point where the stone fireplace met the ceiling. "It's here all right. They're lit-tle, you know. They close up smaller than a fist."

"They won't hurt you, Mom," I said. "They're as afraid of you as you are of them. It says so in the book."

"What book?" Bryan asked.

He'd been watching the whole scene from the top bunk on his half of the sleeping porch, where he'd been sitting since supper building a model of the 1903 Herreshoff Reliance.

"This one." I held the book up to him, knowing he'd like the tiny ink drawings.

A shadow wheeled over my head as Bryan ducked, and my father smashed his racket into the ceiling, cracking the top pane in one of Bryan's casement windows.

"Shit!" Charlie nursed his swollen thumb as the bat dove over us again and sailed into the dark cavity of my parents' bedroom. My father followed. We heard his frustrated swear-ing and the thwap of the racket as it caromed off the bed. Finally, he reentered the living room and sank down onto the couch, where he rested his sweating head on my mother's red-flowered slipcovers.

"Did you get it?" May tiptoed across the room and peered through the shutter doors into their bedroom.

My father's tanned arms quivered, and I noticed the many cuts on his fingers, the red patches on his arms from carrying concrete blocks. Every weekend all spring and for the first two weeks of his vacation so far, he'd been working on the house. He'd torn off the screened porch, jacked up the house to level it, put up the infrastructure of a new porch, and was now rebuilding the foundation. Bryan and I had helped him fill countless wheelbarrows full of wet cement and had hauled concrete blocks from one end of the property to the other. The new columns underneath the porch were halfway done.

"No, I didn't get it. And to tell you the truth, I don't give a damn either. It's been a long day and I'm tired. One little bat isn't going to hurt you."

"*I'm* not sleeping in this house if there's a bat loose, Charlie. Come on, Bryan, take the tennis racket. Danny, get the broom from the kitchen closet."

"I'm not going to hurt her, Mom. I think we should turn out the lights and open the door. Let her fly out by herself," I said.

"Don't *touch* that door! You'll let in more of them."

Bryan didn't want any part of killing a bat, but he couldn't stand seeing Charlie all done in and my mother nervously stalking with the towel still wrapped around her head. My father made room for me as I curled up on my end of the couch.

"Remove all traces of guano," the book said, "because the accumulation of bat droppings will attract additional bats." I peered up into the cracks around the top of the fireplace and wondered what it looked like, this guano, whether it shot out in a stream of milky green, like a bird's. Bryan and my mother were back in her bedroom; I could hear the stiff scratching the broom made as Bryan ran it along the inside of each rafter. My father's head tipped back onto the log wall and he snored peacefully. "If holes are sealed during breeding season," I read, "baby bats may be trapped inside the house. The mother will fly through doors, windows, or other openings to get to them."

My brother swung at the empty air as the bat skimmed the top of the partition around my parents' bedroom and landed in the corner just over my head, where she contracted her wings and flattened herself against the dark wood. My father snored on as I closed the book and walked into my bedroom.

"Did you see it, Charlie? Where did it go?"

My mother was too frightened to give up. She would lie awake in the dark watching for the invisible arc of the bat's wings over her bed. But what could I do? She wouldn't let the bat escape and I wasn't about to squash her, not when the bat was probably a mother with a blind baby waiting for her behind the walls.

*

The next day May asked me to stuff small burlap bags full of garlic cloves. Her newest friend Nini Kelly, whom she'd met at the beach, had told her that bats hated the smell of garlic.

"Never say die, Danny. No bat is going to get into *my* house, not if I can help it."

I held the ladder for her while she hammered nails into the ceiling and hung the bags from short strings. In her own room she hung a whole slew of them. I had to open all the windows to help with the smell, already bad from the chemical we'd painted on the logs to kill the powder post beetles that were creating the intermittent volcanoes of reddish silt that spilled out of the logs and onto the floor.

Afterward, we crumbled wads of newspaper, which we stuffed in every visible crack—between the logs, between the logs and fireplace, between the logs and ceiling rafters, between the logs and window casings. I could only hope the bat had made her way back into the nest and wasn't stranded inside with us. When we finished, even my mother had to admit it was an ugly sight. Tufts of newspaper stuck out everywhere, making the walls resemble a half-plucked chicken.

"Let's go to the beach before your father sees this."

My mother followed slowly across the bridge. She hated the unsettling motion as it swayed back and forth. I shielded my eyes at the way the sun ignited the black cables, looped like a flaming necklace across the blue lake. How easily you could roll underneath the wooden railing and fall into the deep water, or worse, be caught by one of the cables, your back breaking like a twig.

Children's screams carried across the water. I watched the flicker and splash of feet, the bobbing yellow and orange tubes on the children's half of the beach. On the other side, the lanes were already up for swim-team practice. The sand at this end had all but disappeared under a fleet of colored beach towels. Teenage girls were milling around the green legs of the lifeguard's chair, and languidly kicking ribbons of sand into the water. Others leaned over the clubhouse railing, where they whispered and laughed together as they pretended to ignore the boys lounging on the steps.

The *other* boys were diving off the concrete support at the far end of the bridge. You could tell the townie boys right away because they wore cutoffs instead of regular swimming suits. Townie kids lived at Rainy or Disappointment or in the adjoining area all year long, and they attended school in Sparta or Neptune. My father said they swam off the pier because their families weren't members of the Rainy Lake Community Club. Only families who paid the club dues were allowed to use the beach and the clubhouse. Of course, townie kids couldn't be on the swim team either, or the ski club, nor were they allowed to use the club's tennis courts, although many got part-time jobs taking care of the ski-club equipment, driving the retrieval boats, and maintaining the clay courts.

Tucking my book under one arm, I leaned over the railing and watched them goofing around on the pier, as they pushed one another off and then cannonballed on top. They didn't swim the way the swim-team boys did; their strokes were wider, sloppier, and they kept their heads above water. The book hit my foot and bounced off to the side, where it sailed with open wings toward the water.

"Oh, no," I cried and climbed up on the rail, unsure what to do.

27

A boy dove off the pier and swam the short distance to where the book, held aloft by its plastic cover, still bobbed. He shook it, swimming sidestroke with one hand to keep the book out of the water. I ran across the bridge and down onto the white dock, where he was pulling himself up.

I can still see that moment: the curly black top of his head as he rose, his dark-toned skin, the way he looked down on me with that slight, crooked smile. His face fell on me like the clearing in a forest, everything around it dense and closed, all but this one bright place. And there was the smell of water, which I thought was the lake dripping from his slender, muscular arms.

"Thanks." I squeezed the book against my leg.

"What is it?" he asked.

I studied him a few seconds, trying to place where I'd seen him before. "*Jane Eyre.*"

"Is it good?"

"Oh yeah. It's my favorite."

He smiled again and turned back toward the water.

"What's your name?" I asked.

He mustn't have heard, for he dove into the lake and swam back to the pier. On the beach my mother was spreading out her blanket under the elm tree, the one shady spot in front of the children's swim area claimed by all the mothers.

"That was nice of him." She nodded toward the book. "Who is he?"

"Billy Dove." Nini Kelly lifted a huge pair of sunglasses off her face and stretched out a short freckled leg toward my mother. "You stay away from him, Danny. You know his father stabbed Lloyd Sloane last summer right there in the Pink Elephant. Not that Lloyd ever held a warm spot in *my* heart, but to *stab* somebody to death . . . . Raymond Dove's serving over ten years in prison. Like the shoes?"

My mother hooted as Nini modeled her green flip-flops. Orange pom-poms quivered atop her painted toenails. I gazed out toward the pier and saw Billy's laughing face replaced by the image of that boy on the tracks. I took a quarter and two pennies from my mother's beach bag and walked back past the bridge toward Sal and Joey's, a low white building that hunched at the edge of the lake. Through the open doors of the Pink Elephant, right next door, I heard the muffled laughter of men and women.

Crouching next to the railroad tracks, I lined up my two pennies on the warm surface. So far I hadn't walked down the tracks, which ran all along the clubhouse side of the lake and on past Disappointment, but I knew the stories—how the teenagers hung out down there by the spillway where they drank beer and made out on blankets, which they spread all along Lovers' Slope. There was even a place where those kids who had cars could drive to the spillway and park.

The pinball machines were all taken in Sal and Joey's, so I stood by the counter reading the menu and wondered if I could get a plate of french fries for a quarter. Terese Kelly was sitting on a round swivel chair in her red swim-team bathing suit, and licking a vanilla ice cream cone. She was Nini Kelly's daughter, and my mother had been pushing me to be friends with her ever since she and Nini had taken up together at the beach. The fact that Terese had red hair and green eyes and freckles endeared her even more to my mother, May O'Neill Fillian, for whom the Irish were only one step removed from Jesus and Mary.

Terese Kelly was the most popular girl my age at Rainy Lake, which meant, if she were like every other popular girl I knew, that she was stuck up and not very smart.

"How much are your french fries?" I asked Joey.

"Twenty-five cents. You're one of the Fillian kids, aren't you? I met your mother yesterday. What's your name?"

"Danny."

"Short for what?"

"Danielle, but everybody calls me Danny."

I looked into Joey's fair-skinned, freckled face and figured she and my mother had hit it off. Joey was short for Josephine,

29

which wasn't an Irish name, but where else but the Emerald Isle could you get such a complexion? It was odd, too, since her daughter Angie had olive skin, cocoa-colored eyes, and a mane of long chestnut hair. Angie looked more like Sal than Joey, which was ironic since her real father, Vincent Fanelli, had died in Korea when she was only three years old.

That history was part of the fabric of things, like the stories about the spillway and the Pink Elephant, and the townie kids who lived over on Disappointment. Sal and Joey had bought the store six years ago. They had two boys of their own, Nick and Joseph, who played marbles under the pinball machine or ran their Tonka trucks through the doorway into the tiny apartment at the back of the store where the five of them lived. Sal and Angie got along OK, although she refused to give up her real father's name and, in Sal's view, held too high an opinion of herself. Joey should clip her wings, he said, before she went flying into someone's windshield.

Sal ran around the pool table and pulled Joey aside. One of the boys had swallowed something in the back, he said.

"Jesus Christ, Sal, weren't you watching him? Where's Angie?" She rushed across the store and through the curtained doorway.

Joey and Sal made an odd pair; she was plump and almost five foot nine, and he was skinny and the same height as my mother, who was only five foot three. Joey was real friendly to everybody, while Sal hardly said a word, except if he was in the Pink Elephant, where my father said Sal was a pretty lively guy. I couldn't see it, not with that sour expression he always wore. He had this flat top, too, which made me nervous. It was so stiff and straight, not a hair out of place. You wouldn't want to cross him, or break anything in the store.

"You ever try the french fries at the lodge?" Terese asked.

I looked at her sidewise, not giving her my full attention. "No, why?"

"Come on, I'll show you."

She hopped off the chair and loped out of the store. She had long legs, which must have been from her father, Tim Kelly, since Nini was shorter than my mother. Her hair swung back and forth in a ponytail that reached halfway down her back. One thing I had over her was being able to tan; already I was a soft burnished brown, which helped camouflage the freckles, all of them blending together. Terese's pink skin peeled in angry patches on her nose and shoulders.

I followed her across the tracks and parking lot to the back door of the Rainy Lake Lodge. Terese swung open the screen and marched in. I had to blink a minute, it was so dark in there. Hamburgers sizzled on the grill.

"What'll you have, Terese?" A short woman with black hair rolled under a net spilled french fries into a wire basket. "Need I ask?"

"I'll share 'em with you, OK?" Terese said. "Otherwise, I have to go back and ask Nini for another quarter."

"You call her Nini?"

"In the morning when she doesn't have any makeup on yet, I call her Mom. Whadda you call your mother?"

"Mom, or Mommy." I shrugged, keeping my eyes on the droplets dancing a few inches over the wire basket.

She tipped her head to the side and smiled, as if she was trying to figure me out. *Go ahead, try.* I handed the woman my quarter and we walked back across the white-pebbled parking lot.

"Ever been down the tracks?" she asked.

I shook my head. Some girls would have lied, but I wasn't like that. The sun smouldered on the metal tracks, and motors hummed through the screen of trees. We hopped from one railroad tie to the other, and passed the brown bag between us. In time the paper was splotched with dark circles, and the ends of my fingers were slippery with grease. Terese had been right about the french fries; they were the best I'd ever eaten. I can still remember that sensation of biting into one, its crisp, hot skin and then the full taste of it, just a second or two before it disintegrated, leaving only the memory.

31

When we reached the spillway, I looked around for the blankets, but there was nothing, just a flat clearing and then a slope that poured down into a heap of empty beer bottles and cigarette butts. You could tell it was totally private; a ring of dense shrubs protected the clearing from the lake, and a bank of birch trees hid the bottom of the slope from the road, at least ten yards away. We sat on top of the concrete spillway overlooking the big middle of Rainy Lake. This was where the skiers made their widest turns, as they tilted almost parallel to the water while the spray erupted around their ankles, and the long lines of the ski rope billowed and dipped and then tightened, jerking them upright as they sped back toward the beach.

"Isn't that Angie Fanelli?" Terese asked.

Shading my eyes with one hand, I peered at the tall girl skiing slalom behind Jimmy Piper's black sixty-five-horsepower engine.

"She sure is good," I said, admiring the daring way she hugged the surface of the water, the muscles visible in her tanned arms.

"It amazes me how she gets away with it. She's *supposed* to be working in the store, yet there she is skiing off the best boat on the lake. You'd think she'd grown up in the Everglades."

"Don't you like her?" I asked.

She shrugged. "She's OK. It's just that she *acts* bigger than she is, like she grew up in a really rich family."

"Maybe that's the way she sees things."

"What, living at Sal and Joey's? You've gotta be kidding."

The boat spun around, dissecting the swell of its own wake. The sun tossed up colors from the water, which slapped against the concrete wall. Angie's periodic laughter and the buzzing motor were the only disturbances to the easy silence that had fallen between us. Several times I pointed out a fish to her—a big bass circling in the weeds, a mossy-colored perch dozing next to a black rock. Once Terese asked me if I played cards and I said only gin and crazy eights and euchre but that

I loved games and would try almost anything. Before we left she asked me if I had any favorite books.

"*Jane Eyre* and *The Wide, Wide, Wide World.* That was my mother's when she was a girl and she gave it to me."

"Not many of my friends like to read," she said.

"What about you?"

"It's the thing I do. I could read all summer and never come up for air."

I thought she was kidding but she wasn't. "You should come over to our house. The old-maid music teachers who owned it before we did left all their books. That's where I found *Jane Eyre.* We must have over a hundred books."

When we reached the beach our mothers were gone. Halfway across the bridge I could hear Nini's high-pitched giggle and saw the two of them floating side by side in the black inner tubes my father had bought for us. Charlie was standing on the ladder and tapping cement around the base of another concrete block. Beneath him Bryan stood, diligently holding the ladder; his face and arms were streaked with tails of dried cement. As we started up the stairs, he said "hi" to Terese and made a joke about how Charlie was turning him into a piece of concrete. Thinking how corny the joke was, I held the door of the porch open, and saw in her face a look that made me think right away of Billy Dove—a look as if all the leaves had fallen from the trees in that one minute and she was the only one who'd seen it happen.

*

I turned down the yellowed corner on page 213 of *Drag-onwyk.* Last winter I'd read my mother's library copy of *Desiree,* so when I found two more Anya Seton novels in the cabin, I hid them in my room for me and Terese. Outside, my father was nailing up the new screens in the front porch. The room was warm and silent but with that air of waiting I'd come to anticipate on these sleepy afternoons. I listened: faint calls from the beach, the creak of the bridge as someone padded across, and suddenly, as if on cue, that eerie squeaking behind the walls.

My mother climbed heavily up the stairs and stopped when she heard the noise—the steady scratching, the high-pitched drone of their voices. The folded towels she'd been carrying thudded to the floor as she ran to the window.

"Charlie, come up here. *Hurry!*"

We'd been through it often in the past weeks. Each time it was like a spring tightening inside her head. We'd stuffed so much newspaper into the logs it didn't even look like a log cabin anymore. Twice the bats had appeared and flown around the living room. Bryan's and my efforts at chasing them were fruitless, but it seemed to ease her, especially since my father had returned to work and could only come up on weekends. When she asked me to sleep in my father's bed, I couldn't refuse. Not after I'd seen her lying like a mummy under the sheets, her turbaned head awake and restless on the pillow.

On that Saturday, my father was at the cabin. Tired as he was of all the construction, even he was moved by her anxious face, the flattened look of her hair from all those nights under the towel. He and I knew the bats were not concentrated in one place—all you had to do was listen. But the worst noise was in the pitched corner over their bed.

"I'm going to have to insulate the walls in here," he said. "Ask Eliot for another week off and put up Sheetrock."

"But Charlie, the logs . . . "

"Nothing else to do, May."

"What about now?" she asked.

Hang tough, Dad, I thought. *Don't do anything drastic.*

He sighed. "I suppose Bryan and I could flush them out, at least on this side."

When she lay her cheek against his arm like that, his face went soft as butter, and I knew the bats were history. It wasn't fair, the way my parents thought they could just get rid of the bats, as if once you owned a piece of property, nature lost any claim.

Bryan reluctantly dragged the aluminum ladder onto the rock on the north side of the house. My father climbed with a crowbar under one arm and started prying away the wooden soffits under the eaves. Word spread quickly along that end of French's Grove, and soon kids were gathering on the steps and the dock below. My mother had complained so about the bats that all the women under the elm tree knew, and so when May told Nini that Charlie was finally going after them, the news traveled across the bridge and back again. Everyone wanted to see the bats flying out of the house in broad daylight.

Once my father had the soffits off, he tied a handkerchief over his nose and mouth and sprayed something foul into the opening. The first bat stumbled out, dropped a few inches, and then took off around the corner of Maudie McDonough's house next door. One after another they followed, unnerving my father, who ducked under the stream of black wings. I held a fist tight against my chest, wishing he'd left it alone. The bats could have stayed there, could have flown in and out without bothering us once the Sheetrock was up.

Then Charlie stabbed the fireplace poker into the opening, and moved it back and forth like a pendulum. A few more bats flew out, smaller ones this time, and he jabbed the poker in again and scraped it over his shoulder, hurling the tip into open air. Several black balls tumbled onto the rocks.

As I stared at the tiny, quivering forms, Lou Sullivan and his brother Ed, who lived four houses down, pelted the bats with stones. My scream ricocheted off their surprised faces, and I ran forward and stood spread-eagled over the bats.

Bryan stood next to me. "Go home, guys. There's nothing more to see."

Four bats lay on the rock. Two were so tiny they looked like black prunes. I touched them lightly with a stick but they didn't move.

"They're dead, Danny," Bryan said. "The best thing to do is to put the others out of their misery."

"No!" The sun was a gold wheel over his head.

I ran into the house and grabbed a wad of napkins from the kitchen. Gently I rolled the bats on top and slipped through the screen door that led from the kitchen into the storage area under the house, that cool, dark space where we stored paint cans and fold-up chairs, inner tubes, and an old baby carriage a previous owner had left behind. After laying them on the thin mattress inside the carriage, I went upstairs and took a brown quilt from the trunk in my parents' bedroom. On my way back through the kitchen, I pulled on a pair of my mother's gardening gloves.

First, I wiped out the inside of the carriage, which was dirty and smelled of mildew. Then I folded the quilt and tucked it inside, placing the two little bats on top. Their eyes were open but they didn't move; not a breath stirred in them. Lying on their stomachs like that, their wings folded tightly into their body, they resembled brown furry frogs. I shook the mosquito net, still hanging from the back of the baby carriage, and stretched it over the top.

The door opened and Bryan walked up beside me. "What the hell are you doing?" He peered inside the carriage and whistled.

"Stay with them," I said and went outside to find a stick, which I put under the net, and positioned across the top of the carriage.

"What's that for?"

"So they can hang if they want. Now I need to get some food."

"What kind of food? Danny, you're not serious?"

"Why not? We kept that baby jay a whole week last spring. You remember, right after your birthday."

"But this is different, Danny, these are *bats*."

"Of course they're bats."

"I mean, they bite. They could give you rabies. How do you know what they eat even?"

"Look at me—I'm wearing gloves. I'll be very careful. And I read the book. They eat bugs, worms, insects, unless they're still breastfeeding. God, I hope they're not breastfeeding. Stay here."

"What am I supposed to do?"

"In case Mom or Dad comes in."

For the next few days I hid them successfully under the house. I told my father I'd buried them and showed him the little crosses I'd made in the dirt next to the back patio. Bryan caught several mosquitoes and flies with his bug net and I dug up a whole container of night crawlers. I chopped them up and lay them on the quilt in front of the bats' tiny, scrunched-up faces. Once I tried to nudge their mouths open with an eye-dropper, but they wouldn't move, so I filled a capful of water and left it there.

*

Terese came by every morning to pick me up for swim-team practice, but I didn't tell her about the bats. Instead, we talked about *Katherine*, the best Anya Seton novel so far. These practices were all preparation since I wasn't officially a part of the swim team, not until I'd mastered twenty-five continuous laps. Terese, who was one of the best swimmers in her age group, had been coaching me, but, hard as I tried, I always gave up after eighteen laps. The first away meet was scheduled for Saturday, in just two days, and Terese was prodding me to make the team so we could ride together on the bus to Lake Hiawatha. We walked to the beach, where I dove into the water and swam back and forth in the lanes. Just as I'd completed the seventeenth lap, a cramp festering in my right side pulled me up double.

Facing me was the white number four on the green dock. Barrels floated underneath, one open space among them. If you dove exactly at the spot in the middle of the fourth lane where a wedge had been cut, you'd emerge into that opening. Then you could duck under the other side of the dock, swim to the far steps, and escape the beach unnoticed.

Gauging my distance carefully, I inhaled deeply and plunged toward the wedge-shaped opening in lane number four. I made it through the wedge all right, but when I looked up toward the surface I met only the foggy bottoms of barrels, one after another. I tried to retreat through the wedged cut-out in the bottom of the dock, but couldn't locate that either.

Don't panic. If you can't find the opening in a few seconds, swim beyond the barrels to the other side of the dock. You'll make it.

I banged from one barrel to another, hearing the sound of my hand against metal like the tolling of a great bell. Then a light flashed in front of my eyes and a white arm swept past. I followed the phosphorescent tail of her hair through the encroaching dark, the tiny flames of red and yellow before she broke the surface. My shuddery gasp echoed eerily, eclipsing the metal clink and suck of barrels. That close, I could see the spark of water on her eyelashes, the fine brown hairs marking her temples.

"Cutting out?"

I stared back at her, unable to speak.

"You did the same thing yesterday. You're Danny Fillian, right? I'm Angie . . . "

"I know who you are."

"Most kids reach a point like this when they think they can't make it. That's when you have to try your hardest, you know, just keep swimming. Otherwise, you'll never know what you might have done, will you?"

Angie held the league record for the hundred-yard freestyle. Since Sal and Joey couldn't afford the club membership dues, the coach, Linda Hailey, had given Angie a job. She was allowed to swim on the team in exchange for helping to coach, and doing the team paperwork.

I followed her under the last row of barrels. We came up on

the children's side of the green dock, where we saw a bobbing sea of life preservers and animated tubes. Terese was sitting on Nini's blanket underneath the oak tree, pawing through her mother's beach bag.

"In the spring I come here after school and swim until supper. There's never anybody here then. The water makes everything different. If you swim long enough, your body disappears. You should try it."

When the swimmers had finished their laps and Angie was curled up on the sand next to the lifeguard's chair, where she was scribbling the day's times into the team notebook, I tried again. The twelfth lap was the hardest, but after that I didn't feel it—not the eighteenth or twenty-first lap either, only the last leg of the twenty-fifth—my weightless body, the warm water, the hard wall against the palm of my hand when I touched one last time.

*

The darker-colored bat ate the worms, and one afternoon I found it hanging on the underside of the stick. The other bat grew stiller and more shriveled every day. By the tenth day it was dead. I wrapped it in Kleenex and buried it next to the others. As I sat on the half-finished patio I listened to my father's voice singing cheerily inside the cabin. He was almost done with the Sheetrock, which at least covered all the newspaper, but the effect of living inside a log cabin was gone.

The two bats weren't related, since bat mothers had only one baby at a time, but I'd thought of them as if they were. Or maybe they were simply friends, like Jane Eyre and Helen, both of them orphans and weakened by the bleak life at Lowood. Only Helen had died while Jane toiled on, determined not to quit. What was it in the one that had made it survive when the other couldn't? Maybe one of the bats was younger and needed its mother's milk still. Maybe one was more sensitive than the other, or simply weaker, and the shock of separation, the bad fall, had been too much for it. Maybe one had simply refused to give up. I looked down at the little crosses, and a sob welled up and shook me.

A few nights later I held the living bat in my gloved hands and walked to the middle of the bridge. My parents had gone to the Kellys' for cocktails and cards, and Bryan was playing pool at the club with Ty Malone. I looked up at the purple sky and murmured a prayer that the bat would fly. Holding my cupped hands high over the railing, I lofted the bat into midair. For a moment it shuddered, as if rousing from sleep, and then spread the black web of its wings and soared over the cables and out into the summer night.

HAWAIIAN LUAU (1965)

H OW DO THEY EXPECT TO GET ON WEARING those ski belts?" Terese asked.

We leaned over the railing of the bridge to see better. Our mothers floundered helplessly as the white belts encircling their waists caught on the edge of the boat and anchored them; their breasts were flattened against the deck and their white legs flailed at the water. Terese and I looked at each other, shock at our mothers' stupidity vying with the sheer pleasure of watching something that funny. May reacted each time with loud laughter, her head thrown back so that the pink floppy flowers on her bathing cap touched the water. Nini responded with her high-pitched, lilting giggle and lots of orders: "May, grab here." "No, no, not that way." "Watch it, you're tipping the boat!" "Come over here and push me from behind."

Their voices reverberated across the water, until the men in the Pink Elephant threw open the casement window and saluted them with beer bottles. Finally, my mother swam over to Nini and got behind her, pushing up on Nini's behind. Nini giggled louder, but her giggles were broken by the loud grunts she made as she inched herself forward onto the boat. The ski belt kept May from going under; she was laughing so hard and Nini had kicked her several times on the chin with her little, chubby feet as she pulled herself up.

Once Nini was on she tried to pull May up, but of course she couldn't. When they spotted us, as the boat drifted under the bridge, Nini yelled up.

"Terese, you and Danielle come down here. You dive right in and push Mrs. Fillian up onto the boat."

"You've got to be kidding." Terese sucked on her lips, trying hard not to laugh.

"Danny," my mother hollered, loosening the bathing-cap strap under her chin. "Come in and help me."

"Mom, just take off your ski belt. Then you can get on by yourself."

The women looked at each other and shrieked. Nini was giggling so hard it looked like she was going to roll back into the lake. Leaning forward with one hand on the mast, she helped steady my mother, who was unbuckling the ski belt. Once it was off she got herself on past her waist, and Nini grabbed her by the seat of her lime-green bathing suit and hoisted her up the rest of the way.

Our mothers stood on the deck of the sailboat; May, the taller, gripped Nini's freckled shoulders while Nini clung to May's soft, round waist. I shook my head, hoping they wouldn't fall off. It was their first time out and neither one knew a thing about sailing. They were like two girls the way they carried on.

Two women stopped on the bridge and watched them enviously. Nini Kelly had been coming up to Rainy Lake for years and was more popular even than Terese, but as soon as my mother joined the club, it was just the two of them. Nini didn't even go to the beach anymore; she preferred to sit in the shade with my mother, May's rock garden at their backs, as they knit or read or practiced their bridge hands. When our fathers arrived on Friday evenings from work—Tim Kelly from Staten Island and Charlie from New Jersey—the women had everything ready. Whisky sours or Pink Ladies for them, Manhattans or martinis for the men. Bowls full of potato chips and cheese doodles, plates piled high with Ritz crackers, and Velveeta cheese sliced into tiny heart shapes. The four of them drank and swam before separating for dinner.

"Terese," Nini called up. "Do either of you know how to work this sail?"

42

Terese leaned farther over the railing so her mother could see her. "Why don't you ask Bryan?"

May pivoted, almost knocking Nini into the water. "Where *is* Bryan?"

In the distance, at the bend leading into Catfish Cove, my brother sat motionless in the motorboat. It was only a small boat, the engine too small for waterskiing, but it was fine for fishing. Bryan had begun work on the Chris-Craft in June. He'd painstakingly loosened the dozens of screws, removed the rotted planks, and treated the others with a chemical restorative he laughingly called "rop rot juice." Anyone could see how long it was going to take my brother to refinish that boat, so when Charlie announced he could get a small fishing boat cheap from the boat works in Neptune, we begged him to buy it.

"Bryan!" May's voice careened off the blue water. "Bryan!"

"Mom, he can't hear you." I squinted through the slats in the bridge. "Why don't you go back to the dock and read the instructions?"

"*What* instructions?" Nini hollered.

"Maybe somebody over at the Pink Elephant knows what to do." Terese pulled my arm as our mothers whooped and giggled again. We cut in front of the boat house next door and stopped beside the upturned hull of Bryan's Chris-Craft. The boat, lumber, and supplies took up half the patio.

"What do these numbers mean?" Terese pointed to the white markings Bryan had made on the old planks he'd taken out of the bottom of the boat.

"It tells him where each board came from, so when he's ready to cut the new one he can use the original as a template. It has to be a perfect match."

Bryan's paper-route money had paid for the new mahogany boards. So far he'd managed to remove all the rotted planks from the bottom and stern and had recut and installed a new transom frame and ribs. I'd come to count on the sight of

43

Bryan's blonde head bent over the worktable in the mornings. He was careful not to turn on Charlie's band saw too early. The first time he'd done it, Sal had flung open the window in the back of the store and hollered across the water.

"You'd think he'd get tired of it. Why won't he come to the beach?" Her eyes followed the yellow flag of Bryan's hair as he rounded the cabin on the point and disappeared into Catfish Cove.

I touched the neat rows of files and chisels lined up on the table. "I've told you a hundred times—he *loves* this boat. It's a Chris-Craft, which means it's a classic, one-of-a-kind. They're irreplaceable. We could never afford one, not even one as beat-up as this. It means he has to do everything just right, which is why he sent away for the plans. They give you the exact sizes of things, the names of screws and rivets and hardware. Bryan likes doing it this way—going back to the beginning and starting over, making sure it's perfect."

"My father says you'd be better off with a fiberglass boat. By the time Bryan gets through with this, it'll cost just as much. Fiberglass is lighter and more durable. You can't water-ski off a big, heavy boat like this." She looked again toward the Cove. "I just wish he'd come to the beach."

"He *does* come to the beach, every morning for swim-team practice."

"I mean later during the day, when all the other kids are there."

It was useless trying to explain it to her. Except for a few boys, like Ty Malone and Jimmy Piper, who were on the swim team and liked to fish, the kids on the beach bored Bryan. All they ever wanted to do, he said, was lie around on beach towels or shoot pool in the clubhouse. He liked the volleyball games down in the pit between the railroad tracks and the club, but the boys didn't take the game seriously. They were playing to show off, to see who could smoke and hit at the same time, whose muscles were bigger, who could attract the most attention from the girls watching through the Cyclone fence.

And his thing with boats, you'd need something in your own life to compare it to, or else how could you understand? Charlie's tools were lined up with the same devotion Bryan showed when he used to prepare the altar on Sundays. I could see it in his face, the same way I felt as I sat in the channel leading into Disappointment—the line wheeling its graceful, mercury arc over my head, and freezing me in that momentary death whenever the lure penetrated the still surface.

Looking at Terese's sorrowful face, I wondered again how she could want Bryan so badly and not understand him. They weren't alike at all, except the way they could each walk across a room and people would turn involuntarily to watch them. I used to think it was her mother's reputation that had done it for Terese, but I was wrong. You'd think at fifteen Bryan would have been more interested in girls. For Terese's sake I hoped he'd wake up one morning ready, and there she'd be waiting for him.

While I filled a bowl full of barbeque-flavored potato chips, Terese placed the chessboard on the kitchen table. Bryan and I had started playing chess at the beginning of the summer, and I'd taught Terese. I was better at it than Bryan, which surprised everybody. It's all a matter of making it up in your head, I told Terese, like a story—plotting the moves in advance, being able to alter your scheme at any minute. She was a quick learner but so far that summer she hadn't been able to beat me, and that was the gnat buzzing around her ears, and making her moves hasty and a little desperate.

"I keep telling you, Terese, you shouldn't take my piece if you know you'll automatically lose yours right after. It isn't worth it."

"Easy for *you* to say. How else am I gonna get anything?"

"You have to think ahead."

"I know, I know, it makes me dizzy. Your father have any new books?"

Finding the Mickey Spillane novels in my father's bureau drawer was like striking oil. He'd covered the books with brown paper, which we'd peeled off right away to see the covers. I was disappointed to find everybody fully clothed, especially the men, who wore white shirts and dark suits. The women were better but it was all the same: tight skirts and blouses and bulging breasts. We read aloud all the dirty passages we could find before re-covering the books and sliding them back beneath a pile of bleeding madras shirts.

Charlie believed there was a real difference between a book like *Anna Karenina* and *Sisters* by Kathleen Norris. He wanted me to be more discriminating in my reading, to be able to distinguish good literature from bad. What I cared about were the *stories*, whether they kept me awake at night, whether I loved the characters and wanted to be like them.

Take Jane Eyre, for example. I still had a soft spot for her, being put in the red room like that, having to stand on the stool in front of the Misses Brocklehurst while Mr. Brocklehurst cut off her hair—all the years of one disappointment after another and still she kept her loving nature. I admired girls like that who defied the odds. I most loved the part when Jane spent the night with Helen Burns, cradling her friend's feverish body in her own thin arms, and waking to find Helen's cold face against her neck.

"Nah, he's been too busy designing the deck to do any reading."

It had taken all this time for my father to renovate the house. Last spring, buoyant with the well of energy he'd discovered in November when he left the firm and started his own architectural practice, he'd started designing the deck. He and my mother had turned the porch into an office. His drafting table was at one end; her garden and plant books formed tall piles all along the screened walls. They'd hung up pictures of the Hanging Gardens of Babylon, the Alhambra, and the Villa d'Este for inspiration.

Not too elaborate, my father said. The deck had to fit with

the site, look good from the water as well as from the porch, and reflect the nature of the house itself. It should also camouflage the columns and unsightly underbody of the house, blend into the dock and patio below, and give both of them little opportunities for beauty: a potting shed, a pergola, the shaped cutouts of one-by-sixes he'd designed for the railing, and one-of-a-kind planting boxes. They'd designed a patio that resembled the stone walkways in the Alhambra.

"*Here* you are, Terese. I've been looking everywhere."

Carline Gland stood in the kitchen doorway and popped a purple bubble all over her Pink Tango lips.

"Don't you believe in knocking?" I asked.

"I *did* knock. You must have been too interested in your *chess* game to hear me."

Terese waved Carline over to the table.

"What in *hell* are your mothers doing out in the middle of the lake in that sailboat? They are making such a *racket*. I don't think they know *what* they're doing."

Terese laughed and held out a plate of Ritz crackers.

"It's official. I just checked the bulletin board. You have to be fourteen to get into the luau next week."

"We know that, Carline, and we're not going. We're only thirteen."

Carline rolled her eyes. "You're not gonna let *that* stop you, Terese. All you have to do is tell Mike Cooper you're fourteen. You know he'll let you in."

"I don't think so. I heard they're being pretty strict this year. Besides, I'm having a sleepover."

I looked at her, wondering when she'd thought that up.

"Who're you having?"

"Just me, you, and Danny. Wanna come?"

I could see the struggle on her face. She wouldn't want to pass up the chance to sleep over at Terese's, even though she was fourteen and all her other friends would be at the luau. Terese was still the top of the pyramid at Rainy Lake. Carline couldn't figure out why Terese was spending so much time with me, anyway. The way she eyed me up and down as if I were deformed, and stared at the flat expanse of my red swim-team bathing suit. Once she asked me on the beach why I didn't get my hair straightened. Everyone knew the *in* look was peroxide streaks and very straight hair teased on top, she said. I told her I could get the same birdsnest effect just waking up in the morning; I didn't need to shell out fifteen bucks at the beauty parlor to look like that.

"So, what are you gonna do? Go to the luau or be with us?" Terese asked.

Carline's painted eyes leaped over my head and landed on Terese. "What time should I come?"

"Meet us at my house at seven-thirty. My parents will be gone by then."

Carline nodded and left, her high-heeled slingbacks clattering down the wooden steps. I watched her thin body sashay across the bridge. Skinny as she was, she had great legs, long and muscular like my brother's. She should be on the swim team, I thought, it would build up her upper body. The water would ruin her eye makeup, though. The sun did a good enough job on it, melting the layers of blue eye shadow and mascara so that by the end of the day her eyes resembled two cobalt moons.

"Where are your parents going on the night of the luau?" I asked Terese.

"Where do they go every Friday night? To the Pink Elephant with your parents and then back here for bridge or swimming."

"I don't see why you had to ask Carline." I reached for my black knight.

"Don't worry about Carline. She's all talk."

Easy for you to say. I set my knight in position to take Terese's bishop. I'd have to watch while Carline took off one of those pink shells she wore every night and displayed her bra. Of course, the bra did have those tiny points that meant it was padded. Maybe she didn't have anything at all under the

48

bra, although I knew there was no way Carline was going to let either of us see *that*. But I loved sleeping in Terese's room, which used to be the Kellys' storeroom under the house until Mr. Kelly fixed up the back part for Terese. It had a little window next to Terese's bed, where I had to yell for her most swim-meet mornings, since Terese never rose before nine on Saturdays.

"Hey, we'll do your hair before the sleepover. Carline won't believe it." She swallowed my protest with a sweep of her hand and took my knight with her own, a move I hadn't foreseen. "I hear they're giving out leis at the luau. I'll ask Fern or Maizie to get us each one. We can hang them on our mirrors."

*

The morning sun intensified the smell that was searing a hole between my eyes. I tried to loosen the sheet, which Terese had tied tight as a choker around my neck.

"Can't we just iron it?"

"We did iron it, *twice*. You accused me of burning your earlobes. You also said it was making your hair frizzy. I had to give my mother four dollars for this stuff, so the least you can do is sit still until I finish."

Terese pulled on a pair of rubber gloves and started working the solution into my hair and scalp.

"It smells like Drano."

"That's 'cause there's lye in it."

"Lye! Are you sure this is safe, Terese?"

"Of course it's safe."

"What if my hair falls out?"

"I specifically asked my mother to find that out. Her hairdresser says this is the best product on the market, which is why it cost *four* dollars, and, if done properly, will straighten the hair with no problems whatsover."

"She said 'if done properly,' Terese."

"What's that supposed to mean?"

"She's a beautician, that's what."

"Look, Danny, I watched the other hairdresser in the shop do this to a black lady while I was waiting for Nini. That's how I got the idea."

I looked glumly into the mirror. The hair rolled in a creamy wave away from my face.

"It's burning my skin, Terese."

I could tell by the contorted expression on her face that the smell was getting to her, too. She moved the comb rapidly down the back of my head. The sheet bound my hands so I couldn't wipe away the solution, which leaked continuously into my eyes beneath my roasting forehead.

"Hurry, Terese!"

"There. Now we can rinse it out."

We ran to the bathroom, where I ducked my head under the faucet, sighing in relief under the rush of cool water. When I stood up, we stared open-mouthed into the bathroom mirror at my hair, which fell in straight, stiff lines to my shoulders.

"It's gorgeous, Danny."

After we'd rolled up the sheet and capped the lethal-smelling bottle, Terese emptied her beach bag onto my bed-spread.

"Come on, just try it."

"I told you, Terese, I'm not wearing it. You don't think people are gonna know?"

I gestured to her lap, where she'd laid out one of the new two-piece bathing suits Nini had bought her. The points of the bodice reared up like twin ice cream cones.

"In a few days no one will remember. Put it on, you'll look great."

"I'll feel like a total fraud. Look, I know you won't believe it, but I'm glad I don't have breasts. You think I want boys looking at me like that? It gives me goose bumps just walking behind you on the bridge. At least they leave me alone."

"That's the point, Danny—you don't want boys to leave you alone. You want them to notice you."

"You think they're gonna notice me if I wear this?" I held it up and faced myself in the mirror. "They'll be looking at *these*, Terese, not me. Don't kid yourself."

I gnawed the underside of my lip as the light waned in her face. It wasn't her fault that she'd sprinted ahead of me: she was several inches taller and already wearing a B cup. The boys, especially Jimmy Piper, were all over her. I knew she had my best interests at heart. She just seemed to be growing up so fast, and much as I tried to keep up, I hated the thought of putting on makeup or stuffing my bra to make me look like what I wasn't. We'd argued so much that when she'd turned her attention to my hair I weakened. Even I could see the hopelessness of my unruly hair, so thick and curly that nothing could tame it.

"Let's show your mother."

We picked our way through the mounds of tracing paper on the screened porch and leaped down the new stairs and onto the half-finished deck. My mother was standing on the lowest level holding one end of a plank while my father hammered the other into the side of the new potting shed.

"This deck sure is gonna be something," Terese said admiringly.

"*If* they ever finish. The plans they've made—you'd need a team of builders to get it done this summer."

My mother's blue eyes turned absently upon me, then shot into focus when she saw my hair. "It's straight."

Terese laughed out loud. "Of course it's straight. What do you think?"

May rubbed a lock of hair back and forth between her fingers. "Why is it so stiff?"

A cloud touched briefly on Terese's forehead. "It's still wet, that's all."

"How long's it going to smell like this?"

I swallowed and looked up toward Terese. "Not long. We haven't even shampooed it yet," she said.

"Looks good, honey, although I'll miss the curls." My

51

father winked at me, loosening a cloud of sawdust from his eyebrow.

"Like it, Mom?"

"Sure, Danny. I worry about the chemicals, that's all. You like it, don't you?"

I nodded vigorously, although already I yearned for the familiar, bouncy weight on top of my head, the fly-away tendrils drifting into my eyes. At the sound of a familiar whistle my father waved to Paddy Doonan and Ed Casey, who were walking across the new flagstones my mother had laid in the patio. The men had been coming pretty regularly to watch the progress on the deck. Sometimes they pitched in and helped, although mostly they sat on the new steps and hollered advice up to Charlie. He'd designed eight decks already at Rainy Lake, and the men were curious to see what kind of deck he'd make for himself. If they stayed long enough, my father would bring down a trayful of gin and tonics.

Terese and I dove off the dock and raced toward the pier. She out-touched me by inches, which she still managed to do nine times out of ten. We sat side by side on the ledge, our backs resting against the concrete support. My mother's laughter and the rhythmical thwack of the hammer echoed across the water.

"My dad says your father's pretty happy having his own usiness."

"Oh, yeah. He still has to please his clients, but it's different v. One thing leads to another—that's what my mother says. if my father hadn't been so frustrated at the firm, he dn't have done such a bang-up job on those patios, which that article in the magazine, and then people started him to do houses. You should see the swanky house igned on Panther Lake. They even have an indoor g pool, can you believe it? Bryan doesn't like the use the guy doesn't have a regular job. He says the be a crook to have so much money."

lucky you can talk to your father about his work.

Sometimes my father tells my mother things, but they clam right up if they know I'm listening. He's had to identify dead people, I know that much."

Tim Kelly was a homicide detective in the Bronx. You'd never know it by talking to him because he seemed like a happy, good-tempered guy. Even my mother said she'd pick Tim for a car salesman but never a New York City cop. Charlie said he could imagine Tim being really tough if he had to, that he'd seen terrible things on the job.

"Now all we need is the money for Bryan's engine," I said.

Both of us looked over toward the Chris-Craft, perched like a miniature arc on Maudie McDonough's patio. Maudie was the widow who lived on the other side of us. Her husband Pat had been in the Navy and was always dragging her off to look at boats, so she'd taken a real shine to Bryan. Last weekend she'd offered to let him move the Chris-Craft onto her property where Bryan could work on it without all the sawdust from the new deck blowing down on him. She'd even volunteered to help him re-upholster the cockpit cushions; already she'd salvaged the horsehair stuffing from the original seats and sewed brand new red Naugahyde covers.

"I can't believe how long it takes him to refinish one old boat. He's gonna be in college by the time he's done," Terese said.

The door under the house slammed, and Bryan appeared on the landing. The blonde hair rose on Terese's legs as my brother hopped over Maudie's railing and set down his tools next to the boat.

When we heard Linda Hailey's voice on the beach, we plunged back into the water. Linda was a tall, blonde woman whose bellow chugged across the lake like a locomotive. She'd been an all-league champion four years in a row when she was a teenager, and she was grooming Terese and me for the end-of-the-season heats.

Bryan smiled as Terese climbed onto the dock and dried herself with my beach towel. That summer her hair was cut short with long, spiky bangs. I admired the way her new haircut thrust her face forward all by itself; now you could see clearly the tiny blue veins under her skin and her big eyes the color of seaweed. Maybe Bryan was taking notice, for when she passed by him he managed one of those big smiles that showed his perfect teeth.

As we neared the seated throng of teenagers on the far end of the bridge, I felt the hot pricklings of self-consciousness. Not that I minded their eager eyes all over Terese's body or the way she kept her back straight and puffed out her chest. But she seemed in those moments to leap into an atmosphere out of my reach, and I was left with this sore cavity I couldn't seem to fill.

On that day I shook my head hard, feeling the stiff hair against my shoulders, and tried to look as if I were totally bored. Midway through the gauntlet of boys I saw Billy Dove. I bottomed out right there, like someone had kicked me hard in the softest part of my stomach. What made it worse was that he was ogling Terese the same as everyone else.

I'd just passed him when his voice descended on my shoulder. "Hey, Jane."

Terese stopped suddenly and I banged right into her. "What'd you say?" She peered at him over the top of my head.

Only he wasn't looking at her anymore. "Jane, isn't that your name?"

His face was the same, smooth and dark with that crooked smile and eyes the color of sun falling through trees. Lou Sullivan laughed out loud. "Who, her? That's Danny Fillian, Bryan's sister. The bat girl—that's what Ed and I call her."

Ed Sullivan was Lou's idiot brother, the one who couldn't keep his finger out of his nose. What did his parents expect, naming him after the ugliest guy on TV? I remembered the two of them tossing stones at the bats. I stepped forward, stopping an inch from Lou's bony knees.

"Oh yeah," I said, "you oughta tell your brother to floss once in a while, clean the worms from his teeth."

Billy leaped down and stood so close to me I could smell the water again. Only this time he was dry, not a drop on him.

"Danny, huh? I could have sworn it was Jane."

"That was the name of the book."

"Book?" Terese said.

The light flared in his eyes. "Yeah, that's right. What was it?"

"*Jane Eyre.*"

Terese was gaping at me. "What are you talking about?"

"Nothing. Come on, Linda's blowing her horn over there."

I nudged Terese forward, and we hit the beach running. Angie Fanelli was sitting on the edge of the dock next to Joe Malone, the oldest of the Malone boys and captain of the swim team. Joe's father, Doc Malone, was a Yale man who had a busy practice in Huntington, Long Island. Everybody knew Joe was headed for Yale after he graduated next summer. He and Angie had been hanging out a lot together, which had caused a gaggle of raised eyebrows among the women at the beach.

The cold swallowed me as I plunged into the brown well of water. I felt the weight of the lake on my eyelids as I surfaced and sped toward the green dock. Terese was breathing down my ankles. Try as I might, I couldn't match her time for freestyle or backstroke, although I knew if I mastered the flip turn I'd have a better chance.

When I reached the dock I waited as Terese flipped around and raced back. Angie sliced neatly through the water and stopped in the lane next to me.

"What's the matter?"

"The flip turn. I can't do it."

She ducked under the lane and bobbed up next to me. "Watch."

She swam back a ways and modeled the turn for me. Her dark head disappeared in a sudden flume of water as her ankles whirred around. I heard the thwack of her feet on the board, and then I saw the blurry outline of her body sliding past me underwater. After she redid it several times more slowly, she guided my body through the turn. She was laughing as I rose out of the water. Joe Malone was standing behind her, squirting a stream of water into her long brown hair.

"Practice!" she shouted as she leaped after him. The muscles rippled across her back as she lifted herself onto his shoulders.

When I joined Terese on the beach, she inched onto my towel, her green eyes hungry. "So what's with this *Jane Eyre* stuff?"

"It happened last year. I was coming across the bridge and I dropped my book in the water. He got it for me, that's all."

"He has a good memory."

I took out my Coppertone and flipped the cap nonchalantly onto the sand.

"I can't imagine having a father in prison, can you?" she asked.

"No."

"Douglass Dove dropped out of high school last winter, did you know that? Why would anybody do that in the middle of his senior year?"

"Maybe he wanted to give people something to talk about."

She rolled toward the lake, where Angie was illustrating a water-ballet dive for Joe. "Just look at her. I can't believe how she throws herself at him."

"It's the other way around, if you ask me."

"She's gonna have a rude awakening if she thinks he'll ever ask her to go steady. His parents would have a cow."

"He could do a lot worse."

She studied me. "Well, I wouldn't fall for somebody I couldn't have."

"Oh yeah?"

She flushed. "I mean somebody really different from me, you know, like Angie and Joe or like Shirl Daniels and Douglass Dove. Mr. Daniels wouldn't let Shirl go out on a single date with him. Or think about dating a boy who's *all* black or a Jewish boy. I wouldn't mind a Jewish boy, but their mothers never let them marry a girl who's not Jewish."

"We're only thirteen, Terese. Who's thinking about marriage?"

"Well, I wouldn't want to fall in love with a boy I could never get serious with."

"I think if you loved him it wouldn't matter. You'd have to be braver than the people around you. The world is made up of narrow minds, Terese."

"Well, thank you, Madame Einstein. Listen, Danny, you can't ignore the rest of the world. They'll ruin it for you sooner or later, so why take the chance?"

*

I spent that afternoon with my mother setting bricks into sand. May had designed a herringbone pattern for part of the patio, which meant digging up and leveling the whole area, shoveling in a layer of sand, and packing it in with bricks. She'd already laid a pattern of flagstone and pebbles, so the bricks were the finishing touch. The rock garden along the north side of the house was mature enough now so that the plants tumbled down the hillside in a profusion of color.

When I think back upon this time, I remember my parents' constant industry and what that meant for me and Bryan. My father rarely fished with us anymore, certainly not the way he did during the summers we rented, when we made all those early morning trips into the old lake and he talked to us about his life and dreams and the natural order of things. I missed the easy way he lounged in the boat and gave us advice about fishing. My mother, too, had launched into her own world. She was rekindling her girlhood with Nini Kelly and fueling, with dauntless optimism and energy, my father's building projects and her own formidable gardening.

Yet I remember too my father's smiling, determined face that summer. The way he and my mother worked shoulder to shoulder on the deck, the burn of pride in their eyes as they surveyed the results of their labor at the end of each day. Bryan, too, sanding and scraping diligently on Maudie's dock. Often I joined them. I followed my father's directions as I sawed a plank for the railing, and rubbed my sandpaper with the grain of the wood to avoid the hateful whorl marks Bryan warned me against. Or I perched with my mother on the lip of a gray rock, our hands up to the knuckles in soil, as we loosened and fertilized before planting the bulbs and seedlings that May had spent the winter arranging in her head: the blue-flowered veronicas, the nodding white bellflowers and columbine, the bright yellow St. John's wort and ornamental thymes, the goldenrod and basket-of-gold and sedum.

"Wanna come?" Bryan stood on the dock with his fly rod.

"Nah, think I'll go for a walk," I said.

My mother leaned over the railing. "Would you get me a pack of cigs, Danny? Take sixty-five cents from my pocketbook."

I strolled across the bridge, feeling the sun on my shoulders. The cigarette machine was broken, so Joey handed me a pack of Chesterfields from the stacks under the counter. Her pale blue eyes were rimmed in red, and sweat pooled in the folds of her throat and arms. She was so pale compared to everyone else in the store. Sal was dark-skinned to begin with and fished often with the boys off the dock out back of the store, so the three of them looked alike: skinny and bronzed, with the same flat-top haircut. Joey hovered in their midst like a white, over-sized flower.

"I see your parents working over there day after day. You're gonna have a mighty pretty house, young lady, once they finish."

I nodded, curious about why she'd been crying, if it had anything to do with the angry voices that carried across the lake at night. It seemed they led a difficult life in that cramped apartment in back of the store. Everybody knew their business—how much time Sal spent in the Pink Elephant, how they hollered at the boys to keep out of the store or to stay in the small, weedy yard and off the beach. Sometimes at the end of the day the boys swam in the lake with their life preservers. Hunched on the gray dock, Sal would watch them, with a cigarette clenched between his teeth.

"Can I have some french fries, Joey?"

"Thought you preferred the ones over at the lodge." She grinned at me and dropped the wire basket into the oil.

"Say, what'd you do to your hair?"

I reached up to touch it, and was surprised at how stiff it was. "Terese straightened it. Can't you tell?"

She reached out a big hand to touch it. "You got too much hairspray on this, Danny. Why you girls think you need all that stuff . . . "

"I don't use hairspray. The chemicals just made it a little stiff, that's all. Terese said it'll wear off, probably once I shampoo it again."

I ran my hand through it, hoping to find a soft patch somewhere. When Joey handed me the bag hot with fries, I noticed several strands of hair wrapped around my fingers. Giving Joey an uneasy wave, I left the store and headed down the tracks. Splashes and squeals resounded from the beach, and I breathed in hard, in love with the smell of water, the unbroken line of metal track that spun out ahead as if it were a road right into my future. At this time of day there was no one on the tracks or walking along the path that ran parallel to the lake. That's why I liked it: the sounds of the world audible only through this green bubble of trees and shrubbery.

I was almost upon them when I saw the blanket on Lovers' Slope. Angie was on top, her long brown hair spread out across Joe's shoulders. His eyes were closed. One arm was flung out on the blanket, the other curved round her shoulder. I saw the white line of her bikini strap across her tanned back, the dark hair and pale arch of his penis half-hidden by her knee. They were mindless of the sun and the whir of boats, as if they were lying in a private room no one could enter.

I couldn't take my eyes off them—the curve of their bodies, the sleepy doze that held them like children. When Angie sighed, Joe wound his fingers through the brown fan of her hair. I turned and strode back up the tracks, holding the memory of his white thigh, and the mahogany glow of her hair as the sun hit it.

*

We could still hear the band, even though Terese's house was a five-minute walk from the lake, through the trees and up a steep hill. I crumbled my Fritos bag and pitched it into a trash basket.

"When I came across the bridge before, I saw your brother with Sandy Day. He had his arm around her and she was talking in that breathy little voice of hers. God, how *anyone* can wear that white lipstick, it's been out for *months*."

Carline's beehive was bigger than I'd ever seen it. The hairspray was so thick some of the little hairs were standing straight up all by themselves. The top of her head reminded me of a porcupine perched under a bush.

"Where're your glasses, Carline?" I asked. She was supposed to wear them all the time but she refused. Why spend all that money on eye makeup if nobody could even see your eyes?

She shrugged. "I can see just *fine*, Danielle."

"You *can't* see just fine, Carline, because my brother isn't at the luau tonight. He's at our house working on his boat with Ty Malone."

"Should have figured . . . .Well, it's just as well I didn't go. I'd have to watch my sister making a fool of herself anyway."

Terese smiled at me. Marilyn Gland was sixteen and had been going down the tracks with boys since last summer.

The two sisters were like water and oil. Marilyn was short and bosomy with a quiet, docile air about her, while Carline was all angles and brassiness. They were a little like Mr. and Mrs. Gland, at least in the way they acted on the outside. Even

60

then we were aware of the fact that Gerry Gland had affairs with other women, and his wife knew all about it. How could she not, Terese said, when some of the women were Frieda Gland's own girlfriends? Carline had seen her father's truck, Gland's Appliances, parked in front of the women's houses in broad daylight.

"She still have a thing for Billy Dove?" asked Terese.

I leaned forward and played with the fringe on my cutoffs.

"She should have her head examined. It isn't as if they're *going* together. He won't even take her down the tracks. She *asked* him, can you believe it? That's how gone she is. I swear, she has as much pride as my mother. And he said no, he doesn't go out with Rainy Lake girls. Who does he think he is? It's not as if he can afford to be choosy, or that those *Sparta* girls would win any beauty contests."

"Well, after all, Carline, look what happened when Douglass wanted to go out with Shirl Daniels," Terese said. "Her father threatened to send Shirl home to Staten Island if he caught them together."

"I still think Marilyn's off her rocker. Have you seen the Doves' house on Spirit Road? It's not even an all-year-round house. His father's a murderer, and just look at his *mother*."

"I think she's pretty," I said. "Besides, Billy isn't that much darker than Sal."

Carline's lip curled. "Sal may be poor, but he's not a *Negro*."

I leaned back against the red-and-white-plaid pillows on the couch. The smell of pine blew through the screens, and I felt that hollow ping inside my chest, the sensation that I was floating in a vast wilderness with no lifeline to anything tangible I could see.

"Got anything to drink around here?" Carline asked.

"There's some soda in the refrigerator," Terese said.

"I don't mean *soda*, Terese. You got any beer?" She stood up and walked into Terese's small kitchen. I could see the muscles in her butt as she leaned into the refrigerator.

"Jesus, Terese, there's all kinds of mildewed stuff in here. Doesn't your mother ever clean it out?"

Terese shrugged her shoulders and grinned at me. "My mom isn't much of a cook, Carline, especially in the summmer."

Neither one of our mothers liked to cook, which was yet another of the links in the chain that bound them together. It was a big disappointment to my father, who enjoyed a gourmet meal, especially when it was presented with an artistic flair. May never kept more than six spices in the spice rack; names like tarragon and rosemary, cardamon and coriander were foreign to her. Potatoes were a staple, boiled or mashed, nothing in between. Her summer passion was macaroni salad, which she and Nini piled onto their plates for lunch.

Carline was cradling three beer bottles against her chest. "My mother would *flip* if she looked into that refrigerator. Not only is our refrigerator absolutely clean, but everything's *arranged.* Frieda wouldn't *dream* of putting the ketchup on the wrong shelf. Here, have one."

Terese busied herself with the can opener as I pushed the bottle away from me. "I don't want it, Carline."

"*That* figures." Carline flung her shoulders back so that her pinecone breasts stuck out.

Carline and Terese sat at the picnic table in the middle of the room and drank their beer. Under the hanging light Terese's hair erupted like a volcano. I tucked myself into the couch and pressed my forehead against the window. The glass moved with dozens of insects. I couldn't take my eyes off their spidery black legs and fluttering, phosphorescent wings. Outside, the Japanese lanterns Mr. Kelly had hung shone red on the new cedar deck. It had been the first one my father had designed on Rainy Lake, and the Kellys were proud of it. I liked the way it undulated around the house, and ended in a wide, cantilevered arc that floated over the rocks below like the bow of a great ship.

I pushed back the thick headband my mother had bought

for me and inspected the front of my scalp. Beneath my finger-tips I could feel the bald patches along the hairline, the splintered ends that resembled stalks of corn sheared off at the ankles. So much had fallen out in the past week that it looked as if I'd mowed a ring around my face.

"It could be worse." Carline pressed a glass into my hand. "You could have had great hair to begin with."

"Shut up, Carline," Terese said.

"It's what you get for trying to look cool." Carline shook her head.

"It's what I get for trying to look like what certain people *say* I should look like." I glared at Terese and tossed the glass onto the rug.

Five bottles were standing on the table. "I can't believe how much liquor your parents have. There's so much stuff here they'll never even miss any." Carline worked her way through another shelf of bottles in the knotty pine cabinet on the far side of the living room.

"Are you sure you should be doing this?" I asked Terese.

Terese smiled and wiped her mouth with the back of her right hand. "Don't worry, Danny. Carline's right—my parents won't even notice."

"What if they come home?"

For a moment the film over her green eyes cleared, and Terese squinted, her forehead crumpling under her strawberry bangs.

"No problem!" Carline said. "We'll just take a few bottles down to Terese's room. We can put them back in the morning."

I didn't like the taste of any of them, although the Southern Comfort didn't burn as much going down. Out of curiosity I sampled each one: gin, which Terese said to mix with tonic water; bourbon, which they were mixing with ginger ale; and something awful called Benedictine, which they were drinking straight. After a while Terese and Carline were guzzling the

63

liquor right out of the bottles, and letting it pour down onto their clothes.

That's when I went upstairs for crackers. I remembered my mother saying once that you shouldn't drink on an empty stomach. I set a plateful in front of them and hid the bottles behind a pile of black inner tubes in the storeroom. Not long after, Carline threw up all over Terese's patchwork quilt. By the time I'd hauled her off the bed and onto the straw mat on the floor, Terese's face was green and her shoulders were heaving up and down. Grabbing a small wastebasket, I shoved it under Terese's face, just in time to catch the first deluge of vomit.

"Jesus!" I yelled. "Could you wait a minute?"

Carline was up on her hands and knees, puking into the straw mat. I hurried into the storeroom and found a plastic bucket, which smelled peculiar but not as bad as the room. The stink was so rancid I had to open a window.

For the next hour I raced back and forth between the two girls. I propped Carline's lipstick-smeared chin on the lip of the bucket and held Terese's damp hair back as she dry-heaved into the wastepaper basket. Soon there was nothing left to throw up; the last few times each girl had dribbled out only a spoonful of green bile. Terese had curled up like a pretzel on the floor and fallen asleep. Since she didn't have much vomit on her clothes, I covered her with a wool blanket I found in the closet.

Carline was a different story. The whole front of her was soaked; tiny particles of Fritos stuck like confetti to her once-pink shell. An oatmeal-like paste clung to her hair and oozed out of the frizzy walls of her beehive.

Gingerly I peeled Carline's shell over her head and unsnapped her bra, which was wet and stained a sickly shade of peach. As she pitched forward, I smiled at her tiny breasts. The nipples were as blue as Carline's lips. After taking one of Terese's nightgowns from her bureau, I stripped off the rest of Carline's clothes and slipped the nightgown over her head.

There was nothing to do about her hair, which I was afraid to touch anyway.

The yellow alarm clock next to Terese's bed read two-thirty, yet I still hadn't heard Mr. and Mrs. Kelly come home. Carefully I rolled up Terese's quilt and straw mat and put them in the store room. The sheets smelled bad but they weren't wet, so I stretched out on the bed as close to the window as I could get and tried to sleep. The lanterns swung in the breeze, and vermillion lights vibrated on the rocks outside. Sometimes, when the wind blew, I could smell the new cedar, which momentarily obscured the room's odor. The alarm clock ticked loudly, and I realized how badly I wanted to go home, to my own room with its pale green curtains swimming over my head.

When I woke my shoulder was cold, and the first ribbons of pearly light were defining the shapes of bushes and trees outside the window. Cool, rainy air filtered through the screen. I knelt down beside each girl and listened to her breathing. I took an old bathrobe from the closet and draped it over Carline, whose thin arms were crossed over her chest. Then I left.

My sandals thudded on the road as I ran down the hill and up the short road leading to the back of our house. A light rain was falling, splattering the green leaves of the lily-of-the-valley my mother had planted along the steps. Slowly I opened the back door, hoping the creak wouldn't wake anyone.

Just inside the door I smelled it again. Bryan was sprawled out on the couch, one arm dangling over the edge. Underneath his fingertips sat the blue-marbled mixing bowl we used for throwing up. I tiptoed across the room and studied the capful of water in the bottom of the bowl. As my knees brushed his leg, Bryan jerked and sat up.

"Bryan, are you sick?"

He stared at me a minute and then motioned across the living room toward the open door of my parents' bedroom.

"No . . . it's Mom and Dad."

My father was lying on his back with his mouth open. My

mother lay with her face to the wall. A breeze through the open window blew the smell of lake water and rain across the room.

"Are they all right?"

He walked over and peered at them closely, as if to make sure.

"They're sleeping, finally. They were on the porch half the night drinking and playing cards with Mr. and Mrs. Kelly, arguing about the election again. Mr. Kelly said Johnson isn't doing enough on crime and doesn't think his idea for a Great Society is going to change the lot of blacks or poor people one iota. He claimed Goldwater will get the job done better and faster in Vietnam, too. That set Dad off. He said Tim didn't know his ass from his elbow about combat, since he'd sat out World War II with a deferment while Dad was kicking butt in the South Pacific. After a while nobody was making any sense. Mr. Kelly rambled on about all the thefts and murders in Staten Island; Dad was quoting Adlai Stevenson; and Mom and Mrs. Kelly were singing along with one of those Jeannette McDonald and Nelson Eddy records.

"I'd just fallen asleep when they came upstairs. Dad fell down in the living room and started throwing up. You know, with his ulcer so bad he shouldn't be drinking. Geez, Danny, I was so scared when I heard the thump he made. I thought he was dead."

"And Mom?"

"She tried to help but she was too drunk. I put her into bed. I was worried about Dad; he's been so anxious over the Hawkman thing. Geez, I hate that guy."

"What Hawkman thing?"

"You know that big house Dad designed on Panther Lake? The guy owes Dad over ten thousand dollars. Now he claims there's some flaw in the design, and he says it's Dad's fault the house is costing so much."

"That's not true, is it, Bryan?"

"Course it's not. Dad has the documents to prove the

design problem was the contractor's fault, not his. Something about the height of the entryway. You think it was Dad's idea to build an indoor swimming pool, or order Italian marble for the bathroom? We'll just have to fight him. God, what a night. I didn't think he'd ever stop throwing up."

"Poor Bry," I said, rubbing his arm. His face looked tired and drawn in the dim light.

"What are *you* doing home so early?"

"I just wanted to come home."

The rain fell past the window in a sheet of silvery needles. I closed my eyes at the steady drumming on the roof.

"Do you think the bats are ever coming back, Bry?"

He peered up at the ceiling. "Oh, they're back, Danny. I see them circling outside at dusk."

"I read that they usually come back to where they nested."

"They're in here all right, behind the walls."

I examined my father's meticulously taped and sanded Sheetrock and listened. Nothing. No unnerving squeak or scratch.

"You know anybody who's part black, Bry?"

"What do you want to know that for?"

"I just do."

He shrugged. "Some kids at school . . . . I know Jimmy Hicks is. He's in my math class."

"Sometimes it's hard to tell if somebody's black or white, isn't it?"

"Not with Jimmy. Anybody can tell he's black."

"But isn't he white, too?"

"Yeah, though he's more of a yellow color than black or white. Kids pick on him. That's why he quit the swim team, because the guys were calling him names."

"White kids?"

"Both."

The smell of vomit was strong, and I realized how badly my head hurt. I felt the burn beneath my eyelids.

Bryan glanced again into the bedroom. "A couple of times

this week I've seen Tim Kelly head over to the Pink Elephant. Then he crosses the highway and goes into the Tamarack."

"He's on vacation, Bryan. All the men go to the Pink Elephant."

"Dad never used to, not in the afternoons. Now he's doing it, too."

"You worry too much, Bry."

"Something's happening, Danny. Can't you see it?"

I looked at him, confused, and tried to stop myself from crying. He put one arm around my shoulders and squeezed, leaving a tiny indentation in my skin.

BYOL PARTY (1966)

THE BOAT-HOUSE GATE SLAMMED, AND MY brother's blonde head appeared on the bridge. Despite his muscles and height, Bryan seemed to be slowly shrinking. Maybe it was my own leap forward, the climb so swift and sudden my heart had to beat double time just to keep up. Overnight, it seemed, my body had lengthened and filled out, and there was something at long last in my face: my mother's fine bones finally emerging, my dusty green eyes, my hair all grown in and wild. Maybe it was the loss of light I'd always associated with Bryan, that orb of hopefulness and daring that spun like a planet in the blue centers of his eyes.

Bryan was working part-time in the boat works at Neptune. By the end of the summer he figured he'd have enough to buy the Kermath inboard motor he'd been hungering for ever since he'd stroked the last coat of varnish on the boat. Although the sleek, finished lines of the Chris-Craft didn't give him much pleasure this summer. He didn't glance back now when he crossed the bridge the way he used to. I knew he couldn't bear the sight of Charlie's unfinished deck staring forlornly across the water.

My mother said it was Bryan's age erupting inside him like an abscessed tooth that made him moody and argumentative. But it was more than that. Charlie sensed it too and gazed back at us with wounded eyes during supper as he toyed with the olive in the bottom of his martini glass.

I kicked the wrought-iron table, laden with vases full of gladiolas and snapdragons, and swung lightly in the swing. The air was ripe with impending rain, which was the reason Bryan was heading over to the beach this late in the day. He knew everybody would be gathering in less than an hour to arrange rides to the baseball field on the north end of Disappointment where the fireworks were held every year. But diving off the high dive in the rain gave Bry the kind of thrill the other boys got after they'd drunk a few bottles of Ripple or rolled some of those reefers Mike Cooper kept stashed in his sneakers.

Bryan dropped his towel on the bench behind the lifeguard's chair and walked in his slow, fluid fashion onto the white dock. He climbed to the top of the high dive and stepped gracefully to the edge, where he balanced himself, toes hugging the board, arms flat against his sides. I inhaled deeply. The air was sweet and heavy. The breeze blew infinitesimal droplets of water through the screens and onto my skin.

He waited like that on the end of the diving board until the rain cratered the surface of the lake, and I could see his hair blowing out to one side. Then he turned and walked back a few paces, turned again, and took two long steps forward— one, two, the second step rising in a leap, the board springing under his feet as he landed with a dull boom and flew forward into the rain, his arms splayed open like a dancer's.

He followed with a forward double somersault, a jackknife, and then a backward double. All the time the rain continued to fall, stirring up the smell of leaves and fish, gasoline and wet wood, the black earth in my mother's garden. Something changed in my brother during moments like these. An exuberance traveled up from the deepest part of him, freed somehow by the weather's raw, primal force.

Behind me in the kitchen a glass shattered.

"Shit! Why do we have to have these blasted flowers everywhere? May? You'd think we were living in a damn greenhouse. *May!*"

The swing shook slightly as my mother clattered down the stairs. "For crying out loud, Charlie, I was in the bathroom."

In the kitchen the door leading into the storage area under

the house banged against the old refrigerator we kept there. "Oh, Charlie, what are you doing here?"

"What am *I* doing? What are all these *flowers* doing here?"

"You know damn well, Charlie, they're for the dance next weekend. Now you pick up this glass while I find something to put the dahlias in."

"Where's the beer?"

I knelt up on the swing and peered through the open window into the kitchen. My parents were standing face to face in the doorway. Even from the swing I could see my mother's flared nostrils.

"The beer's stacked against the wall." She pointed. "There, underneath your tools."

"Christ, May, it's gonna be warm."

"You just had a martini, Charlie."

He followed her back into the kitchen, where she stood at the sink filling a jar with water. His face was pale, his expression dogged and fixed, the way it had been all summer. It was as if he were swimming underwater; he was convinced that all he had to do was keep moving forward without hesitation, not taking too much in or letting his vision stray too far.

"It's Saturday! Can't a man have a drink in his own home?"

"Of course you can, Charlie. I just worry that . . . "

"That what?"

"You know what, Charlie. It's been like this for months. You're always . . . "

"I don't want to hear this now, May." He sat down heavily at the kitchen table.

She sat across from him. "It wasn't your fault, Charlie. You didn't have a choice . . . "

"Just when everything was going so well, too. Now the whole lake knows. You'd think a man could at least get some support at home. Bryan . . . "

"Bryan's just a boy, what does he know about business?"

"I could have borrowed the money to pay the deductible and gone to court. They know what they're doing on that

71

insurance, especially for a guy like me out on his own. I wish I could have seen it coming."

I'd asked myself the same thing more than once. Why hadn't he known more, why hadn't he taken action when Hawkman stopped paying him? Instead, he'd kept on working, borrowing money to keep the business going, sure the man was good for it. Just like he'd assumed Hawkman would know that all those extra things—the imported Italian tile, the nine-thousand-dollar chandeliers—were driving up the costs. "He's not paying his bills," my mother kept saying. "He'll pay, he'll pay," Charlie replied. "The man's a millionaire."

"It would have been suicide to keep borrowing, especially when there was a chance you could have lost the case. You said it yourself, Charlie, there was always that chance."

Not wanting to look anymore, I sat back in the swing. His face was so drawn and quiet, and the muscles were bulging in his cheeks. I often wondered why my mother continued to insist that he didn't have a choice about going to court. Maybe she was trying to convince herself that she'd done the right thing by lobbying for him to settle.

Shutting the screen door softly, I walked along the catwalk on the south side of the house and into the living room. In the bathroom I ran a pick through my hair and applied the lavender eye shadow I'd bought in Woolworth's.

"Whoa," Terese said from the doorway, "you can't even tell the difference."

My mother had made my blouse and Bermuda shorts to look just like the Villager outfits Terese and I were crazy about.

"Try some of this." She held out a tiny bottle of L'Aimant perfume. "It's my grandmother's. They're up for the weekend and she let me borrow it."

Behind me in the mirror her green eyelids shone. Her hair was cut short on one side and hung forward over one eye and down to her chin on the other. It was a sharp hairdo, and she didn't mind at all that it made her look taller than she already was. I dabbed the perfume in the base of my throat and behind each ear. The sweetness hit me like a club, and I rubbed the spots with a towel.

"What're you doing?" Terese yanked the towel away from me.

"It's too strong."

"Jesus, Danny, you hardly have any on. It smells great."

Bryan stopped in the middle of the living room. "Watch out, killer bees on the warpath." He slung the towel over the railing at the top of the stairs.

"It's not gonna dry there," I said. "I keep telling you to hang it outside."

"I like it here."

"That's because it's easier than going outside. What if we had guests, where would they sleep? The whole bottom bunk in your room is piled high with junk."

"When do we have guests? You're going to wear out early worrying so much, Danny."

"You think I like the fact that you leave your toenail clippings all along the window sills? Apple cores fermenting under your bed? You've got bugs in your room, Bryan, and they're gonna be heading my way next."

"If you had enough stuff to keep you busy you wouldn't be noseying around where you don't belong. You know what they say about people like you, Danny—anal retentive. Besides, you've got dirty books under *your* bed."

Terese gaped at him. *The Harrad Experiment* had her name written on the inside cover. "How do you know what's under my bed?" I asked.

" 'Cause I saw you stick it under there. You better watch it, Danny, too much reading'll give you warts."

"You're a disgusting armadillo, Bryan."

Downstairs the refrigerator door opened, and we heard the plink of cubes, the pop of the can opener.

Bryan made a big show of draping his T-shirt over the railing. "You two have a ride to the fireworks?"

"We're going with Marilyn," Terese said.

"I thought you said Jimmy was driving us." I took the end of Bryan's damp towel and rubbed it over my throat. Watching TV might be better than listening to Carline Gland bleating into my ear all night, that is, if she was coming to the fireworks. Twice a week she and Frieda drove home to Staten Island; she'd probably failed something and was taking a summer school course.

"Who wants to go with him?" Terese asked. "Marilyn's father said she could take the Mustang. We can put the top down."

Bryan grinned. "I'll have to go with Jimmy then, cheer him up a bit."

Terese had toyed with the idea of asking Bryan to come with us, but she didn't. She'd been brushing Jimmy Piper off for weeks now, thinking that since he and Bryan were best friends, it was hurting her chances with Bryan. I'd had my fill of it.

Bryan turned on the TV. He couldn't get through the day without tallying up the latest casualty figures and worrying over the new "search and destroy" missions that were supposed to kill as many Vietcong as possible. From what we could see on the news, it looked like whole families were getting killed. Already there were over half a million refugees, peasants who had nowhere to go.

"Here we are, going to the fireworks when just this week Johnson sent bombers over Hanoi. It doesn't seem right," he said.

My mother's high-pitched voice carried up the stairs and muffled the sound of helicopters. I pulled Terese by the sleeve, and we left through the back door. Now and then a drop fell on me from a leaf overhead. The intermittent sound of dripping leaves and branches soothed me, and I was grateful, as I always was, for Terese's silence.

As we walked across the bridge, I glanced back once at the house. My father was standing on the porch gazing out on the lake. I lifted my hand in a wave just as he raised his glass, so he didn't see me. I could only hope that if he went over to the Tamarack later, he'd be careful crossing the highway. My mother used to go with him on Saturday nights, but now she stayed home and watched *The Big Valley* on TV.

Marilyn was propped up in the front seat of her father's yellow Mustang. She was dating some boy from Staten Island who looked like Ringo Starr and could only come up every other weekend. With time on her hands, she didn't mind chauffeuring us around.

"Terese." Jimmy Piper leaped out of the line seated at the end of the bridge. He had a round freckled face and a mouthful of braces. He was short, too, which didn't help him with Terese, who was at least three inches taller. Nobody could beat him for personality, though. He was like his father, Jay Piper, who was chairman of the board of governors at Rainy Lake and a member of the city council in Cherry Hill, New Jersey. The two of them were always right out there with an opinion or a joke. Much as Jimmy bugged me, the way he hungered after Terese, I thought if I had to be stranded in an elevator with any boy up there, excepting Billy, it'd be Jimmy Piper.

I felt sorry for him when Terese breezed by and hopped into the Mustang next to Marilyn. It meant that I was stuck in the back seat with Carline, who was strolling out of Sal and Joey's with a new pack of Camels.

"She's up," I said flatly.

Terese laughed. "Of course she's up. You think Carline would miss the fireworks?"

The two Gland girls could have been adopted, they were so different. Marilyn, who was short and looked just like Ann-Margret, dressed in feminine, cute-looking clothes, while Carline was all greaser, clothes flashy and tight, the seams ready to go at any minute. Carline was tall and thin with a long neck and the pointy, padded breasts that were her trademark. These days she was letting her hair go back to its natural, dishwater color. She had a wispy, uneven cut that made her look just like Twiggy.

Next to Carline, you couldn't help liking Marilyn. I didn't used to, especially when she was chasing after Billy Dove. She had a bad reputation with boys, still swam the doggy paddle, and had a helpless look about her, even though she'd just turned seventeen. She had this beautiful voice, though, high and melodic with a range like Joni Mitchell's. The first time I'd heard her sing was at one of the dances last summer when the lead female singer had dropped out and they'd asked Marilyn to take her place. There she'd stood on the platform, dressed in an apple-green-checked culottes outfit and not fitting in with the band at all. Yet when she opened her mouth, you couldn't think of anything but her voice and the way the song showed in her face. I had the feeling she could be a star someday, if some guy didn't knock her up first.

Plus she was genuinely friendly, unlike her sister, whose voice was like hot wax boiling in my ear.

"Who's got that *godawful* perfume on?" Carline sniffed in an exaggerated way, coming so close to my neck I almost belted her.

"Cut it out, Carline." Terese leaned over the front seat, and a new wave of L'Aimant washed over us. "This perfume happens to cost thirty dollars an ounce."

"Well, I've got something here that costs less than that but will make you feel *a lot* better." She held up a bottle of Mott's apple juice.

"The wires upstairs starting to short out, Carline?" This close to her, I could see a sprinkling of bronze-colored freckles across the bridge of her nose.

"Here, have some." She handed me the bottle.

"What are you up to, Carline?" Marilyn asked.

"Start driving. You want everybody in here with us?"

I unscrewed the lid and tipped the bottle toward my lips. The unmistakable smell of alcohol brought immediate tears to my eyes. "What the hell *is* this?"

Carline laughed. "Bourbon."

"You took that from home? Dad's gonna kill you, Carline, when he finds out," Marilyn said.

"There's the beauty of it, he's not gonna find out. I've been siphoning this off since last May, a little bit out of every new bottle. He's never even noticed."

I looked at her with admiration. "I gotta hand it to you, Carline."

Terese shook her head. "The police catch us driving around with that, we're dead. You better hide it."

"Loosen up, Terese. We're just having a little apple juice. Here, have some."

Terese chewed her lip. Ever since she'd gotten drunk at her house last summer, she'd drunk only an occasional beer or bottle of Ripple.

"Well, I don't want any." Marilyn slapped her hand on the steering wheel. "You kids are gonna be up to your necks in it if we get caught. Besides, Carline, what about Toni? She won't like you showing up with a hangover."

"Aw, I've been good all summer. I gotta live, don't I?"

"Who's Toni, your summer-school teacher?" I grinned.

Terese took a sip and grimaced, handing the bottle back to Carline and me. "Summer school? She's talking about her coach."

"What coach?" I asked.

A few drops dribbled down Carline's long neck as she swallowed. "Here, have some."

"You have anything to mix it with?" I asked.

Carline reached into her bag and pulled out a bottle of ginger ale and two paper cups. Her eyes were fairly burbling over, she was so pleased with herself. I grinned, filled a cup half-full of ginger ale, and topped it off with bourbon.

"Geez, Danny, you better watch it," Terese said.

It was pretty smooth going down, and I thought about how many times my father had described a drink like that—*smooth*. By the time we reached the field off Disappointment,

I'd downed two glasses. Carline had already spilled enough to soak the whole front of her shirt.

It was still light when we arrived. The field was moving with kids, and there were blankets spread out everywhere. Through the trees I could see the blue-gray glint of Disappointment Lake. Marilyn put down a green plaid blanket for us. I remember rolling up against Carline's knobby shoulder, lifting the bourbon to my lips, and drinking it straight. Most of all I remember the black night and the fireworks—bigger and grander than I'd ever seen. The whole sky was smouldering and popping as if wired with electricity.

"Danny, would you sit up? You're kicking me." Terese was propping me up, which brought the sky even closer. I threw my head back against her chest, and saw the red glow of her hair against the fireworks.

"Ow, that hurts."

"Jesus, Terese. I've never seen it like this. Jesus, sweet Jesus. Red, blue, look at it, *look, look,* shit, it's purple, pink, yellow. Aw, when it starts to crumble like that don't you think it's sad? I do, shit, *shit* I think it's sad."

"Danny, keep your voice down. Geez, is she ever loaded." Terese's hands were on my shoulders, pulling me up every time I slid down. Marilyn's face was a pale, worried disk in the evening sky. She had enough to handle with Carline, who'd tumbled face first onto the blanket.

"You should hope she doesn't start puking all over like she did last time. Remember, Terese? Remember? Shit, it was just about the worst. My father, that's it, my father was sick too. Drinking with *your* father. The two of them, they're turning out to be just drunks, aren't they? All this trouble with his business, my poor father, you never know who's gonna try to do you in. Jesus, oh Jesus, look at the sky, Terese. Look at it, *look*—it's falling, do you believe how loud it is? Somebody's gonna get burned the way those sparks keep flying."

"What's going on?"

78

I stared up the dark street of Bryan's leg as he stood over us, his blonde hair lost in the fireworks.

"Bryan, *Bryan*, whoa boy, you won't believe what's happening. Your head is absolutely going to be history if you don't duck. All that friggin' red and orange . . . Christ, Christ, get out of the way."

"Is she . . . ?"

"Absolutely," Terese said.

"How did this happen?" He knelt down, and the two of them rolled me up to a sitting position.

Terese pointed to Carline. "Quasimodo here brought a full bottle of bourbon. We kept telling them to quit. Carline didn't have as much as Danny, and she's out like a light. I don't know what's going on at your house, Bryan, but she's been itching for trouble ever since I picked her up."

"You want me to drive you home?" Marilyn asked.

Bryan nodded. "Let's get Danny to the car first, then I'll come back and give you a hand." He nodded toward Carline, who was curled up like a bony donut on the blanket. Terese helped him to lift me. With one arm hooked around each of their necks, I wobbled across the field.

When I heard Billy Dove's voice, I concentrated on holding my head up, and saw faces rocking by in billows of colored light. "Terese, Terese, what's he doing? Christ, he's gonna go find Marilyn now or is he with somebody else? Shit, Terese, won't you tell me what's happening?"

"Danny, just shut up, would you? I don't know what you're talking about."

"Sure, sure, nobody knows but me and what does that prove? Oh, Jesus, look up, there it goes again. I'm gonna be sick with all this color, this *friggin' color.* Look, look!"

"Quiet down for God's sake." Bryan was practically dragging me now; my feet were collecting pebbles from the gravel lot down by the lake.

I felt the thud of the seat travel into my throat. My head

rocked forward, and Bryan tipped it back, holding his hand a minute on my forehead.

"When are you gonna let up on Daddy?" I asked. "Everybody thinks they know all the answers. Well, I'll tell you something—that man did Daddy in and nobody can tell me otherwise. Jesus, I wish I could meet that son of a bitch shitty friggin' bastard face to face and you know I'd let him have it. So Daddy didn't know everything, is that a crime? Is it a bloody crime to be naive, Bryan? Is it? Jesus, nobody wants to admit anything. Terese better wake up and see what she's letting herself in for, mooning over Mr. Perfect your highness, never give anybody a break . . . *shit*."

"He went back to get Carline. Would you be quiet?" Terese's voice was ragged, and her face bobbed up and down like a buoy next to me.

"Sit still, Terese. *Jesus*. What about Billy, you never said anything—who was he with? Some girl, that's what, some big-breasted girl like Marilyn. He'll never like me, Terese, never, never, never, only big girls with high voices who are older and go down the tracks with him. I would, in a *second*, you can bet your sweet life on it."

"Don't say that, Danny, you're too young for that stuff. Billy's not the right kind of boy for you anyway. I wish you'd see it."

"Whaddaya mean? What's not right about him? He's as good looking as Bryan any day, you know he is."

"OK, he's good-looking, so what? His father's a convict and his mother's black. For crying out *loud*, Danny, do I need to spell it out?"

"So what, so what, so what? Jesus, Terese, what the damn hell do I care?"

"You have to care, Danny. It'll matter, one day it'll matter. You know your parents wouldn't like it."

"They won't even notice. Besides, my father isn't like yours—he's a Democrat, and he's not prejudiced either."

"You're saying my father is prejudiced?"

"Shit, Terese, give me a break. *You're* prejudiced, look at what you just said about Billy."

"That's not prejudice, it's common sense. Billy isn't right for you; you have *nothing* in common."

"Besides which he's not all black anyway. He's only half black."

"Half black, all black, who are you kidding? You better stop pretending he's white, Danny, cause he isn't. You're no better than me, pretending the black part of him doesn't make him black."

"Black, white, all this color anyway, it's giving me a friggin' headache!"

"Move over." Bryan swung open the door and Carline tumbled in beside me.

"Yuck, she's throwing up." Terese said.

"That's just the smell. She did it already." Marilyn slid into the front seat next to Bryan, and we turned onto Route 206.

Carline's head bumped gently on my shoulder, and I could smell the odd, incense-like fragrance of her skin. Every now and then she moaned softly. Even in my wasted state I felt myself softening toward her; Carline asleep seemed to bring that out in me. Awake I always wanted to haul off and hit her.

I have this image of the Glands that stays in my mind. They're sitting at the dinner table—Gerry's rattling on about how many dishwashers he sold that morning, not looking at his wife sitting next to him staring at her plate or at his daughters, each of whom knows exactly who he is and handles it in her own way: Marilyn by going down the tracks with one boy after another, Carline by arming herself to the nines with peroxide and mascara, and holding the world an arm's length away.

Bryan and Marilyn were talking softly in the front seat. I tried to listen but the noise in the open car blew away their voices. Wouldn't that be a pair, I thought, Bryan and Marilyn Gland? Well, it would probably be good for him. It might shake loose some of his backed-up hormones.

When Marilyn dropped us off on the dirt road in back of our house, a momentary blackness descended on me. I remember wondering why they didn't bring me to Terese's house. Bryan could have said I was sleeping over; nobody would have known I was drunk, and the evening would have passed almost peacefully. Now I think he did it on purpose, not minding his own trouble as much as he wanted my father to see it, to have it out at last.

Bryan propped me up in front of him and banged on the back door. The lights beamed through the window next to my right ear, and I saw the black stove, the TV antenna, my mother sitting on the red-flowered couch. When the screen door opened, I pitched forward past my father's stomach onto the wood floor.

"Dad." I gawked at the scuffed tip of his brown loafer.

My father's eyes were locked open in surprise. His thinning blonde hair stuck up on top as if he'd just run his hand through it. He leaned down to pick me up, and that's when I started laughing. It was an out-and-out fit. Laughter rolled out in reels of sound, shrieking, gasping, quivering. My parents and Bryan stood there looking dumb. Finally, my father reached out and slapped me—once, but hard enough so that you could hear the sound. I bit my tongue and tasted the eggy blood inside my mouth.

My mother took my arm and walked me over to the couch, where she pushed me back lightly so my head rested against the cushion.

"She's drunk!" my father said.

"No kidding." Bryan sat down on the rocking chair, and glanced from my father to me.

"And what are you looking so smug about? How dare you bring her home like this . . . ?"

"Where else was I supposed to bring her?" Bryan's hands tightened on the arms of the chair.

When my father stepped toward him, it looked as if his whole body were swelling up, all his muscles pressing to the surface, his head growing bigger and bigger. "You've been pushing the limits all summer, Bryan, but this takes the cake. You've got one hell of a nerve bringing your sister home like this!"

"Wait a minute, you think *I* got her drunk?"

"Shit, Dad, Bryan didn't do anything." My head was weighted down with bricks, and I could hear the gurgling in my stomach.

"You can just shut up, young lady. You've done enough as it is."

"Maybe you should ask her," my mother said.

He whirled around. "*I'm* handling this, goddamit!" My mother recoiled as if he'd slapped her. "You're the oldest, Bryan. I expect you to be responsible enough to look after your sister. Whose car did you come home in? Was the driver drinking? Both of you could have been killed! And what if you hadn't been there? Anything could have happened to her—she's only fourteen, for crying out loud."

"I'm trying to tell you, Dad, Carline had this apple juice in a bottle only it was bourbon and we were drinking it. Then we got to the fireworks and holy Jesus you should have seen it . . . why, the whole place was lit up like a friggin' bonfire. I thought Bryan's hair was gonna blow once, I sure as hell did."

My mother was staring as if I'd suddenly mutated. "Listen to her *language*! Jesus, Mary, and Joseph!"

"*They* were there, *they* were there. Goddamit, the whole friggin' lake was there."

Charlie was standing practically on top of me. "So you were with your brother?"

"What does *he* have to do with it? No, I told you already. Though Terese wanted him to. Jesus, what a case that girl has. You'd think you could give her the time of day, Bryan. At your age you should have a girlfriend, or people are gonna think there's something wrong with you. Nobody likes the one who likes them, and that's the God's honest truth. Shit, I wish things would stop moving around in here . . . . I'm gonna throw up, Mom."

My mother raced downstairs and then up with the blue-marbled mixing bowl, which she put in my lap. I could hear it bubbling around in my stomach, my hiccups loud and fast. When I started vomiting, I was aware of my father's feet over by the rocker, Bryan's sneakers circling, my mother's hand on my hair.

She took the full bowl and disappeared into the bathroom. My father and brother were standing face to face, Charlie red and big, Bryan pale as a new moon, with tears brimming in his eyes.

"I don't have to take this. Go ahead and think what you want. You're always looking for a scapegoat, aren't you, Dad? Someone to blame for things. Like Danny couldn't have gotten drunk all by herself, I had to do it to her. Maybe she was upset about something, you ever think of that? Hanging around here the way she does, chewing her nails and reading books. She sees *everything*. Nobody thinks a thing of it, you and Mom going at it, the whole group sitting around having drinks—or worse, you heading over to the Pink Elephant . . . "

"Bryan!" My mother moved toward him, still holding the washcloth she'd just wiped my face with. "Watch how you talk to your father."

"Why? It's true, isn't it? I don't see how he has the right to be so mad at Danny, considering the way he drinks. He won't do a damn thing on the deck . . . "

I saw it coming: my father's hand clenched hand rising, the left side of his jaw throbbing as if he were carrying something live inside his cheek. The blow sent Bryan into the bookcase. A whole shelf tumbled down with him onto the braided rug.

"Charlie!" My mother stepped forward, and the shock resounded in her face. It was one of my father's strictest rules— he didn't hit us and, no matter what happened, we weren't to hit each other. Even when Bryan and I were little and neighborhood siblings were pummeling each other in the back seats of cars, we knew it was forbidden for us. Talk it out, Charlie said, or walk away.

My father seemed to be imploding before my eyes. His skin was drawn and gray; his cheeks sagged as if the flesh were being suctioned from within. Bryan was stiff and pallid; the whole sad year was swimming in his face. He opened his mouth as if to say something, then strode out of the house, leaving the door open behind him.

"Bryan!" I lurched toward the door. My brother's blonde head disappeared down the dirt road.

"It's not his fault, it's not." Wishing I could see them better, I turned back to my parents. "He didn't come along till *after*, Dad. I swear to God it's true. Bryan helped me to the car and brought me home. You can ask Terese, she was there. Shit, Dad, Bryan's already told you. He doesn't lie, you know he doesn't. Why the hell didn't he bring me to Terese's house? Now *this* has to happen."

"Go after him, Charlie," my mother said.

"He'll be all right. He can't talk to me like that, May, I won't have it."

"Please, Dad, he didn't mean it." I was vaguely conscious of my parents holding me between them and walking me back and forth. I remember stumbling downstairs and sitting at the kitchen table, where my mother set a cup of coffee in front of me. When I tried to drink it, my forehead crashed onto the rim of the cup, splashing the steaming coffee back at me.

Finally, as the objects in the room settled, I started to cry. My head hurt, my stomach hurt, my forehead smarted from the hot coffee. As Charlie's hand moved in circles on my back, the callouses on his fingers snagged on my blouse.

"Why is this happening, Dad?"

"I don't know. It's been a bad year, Danny, for all of us."

"It wasn't your fault, Dad, was it? I don't understand how he could get away with it. All your wonderful ideas. Now you have to work with those other architects again. I don't see how you can stand it."

"It's the way things are, Danny. I needed the job." My father handed me a Kleenex. There were so many lines tracking across his skin, like tiny Chinese characters.

Some things I knew: that Hawkman had sued my father and the contractor, that Charlie had declared corporate bankruptcy and settled out of court, that Bryan believed Charlie should have fought it. Later, I learned how much money my parents had borrowed, which was why Charlie was so scared of losing more.

"Terese says her father thinks Mr. Hawkman planned it, he and his lawyers . . . " I said.

"What does Tim know?" my mother said.

"Maybe he did. Hawkman's got a whole team working for him. They know all the ins and outs of insurance, you can bet your life on it. Who kept jacking up the price, anyway? He just didn't want to pay for it, that's all."

"Maybe if you'd had more experience with this kind of project, Charlie, or if you'd asked someone."

"What are you saying, May?"

His face had regained that scary stillness again. My mother bit her lip; her blue eyes darted back and forth.

"Nothing, Charlie, only that maybe you'd have estimated differently. I said 'maybe', Charlie, no one knows for sure."

"Well," he said bitterly, "it's over now."

"I'm so sorry, Dad," I said, the tears rising again.

"Take her up to bed, May."

"Are you gonna look for him?" I asked.

"Let's go, Danny." My mother put her arm around my shoulder and guided me toward the stairs. I heard the refrigerator door open and the clink of ice dropping in a glass.

*

The next morning I crawled out of bed and pushed aside the striped curtain in my doorway, then Bryan's. He was lying spread-eagled on the top bunk. One bare foot dangled over the side. His mouth was open, and the pillow he hugged close

86

to his body at night had tumbled onto the floor by my feet. I picked it up and sniffed my brother's familiar odor: balsam wood, hair oil, and the comfortable smell of worn flannel. I tiptoed past my parents' room to the bathroom, where I took two aspirin and a hefty swig of antacid. A long sigh emptied out of me as I slipped back into bed, relieved I didn't have to worry anymore.

It must have been late morning when I woke again, for the sun was falling in bisque-colored strokes onto the blue leis hanging from my oval mirror. I reached down and grabbed the novel, *My Antonía*, lying open face-down on the rug. Later, when I walked onto the porch, my father was standing on the deck sanding the edge of a freshly cut piece of wood. Bryan was kneeling a few yards away on the steps, hammering a two-by-four into place.

It was quiet, just the occasional "hand me the chisel" and "the level OK?" A summer ago Bryan would have been firing questions about politics or buildings or boat design, and Charlie would have responded in his slow, thoughtful way. Across the lake children called out, boats chugged by, and one of the Conroy boys rode his bicycle across the creaking bridge. My tongue licked the cottony surface of my teeth. I sat in the swing and leaned my throbbing head against the cushion. I was happy the world was stationary again, that my father was working on the deck, that my brother's voice was only a few yards away.

*

My mother's flip-flops pattered up and down the wooden steps. I kicked back the covers and thought about which was better: not having to dive into the algae-thick water at Lake Hiawatha (my mother had told Linda that I'd be missing the swim meet), or helping May transport forty flower arrangements over the bridge to the clubhouse.

She'd been up most of the night. Flowers and greens were strewn everywhere; our refrigerator and four others were filled to capacity with arrangements. The women came and went, watching my mother's deft fingers as they sorted and shaped. She'd even managed to rope my father into the act, for he stood at the kitchen table dutifully tying bows around the base of each basket.

"For God's sakes, get dressed, Danny. I want to take these over first, then we've got to go to Nini's, and then over to Caseys'."

My father peered at us between purple spokes of hianthus.

"Take those two arrangements, Charlie. Danny, we'll meet you over there."

Gladiola cascaded over my father's shoulders as he made his way carefully down the steps and across the patio. After I'd eaten my third slice of Entenmann's coffee cake, I foraged through the forest of greens under the house to find the white swan. It was my favorite arrangement—tight bunches of white carnations twisted into an underwire figure of a swan. I loved the long and graceful neck soaring through a tangle of ferns. "Your mother's a genius with flowers," the women kept saying, as if I needed convincing.

We must have made eleven trips back and forth by the time we'd ferried the last arrangement across the bridge. Inside the clubhouse women were setting up tables, laying tablecloths, choosing among the rows of arrangements lined up along the wall. They looked so funny, most of them in rollers and spit curls plastered to their cheeks with Scotch tape. Usually my mother sewed a new dress for the opening BYOL (Bring Your Own Liquor) Dance, but this year the flowers had taken all her time. The night before, Charlie had handed her a fifty-dollar bill and told her to go into Neptune and buy a new dress. That was another reason she was hurrying, so she and Nini would have time to hit the new dress shop where Rita Casey had bought hers.

The men were gathered on the clubhouse porch. I figured they'd be discussing the latest bombing of Hanoi, so I sat quietly on the wooden bench that ran the length of the clubhouse.

I had to laugh at Ed Casey, who was wearing a pair of bleeding madras shorts with another, different, bleeding madras shirt. One thing about Charlie, he sure did have a sense of style. He looked a little like Alan Ladd as he stood there tall and lean in the midst of the other men, most of whom were a few inches shorter than he with Dunlops already started around their middles. Ed Casey leaned over Charlie's shoulder and jabbed his finger into the open air.

"You know damn well, Charlie, our property value, *everybody's* property value, will drop if we allow J.D. Hicks and his family into the club. Jay talked to a realtor, who told him what happened over at Jewell Lake. Why, he can't even sell a house there for more than ten thousand dollars. You know those houses are worth at least twenty."

Jay Piper shook his head sadly. "That's right, Charlie. A realtor from over in Dover said he's seen it happen that way before. Said once the colored infiltrate a neighborhood, white folks leave in droves. You can't ever recoup the value of your property."

"It's wrong," Charlie said. "I can't vote against a man simply because he's black."

"Well *I* can," said Paddy Doonan. "There isn't another Negro family on the whole lake. Why can't he rent over on Disappointment? The fishing's just as good, houses are *a lot* cheaper, and there are Negroes living on the lake already—you know, Marcella Dove's folks."

"We'd be doing him a favor," said Ed Casey. "Rita says his wife's not any too anxious to stay at Rainy. She knows the score. J.D.'s just got his dander up and wants to make a statement. Look, I'm as much for civil rights as anybody. Hell, they're busing Negroes into our schools from downtown Newark. Oughtta see what a difference it made on the varsity basketball team, changed some folks' tunes in a hurry, I can tell ya. But when it comes to your own property, losing money, you gotta defend yourself."

"I wouldn't rent an apartment in *their* neighborhood. I wouldn't belong, pure and simple," said Paddy.

"The bottom line, Charlie," said Jay, "is that you'll lose the money you've put into your house. All that fancy work you're doing, it won't be worth a nickel."

"I'm telling you I won't vote against him."

I could see the tension in my father's back. His shoulders were curled inward as if to ward off the men closing in from both sides. Jay Piper mentioned the bankruptcy then, how much money Charlie had lost, which surprised me since I assumed my parents had kept it quiet. The way they were yammering on about their property values, you'd have thought the whole lake was in danger of being mortgaged.

"Everybody on the board'll be at the dance anyway," said Jay. "We can vote there, save us an extra meeting next week."

The screen door shut softly behind me, and I walked to the center of the room and surveyed the blur of candy-pink table-cloths, pink plastic cups and ashtrays, and pink and white balloons tied at the head of each table. The sweet, heavy smell of my mother's flowers was like a drug, which made the women floating back and forth seem like so many bubbles colliding without a sound.

Less than an hour later my mother was sitting next to me in the swing, sewing the cuff on my father's navy blue dress pants. I knew by the way her foot was jiggling up and down that she was nervously waiting for Nini. She wished the new dress was already bought and hanging in her closet.

Bryan pushed open the screen door and came in. He was breathing heavily, as if he'd been running.

"Who won?" I asked.

"We did, by seventeen points."

"Did you beat Mark Hennessy in butterfly?"

"Yeah. Where's Dad?"

"Here I am." Charlie walked out of the kitchen, rolling a long streamer of yellow ribbon back onto the spool.

"Ty says his father's going to vote against the Hicks family joining the club. Whaddya say to a guy like that?"

Charlie placed the spool carefully onto the table top and took a deep breath. "We were just talking about that over at the club."

"What are you going to do, Dad? They can't get away with this, can they?"

My mother still had her needle lifted; the blue fabric was frozen in her left hand.

"I'm going to do what I think is best, Bryan, for all of us."

"I know that, Dad, but what about the rest of them?"

"The men have nothing against the Hicks family, Bry. The sad fact is that once a Negro family moves in, people get nervous. As soon as one person sells, it's like a chain reaction. Over at Jewell the property values have dropped so low you can buy a house there for a song."

"If they want to sell, let 'em. Things'll level out sooner or later, won't they?"

"It's not that simple, son."

"Well, *we* don't have plans to sell. Neither do any of my friends' parents, not that I know of."

"No, we don't. But we do plan to use this house to help finance your college education. Either we'll sell it or refinance. That's only a few years away for you, Bryan."

"Come on, Dad, we're talking about one black family here."

"Once the Hicks family joins, who's to say other blacks won't try to rent, or even buy at Rainy?"

"What if they do?"

"*That's* what I'm telling you. It means the value of our house will go down. We might not get back what we paid for it, much less all the work we've done."

"Are you saying *you're* going to vote against him?"

There was a whizzing noise inside my head as if a dozen birds were flying very fast, their wings catching on the roots of my hair. My mother looked down into her lap.

"I'm saying, Bryan, that I want to be able to borrow against the house when you're ready to go to college. After this year . . . well, we've got a lot to pay back. This house is all I have to put you kids through college."

"Bryan and I could take a loan, Dad," I said. The three of them looked at me as if I'd dropped through a hole in the roof.

My father shook his head. "Bryan will probably have to take a small loan anyway. I won't let *you* take a loan. Mark my words, a boy'll think twice about marrying a girl with a loan."

"Marry?" I said. "What has that got to do with any-thing . . . "

"Look, I don't like this any more than you do, Bryan. I'd never vote against him under normal circumstances. They could all hang before I'd do it. If it weren't for this financial mess we're in . . . . Besides, the Hicks family will be better off somewhere else, somewhere they fit in."

"You gotta be kidding me, Dad." Bryan's sunburn looked splotchy and red.

My mother stood up. I knew by her eyes that she didn't agree, that she believed it was a weak and cowardly act no matter how good the reasons. But her chin was set on the high sweep of her neck, and I knew she wasn't going to question my father's judgement. This time, like it or not, she was going to be in his corner.

"You don't understand anything about money, Bryan." Her blue eyes dropped onto me. "You either. The men on the board can't do what they might like to do here—they have to consider the larger picture."

"Some men on the board won't mind at all." Bryan's voice fell like a stone at my father's feet.

"I'm not like them, Bryan," Charlie said quietly.

"Oh yeah? You're always talking about justice. The color of a person's skin doesn't matter, his religion doesn't matter. Whether he's educated or middle class or lives in a friggin' cave isn't supposed to *matter*. Everybody deserves the same opportunity, isn't that what you said? Or is it only when it's convenient, when it doesn't demand anything of you?"

Bryan's eyes, fixed on my father, burned. Charlie's mouth opened and closed, and on his face loomed the same shadow that had been chasing him all summer. I brushed the side of my head where the whirring patter of wings was the worst, and wondered if you needed your parents' consent to get a student loan.

"There are some facts of life you can't ignore, Bryan." Charlie's breathing was loud and labored. "My vote won't matter anyway. Even if I were to vote for J.D., the others have a majority."

When we heard Nini Kelly's giggle at the back door, my mother tossed me Charlie's pants and clattered up the stairs.

"You'd better get dressed, Bry, or you'll miss your bus. You don't want to be late for work. I'll fix you some lunch," I said.

He stalked past me and up the stairs.

"Come on, Dad, why don't you clean this mess off the table while I make us a couple of sandwiches?"

Charlie stood mutely on the porch, his arms droopy and long at his sides. When I nudged him, he shuffled into the kitchen, where he busied himself clearing the table of pieces of curling ribbon, ferns, and discarded, brown-tipped buds. I packed a ham-and-cheese sandwich and the last two slices of coffee cake for Bryan. I'd just set it by the bottom of the stairs when I heard running footsteps on the bridge and glimpsed the back of Bryan's head as he loped across. A few seconds later the engine turned over in Nini's yellow Volkswagen as the two women headed off to Rodeo Dresses in Neptune.

*

When my mother arrived home at five-thirty, she called down from the screened porch. I could tell by the high, joyful sound of her voice that she'd found a dress. Charlie finished hammering his end of the railing into place and took mine into his own hands.

"I can finish this myself, Danny. Go on upstairs."

Tissue paper whispered, and my mother's feet thumped across the floor.

"Mom?"

"What do you think?"

Hanging from the curtain rod was a hot pink, sheath-like formal with a cowl neck. May's face was flushed nearly the same color, and her blue eyes flew from me to the dress.

"Well, do you like it?"

I swallowed. "Yeah, sure, Mom. It's just, well, it looks kind of . . . narrow. You never make this kind of dress."

"I know, and that's why I thought I'd give it a whirl, try something new. Nini thinks the color's perfect for me. Look, I bought lipstick in Woolworth's to match."

I glanced from the pink dress to my mother's blooming face. There were other colors that would have been better, but it was the size that worried me. As she bent over the bed to unwrap another package, I couldn't imagine how she'd fit into it. She usually wore empire dresses or designs with a loose-fitting waistline.

"What size is it, Mom?"

She spun around on her blue sneakers. "Twelve. Wait until you see this!" She held up a white garment: a one-piece girdle and long-line bra.

"Twelve . . . . You wear a size sixteen, Mom."

"Fourteen, Danny. Remember, I lost five pounds last week when Nini and I went on that grapefruit diet. The salesgirl said it ran large."

"Did you try it on?"

"Not exactly . . . . I needed one of these first."

"What is it?"

She smiled. "An all-in-one girdle. Nini says they're the newest thing. The salesgirl *assured* me there'd be no problem if I wore this."

Not wanting to hurt her feelings, I nodded. Her eyes were

so shiny blue, and the breeze from her rapid movements rustled the tissue paper on the bed.

"You go downstairs, Danny, and heat up my ziti casserole. I'm going to shower and do my hair. And call your father up. I want him to have plenty of time to dress. Did you finish his pants? Oh, and ask him what shirt he plans on wearing—you may have to iron one for him—no, never mind, check with me before you iron anything. You never know what he'll pick out, and I want to make sure he doesn't wear one of those paisley shirts you kids gave him for Father's Day. They'll never go with my dress."

I served the ziti, but my mother wouldn't eat any; she didn't want to put anything in her body that might show. When Bryan had come home, he'd stopped next to my father on the deck, picked up one of my neatly sawed lengths of wood, and continued on the latticework right where I'd left off. Now the two of them sat at the table talking in abbreviated sentences about silicon carbide reamers.

"Danny, could you come up here?"

"You better take your shower, Dad. She'll get mad if you're not ready in time."

He waved me away with his fork. "Don't you worry, it only takes me fifteen minutes to shower and dress. You go upstairs and help your mother."

At the top step I heard a loud thump from the bedroom, as if someone had fallen.

"Mom?"

My mother was on her knees, hands on the top of the all-in-one, an elbow against the bed.

"Help me up, Danny. This thing is so hard to get on I lost my balance."

I pulled on the back while May yanked up the front, squeezing her face in pain.

"Mom, are you sure this fits?"

"Just hook up the back, Danny."

"You're gonna have to suck in, Mom, 'cause it doesn't close across your back."

May took a deep breath while I tugged the back ends together, breaking a nail in my struggle.

"There!" My mother reached triumphantly for the dress.

From behind I could see the flesh spilling over the top of the bra.

"Mom?" I pointed to the bulge along the edge of her armpit.

"Oh, that doesn't matter. The fat has to go somewhere—you won't even see it."

She slid her slip over the girdle and motioned for me to hold the dress so she could step inside. The pink dress went on without too much trouble, although I had to strain to get the zipper up. My mother took several small steps over to the mirror on the back of the bedroom door.

"What do you think?"

I studied her figure, unable to overlook the rolls protruding through the pink fabric. What was even worse was that you could see the elastic binding on the girdle, which resembled rows of downward-pointing arrows. It looked as if she'd fallen asleep in her dress on a patterned bedspread and woken up to find the design imprinted on the surface.

"Looks good, doesn't it, Danny?"

I hesitated, torn between telling the truth or lying to make her happy.

"Sure, Mom."

May's blue eyes flashed past me and she smiled.

"Like it, Charlie?"

There was my father's face, mouth open as if he'd just swallowed something too big for him. "You look real . . . snappy, May. That's some color, isn't it?"

My mother whooped and minced over to the bureau, where she fumbled in her makeup case. "Wait till you see Nini's! It's the living end."

"I can hardly wait." Charlie turned and headed for the bathroom.

*

Bryan and I rocked on the swing. The low table in front of us was littered with soda cans, Ritz crackers, and Velveeta. Late arrivals to the dance swayed across the bridge. The women were stiff in their high-heeled shoes, which caught now and then in the open spaces between the slats. When one did, the woman cried out or laughed while her husband held her by the arm and tugged her ankle, taking care not to drop the brown bag holding their bottles for the BYOL dance.

"It's hot." Bryan fanned himself with a copy of *U.S. News and World Report*, which he'd been reading regularly ever since he'd joined the debate team at Westfield High.

"Think it'll rain?" I asked.

"Nah, sky's too clear. Let's swim—I haven't done laps in a couple of days."

We swam back and forth between the dock and the bridge. I loved the quiet, lukewarm lake at this time of day: the way copper lights flared in the darkness when you opened your eyes underwater, the sudden motion as a fish, its oily scales shining, flickered out of sight. After the initial fatigue wore off and I'd found my rhythm, I could swim without consciousness. It was like a prayer, this steady movement through water, the way it happened sometimes when you slipped into church for confession and there was no one else there, just you and the priest and the gleam of candles.

Bryan had two laps on me by the time we climbed onto the water-level ledge that topped the base of one of the bridge's two concrete supports.

"What do you think Mr. Hicks will do?" I rubbed my back against the concrete.

"If they'd rented on the water it wouldn't be such a problem. They could still swim and fish off the dock. But now, since they can't use the beaches, what good is it? He'll probably go somewhere else. I suppose he's used to it."

My white legs circled in the ruddy dark. "What would you have done?"

"Voted to let him join and then threatened to resign my own membership if they rejected him."

"But then we'd have to leave Rainy Lake."

"No we wouldn't. We own the house; nobody could change that. But we couldn't use the beach or club."

It was the first time I'd ever thought about membership in the Community Club. Without it, you couldn't be on the swim team or the ski club, you couldn't use the tennis courts or play pool in the clubhouse. And you could forget about the dances and other events on the beach and in the club, even Mass on Sundays.

"I'm not saying it wouldn't be hard, but what's better, being a racist?"

"Daddy's not a racist, Bryan, and I don't think Mr. Kelly is either."

"Most people don't think they're racists, Danny, especially liberals like Dad. It's easier to spot it in people like Paddy Doonan. The real truth is it's everywhere—it keeps this country ticking."

"Is that what Mr. Leibowitz told you?"

Herb Leibowitz was Bryan's history teacher at school as well as the debate coach. He was a Jewish man who'd grown up in Bedford Stuyvesant in Brooklyn, fought in Korea, and had already caused waves among parents at the high school for his activism regarding civil rights and the war in Vietnam.

"Mr. Leibowitz is a smart man. It's more than what you see on the surface. Good people do bad things, and usually they can't even see it."

"I'm not saying Daddy's right, Bryan, just that I can understand his reasons. Like I can understand why he settled out of court and went back to work in the firm. It's all connected—he's scared of losing more money . . ."

"It's not the same thing at all."

"It's why he's acting this way. Now with you down on him for this, he's gonna feel even worse."

"Don't pin it on me, Danny. I know Dad's had it rough. Hawkman exploited him pure and simple. Still, he's my *father*. He has to pick himself up like everybody else. Mom's not helping him any by defending him. She knows it's wrong."

"She's not gonna kick him when he's down, that's all."

"What are you talking about? This isn't about his feelings, Danny. It's about whether Mr. Hicks should be admitted to the club."

"There's more to being right, Bryan, than just standing up for something. There's all those things about people you don't even see, like how you make them feel."

"That's bullshit. I'm not gonna make Dad feel comfortable about acting like a racist."

"You think you're so perfect, Bryan."

He stood up and reached for one of the steel cables overhead. "What about you? You think that if you feel sorry for him he's gonna stop drinking?"

Bryan pulled himself to the top of the concrete support and then up again to stand on the black metal platform we used as a diving board just beneath the railing.

"Jackknife!" He touched his toes and disappeared with hardly a splash.

I waited on the platform until he'd swum back to the ledge. "Swan dive!" I leaped toward the lavender sky.

When I surfaced, rubbing my smarting thigh, Bryan was standing on the railing of the bridge. "You can't do a swan dive without a diving board. You have to *spring* to do it right. Watch this. Forward somersault!"

Jumping from the railing was more dangerous because you had to maneuver your body through the cables. Bryan hit the water too soon, slapping the surface with his ankles.

"Cannonball!" I hurtled down, knees huddled against my chest. The wave of water almost submerged him.

"All right, you watch."

I tread water by the ledge while he climbed. "Where are you going?"

From the top of the railing he swung onto the longest cable and wrapped his body around it as he inched his way up. The muscles in his arms and legs pulsed under wet, gleaming skin.

"Bryan, that's *dangerous!* You're not supposed to do that!"

I climbed onto the ledge. He'd reached the highest point on the bridge, the dark steeple above my head where the two arcing cables joined. Carefully he raised his body from a crouch to a standing position. He bent forward slightly, his features shaded by the growing dusk.

A band wrapped round my chest and squeezed. I plucked my bathing suit, sure I was being crushed. I could hear the strange warble my voice made, as if a frail bird had nested in my throat. Bryan flew forward past the cables, sailing in a graceful curve and cleaving the water without a ripple.

I cradled my chest as he surfaced and slapped the water with his hand.

"Did you see that? Did you *see* it!"

Red lights flashed as I swam toward the dock. I dressed in the bathroom, the only room in the house with a lock on the door. A bunched-up towel muffled the sound of my weeping. I didn't know if it was the sight of Bryan on the top of the bridge like that, the empty bottle of bourbon in the wastebasket, or my own face in the mirror. Was I wrong to love my father so much that I couldn't bear his sorrow? Did it make me a racist, too, that I wished Mr. Hicks and his family would disappear so Charlie wouldn't have to vote?

I was sitting on the porch when Bryan laid his hand on my shoulder.

"I'm sorry, Danny. I didn't realize it would make you so upset."

I looked up at the curve of his jaw and wondered what drove him to those edges. He wasn't a braggart like some boys who tried to be daredevils. But he had this desire in him, not for danger really, more for the thrill of pushing himself to the brink just to see what would happen.

"I won't watch that ever again, Bry. You want to hurt yourself you do it far away, where I won't be able to see you."

He made me a root-beer float and set up the chess game. It was almost midnight when I finally beat him. The music from the dance had stopped, and I could hear the lake again, lapping against the rocks like a million tiny, clapping hands.

"You like any of the girls up here, Bry? You know, enough to go out with?"

"Nah."

"How come?"

He shrugged. "Nobody really interests me."

"But aren't you even *attracted* to anybody?"

"Yeah."

"You are?"

"Don't look at me like that. Sure I am."

I peered at him through the dusky porch light; his face was etched with thought.

"What do you think of Carline Gland?" he asked.

I lay the last pawn in place and set the lid on the box. "Who brought *her* up?"

"Do you like her?" he asked.

"I like her fine when she's asleep."

"There's gotta be *something* about her you like."

"Well, if I were being jumped by somebody, I expect she'd help me clobber the guy pretty good."

"Anything else?"

"You could sit her down next to somebody you wanted to get rid of and start her talking. That'd do it."

"Come on, Danny."

"Look, I'm trying. Terese says she's OK. I feel sorry about her parents, how weird they are."

"Did you know she's an ice-skater? Jimmy says she's pretty good."

"Jimmy's full of it. Carline wouldn't know the difference

101

between an ice skate and a roller skate. Look, don't tell me you like her 'cause if you do, I'll slit my wrists."

"Nah, it's just that . . . the other night when I was carrying her to the car she looked up at me and sort of smiled. I'd never actually seen her before, up close I mean. It's like you could see right through her skin, it was so fine."

"Beats me how you could see her skin with all the makeup she wears."

"She has these tiny freckles across her nose, too. I was thinking . . . someone who acts so tough, you know, and yet you can see right through her."

"You'd better be careful, Bryan, especially if she's like Marilyn. You could get in trouble with a girl like that."

He laughed. "That's what she *wants* you to think. She'd be too afraid to go down the tracks."

I stared at him, thinking how dopey boys were. The thought that Carline Gland was afraid of *anything* . . . maybe a double-barreled shotgun pointing right at her.

The bridge was alive with people: their voices and laughter, the tapping of high heels against wood. My parents and their friends stumbled past us on the dark porch. I don't think anyone even noticed Bryan and me. May was laughing, but I could tell by her pinched face and tortured walk that the dress was killing her. Bryan nudged me when Nini Kelly flew by in a blur of dark green trailing a feathery tail studded with sequins. Not long after, my mother returned, sighing happily in her blue-flowered swimsuit. Soon the dock was crowded with grown-ups, half of them still in party clothes, the rest in bathing suits. Glasses clinked and the outdoor spotlight shone on the green and brown bottles lined up on the railing of the deck.

A man started singing "My Wild Irish Rose," and the others joined in. May's voice soared above the crowd, ringing in my ears like the perfect notes of the noonday Angelus. They rocked back and forth and sang one song after another: "Wait Till the Sun Shines, Nelly," "Begin the Beguine," "The Rose of

Tralee." I drank another root beer and watched as one woman in a black gown fell in. Then a man got pushed, and soon the whole group was floundering in the water. They hooted and squealed and called each other names. One by one all the lights on our side of the lake blinked on, and people yelled from their houses for them to shut up.

Slowly they straggled out of the water, giggling and squabbling like children, and the clink of glasses resumed. That's when I noticed the black shape leaning against the railing of the bridge. For a moment he straightened, and I saw how tall he was, with broad shoulders and iron-gray hair that shimmered in the moonlight. The band tightened round my chest when I realized who it was.

"Bryan."

He followed my finger and saw, too, the big, shadowy man hunched over. His head was rolling from side to side as if he were laughing. Suddenly he called out and his deep baritone voice rumbled across the lake.

"You all better watch out you don't catch your deaths out there. My, my, what a party."

His shoulders shook as he leaned his head down on the railing. The group on the dock quieted immediately, as if a gun had gone off. Paddy Doonan called out: "Hey, Mr. Hicks, you won't be laughing so hard when you hear the news. No new members in the Community Club this year."

I flexed my arms, trying to ease the grip on my chest. Bryan had risen and was leaning with his hands flat against the screen. He was staring at the back of our father's head. Charlie stood next to Paddy Doonan, one hand on Paddy's wrist. I couldn't hear what they were saying, but my father's gestures were angry, and Paddy was trying to shrug it off. His face hidden by the dark, J.D. Hicks reared up very straight and walked slowly across the bridge. Tim Kelly draped one long arm around Charlie's neck and said something, then laughed loudly as he pointed at Paddy. He was trying to make peace between the two men, Paddy Doonan being the brunt of some joke that was supposed to soften Charlie up. My father smiled finally, and the drink winked in his hand.

Bryan walked into the kitchen as I continued to gaze down at the floating heads. My mother was standing uncertainly by the ladder, her head tipped toward the bridge. I didn't expect her to say anything, although I wanted her to. Even now when I think of it, I wish with a live ache that she would have walked over to Paddy and told him to leave.

When I heard the sound of breaking glass, I scanned the surface of the deck, wondering whether someone had knocked over a bottle, and if they'd have the presence of mind to search under their bare feet. As the second glass shattered, I ran into the kitchen.

Bryan was standing at the sink, an unopened bottle of gin held over his head. He heaved it full force onto the metal faucet, where it exploded into a pile of green and amber glass in the bottom of the sink. The gin sprayed in our faces and I leaped back, pulling Bryan by the collar of his shirt. He was still holding the neck of the bottle; his face was wet and two shards of glass were sticking out of his forehead. Blood dribbled unnoticed down his left cheek. He was laughing high and shrill, the way he sounded at night when he called out in his nightmare voice.

"Did you see that! It looks like stained glass, doesn't it? Whaddya think this'll do?"

I grabbed his wrist as he reached for a bottle of bourbon.

"Look at all this stuff. It's like a friggin' liquor store in here."

I hadn't noticed anyone carrying bottles when they came in, but there they were, clustered on the countertop.

"You've got glass in your forehead, Bryan."

He tilted his head, as if puzzled, and I pulled him over to the mirror that hung on the wall at the bottom of the stairs. Gingerly he reached up, pulled out each piece, and stared at them as they lay in the palm of his hand. I ran a towel under cold water and held it against his forehead.

"Press down," I said, and ran upstairs to the medicine cabinet.

I placed two Band-Aids across the wounds on his forehead. "This oughtta do it—they're not that deep. Go to bed, Bryan; I'll clean up."

"Leave it for them," he muttered as he climbed the stairs.

What good would that do? Drunk as they were they'd only cut themselves, and I'd have that to worry about, too. My mother's voice sailed above the others as they sang "I'll Take You Home Again, Kathleen." I blinked back tears as the haunting melody reverberated off the water.

*

I was dreaming of my mother marooned on our dock, which bobbed like a cork in the middle of the lake. As I sat up in bed, gazing into the cobwebby dark, the sound started again. I leaned my head against the screen and listened. There it was: the low, choking sound of a woman weeping.

I crept downstairs and stood at the closed glass door leading onto the porch. My mother's bare toes and the white edge of her nightgown shone in the dim light. After setting a chair down by the window, I stood on it and pulled the half-open window wide, peering over the sill at my mother huddled at one end of the swing. Her pale neck was visible beneath the line of her hair, which tumbled forward on either side of her face. She was rocking slowly back and forth, her arms cradling her knees. Sobs slipped down the front of her nightgown and seemed to strangle there. I could hardly catch the few muffled words.

"Never . . . what does it matter . . . never, never . . . not once . . . not in my whole life."

I'd so rarely heard my mother cry. It was even more rare for me to see her like this—all alone, not a mother or a wife, just a woman who'd once been a girl. There wasn't a thing I could do to help her.

KING AND QUEEN DANCE
(1967)

THE PROTESTANTS STARTED UP AT EIGHT-THIRTY in the morning. For years I believed the clubhouse had a real organ, hidden under a sheet in the storeroom and rolled out every Sunday. Carline Gland laughed and said it was only a tape. It must be the water, I thought, which amplified the tone like that. No way did the Catholics, no matter how seriously we sang, sound like we were sojourning in purgatory, our red hearts hungry for Jesus.

There was something different about the Protestants, even in the way they walked—straight-backed and sober as if they were thinking about balancing a checkbook or attending a funeral after brunch. The Catholics, on the other hand, skipped across the bridge in a flurry of jovial energy. Maybe it was because the Catholics had so many children, all of them anxious to arrive at the club early while there was still chance of a seat.

I knew all about rhythm by this time—those days of the month when the egg was ripe and you had to abstain. "No lounging around naked on the bedspread for *us*," my mother said, referring to the college students in Terese's book, *The Harrad Experiment*, who spent their afternoons studying in the nude. May had been upset that I was reading it, but I detected in her tone a wistful regret. What would it be like, I wondered, to make love under a blanket only a few days a month?

Terese's grandmother, Rosie Luchow, started across the bridge next to her new husband, Al. Terese followed a few paces behind, bouncing the flat of her hand along the railing. Nini and Tim Kelly had remained in Staten Island this summer, so Nini's mother and Al were looking after Terese. Rosie was a short woman, like Nini, with platinum blonde hair swept up in a French twist. She wore suits to Mass, short lavender jackets with tight straight skirts that showed off her legs. Al strutted along beside her, a cigar lodged in the corner of his mouth. He was frumpy and bald, with a voice that sounded like he was drowning in gravel. Charlie said Al had made his money on some kind of plastic packaging, the kind you see everywhere—on toys, brushes and combs, jump ropes, and screws, *everywhere.*

Although she was happy for the Kellys, my mother sorely missed Nini. The counselor at the treatment center where Tim was a patient said flat out that they should avoid any situation that might threaten Tim's recovery, especially since he was doing so well and couldn't return to the force until he'd taken care of his drinking problem. Terese had told me all about it, how they'd talked in their family sessions about the amount of drinking that went on at the lake and how, no offense, Charlie and May were a bad influence.

My mother hollered down from the top of the stairs, and the four of us left through the back door. My father took May's elbow as he always did when she wore high heels; it was one of those involuntary, gentlemanly acts of his. He was chewing a stick of Dentyne, which wasn't necessary. Charlie didn't drink in the morning. Sometimes whole days would go by without drinking, particularly if his ulcer was acting up. But on weekends somebody was bound to stop on his way to the Pink Elephant or the Tamarack, and Charlie would go along. His face showed it—not florid the way Tim Kelly's used to be, more as if he'd spent too much time indoors without the proper nutrients.

Bryan hummed a tune by Cream and played an imaginary drum with his hands. The ends of his hair slipped underneath the collar of the shirt I'd ironed for him. Years later I gave up ironing altogether; then, I felt only pride in those shirts, their laundered smell and crisp folds, as I stood at the ironing board facing the lake through the screens. From the radio on the kitchen counter slid the voices of Nat King Cole, Andy Williams, and Robert Goulet crooning my mother's and my favorite songs: "Moon River," "Unforgettable," "Camelot." I sang along, not caring that Bryan ridiculed me by calling it elevator music. The music suited me and the pile of his wrinkled shirts just fine.

When he wasn't working in Neptune, practicing his diving, or tinkering with the engine he'd bought, Bryan was lying on his bunk listening to the Rolling Stones and reading some heavy book like *The 900 Days*, which was all about the siege of Leningrad. At Westfield High he was the high scorer in debate, which ordinarily would have put him in the same class as those boys who wore dickeys and bow ties to school, but Bryan got away with it. It didn't hurt him, either, that he could cite a suitcase full of facts about the history of Indochina, the "Domino Theory," the Van Thieu government in South Vietnam, the effects of napalm, biographical data on the entire Johnson cabinet, or the makeup of lysergic acid diethylamide, otherwise known as LSD. One side of Bryan's bedroom closet was stacked with boxes full of old issues of *U.S. News and World Report, Time,* and *Newsweek.*

Terese was leaning against the railing at the end of the bridge talking to Jimmy Piper. God had smiled on Jimmy finally, sending him up five inches in one season. With his braces removed and his brown hair dipping across his forehead, Jimmy was one of the most sought-after boys for a date to the King and Queen Dance. He was waiting to ask Terese, who was waiting for Bryan, who was oblivious, as usual, to the fact that the most important dance of the summer was two weeks away.

"Hi, Danny."

Lou Sullivan leaped off the railing and slouched along beside me. He'd been dogging me for weeks, and I didn't know who to thank for my unexpected good luck. I'd have much preferred one of his old insults over this newfound, sticky attraction. It wasn't that he was ugly, except for his ears, which fluttered alongside his head like two kidneys, more that he was a suck-up kind of boy who didn't have much backbone.

"You going to the dance?" he asked.

"Yeah," I said, walking faster.

"You got a date?"

"I don't go in much for dates."

That shut him up. My mother turned a warm eye over her shoulder, and I could read her mind. She liked Lou's parents, Lois and Dan Sullivan, and had told me more than once that I was too picky when it came to boys. Not that she wouldn't have been wild if I'd have *really* gone for somebody, necking up and down the beach like Marilyn Gland or Fern Daniels, but she was always listening to Nini rattling on about the dates Terese got asked out on, and I think she felt I was making her look bad. My father liked Lou because he had the same name as Louis Sullivan, a famous architect. "A name like that, the kid's got promise," he'd said more than once. I didn't see a hint of visual or spatial talent in Lou Sullivan, whose entry in the boat parade last summer had sunk right after it passed the clubhouse.

Terese flagged me over to the bench at the top of the stairs leading down to the girls' bathroom. I squeezed in beside her, relieved that Lou had remained on the porch with the other boys. Bryan, of course, was sitting inside the clubhouse, where he listened with an almost painful intensity to the service. These days he liked to critique the priest's sermon to whoever would listen, usually me and Jimmy, and rank each priest on a scale of one to five. Since Rainy wasn't really a parish, it didn't have a regular priest. We were assigned priests from St. Mary's Church in Neptune and from the Abbey five miles up the highway. The St. Mary's priests meant well but they were boring. The priests from the Abbey weren't much better, although

Bryan liked to lecture us about how these men were committed to a higher purpose in life that we could all learn from. He hated the fact that the priests didn't seem to care about politics or the hundreds of thousands of boys we were sending over to Vietnam without declaring war.

What *I* noticed, which didn't occur to Bryan, was how oblivious the priests were about girls. You'd never catch a girl up on the altar helping with Mass, and the only time we were ever mentioned was when it came to sex and marriage. Then we were supposed to stay pure, remain in the background, and obey everybody. We should have been flipped around, Bryan and I, because he was happy thinking about purity whereas I was fixated night and day on underarm hair. *Any* kind of body hair, actually, although boys with too much chest hair scared me. It seemed unnatural having all that hair so young, and if these boys were anything like Mr. Casey, the hair was likely to keep growing over the shoulders and right down the back.

Take Rickie Brazil, for example, sitting two rows away with his wife, Shirl, who was Fern Daniels's older sister. I couldn't look at Rickie Brazil without imagining what he was like with his clothes off. It was rude since he was such a hard worker and there, sitting next to him was his wife, my friend's sister no less, but the thought of him naked raised beads of sweat at the base of my throat. That was where I fantasized being kissed, not by some big-eared bore like Lou Sullivan, but by a man who looked like Rickie, or a boy like Billy Dove, who knew how to approach a girl—quiet and strong, with part of him held back, the part you most wanted and were willing to wait for.

I should have worn sunglasses because everywhere I turned I could see tendrils of hair poking out from men's shirts, damp dark patches under their arms, the bulge in their pants I tried to ignore but couldn't. I was supposed to be praying, too, which made me feel really dirty, like I was one of those girls who went down the tracks.

On that day it was Father Downs, the priest who stuttered.

111

I tried to expunge my guilt by hanging on every word, by putting myself in his place—a boy no one had listened to and here he was talking to a whole congregation in spite of his difficulty—but after a while I couldn't help imagining what *he* looked like underneath that black robe, whether his chest was as pale as his face with black hair or smooth like my father's with a tuft of strawberry gold. When Terese slipped down the girls' bathroom stairs, I sighed gratefully and followed.

She made room for me on the windowsill and I handed her a cigarette. We blew the smoke out the open window and watched it evaporate into the blue sky over the chin-up bars.

"Not as good," she said.

We were smoking Marlboros, but since we'd finished our last cigarette the night before, I'd dug two Chesterfields out of the bottom of my mother's pocketbook.

"Rosie and Al ever smell it on you?" I asked.

"Are you kidding? My dad would smell it though. Now that he's giving up smoking too, he can detect anything."

"That's gonna be rough when they come back up."

"I don't know if they *are* coming back up."

"What do you mean?"

She hesitated. "They're talking about selling the house."

"Why?"

"My mom says maybe we should do something else in the summer. They don't think they'd have a good time coming up."

"But they love it up here, Terese."

"Not anymore."

"Is it because your father stopped drinking?"

"They don't think they can enjoy themselves when everybody's going on as usual and they can't join in. I mean, what did my dad ever *do* when he was up here? He slept in late, read a little, and went over to the Pink Elephant. In the evenings when they get together to play cards, you know they're drinking."

"Why couldn't he just drink ginger ale or something?" I

didn't like to think what my mother might do if she heard Nini was never coming up again.

"Maybe he doesn't want to. He's different now, Danny, you haven't seen him."

"Different how?"

Sometimes when the sun hit Terese's face she looked just like Rita Hayworth. Her hair was down to her shoulders again. Often she curled it, but I liked it best the way it was then, tied back loosely with a blue ribbon. She'd toned down the makeup so you could see more of her own color, all green eyes and peachy skin, a disappointment to Terese, who wanted to tan dark as acorns like me, but which I thought was simply beautiful.

"He likes to talk about things now—what he's reading, movies, anything. He even talks about being a policeman; he talks *a lot* about that and I tell you, sometimes it's so gross I don't want to hear it. The best thing is that he and Nini seem so happy. She says it's like starting over."

"So why couldn't he talk to people here? My mother loves to talk."

"He says it's that people at Rainy only know him a certain way. He's not sure they'll like him as much now."

A wave came over me then as I noticed the pile of cigarette butts at the base of the clubhouse, and the tracks traveling past the scrim of trees, farther than my eyes could follow. I saw my father sitting at his light table, a blueberry-colored pencil rapidly filling in the petals of the clematis vine that clambered greedily all over the wooden frame of the pergola. All his dreams about architecture, my mother's hands coaxing green life from the neglected soil, their happy voices drifting through the screens.

"I thought that after he went back to work for his old firm, after he got used to it, things would be all right. But it doesn't get better, you know, no matter how hard I try. It's like we're living in this play—everybody's acting out their parts only the story's all wrong. He won't even listen when my mother tries to tell him about your father and Nini."

"You know, Danny, the department *made* my father do it. He screwed up on an assignment . . . . I think he took something. Don't ever tell anybody. They said he could either take a leave and get some professional help, or be suspended."

"So what has to happen? Some terrible accident? My brother goes away to college and never comes back? They burn the house down during a bridge game? All I want is to go back the way it was, when we were happy."

"I wouldn't want to go back. This is the first time in my whole life I can truly say I have a happy family." She ran her tongue along her upper teeth the way she did whenever she was ruminating over things. "Carline invited me to stay with her next summer, *if* my parents sell the house. Marilyn won't be up—she's going to beauty school—and I can have her room."

"Terese, you could stay in *my* room, with me."

Her face puckered with sadness. Much as she'd always liked Carline, I was her best friend and it didn't make any sense.

"Is it because you wouldn't want to live with Bryan?"

"No." The tears sprang out of nowhere, covering the surface of her eyes like a coat of clear lacquer.

"What *is* it?"

"It's just . . . God, Danny, I don't want to say anything that'll hurt you."

"For crying out loud, tell me."

"I don't think my parents would let me stay with you."

"Not *let* you! They hardly even know the Glands."

The steady drip of a faucet was the only sound. "It's 'cause of my father, isn't it? His drinking."

She looked down at the blue belt on her miniskirt.

"I suppose they think it would be better for you to be with Gerry and Frieda Gland all summer, huh? Driving into Neptune in that appliance truck with all his girlfriends' hairs all over the place . . . . You'll have to carry a whisk broom with you, as if you had a *dog*. Frieda sitting there in the front seat with that mummy face of hers, not saying a word. *Geez, Terese, it isn't fair!*"

I put my hands over my face, unable to hold back an eruption of shuddery sobs. She wound her long arms around my neck and pulled me close. It was such a lousy view out the back window of the girls' bathroom: the black bank up to the tracks, the sand scarred with pieces of garbage and empty bottles, carvings and graffiti splayed across the logs.

Charlie wasn't an alcoholic anyway, no matter what Tim and Nini thought. He didn't drink every day the way Tim used to, and some Friday nights he'd stop after two Manhattans. He was still the best designer in his firm, which now employed over forty architects. Even if he had to alter his schemes and please a million different people, he was still an artist at heart. What was my mother supposed to do, throw him out? She didn't drink much herself anymore, just a cocktail or two to keep him company on weekends. What do you do when someone won't stop, when you hear crying in the middle of the night, when you can't even talk at the dinner table without somebody turning it into an accusation?

I don't know how long I cried, harder and longer than it seemed possible. Terese hung on the whole time, her silence and strawberry shampoo smell giving me such comfort, more than her steady arms or the little bell announcing the presence of Jesus over our heads.

"If I live with Carline, it won't change anything, between us I mean," she said.

We slipped out the window and joined the teenagers clustered around the railing on the front steps. Even with the fishy water right there and gasoline wafting up from the engines tied along the catwalk, the smell of perspiration and deodorant was strong. It seemed hotter than usual that summer; my clothes were damp by midmorning. Ty Malone was flirting with Terese—who didn't?—and as I sat there watching the sun on his face, I remembered his brother's naked body lying under Angie Fanelli, how the sun had turned Joe's hair the same color, a mahogany luminous as newly finished wood.

"Can we use your boat later?" Terese asked.

"I guess so, why?"

"Carline wants us to pick her up so we can spend the afternoon on Rock Island. If I'm gonna wear that dress Nini's making me, I need to do something about this tan."

"But you never tan," I said.

"Carline has this stuff you put on that turns your skin dark. I'm gonna try it."

"You better be careful, Terese. Your skin's liable to fall off, just like my hair, and you'll be the first Queen of Rainy Lake sitting on her throne like a piece of fruit, your skin lying on the floor in a pile of tanned peels."

"You're a real comedian, Danny. Who says I'm gonna be Queen?"

"Give me a break, your whole life has been nothing but preparation."

"Your dress is wet."

"Where?" I peered under my arms and hoped I wasn't going to be one of those women who had to wear underarm shields.

"Down the middle of your back."

I reached behind and fanned the fabric while averting my eyes from the sight of Ricky Brazil's long neck, the shadow across his cheeks and chin that I could just bet Shirl ran her hands over a dozen times a day.

*

My mother looked so small sometimes, her red shirt leaping like a poppy from the carpet of green sedum under her bare feet. She was singing "Three Coins in a Fountain" as she tapped her trowel in rhythm on the rock wall. The garden was almost complete and it was a true masterpiece. I had to give her credit for not caving in like Charlie. She'd continued to plant and prune, had carried on according to the plans they'd drawn up, long after those plans had been taken down from the wall and stored away, the details etched indelibly on her memory.

The patio and the lower portion of the deck, including the potting shed, were the parts they'd finished. The upper tier loomed overhead like an unwieldy scaffold, the rough frame darkened by time and weather. May had planted boxes of clematis at the base of the unfinished pergola. She had hoped to train them up the sides as an inspiration to Charlie, but they'd shriveled up at the end of last summer, prey to a scourge of mealybugs. It was so unlike my mother not to plant something in its place. She walked along the upper deck as if it were invisible, her eyes aiming for the red and yellow daylilies rimming the edge of the lake.

The house and deck were a pasticcio of fits and starts: the parts that were done represented the best my parents had to offer; the rest was a reminder of all that was slipping through their fingers. At the base of Maudie McDonough's stairs sat the Chris-Craft, covered with gray canvas. Beside it and taking up most of Maudie's patio was the dismantled engine Bryan had bought last spring from the boat works. He'd rented a steam-cleaning machine to blast off the old grease and oil, and then, as delicately as if he were tying a Royal Coachman for his new fly rod, he'd extracted the pistons, rings, and valves, cleaning and examining each one, poring over the cylinders for scratches and cracks.

There he was in his usual spot, sitting on an old bench with a lapful of metal.

"Where're you going?" he asked, as I tossed my beach bag into our small fishing boat.

"Rock Island. Terese's working on her tan."

"Carline going with you?"

"Yeah, why?"

"Tell her I've got the drawings of the engine. She wanted to see them."

"You're kidding."

"No, she likes this stuff. She even asked to see the design drawings of the Chris-Craft."

I rolled my eyes and climbed into the boat.

"I was wondering if you could ask her to ask Marilyn to do something for me."

"What do you need Marilyn for?"

"Because she knows Billy Dove real well, and I want to ask him a favor."

"What kind of favor?" The perfect lines in my brother's face, his tassles of golden hair, were like a painting.

"They don't make these parts anymore. Some are so worn out I need to get new ones made. A couple of cylinder cracks have to be rewelded, too. Billy works part-time in a tool and dye shop in Sparta . . . it's where his father used to work." He looked up at me. "You know, before he went to prison."

"You said something about a favor?"

"I want to know if he can get these parts made for me."

"Why don't you ask him yourself?"

"Come on, Danny, I don't really know him."

"How long have we been coming up here? He knows who you are. You don't have to be friends to ask him."

"I feel funny . . . . Just ask Carline, would you?"

"So what exactly am I supposed to say?"

He handed me a small burlap bag. "Ask her to ask Marilyn to give these to Billy and see if he knows anyone at the shop who'll make new ones. I'll pay him."

I set the heavy bag on the floor of the boat, pull-started the engine, and maneuvered away from the dock and under the bridge. Bryan was kneeling next to the engine now; a few yards away my mother's hands rose and fell in concert with her voice. It had been four years since I'd first laid eyes on Billy Dove, and Terese was the only living soul who knew how I felt about him. Some days I was sure there must be something wrong and misguided about my instincts, for I'd never spent more than ten minutes with Billy, and he still only dated girls from Neptune or Sparta.

Yet even as I told myself this, I'd look at the other boys and my heart would go limp as a noodle, my body deader than the engine sitting on Maudie's patio. I chided myself that maybe it was pure sex appeal, which probably explained the hot flashes I was experiencing twenty-four hours a day. My deepest fear was that if left unchecked, I could be one of those sexual deviants you read about. All it took was for Billy Dove to pull up to the parking lot in his brother's beat-up blue Camaro and lean his head out the window to talk to Maizie or Fern, and this hot mash of impulses would stampede right through me.

Good God, I prayed at these times, show me some mercy or I'm going to end up down the tracks sooner than I'm ready. It made me feel almost tender toward girls like Marilyn Gland, who must be tormented by the same stew of perverse and oily sensations. Boys seemed to have these feelings without adverse consequences; they certainly weren't labeled as tramps or sluts. "Dirty linen" was what my father said.

Terese was dangling her white legs off the edge of the public dock near her house. I knew she was going to be sorry. Some calamity was bound to follow from any solution Carline had cooked up, or she was going to burn to a crisp as she usually did and have to go to the dance with blisters and a new rash of freckles on her shoulders. When we passed the five-mile-per-hour buoy, I gunned the engine and took off as fast as the little boat would go. Terese and I liked to pretend we were driving a sixty-five-horsepower boat; it was a big joke and we laughed out loud as a light spray blew into our faces.

I slowed down as we entered Weaver House Cove, and steered the boat around the big rocks which protruded shiny and black during the day, but which had ripped the hulls of boats trying to whizz by too fast in the dark. I cut the motor and bumped gently into Carline's half-submerged dock. It was odd, all the years I'd known Carline, and I'd never once been to her house.

119

"Come on." Terese hopped onto the dock and walked across the front yard. I followed slowly, feeling unexpectedly nervous about going in.

The cottage needed a coat of paint, but inside it was clean and cosy—antique chairs and rockers with little pillows covered in the same red-checked gingham as the curtains. Terese pushed open the door to Carline's room. There she was, lying on a bed and cutting out a picture from a magazine. Marilyn's side of the room was decked out in white eyelet, stuffed animals, and those embroidery panels with sappy sayings framed on the wall. Carline's side was the real surprise.

It wasn't the Indian blanket on the bed, the dripped candles sticking up out of Mateus bottles, or the sticks of incense burning on the dresser next to a ton of makeup paraphernalia. It was the pictures of bridges and skyscrapers interspersed with ice-skating posters that covered half the room: the Brooklyn Bridge, the Chrysler Building, the Eiffel Tower, the Statue of Liberty, and Peggy Fleming and other skaters lit up in daring and athletic poses on the ice. When Terese sat down on the bed, she picked up the magazine and more skaters tumbled out.

"Who's this?" I pointed to one of the men skaters.

"That's Scott Allen. He won the bronze medal at the 1960 Olympics and was the national champion last year," Carline said. "And here's Carol Heiss; she won the gold in 1960."

"You don't have any more room in here," Terese said.

Carline walked across the room to her closet and swung open the door. "Voilà!" More pictures hung on the back of the door and across one wall. Shelves ran the length of the other wall, and they were stacked floor-to-ceiling with trophies and medals.

"Bet you didn't know Carline was a skater." Terese sat there with a Cheshire grin on her face. I shook my head.

"She's won these awards all over the state. Last spring she placed fourth in the Novice Regional Championship."

"Is that good?" I asked.

"It's very good," Terese said. "It means she's on her way to qualifying for the Nationals."

"Let's not get carried away, Terese," Carline said.

"How long have you been skating?" I asked, glancing at her lean, muscular legs.

"Since I was four years old."

"I didn't know you could skate that little." My experience in ice-skating was limited to once or twice a winter on the lumpy surface of Cedarbrook Pond.

"There's a rink in my neighborhood. My mother used to take me and Marilyn over to watch the classes. She was killing time, but I loved it. I begged her to let me take a class. By the time I was eight, I was in private lessons."

I was having a hard time connecting Carline with my image of champion skaters. Still, there were all these trophies.

"How often do you skate?" I asked.

Carline shrugged. "I do patch every morning before school, then I skate after school and a couple of evenings. Since June I've been getting a ride home with Mr. Casey three times a week. My coach would like me to do more, but my mother wants me up here with her."

"You wouldn't believe how expensive it is," Terese said.

"My mother took a part-time waitressing job last year to help pay for it. My father wants me to quit. He says it's too much money. As soon as I get my license, I'm applying for a job." She walked over to the closet and banged the door shut.

"Is Marilyn here?" I asked.

Carline shook her head. "She'll be back in a while. She drove my mother into Neptune to get her hair done."

"Doesn't your mother drive?" I asked.

"Only when she has to. It makes her nervous."

"It's because of her accident," Terese said.

"What accident?" It seemed I didn't know anything about the Glands.

"Two years ago, Carline? She rear-ended somebody on her

way to Shop-Rite. Carline says her mother saw her father's truck parked in front of Nola Coyote's house."

Carline leaned against her dresser. "Nola used to be my mother's best friend. They were in Sweet Adelines together. Dad said he was selling her a dishwasher . . . . It wasn't until a year later, after Nola and her husband had split, that my mother went over there and saw they didn't even own a dishwasher."

Carline's face shrunk, her profile all points and angles. I felt sorry for her, having a father like that.

"What about these?" I pointed to the picture of the Eiffel Tower.

She walked over to the wall. "Did you know that the Eiffel Tower and the Statue of Liberty were designed by the same man, Gustave Eiffel? In the Tower you can see how everything's supported, like a skeleton, whereas here . . . " She pointed to the picture of the Statue of Liberty. "Here the structure's completely invisible. You wouldn't think it'd be that complicated but it is, with her holding up the torch like that."

"Bryan said to tell you he has some drawings of the boat," I said grudgingly.

"We're gonna miss the best sun if we don't get out there," Terese said.

Rock Island was situated smack in the middle of the lake. From one side you could see Rose's, the small beach where we'd all taken swimming lessons. Across on the other side was Cranberry Island, which was another place where kids went at night to neck under cover of the dense, high-bush cranberries.

While Terese and Carline spread out their beach towels on the flat rocks at the highest point on the island, I rigged up Bryan's fly rod, tying on a mayfly. Although I preferred the bigger and more exotic bass flies, I was aiming for a sunny, whose tiny mouth needed something small and delicate. After placing my hand on the rod the way Bryan had taught me—firm not tight—I pointed straight down toward the water, then lifted smoothly with my forearm to eleven o'clock. The line rose in the air as my arm reached higher, bending my wrist back to one o'clock, the line hissing out behind me like music—forward and back, forward and back—the loops beautiful and wide, unfurling finally so that the fly hit the water without a dimple.

What did I care if I caught a fish? It was enough some days just to see that shiny filament singing over my head and the way the fly fell like a leaf onto the surface. I must have been at it for almost an hour when Terese climbed down and sat next to the boat.

"Doesn't your arm get tired?"

"I never think about it."

"Well, put it down so we can swim. You're being totally antisocial."

Her skin was smeared with a copper-colored cream. "Won't it come off?" I asked.

"It's waterproof."

We swam around the circumference of the island. As always happened when I was in the water, all sense of my physical self vanished, and I became another moving billow on the surface. Children's voices from Rose's Beach, the lapping lake, the rumble of motors grew dim as I disappeared into the echoey, underwater silence.

Terese grabbed my ankle, forcing me to look up at Carline lying on the summit of Rock Island, her pointy breasts hiding her head from view. When we were finished we stood over her and let our wet hair drip onto her oiled stomach.

"What the *hell* are you doing?" she asked.

I couldn't help laughing at her aggrieved face.

"None of us even has a date for the dance," Terese said.

"All you have to do is give Jimmy the word and he'll take you. He's gonna get the most votes for King anyway," Carline said.

"Is Bryan even going?" Terese asked me.

I stretched out on the rock. "Oh, he'll go. Don't hold your breath for anything."

"What about Lou Sullivan?" Carline rolled over, her face a few inches from mine. "He asked you yet?"

"I got out of it."

"How come?" Terese said.

"Yeah, I'd like to see *you* going with him. Those ears, they're like giant peaches, and he's gotta be a wet kisser. You can tell from all the saliva that collects in the corners of his mouth when he talks."

Carline laughed. "I wonder about you, Danny. You should write for a TV show someday."

She was the one to wonder about—greaser by night, Sonja Henie by day.

"I'm going to be an airline stewardess," Terese announced.

"You're kidding," I said. "Aren't you going to college?"

"All that studying, I couldn't hack it. Think of the kind of life I'll have, traveling all over the world for free, getting to wear those neat outfits. Nini says you have to be just the right height and weight and be pretty enough to qualify. Otherwise, they give you a job on the ground."

"Why don't you go to college first, then become a stewardess?" I said.

"What's the big deal with college?" She slopped another handful of Carline's brown cream on her shoulders and arms.

"There's so much to *learn*, Terese. Besides, college is where everything's happening. Students on campus are *involved*; they care about what's going on, especially in Vietnam."

"Don't start," said Terese. "My father says they're all a bunch of rabble-rousers. You actually want the communists to walk away with Southeast Asia?"

"People have communism on the brain. How do *we* know what those people want?"

"Well, they don't want communism, that's why they asked us to come over there. Look, can we change the subject? Vietnam morning, noon, and night, it's all you hear about. I'm sick of it."

"OK, then, what about expanding your mind? College will show you what's possible," I said.

"While you're reading about it in books, I'll be *seeing* the world firsthand. As long as my looks don't change, I think I have a pretty good chance."

"What do *you* want to do after college?" Carline asked me.

My father said I should be a teacher. Bryan, of course, would probably major in sociology or political science and then go to law school. Charlie had dreams of Bryan becoming a trial attorney or running for congress.

"I don't know. I like the unknown, going somewhere no one's ever been, creating something out of nothing. I'd become a composer if I had any musical talent."

"You could be an astronaut," Terese said. "They're gonna let women go up sooner or later."

I shivered at the thought of all that empty space.

"I'll go to college as long as I can keep skating," Carline said. "My father thinks I should major in engineering because I'm so good at math. What does he know? I just want one thing that makes me stand out, so I won't look back on my life and think I've wasted it."

I was struck by the bitterness on her face and by the fact that her eyes were the same dove gray as the surface of the water. It was true what Bryan had said the night of the fireworks: you could see through Carline's skin to the blue veins underneath. I'd always considered myself a good judge of character, but more and more I was finding out how blind I was. I'd never have believed that Carline Gland was fueled by dreams even brighter than mine.

*

When we returned to Carline's dock later that afternoon, Marilyn was sitting on the lawn working on one of her needlepoint squares, a kitten and a blonde-haired girl crouched on the front steps of a red-bricked house with "Home Is Where the Heart Is" stitched in blue across the top.

"Oh, good," I said. "I need to ask her something."

Taking the burlap bag, I explained Bryan's problem with the engine parts.

"Why doesn't he go into Sparta himself?" Terese asked.

"I'm sure Billy would be glad to do it," Marilyn said, standing up. "Let's drive over and ask him."

"Now?" My abdomen went into an immediate spasm.

"Sure, why not?" Terese's big smile left hairline white creases in the coppery surface of her face.

By the time Marilyn emerged from the house with her keys, Terese and Carline were huddled together in the back seat of the car. I slid in the front, grateful for the car seat between me and their hyperactive elbows, the high-pitched anticipation in their voices.

"You've actually been inside his house?" Terese said.

"Yes, I've been in his house. Billy and I are friends, remember?"

"What do you *do* there?" Carline asked.

"None of your business. Sometimes I visit his mother when Billy isn't even there."

"You visit his *mother*?" Carline was practically salivating. "God, Terese, she visits his mother. Good old Marilyn." The two of them rocked back and forth; with their shrieky giggles they made me think of a couple of monkeys.

When Marilyn glanced my way, she rolled her eyes and pointed with her thumb toward the back seat. *Two lulus on the loose,* I thought, and smiled in agreement. The landscape changed as we drove along Spirit Road. There was more land in between buildings, and stretches of woods. The houses themselves were small and patchy, a few nothing more than shacks. We knew some of the kids who lived along there— Trish Foster and her brother Dale, the Goethalls twins—poor white families whose parents worked in the cement plant near Sparta or in the many diners and vegetable stands scattered along the highway. Through the trees I could see a sparkle of lake beyond the piles of stacked firewood, discarded appliances, and the carcasses of cars mounted on concrete blocks.

"What a bunch of slobs," Terese said, pointing to one house.

She and Carline literally hung out the window as we drove up Spirit Road toward Billy's. I'd seen that same mixture of curiosity and dread on the faces of children standing in line for the roller coaster. Now I understand what made the name Dove blink on and off in people's minds like a neon sign. Was it like this for me? Did my feelings for Billy give me an innocence other white people lacked? I can't answer even now. Maybe the truth is that way down deep in each one of us there is a stain stubborn as original sin that makes it impossible to look at kids like Billy except through a window of colored glass. Me believing I was totally colorblind, Terese and Carline so governed by color they couldn't see anything else.

The car turned up a dirt road that curved through dense trees, and there was the house, a small, square central building with two rooms added on, one in the front, one on the side. The whole cluster sat low on a rise that sloped down to the lake. Under a huge, thick-leafed climbing tree were two rusted-out cars: a blue Thunderbird and an orange Volkswagen bus. I knew my father would let out a long whistle at the roof—layer upon layer of tarpaper slapped on unevenly, gobs of tar creating a shiny grid of roads that crisscrossed back and forth. Underneath each window was a wooden flowerbox brimming with red geraniums, dusty millers, and lobelias. On the southern side of the house a large vegetable garden was thriving: tomatoes, bell peppers, cucumbers, corn, green beans, and several different kinds of lettuce. The smell of lavender was strong.

Marilyn knocked at the screen door and hollered inside. "Billy, you home?"

A dark hand rested on the screen, and the door opened.

Marcella Dove blinked in the sunlight, then smiled when she recognized Marilyn.

"He's out back. Come on inside while I call him."

Suddenly shy, Terese and Carline lagged a few steps behind as I followed Marilyn into the house. Marcella walked across the room to another screen door, which she opened part way to call loudly for Billy. The body of the house was the square living room, with a wood-burning stove at one end and a large braided rug, similar to ours, in the middle. There were several faded but comfortable-looking chairs, a long sofa, and built-in shelves that held an assortment of china figurines. Potted plants—English ivy, philodendron, at least a dozen African violets—crowded the surface of a row of wooden boxes draped with brightly colored scarves. From the kitchen came the brown sugary fragrance of baking ham.

"He's coming," Marcella said. "How about some lemonade?"

Carline's polite "No thanks" was cut off by Marilyn's enthusiastic "Yes, please!" She followed Billy's mother into the kitchen, where I could hear Marilyn's soft laugh and Marcella's deeper, huskier one.

"What are they laughing at?" Terese made a slow circuit of the room as she looked curiously at the figurines on the shelves.

The screen door slammed and Billy stood a few inches away. His face was streaked with grease, and a bead of sweat rolled from the curly edges of his hair onto his neck. I swallowed, thinking that if I touched his face there in the pale moon underneath his eye, it would feel soft as butter. He was sleeveless under a pair of denim overalls. I was aware of the muscle in his upper arm and the smell of water mingling with something earthy—dirt, maybe, or perspiration. He looked from one of us to the other.

"I thought I heard Marilyn."

"You did." Marilyn swept out of the kitchen carrying a tray of tall glasses filled with lemonade.

128

"Sit down, girls." Marcella stopped next to Billy, swiping at his soiled face with a dish towel.

Billy grinned. "What's up?"

"Danny has something to ask you." Marilyn nodded in my direction.

I stood still, ice water lapping around my heart.

"The bag, Danny." Marilyn pointed to the burlap bag in my lap.

"Oh, yeah. My brother Bryan, you know Bryan, don't you?" Billy nodded, his eyebrows raised slightly. "He's been working on this boat forever, well, a long time, anyway. It's a Chris-Craft. He's refinished the whole thing, and now all he's got left is the engine." I reached into the bag and pulled out one of the metal parts, displaying it on my open palms. "I'm not sure exactly what these are—valves and things—he said you'd know." Billy nodded again as he took the part from me. "They're broken. Some of the cylinders need to be rewelded, too. He wants to know if you could find someone at the shop where you work who would make new ones for him. He'll pay you."

Billy turned the piece over in his hand. "Sure. When does he need them?"

"Whenever you can do it, I guess."

He crouched at my feet and placed the part back in the bag. His arm was warm against my knee. After pulling the drawstring tight, he looked up at me. "No problem."

I lifted the cool glass of lemonade to my lips. The shock of tiny ice cubes falling onto my tongue sent an arrow clear through me. Even the trees sheltering the house failed to move in the midafternoon heat. I could almost hear the tar softening on the roof, sizzling and popping like a dying fire. Marilyn introduced each one of us to Mrs. Dove, who smiled politely. Billy walked over to Marilyn and whispered in her ear something that made her laugh. Carline and Terese had their heads together, their gaggly voices making it sound as if there were a flock of girls in the room. When Marcella stood up and left the room, I followed her with my empty glass.

"Thanks." I set the glass on the kitchen counter.

"Why didn't your brother come himself?" Her eyes were the color of chocolate and sharp, as if she knew something about me and my family.

A long blade of shame shot through me. My brother's not like that, I wanted to tell her. I knew that Bryan's liberalism was not immune to cracks. Neither was my family. She'd know something about that, though, with her own husband in prison. She might even understand if I told her about the bankruptcy and Charlie's drinking.

"He said he doesn't know Billy very well and I know Marilyn, and Marilyn and Billy, they're friends, so he thought if I asked her it would be better." When her face didn't move, I opened my mouth to try again.

"That's all right. Must be a pretty fancy boat."

"Yeah, it's amazing how he's fixed it up. You'd think he'd bought it right out of a showroom."

"Boys," she said fondly, "they sure do like their engines."

I looked out the window at the garden. "My mother loves to garden. What kind of herbs do you have?"

"Come on out and I'll show you." Her step quickened as she crossed the neatly mowed grass. "This here's basil." She knelt down and pinched a cluster of leaves for me, holding it up to my nose. "It's been said that if you give a sprig of basil to a man, he will fall in love and never leave you." Her husky laugh rolled over me as she stood up. "I recommend it for stomach cramps, and of course, you can't beat it in tomato sauce." Her long finger pointed toward each leafy plant. "That one's savory, and fennel, rosemary, chives, chamomile, lavender, and comfrey. This," she leaned down and picked a few comfrey leaves, "comes from the Latin word, *conferta*, which means 'grow together.' It's been said that comfrey can close wounds and heal broken bones. I've seen it used on insect bites, eczema, bruises, even psoriasis."

"You get her started, you'll be here all day," Billy said. He was standing so close to me I could see the tiny strokes of green in the amber of his eyes.

"Hush yourself. I'm not tiring you, am I? What did you say your name was?"

"Danny. No, ma'am, you're not."

She handed me the green leaves she had folded in her hand. "You take these herbs to your mother."

I nodded and thanked her, then joined Terese and Carline, who were leaning up against the car. Marilyn stayed a few more minutes talking to Billy and his mother; she had draped one sunburned arm over Billy's shoulder.

"She sure does know how to make a spectacle of herself," Carline said.

"I think it's nice they're still friends." Terese held out her arm to us. "Is there something weird about this color?"

Her complexion was turning a dull orange. It was worse on her face, where the lines around her nostrils, under her eyes, and at the corners of each lip remained white while the rest resembled burnt umber. "Maybe you should try soap and hot water when you get home," I said, trying to be helpful.

Carline guffawed. "*That* won't do anything. I told you, Terese, it's permanent. That's what you wanted."

Terese and Carline argued about it as we drove off. I was grateful when Marilyn started to sing, because her beautiful voice drowned out the skirmishing in the back seat. As the leafy woods unravelled past my window, I twirled the fragrant basil under my nose, and thought that if I had known about its properties a half hour earlier, I could have planted the basil in Bryan's burlap bag.

*

On the morning of the King and Queen dance Terese arrived early to set my hair. Rollers would give my hair a tamer, more styled look, she said. My mother had stayed up half the night to salvage the dress I'd made. I'd followed the

131

pattern instructions carefully, but somehow I'd sewn the sleeves in wrong and the zipper backwards. Plus, the dotted-swiss netting I'd bought as a top layer over the yellow cotton had bunched up in places, and the seams had to be ripped out and resewn.

As I sat at the kitchen table wincing under Terese's machinations with my hair, I studied the blue, raised veins on the backs of my mother's hands as they guided the needle expertly in and out of the fabric. May yawned as she re-threaded the needle for the last section of the hem.

"OK," Terese said. "Wrap a kerchief around this and let's go over to Sal and Joey's for nail polish. Joey has just the pink I've been looking for."

"I have rollers in my hair, Terese!"

"Who's gonna notice? Everybody's got her hair up today. Look at mine."

After a week of pure hysteria she was resigned to her new skin color. I had to admit, the ochre cast went pretty well with her red hair, although it didn't pass as a suntan. At first Rosie had blamed it all on Carline, but since then she'd softened her position and was now using it as a lesson in the pitfalls of vanity. Even my mother got a kick out of that, since we both knew Terese's grandmother had vanity written all over her, and if the lotion had worked she would have been the first one to sing Carline's praises.

"Go on, Danny, you can bring me back a pack of cigarettes. And turn up the radio before you go." May bent her head over the dress and hummed along with Shirley Jones, singing "If I Loved You," our favorite song from *Carousel*.

Midway across the bridge I saw Angie Fanelli sitting on the railing next to Wade Fowler, a tall, well-built boy who had graduated from Neptune High School with her last summer and was working for a local roofing contractor. I stopped right in front of her.

She smiled. "Hi, Danny."

I knew she was studying nursing at the local community

college. "How's school?" I asked, ignoring both Wade, who was leaning his head against the cable and blowing smoke rings, and Terese, who'd walked on and was waving at me from the other end of the bridge.

"One more year . . . . It's only a two-year program. I've already had a job offer from a nursing home in Sparta."

"That's great."

"You know Wade, don't you?"

"Sure." I bobbed my head in his direction.

She held out her left hand to show me a small diamond ring. "Like it? We're engaged."

"We're getting married on Thanksgiving." Wade planted a wet kiss on her cheek. "Turkey Day."

After giving them my awkward congratulations, I joined Terese in Sal and Joey's, where she was busy hurling her hips against the pinball machine.

"They're getting married," I said glumly.

"Didn't you know?" Terese looked at me with surprise.

"What does Joey think?"

"I suppose she's happy."

"Yeah, but Wade Fowler! I mean, how boring can you get?"

"Wade's *always* liked Angie. It's nice to see that patience gets rewarded." Jubilantly she smacked her hand on the glass top of the machine as she scored a second game.

While Terese knocked the ball around with a great jangle of bells, I lay my head on the counter. If she loved Wade Fowler and he made her happy, then their getting married was a good thing. The fact that I was disappointed that he was a roofer and not a surgeon or diplomat just showed what a snob I was. Still, I could smell chemistry between people, and all I could sniff up between Angie and Wade was a loose and easy familiarity, not that shivery charge I'd seen between her and Joe Malone. Maybe she wanted something else in a man, something she could count on.

With Joe's name in my head like that, I had a shock when

133

we walked out of Sal and Joey's and there he was strolling across the highway with a tall, dark-haired girl wearing a white tennis dress. He was as handsome as ever, looking real collegiate in plaid Bermuda shorts and a V-necked navy blue sweater.

"Who's she?" I asked Terese.

"Joan Caldwell. She goes to Bennington. Her father and Doc Malone go fishing together."

By this time they were crossing the tracks and heading right for the bridge. I hurried to catch up to them.

"You forgot the cigarettes," Terese called after me.

There was this instant when they looked at each other, Angie silently gazing up from the railing, Joe with his head bent slightly toward Joan, who was chattering brightly, but he didn't stop. Wade went on blowing smoke rings as if he hadn't even noticed. And Joan Caldwell in her white tennis dress breezed past without knowing that this girl whom Joe was ignoring had *made love* with him on a blanket under the trees.

Something inside me shrunk in that moment, as if I'd been made invisible too. I wanted to stop and say something, but what? That I knew they'd been lovers, that I thought he was a mealy-mouthed rind of a person with tinsel for a spine? Angie laughed out loud at something Wade said; the sound of her voice followed their white clothes off the bridge.

*

One look at my hair after the rollers came out, and I leaped into the shower, dousing the curls with water. I shook my damp head once and decided to let nature take its course. My mother had ironed the dress for me and was napping on her bed. I wanted to thank her, but retreated at the sight of her peaceful face resting on the pillow, the webby folds in her throat I'd never noticed before.

She'd redesigned the dress. The puffed sleeves were gone and she'd changed the back. There was a new, shorter zipper and a low scooped back. Good thing I could go without a bra

134

or you'd be able to see the strap. Besides, Charlie always said my back was one of my nicest features. I'd always thought that a little odd, a girl with a nice *back*, but when I put on the dress and studied myself in the mirror, I liked the way my bones rippled beneath my tan.

We'd dyed my pumps yellow to match the fabric; Terese said you *had* to have shoes the same color. I pulled a pick through my hair and shot it a few times with hairspray. Some sea-green eye shadow, a little mascara, and a touch of my new apricot lipstick. Standing up as straight as I could in front of the mirror, I had to admit the effect wasn't half bad. I tucked the dried slip of basil into May's little evening bag. One dab of Shalimar at the base of my throat and I was ready.

When I reached the kitchen, I was surprised to hear my father and Bryan talking on the porch. They'd had so many arguments over Vietnam that Bryan usually avoided the subject when Charlie was around. Not that Charlie approved of the escalation in the war, but he thought it was important to point out the realities of combat to us. He'd served as a Marine in the South Pacific during World War II and retained an unyielding loyalty to the U.S. Armed Forces. He hated the idea that all these boys were being sent to Vietnam without the backing of the American people. How were they supposed to win this war if congress kept one hand tied behind their back? he asked.

"You know how many POWs there're gonna be, with all those planes being shot down?" Bryan said. "And what about the South Vietnamese army? They're deserting right and left, that's what the papers say."

"They shouldn't print that stuff."

"Shouldn't *print* it! Come on, Dad, you want them to *lie* to us?"

"What good's it supposed to do? Morale's low enough. You have no idea what poor morale can do to a bunch of men. Those boys have enough to contend with fighting in the jungle

135

like that without getting letters from home telling them the South Vietnamese are ready to bail out."

"I don't think you should pretend things are one way when they aren't."

"That's fine from where you sit, Bryan, but over there it's different."

"What does that mean, that you're not supposed to tell these guys the truth about their situation or the people they're fighting for?"

"When did I say that? Did you hear me say that?" The steam rose in Charlie's voice.

That was the point at which things usually turned sour. It wasn't that Bryan and Charlie weren't used to disagreements; Charlie had always encouraged healthy debate at the dinner table. Those days, however, Charlie's fuse was pretty short. There was something else, too, the way he got all tangled up when he was talking. He never used to do that, but now that he was drinking steadily he'd go off on these long-winded monologues that ended up so convoluted that they didn't make sense.

Sometimes it seemed as if he were short-circuiting right in front of me. His thoughts would be moving along normally when suddenly he'd veer off. It drove Bryan crazy, since he was being trained as a debater in all the nuances of logical argumentation, and here was Charlie making one generalization after another and stringing disconnected ideas together as if they fit. He'd start out by talking about when he was in boot camp, then move to what it was like lying in a tent ill with malaria, explosions going off a few feet away, not enough medics to go around, and then how he liked this guy Will Stine in his office, though you couldn't really trust your co-workers anymore, and what a struggle it was working with architects day in and day out who cared more about the number of square feet than what a building actually looked like, and how May really had it easy becoming a partner in Palone's Floral because she didn't have to make the compromises he did. He'd end, finally, with Westmoreland, who he said should drop the heavy artillery over there and take a concentrated course on guerilla warfare.

I walked onto the porch and planted myself in front of the swing, where I pirouetted on my tiptoes like they'd taught us in charm school.

"Like it?" I said.

Charlie let out a low whistle. "You look nice, honey. Nothing like a pretty back to make the boys sit up and take notice."

"Let me see." May stood in the doorway with her arms folded, her face creased with sleep.

She smiled, then looked at my face. "What'd you do to your hair?"

Bryan laughed. "She's letting it go natural. It looks fine, Danny, believe me."

He stood up. His hair was still damp from showering, and he was wearing his good pair of khakis and the light blue oxford shirt I'd ironed for him the night before.

"Let's go."

When I looked up from the patio for one last wave, my parents were standing together, their faces close to the screen. I liked seeing them like that, Charlie's hand on her shoulder. Maybe they'd pull out the Scrabble game like they used to, or practice their bridge hand. Maybe they'd keep the radio going and dance under the spotlight before going for a night swim. The evening was turning out to be promising after all. Chances were good that Terese would be elected Queen, and once Bryan saw her wearing that crown, even her orange skin couldn't stop him from falling in love. How could it miss? In the pink-flowered dress Nini had sent her, all soft and gauzy, her cleavage showing, she'd be without a doubt the prettiest girl on the lake.

The music swelled loud and bouncy as it hit the water. Bryan joined the line of boys leaning against the railing on the porch as I surveyed the ballooned, streamered room. The band platform was set up in front where the altar was on Sundays,

137

and a few couples were already dancing. Carline was leaning up against the log wall directly opposite me and holding a bottle of Coca-Cola.

Nobody could accuse Carline Gland of not having guts. In the flurry of pastel, flowy clothes, her outfit stood out like a black strobe light in an empty room. She was wearing a short, very tight black dress and fishnet stockings that showed off her legs. Her black sling-back heels clicked across the wooden floor.

"I thought it had puffed sleeves," she said.

"It did, except I sewed them in wrong. My mother did a miraculous job repairing it."

"I'll say, turn around."

She whistled when she saw the back. "I like it. You know, if you teased your hair, it could be incredible."

I laughed. Her own hair was teased lightly on top and clung to her face in long, feathery wisps. When Terese arrived, we sauntered up and down the row of whispering girls. By nine o'clock the band was hot, the boys had started dancing, and I'd broken a sweat. We'd turned in our ballots for the King and Queen. I'd voted for Bryan even though I knew Jimmy Piper was favored to win. Jimmy was acting pretty nonchalant, strolling casually from group to group inside the clubhouse.

When Jimmy finally asked Terese for a slow dance, I was surprised at the light on her face when she got close to him. He rested his chin on the top of her red head and braided his fingers around her waist. There was a stillness in their bodies, the way they were trying to hold themselves in check as they danced in a slow, fluid circle. I ran my hands up and down both arms, embarrassed at the flood of goose bumps.

Bryan was smiling, as if he'd expected it. Two things hit me: one, that it didn't bother him at all, and two, that he saw their energy as clearly as I did. I wondered if he were attracted to somebody at the dance, a girl he'd been keeping to himself.

Marilyn was dancing with her boyfriend from home, a tall boy in bell-bottoms and a flowered shirt. I didn't see Billy anywhere. By the time I realized Lou Sullivan was heading in my direction for a slow dance, it was too late to run. His body was stiff as we danced, and his hands on my bare back were cold. It took me a few minutes to realize he was getting a hard-on, and I pulled away as discreetly as I could, hating the way it pressed against my thigh. He stayed right there when the dance was over, and I raced through ways of ditching him that would seem natural. It was a relief when the band stopped for a break, and Jay Piper, who was chairman of the board of governors, stood on the platform to announce the 1967 king and queen of Rainy Lake.

When he read Terese Kelly's name, she walked calmly forward as if she'd prepared herself. He set one crown lightly on Terese's head and handed the other to his son with a jokey flourish that made everybody laugh. Terese gazed out over the crowd with glassy eyes. It was her most perfect moment, and she and Jimmy Piper became part of the history of Rainy Lake. You can read their names on the gold plaque that hangs to this day on the east wall of the clubhouse.

As the band resumed its position on stage and began "You Can't Hurry Love" by the Supremes, I tried to retreat onto the porch but Lou grabbed my hand. The crowd stepped back, forming a ring in which Terese and Jimmy danced the first few bars by themselves. My head was cushioned by the sound of breathing, girls' sighs, and whispers rustling like stalks of corn. Bryan's white hair was a break in the clouds as he strode purposefully across the room. The path in front of him led straight to Carline, who was outlined against a smoky window. She jerked upright when Bryan stopped in front of her, and her lips parted in surprise. His back was to me but it didn't matter, for I could tell everything from the joyful wave that billowed across her face.

Lou put his arms around me again, and I moved with him, swept like a leaf into the crush of perfumed, sweaty dancers. I knew Bryan and Carline were dancing, and that his blue sleeve had encircled her tiny black waist. In my head was a silent bubble, the distant sound of breaking glass. Who would have figured he'd fall for Carline, the last girl I'd have picked? Whatever it was that drew one person to another, it lurked in camouflage, mysterious and irrational. When the song ended and Lou kept his hands around me, I pushed back firmly against his chest to escape the wet kiss flying in my direction. The glass was shattering on all sides, and I felt my supper rising. I made it down the stairs to the girls' bathroom, where I leaned out the open window.

Now, I thought, before anything else happens. I dropped onto the sand and stumbled up the bank toward the tracks. If I walked along the beach, Lou or Terese or somebody would see me, and I'd have to explain or go back in and see something else I didn't want to see. I kicked my shoes off, not caring about my stockings or splinters, sighing in relief as my toes spread out on the dark railroad ties and breathed for the first time all evening.

I didn't notice Billy right away. He was sitting on the stone wall in the parking lot, and if I'd have been on the beach I'd have missed him altogether. I saw the glint of the bottle first, then his arm, and the long swell of his throat when he swallowed. Weighing my loneliness, I walked toward the parking lot.

You could smell the liquor on him a few feet away. I knew by the way he swung his head, as if he wanted me to disappear, that I should have. But something had grabbed hold of me, something fierce and sad and full of pressure, and I was going to talk to him once and for all—straight out so he'd remember. I stood in front of him, not minding the silence as he continued to drink. Finally, he set the bottle down beside him.

"Do you *want* something?"

When I spoke I tried to sound as clear and determined as I could. "Yeah, I do."

"What?" As he gripped the wall, the tendons stood out on his arms and wrists.

His anger surprised me. As the clouds broke, a sliver of moonlight fell on his face and I could see the sadness there. I should have been more frightened of him, for I'd heard he was a fighter like his brother. *Like his father.*

"I'd prefer not to be inside that clubhouse one more minute, and I'm damned if I want to go home."

"So?"

Something was really eating at him. I could tell by the way he grabbed the neck of the bottle and closed his fist around it, lifting it to his lips with a barely controlled violence. There was no label on the bottle, but I knew gin when I smelled it. He'd taken such a big mouthful that it spilled down his throat and into the open neck of his shirt.

"What's the matter?" I asked.

"None of your business."

"You're gonna get sick if you keep drinking that."

He glared at me. "How would you know?"

I stepped closer, resting my hand on the stone wall. "Because I do, that's all."

He sighed and studied me. It seemed hard for him to focus. "Jane, right?"

"Danny Fillian. *Jane Eyre* was the book I dropped."

"You were at my house."

"That's right, with Marilyn and Carline. I gave you some metal parts from my brother."

"They're done." He hopped off the wall and stood next to me. He was still holding the bottle in one hand. His skin smelled like water, even with all the liquor.

The clouds lifted again and he scrutinized me up and down, lingering a long minute on my face.

"Want to go for a walk?" He flicked his thumb over his shoulder toward the tracks.

It was surprise and not hesitation that showed on my face but it caught him. "I won't rape you, if that's what you're thinking." He tilted his head, the lopsided smile sliding into place.

We turned in unison and walked. My left arm, which was only inches from his, stung as if sunburned. Neither one of us spoke as we made our way down the tracks, past the clubhouse lit up like a jack-o-lantern, the inky green trees, the glimmering lake. My heart was making me a little breathless, even though we were walking at a normal rate of speed. I was conscious of its loud, physical presence and the way my skin felt cold on the surface and hot underneath, yet, despite this, I was absolutely certain about what I was doing. It wasn't that I believed Billy wanted me in any real or significant way, the way I wanted him, but that I'd set out on a course I was bound to finish no matter what happened.

That's what comes back to me sometimes, the memory that there I was, fifteen years old, so set on going down the tracks with this boy I really didn't know, willing to do anything he wanted. Perhaps it was the power of my sexual energy, or the loneliness that had crested during that moment at the dance when I'd seen not only my best friend but my brother fall for the two people I hadn't counted on. The effect was stunning, this knowledge that things could change in an *instant,* taking you completely by surprise.

When we reached the tire swing Billy grabbed my hand. My feet were picking up every stone and sharp twig, and I considered putting my shoes back on, but he was walking too fast and I didn't want to stop him. Just then the lake opened out in a huge, motionless bowl of light. I pressed my fist against my chest, hoping the weight of it would still the wings beating underneath.

When I turned I was startled by the black, hard surface of his eyes, which I'd always associated with sun and tawny green leaves. For so long I'd assumed that everything people said about the Doves was somehow separate from Billy, that he didn't hear it, or wouldn't have cared if he did. I didn't know much then about the price paid by a boy like Billy, who lived in a white community and passed most of the time for white. It seemed natural to me that he'd see himself more as white than as black, since he didn't look much different from the other kids around him. Except that his mother did, and her family. And then he felt the shame over his father, the fact that everybody knew what he'd done and passed the deed along to Billy and his brother whether they deserved it or not. So something must have been said, or implied, that had sent him into this angry, inarticulate spin. What it was didn't matter to me; I cared only that he sense my sympathy and hoped that my ardor was strong enough for the two of us. He cupped his hand around the back of my head and pulled me toward him. I felt the softness of his lips, and then his tongue was in my mouth, pressing hard. We slid backward off the concrete spillway onto the hard-packed ground. The bottle hit the dirt and rolled with a glassy clatter down Lovers' Slope.

Billy was on his knees, still kissing me, his hand supporting me as I leaned back. His tongue was gentler now, and his lips played over the surface of my face and down my neck. When I felt him at the base of my throat I must have made some sound, for he raised his head and seemed to look at me differently. The black curtain in his eyes had lifted, and I could see filaments of light. A puzzled expression passed over his face, and he ran his hands slowly up and down my arms, resting momentarily on my shoulders before traveling across my back.

When his hand slid beneath the fabric, a cloud of butterflies took flight inside me. His fingertips slipped along the ridges of my rib cage and brushed the slight curve of my breasts. I pressed my lips against his, and he hesitated, his body suddenly still. His eyes were clear and bright as he sat backward on his feet and looked at me.

"How old are you?"

I swallowed. "Fifteen, why?"

He smiled slightly. "I thought you were older."

"How much older?"

"I don't know, sixteen, seventeen."

"What difference does it make?"

He laughed. "Some."

My chin dropped and I viewed the yellow plain of my chest, rising and falling, not much fuller than a child's. Crisscrossing my arms in front of me, I stood up.

"You don't have to go," he said.

"Yes, I do."

"Come on, sit down. I didn't mean to hurt your feelings. It's been a lousy evening."

A boat sped by, shooting a flume of water that rocked in receding waves toward the shore. The shiver that had felt so good only moments before was now continous and uncomfortable, and my throat ached as if I'd been running.

"I'm going."

"You want me to walk back with you?"

"No!"

Not until I was out of sight of the spillway did I realize I'd left behind my shoes and May's evening bag. *The hell with it.* Let him dump the contents on the ground: the comb, my apricot lipstick, a shrivelled slip of basil. His mother should have given *him* the basil. He could have slipped it into the crown of some girl's creamy breasts; she'd look into his beautiful face and forget her own name. "Only you," she'd say, handing herself over, his fingers busy with her dress, his lips riding the wave of her breasts without stopping, kissing, kissing until the two of them tumbled onto the ground.

Crying softly now, I huddled close to the line of trees so I wouldn't bump into any neckers heading down the tracks after the dance. The music echoed off the water, and I wondered whether my brother was standing somewhere with his arms around Carline Gland.

There was no spotlight shining on the patio, and the porch light was off. I curled up on the chaise lounge and indulged in a string of obscenities. Finally, I gazed out at the dusky lake and the red concentric circles of the Ballantine sign from Sal and Joey's. Tiny sparks flared and multiplied as I recalled the feel of Billy's lips, the smell of water, the way his hands had moved over my skin.

An open bottle of rye stood on the kitchen counter amidst a sea of dirty glasses, a plate of broken crackers, potato chips, and a few spoonfuls of onion dip. After pouring the rest of the rye down the drain, I washed the glasses and dishes, emptied the full ashtrays, and picked up the playing cards scattered across the vinyl tablecloth. When I heard my mother's strained, weepy voice in the living room, I hunched down at the bottom of the stairs. She said something and broke into sobs. The couch creaked and her slippers slapped across the floor.

"Why won't you talk to somebody? I've asked you and *asked* you. Is it *me*? Am I too fat? You don't think I'm pretty anymore?"

"May . . . stop it." Charlie's voice was muffled.

"Why, Charlie? Why should I? I want to know! If it's the drinking . . . . Nini said it does this. Did you know that?"

"You talked to Nini about this?"

"Oh, for Christ sake, Charlie. At least when she told me that I didn't feel so awful. It's been months since we . . . look, I know my working at the shop has been hard on everybody, and I know it bothered you when Frank Palone offered to make me a partner . . . "

"That's not true. I'm proud of you, May."

"Then what *is* it? Because I have to know, Charlie. If you're seeing someone . . . "

"Don't be ridiculous."

"What am I supposed to think? You'd prefer not to talk about it—you just pretend nothing's wrong. Well, it *is* wrong. It's terrible, Charlie. I don't even feel like a woman. I can't go on like this much longer. I *can't*!"

She must have buried her head then for all I could hear was a strangled sobbing, so deep and rending I covered my ears to stop it. When the upstairs light finally clicked off, I pulled my

145

feet out from under me. My stockings were a mass of runs, and one foot was completely shredded. A dark patch covered my big toe, and I turned the foot over, moaning when I saw the dried blood there, the dozens of splinters and tiny pebbles imbedded in my skin.

FLY-FISHING (1968)

BRYAN GRADUATED IN JUNE, SALUTATORIAN OF his class, stunning the audience with a rousing speech against the war and a call to students to protest the expansion of the fighting into Laos and Cambodia. He was eloquent and sincere, with a self-righteous fire simmering in his eyes. Like many of his friends, he'd thrown his hopes behind Eugene McCarthy for president, a ludicrous choice in Charlie's view.

"McCarthy doesn't know the first thing about combat. You can't just pull out. Johnson was opposed to the war, too, in the beginning, until he got in there and saw the real picture. Now all this dissent has finished him. Once we leave, you know, they're going to make mincemeat out of South Vietnam. These college kids . . . they don't realize that when you go to war you have to *kill* people. All those trails filtering men and supplies, we have to stop it. The enemy has to be cut off at the roots, the *roots!*"

Our dinner-table disputes were the only time Charlie and Bryan even talked anymore. I was grateful that the war, the upcoming election, the trouble on college campuses at least offered them an opportunity to communicate. They engaged each other with familiar passion, and I loved to see the way their minds worked with such needle-sharp precision. Occasionally I ventured in, but they were like twin steamrollers, drumming by before I'd had a chance to compose my next sentence. I used to think I was too slow or not as smart, but now I know I was paying attention to different things, the way my mother was as she kept the food moving around the table.

Charlie was as proud of Bryan as the rest of us were,

although he rarely showed it. It would have been hard not to feel proud: Bryan was a National Merit Scholar and was entering Columbia in September. My parents were delighted that he was going to school in New York City, which was in their book the undisputed queen of American cities. They didn't seem to notice the fact that Columbia was practically exploding with student activism.

Bryan had had an offer from the public works department in Westfield to work the road crew over the summer, but he turned it down. He preferred spending the summer at Rainy, he said, even if the city did pay more than the boat works. My parents assumed he wanted to be near Carline. I knew better. Not that Bryan wasn't in up to his eyeballs with Carline; I'd seen the two of them cruising in the Chris-Craft after sunset as if it were a barge ferrying them up the Nile. They were such a sight: Bryan with his long blonde hair and cut-off blue jeans, Carline still testing the limits of good taste with skin-tight skirts and halter tops, and with her hair cut short with a white streak down one side. The problem was Charlie plain and simple. Bryan didn't want to stay home with him.

My mother was jumpy and tired, thinner than I'd ever seen her. Now that she'd been made a partner in Palone's Floral, she couldn't take the summer off as she'd done before. She was relieved when Bryan accepted the job in Neptune because she didn't want me staying at the cabin alone. She was driving back and forth, trying to cover both ends, caring for me and Bryan and managing Charlie's alcoholism.

No one ever said the word; my mother's puffy, pleading eyes ensured our silence. Charlie drank at home after work so we didn't have to worry about him driving around late at night. Some days he'd remain lucid until bedtime, but mostly he'd ramble on, then pass out in his chair around eight o'clock. Bryan told my mother to leave him there but she wouldn't; she hated the thought of going to bed while he slept sitting up in his clothes. She fielded his phone calls, too, and it surprised me how much she knew about his business whenever she spoke to one of his partners or to a client. Then I understood the drill she put him through every evening after he'd walked through the door: how were his projects going, what were the problems, which meetings did he have tomorrow?

Now my mother can admit that had she left Charlie to fend for himself, he might have faced up to it. She feared he'd lose his job. I don't judge her too harshly. Today there are treatment centers on every corner; you're considered odd if you *aren't* in therapy. For my parents it was something to be ashamed of. Alcoholics were characters on TV or in novels, never people in your own family.

I'd considered working part-time in the floral shop, but my mother wouldn't hear of it. "You're only sixteen," she said. "This will be your last summer without working, enjoy it." So far I was bored and lonely. The nights May stayed in Westfield, Bryan arrived home from work at five-thirty, dove into the lake for a quick washup and laps, devoured the hot dogs or ziti I served up, and putted off in the Chris-Craft to pick up Carline. Whenever he invited me along, I declined.

It was better with Terese and Jimmy. I enjoyed driving with them up Tamarack Road and into the black labyrinth of back roads that sooner or later spilled into Sparta or Neptune. I was acquiring a real taste for Ripple and for the chocolate fudge ice cream cones we bought in a little ice cream parlor on the outskirts of Sparta. By this time Terese was making big pronouncements about watching her weight, but any extra ounce on me was a blessing.

Jimmy said I was standoffish; it kept boys away who otherwise would have been sniffing at my door. I'm not a dog, I told him. "Those other girls are a dime a dozen," Bryan told me. "You're unusual—a boy is going to *remember* you." Seeing the unusual flower he'd picked, I wasn't reassured.

The swim team kept me busy most mornings, for I'd taken over Angie Fanelli's old job and was helping Linda with paperwork and other team business. The pay was small but enough to keep me supplied with the meager amount of spending money I needed. Terese and Ginny Conroy had hounded me into joining the ski club so I could be the third girl on the bottom of the five-girl pyramid that had become a Rainy Lake Ski Show tradition. For the past two years Fern Daniels had done it, but she'd sprained her wrist and couldn't support the Casey girls, whose bony hands and feet scrambled daily past my chin as they climbed to our shoulders and grabbed the ski ropes we held up to them.

The worst part about it was having to put up with Bud Doonan, who drove the small retrieval boat that picked up the skis the girls dropped once they started to climb. He was a big mouth and a racist like his father, Paddy Doonan, and had gotten the job over a townie boy because Paddy had made a pitch to the board of governors. It wasn't the money Bud wanted; he figured he could impress Ginny Conroy by whizzing around in that little boat and making waves. Bud had knobby knees and narrow, lizard eyes that left a residue on my skin. Practices were harder and more monotonous than I'd expected, but they filled the long, cavernous afternoons.

I was quick to recognize the breathless look that foamed across Terese and Jimmy's faces when they wanted to park the Mustang under a net of black trees and neck themselves into a splotched and sweaty oblivion. On those nights I pillaged the refrigerator for odd and alluring bait, packed a can of root beer and a few slices of Sara Lee pound cake into the small fishing boat, and headed for the old lake. My fishing tackle was pretty impressive at this point, and I hauled in bass after gleaming bass in a succession of quiet but steady hits.

After I'd returned at least a dozen fish to the lukewarm water, I rigged up Bryan's fly rod and practiced casting. The channel into Disappointment was a prime location, but I gave up once I'd lost four or five flies to the long reeds. Most of the time I stayed anchored in the old lake and cast out onto the silent silver dollar of a surface. Around me crouched the willowy grass, the slow, sucking lily pads, the high-pitched thrum of insects.

Worry rolled off me like sweat, and in those moments I thought about God—not crabby or bored the way I was in Mass, but open to it, wanting to be filled up whole without that yawning echo that kept me awake at nights. I'd abandoned the notion that it was a boy I needed, since no one I'd seen that summer had raised the faintest itch, and yearning for my old family wasn't bringing happiness any closer. So I thought I'd try religion, hoping that my desire and Rainy's hushed grace would be all the calling God needed.

This particular evening I was standing in a funnel of ebbing sunlight, lost in the big hoops whirring back and forth over my head, when a voice rose up like a storm behind me. I spun around, thinking in my confusion that it was the sound of God finally speaking.

"Here." He held out a furry pile of flies to me.

I reached out involuntarily and took them. Billy's hair was longer, the soft curls touching the cinnamon sheen on his bare shoulders. I turned and reeled in my line.

"I found them in the reeds. You know if you change your cast a little, you won't lose so many."

I shielded my eyes with an upraised hand. He'd pulled his canoe alongside me, and his upper arm was taut where he held the paddle in the water. His expression was friendly and curious, without one visible clue he even remembered my name.

"Thanks." I was surprised at how mean I sounded.

His eyes twitched, like a switch had gone off, and when that slightly lopsided smile appeared I sat down hard and started to unhook my fly.

"You look different," he said.

I couldn't tell if he was teasing or not. I am one of those people who don't get jokes right away and can't discriminate teasing from pure seriousness. It's infuriating and brings out the devil in others.

"Your hair's longer."

"Thicker. My hair doesn't grow in the back so I keep getting the sides cut."

He peered around at me, trying to see better. "What do you mean it doesn't grow in the back?"

I shrugged as I dropped the first fly into its labeled box. "Just what I said. It's so thick it stops growing as soon as it reaches my neck. Beats me why. I've been to over a dozen different beauticians and not a one can figure it out. They just trim the sides."

I could feel his eyes on my face, or maybe it was the warmth of the sun. "Did your brother ever finish his boat?"

"You mean you haven't seen him? He's out almost every night with Carline. The boat's a work of art."

"Your brother goes out with Carline?"

"Ever since the King and Queen Dance last summer."

I snapped the lid on the last fly box and looked right at him, as boldly as I knew how.

"I remember." He was smiling again, as if he found me real amusing.

"I suppose you do." I moved into the back of the boat and pull-started the engine.

"Where are you going?"

"Home." The boat jerked forward, rocking the canoe in its wake.

"Wait a minute." He'd stopped smiling, and his eyes held me.

"What?" I kept the engine at a low idle.

"Danny, right?"

I nodded. At least he had that right.

He hesitated, working something over in his head. "You know about the stream?" He lifted the paddle and pointed in the direction of the woods just past the channel.

"What stream?"

"If you really want to fly-fish, you've gotta try the stream. Runs from Disappointment clear out to the Virgin River. Ever catch a trout?"

When I shook my head, he paddled swiftly past me, motioning me to follow. I dipped one hand into the lake and splashed water over my cheeks. His steady stroke cut a path through the weedy channel; I kept my eyes on the creamy line at the edge of his shorts. We'd only gone about twenty-five yards when he pulled the canoe up on the marshy shoreline, then waded in to catch the rope I tossed him. After I'd stepped over the side of the boat and stood up beside him, the smell of water lingering with his sweat, I remembered the way he'd cupped my head in one hand, my back flexing like a straw.

He took a bamboo fly rod out of his canoe, flipped his vest over one shoulder, and strode into a grove of birch. The path was narrow and studded with boulders, and I held my eyes on my bare feet so I wouldn't fall. Billy stopped on the bank of a swift-moving stream.

"This way." He moved nimbly along the rocks, not minding the water splashing over his unlaced sneakers.

I had to work to keep up with him, wondering how you'd ever cast with all these low-hanging branches. Five minutes later we emerged into a small clearing. The stream dropped a level into a still pool that tumbled on its downstream end over a cluster of rocks.

"This is a good place to cast." He pulled a box of flies from one of his vest pockets.

"Doesn't your line get caught in the trees?"

"Not if I cast it right." He knelt down to tie on a leader and rigged the tippet end with a Hare's Ear nymph.

Billy's arm ticked smoothly back and forth, the loops inflating overhead, until with the barest flick of his wrist the line sailed forward and landed without a wrinkle on the surface of the pool.

"Why there?" I asked as the nymph sunk out of sight.

"I'm hoping they're trout down there at the head. It's deep enough for them to hide, and they can watch for food washed down by those riffles."

The water bulged as Billy's leader dipped. He raised his rod slightly and tightened the line.

"Did you get one?"

He nodded, his eyes steady on the line as the fish struggled. After pulling out enough slack for it to swim, he reeled it in carefully.

"It's a brownie," he said, dropping to his knees.

"It's big." I could see its shiny, speckled back, its sinuous movement through the water.

Gently he slid his hand under the belly of the fish and cradled it in the stream. Once he'd removed the hook, he waited, the fish suspended loosely in his hand, before letting it go. The tail fanned sluggishly back and forth as the trout swam out of the shallow water and disappeared into the depths of the pool.

"I never saw a bamboo rod like that."

Bryan's was graphite, an inexpensive rod he'd gotten from our grandfather one Christmas. I'd seen the bamboo ones in Charlie's catalogues and knew how costly they were.

"It's my father's. He made it a long time ago."

It surprised me how matter-of-factly he said it, as if his father were trolling out on the lake or sitting on the front porch of their house drinking a beer—not in prison hundreds of miles away, in prison for manslaughter. The way he looked at me then, slow and careful, with the tiniest compression of his eyes, is the look I most remember. It was as if he knew things about me, things I didn't know myself. It made me want to slide underneath the surface of his skin.

"What?" I asked.

"You want to ask me something?"

I dug my toes into the dirt. "I was just wondering when he made it for you."

"He didn't. He made it for himself, but after he went to prison I took it. I figured he wouldn't mind."

"You miss him?"

Later he told me I was the first person near his own age who'd ever asked him that. "Yeah, I miss him a lot. We used to fish along here all the time, or we'd take the canoe over to the Virgin."

"What about your brother, you fish with him?"

"I did before he enlisted."

I was sitting on a tangle of roots a few feet away from where he stood at the edge of the pool. He'd rigged up his line again and was trying for a hit at the tail end. "Is he in Vietnam?"

"Yeah."

I whistled softly. "There's a man in my father's office whose son is a Marine, but I never met him."

"I know lots of guys over there, two who've already died."

"Really?"

"Sure, I enlisted a couple of weeks ago."

My open mouth could have snagged a couple of flies. "You're not going on to school?"

"Nah, maybe later. The Navy'll pay for it then anyway."

"You could get killed over there."

He shrugged. "My cousin got killed driving to a movie in Sparta. Besides, if I enlist I'll have a say in where I go. Guys who get drafted are sent straight to Nam. I want to work on planes."

"You mean be a pilot?"

"You have to have a college degree to be a pilot. I'm going to be an air mechanic. A couple of guys I know enlisted in the Navy same day as me. Ever read the ads "join the Navy and see the world?" If I go to air school I'll be working on F4s and F16s."

"So they won't send you to Vietnam?"

"If things get hot enough they'll send me. I wouldn't mind being on an aircraft carrier; that's where Douglass is."

"What about . . . well, I don't think we should be in Vietnam in the first place. No offense to your brother or anything."

"You're not one of those hippie communist sympathizers, are you?"

I laughed. "God, Billy, you sound just like Terese's father."

It was the first time I'd said his name, out loud as if we were old friends. "I'm not a communist, honest, and not all hippies are either. I just think the Vietnamese people know better than us what's best for them."

"Since when did all the Vietnamese want to be communist?"

"I didn't say that. But countries have been going in there for years telling them what to do. It's time we let the Vietnamese decide for themselves what government they should have."

"As if the Vietcong would ever allow South Vietnam to hold free elections. My father fought in Korea for the same thing: freedom. All these college kids protesting the war—I get real tired of it."

He pulled in his line and turned to me. "Want to try?"

I concentrated on my arm and wrist to blot out the smell of his skin only inches away. Even in this fairly open space, the line snagged on a branch. He showed me how to do a roll cast, which kept most of the line in front of me, and a curve cast, where the line bent into a long, narrow U on either side. Twice he leaned over me, his arms straddling mine the way men do in the movies when they're teaching women how to shoot, and I felt his skin against my shoulder.

"It's getting dark," I said. "I'd better go."

On the way back I stubbed my toes several times on rocks hidden in the dim grass.

"You have a light?" He pushed the canoe into the lake.

I held up a lantern-sized flashlight. "One thing," I called over the purr of my engine.

His chin jerked up in response.

"I could tie better flies than you have."

He grinned. "I *bought* the ones I have."

"I can do better. Which ones are you using—mayflies, caddis, stones?"

He nodded, humoring me.

"I'll make you some of each. Can't beat my grasshoppers either."

156

"I thought you said you haven't fished much trout," he said.

"Doesn't stop me from making flies. My brother and I go to fishing stores all the time, and I've got two books on fly tying. It takes imagination and skill to tie a perfect fly."

When he smiled like that, I tottered, the ground a mile away.

"I hear you're in the five-girl pyramid this year," he said.

"If I don't die first."

"Ty Malone called me yesterday asking if I'd drive his boat next week. He's playing in some golf tournament and can't make the practice. I don't have to be at work until six so I said I'd do it."

"I'll see you then," I said.

As I aimed toward the channel I looked back once to see the pale gleam of his back moving into the murky middle of Disappointment. Just as I reached the edge of the old lake I cut the motor and drifted for a few minutes, my head rolled back and my ears open to the hushed music of the lake. I was aware of a slow, steady burn sealing me to my seat. I shifted uncomfortably. *Damn.* All that long winter's work beating the image of Billy Dove from my mind as I focused on that black moment last summer when he'd hunched back on his heels and regarded my flat chest with sober eyes.

I glanced down at the small mounds beneath my T-shirt and sighed. *Where am I heading?* I wondered, knowing he had only to ask and I'd go with him.

*

I grew up thinking schizophrenic meant split personality, a person rattling between two contradictory selves. Now I know it's more complicated than that, a disorder with many faces. Still, the word occurs to me as I recall how easily I veered from intense, almost painful sympathy for my father to a contempt that shook me to the core.

I sat on the porch each Friday evening, waiting for the train

157

whistle announcing Charlie's arrival. The only difference now as he walked across the bridge was how low his head sat in the hollow of his shoulders. His neck looked rubbery and tired, like a piece of clay rolled thin enough to break. As he pushed open the door this night, I looked up, hoping to meet a lurking spark in the closed field of his face.

"Water's just right, Dad. There's still about twenty minutes till supper."

That seemed to rouse him. "Your brother home?"

"Not yet."

In past summers they'd have raced to the pier after Charlie arrived at the lake. My mother would have laid the folded towels over the railing of the deck and stretched out on the chaise lounge with a whisky sour in hand and Charlie's martini waiting on the flagstone underneath his chair.

My mother's low voice in the kitchen parried his sharper, more agitated tone. She'd gone into the shop at 6 A.M. to finish the arrangements for a wedding and had driven up that afternoon. She insisted on cooking a real dinner on Friday nights, although I told her repeatedly it wasn't necessary. Charlie didn't seem to notice what he put in his mouth, and Bryan paid more attention to the minutes ticking by than to anything on his plate. He was hungering after Carline, I imagined, baffled at the thought. Anybody could see how worn out May was. Her face was doughy with fatigue, but she toiled on in the hot kitchen. Her red shirt bobbed like a balloon as she pulled a bowl of hard-boiled eggs out of the refrigerator.

Charlie trudged up the stairs to the living room just as the Neptune bus stopped in front of Sal and Joey's. Bryan bounded across the bridge; his long legs swallowed the distance in a matter of minutes. A crop of bleached hair preceded him through the screens, then I saw his face, sunburned and moist, sweat darkening his sideburns.

"Hi." He smiled at me.

"Dad's going swimming. We could do laps . . . " I looked up hopefully.

"No time. Carline's been practicing at the rink in Peapack; I said I'd meet her there. Want to come?"

"You're not leaving without dinner, Bry." My mother swooped onto the porch and handed me a strainer full of green beans to trim.

"What time are you leaving?" I asked.

He looked from May to me, measuring the danger of skipping one of my mother's Friday night dinners.

"Right after dinner, I guess."

"Right after dinner what?" Charlie stood in the doorway, the bald front of his head on a level with Bryan's.

"I told Carline I'd meet her at the rink."

"How about a swim first?" Charlie asked.

When my father's shoulders sank forward like that, my throat closed like a fist. Bryan didn't look up. He simply swung past Charlie, his polite "no thanks" trailing after him. I gnawed a thumbnail as Charlie slipped through the screen door, leaving it open behind him. He draped a towel over the railing on the lower level of the deck and set a highball glass beside it. While I snapped off the dead ends of each bright green bean, Charlie swam slowly out into the lake. His long arms wheeled forward like the limbs of a windmill. There was something about the picture he made once he'd rolled over and was floating on his back. I could see myself towing along behind, my small hands curled round each big toe as we took turns singing the Roy Rogers' and Dale Evans' verses in "Happy Trails to You."

"Danny, what're you doing? Stop already, they'll be too small to put on a fork."

After my mother had removed the bowl from my hands, I continued to snap imaginary beans as Charlie climbed heavily up the wooden ladder and stood at the railing with the towel barely covering his big white stomach. Ice cubes clinked as he raised the glass to his lips. He waved to Ed Casey and Paddy Doonan, who called to him from the open window in the back of the Pink Elephant. Their voices traveled in shaky circles across the water: "Gin and tonics . . . nine o'clock . . . your house."

"Bud Doonan's making a complete ass of himself at ski practice," I said at dinner, breaking the silence. "He thinks . . ."

"Watch your language, Danny." My mother wiped a ribbon of sweat from the side of her face.

"He thinks that if he treats the retrieval boat like a hot rod Ginny Conroy's going to fall for him."

"Seems to me you're being a bit hard on old Bud," my father said.

"Hard nothing. Everybody knows Dale Foster wanted that job. Mr. Doonan just . . ."

"Paddy did what any other man on the board would have done if his son were looking for a job. What good's it do to work so hard all these years without a little something coming back?"

"Well, I don't know, Charlie, I didn't see *you* asking the board to give that job to Bryan." My mother spooned a deviled egg and a huge helping of macaroni salad onto her plate.

She *meant* that he wasn't the kind of man to ask a favor like that, especially when the job usually went to a townie boy.

When Charlie glared hatefully across the table at her, something inside me stood absolutely still. Bryan's hand reaching for a pork chop stalled in midair.

"If I'd known Bryan wanted that job, I would have asked. 'Course one of you would have had to tell me first, wouldn't you? In this family, that's too much to expect." Charlie's voice was like an unhealed wound—hardened with pain and the imposition of injury, yet tender to the touch.

My mother sighed. "I didn't mean it that way, Charlie."

"Oh yeah, how *did* you mean it? You think I can't see what's going on? Just remember, when you're all out having your good times, *I'm* the one paying the bills. I bet I'll be good enough in September to sign your tuition check, won't I,

Bryan?" Charlie walked over to the counter next to the sink and poured another glass of bourbon.

"Of course, your mother can tell all her friends about me. A man's personal business isn't his own. It's amazing how someone so inadequate can tie his own shoes in the morning."

I looked away from my mother's stricken face. Bryan was flexing and unflexing his right hand, his eyes lodged on the charred crust of his pork chop. Charlie sat down heavily and took a long drink. I was not deaf to the plea in my father's voice, although I had no idea how to change things. The burden of it weighed on me, and I wished we could have one friendly conversation the way we used to. Even an argument over Vietnam would do, anything but this loud, gelid silence.

Bryan stood and pushed the chair into the table. "I told Carline I'd be there by seven. Can I use your car, Mom?"

"*Her* car?" Charlie asked.

"Yes, why don't you go with him, Danny?" May said.

"Since when is it *her* car? I suppose you think this is *her* house now, too." The sneer in his voice accompanied the collapsing gray matter of his face.

I looked uncertainly at my mother.

"The Caseys are coming over later to play cards, aren't they, Charlie? The Doonans too?" May smiled at me reassuringly.

Charlie remembered the men he'd invited over. "That's right. How's our gin? We're going to need ice, too, plenty of it."

My mother waved Bryan and me out of the kitchen. I had to run to catch up to him, bounding down the back steps two at a time. Once we'd made our way through the winding streets of French's Grove, Bryan floored the accelerator pedal and raced along the two-lane road leading back to the highway. I nibbled my fingernails as the trees spun by, glad for the small Fiat engine, the speedometer that never moved past sixty-five miles an hour. Bryan in a bigger car would have been a fearful thing, the way he bore down in the seat like that, his mind and body focused on the narrow tunnel before him.

"Sometimes I feel like I'm going to have to *do* something," he said quietly. "I don't know what it is. Knock him over maybe, or smash a bottle over his head. I get this picture of him in my mind, the way he used to be, and I cling to it. I imagine him gone away somewhere, that it's just you, me, and Mom. Then something happens and there he is . . . ."

Bryan's skin appeared almost transparent, the outline of his bones as familiar to me as the back of my own hand. I assumed all along that his suffering was greater than mine, because as a boy he needed to identify with Charlie, and there was such a gap now between who Bryan was becoming and who our father was. Of the two of us, I was the more flexible. I didn't expect as much from myself as Bryan did, at least not then. Bryan was the one destined for stardom, after all, and he needed Charlie to point the way.

"You make it harder on yourself than it has to be," I said. "I'm not saying it's your fault, 'cause it's not. If Dad would get help, you know, the way Mr. Kelly did, maybe things would get better. I just think that if you didn't expect so much, you wouldn't be as disappointed."

"I don't expect anything from him anymore."

I bit my lower lip, knowing he would disagree with anything I said. He was wrong, though. The old Charlie was locked into his head as clear as daylight. As long as he kept comparing one man with the other, he was going to be stuck in the visceral grip of Charlie's failures. I understood it, but much as I loved my father I wanted him to travel his road alone, not take me and my brother with him.

"She should leave him. That's what I'd do if I were her."

"Bryan, how can you say that? She *loves* Daddy."

"If she left, he'd sink like a stone. He might do something then to save himself."

Bryan deftly navigated the back roads to Peapack. I tried to picture him and Carline taking this route home from the rink at night, inching the car into tucked-away alcoves where they lay on the red-upholstered seat and necked. It was hard imagining any boy getting worked up over Carline's coat-hanger shoulders, getting worked up at all under the watchful eyes of the St. Christopher medal dangling from a silver chain on the rearview mirror.

There were four girls skating in the rink, but I didn't see Carline. She'd divided up her practice time so she was skating three days here and two days in Staten Island. By that time I knew how much money Carline's skating was costing. Skates, coaching, ice time, costumes, the cost of competitions—it was more than you'd pay for a good private school. Last winter her father had balked, claiming that there was no sense in dumping all this money into figure skating, which was just a hobby anyway.

That was when Frieda had stepped forward with the first of several actions which were to take us all by surprise. It seems she'd been hoarding a safety deposit box full of stocks her father had left her when he died. He'd been a man cut out of the same cloth as Gerry; he'd slept with different women until he actually fell in love with one of them and divorced Frieda's mother. The new wife belonged to some religious sect, which Carline claimed had rubbed off enough on her grandfather to make him renounce adultery once and for all and bequeath to Frieda, his only child, a bundle in stocks.

Terese and I saw the money, which until this time Frieda had kept a secret, as her ticket away from Gerry someday, so when she announced that Carline was going to continue skating and that *she*, not Gerry, would pay for it, my view of Frieda Gland's selflessness changed from scorn to admiration. It must be an amazing thing to reach a point in your life when you consider the possibility that your worth as an individual rests in shepherding a child toward a level of achievement higher than the one you dreamed of for yourself.

Bryan and I sat midway up the nearly empty rows of seats and watched one of the girls on the ice go through her program. The first thing that hit me was how skilled she was with her leaps and spins; she was so elegant in her satiny pink dress that it took all my powers of imagination to envision Carline matching her in any way. She'd chosen a medley of romantic classical music, ending with Debussy's *Afternoon of a Faun*.

Carline appeared at the door to the rink, where she slipped off her skate guards and glided over to one side. After a few minutes of stretching exercises, she skated in fast, powerful strokes around the rink. I leaned forward, surprised by the skill in her footwork and by the ease with which she executed her jumps. She was wearing a black leotard with a translucent red skirt attached. Her white skin accentuated her eyes, outlined in black eyeliner and mascara.

When it was Carline's turn to do her program, she took her place in the center of the rink. Her peroxide-streaked hair was thrown back, and one arm curled gracefully up. As the overture to Copland's *Billy the Kid* began, she snapped her head forward and sped across the ice. She was fast and strong, with a drama in her face and body that made the other girl's performance seem like lukewarm tea in comparison. Her jumps were athletic and bold without a single wobble. She was able to contort her body into odd positions, too, that matched the sweep and turn of the music and gave her routine a quirkiness and originality that I learned later was her trademark. Bryan kept up a running commentary as she skated: "that's a split-Lutz jump," "that's a double axel," "that's a camel-jump-camel-spin," "that's a double Salchow." By the last segment, the "Rumble" from *West Side Story*, I was completely mesmerized by her flashing, spinning body— the glint of silver blades, her long legs, the whir of red against black. What was most inspiring to me was the sheer power she radiated, the sense that she was unequivocally in control.

When she ended on her knees with her back arched and the top of her head touching the ice behind her, I could feel the lurch of my own heartbeat. Bryan was sitting forward, his hands gripped between his legs. On his face was a look that explained everything, a single, unabashed glow of belonging and desire. I bowed my head, chastened by how good she was.

The lights blinked back on and the Zamboni circled the ice.

"I had no idea she could skate like that," I said.

Bryan nodded and glanced toward the dressing-room doors near where Carline had exited.

"Do you think she was born knowing she could do that? I mean, I realize it takes a lot of practice, but she seems so *sure* when she's out there."

Bryan thought a minute before answering. "Carline has an inborn talent and drive that have gotten her where she is. To be a really good skater takes such determination and focus. She has to believe that she can do it, you know, that she's *special*."

I thought of Angie Fanelli, and the way she'd looked skiing off Jimmy Piper's boat, or sleeping on the blanket with her leg slung over Joe Malone. She'd thought she was special, too, but she was married to Wade Fowler now and living in a run-down bungalow on Tamarack Road. On Saturdays she worked in Sal and Joey's to give her mother a few hours off.

"You could learn something from her, Danny."

"What?"

"You always act as if everybody *else* is the gifted one— Mom or Dad, me, even Terese. Sometimes I look in your eyes and I see this whole living world there. I don't think you know how special that is."

I could tell by his face that he meant it, and I was touched. I was too young to understand the advantages of having a *whole living world* inside me, a world that would enable me someday to write about my family, to bring us all back for a short time the way we were in the beginning, to make sense out of what happened. In all my thirsty poring over books I hadn't yet made the connection that I had anything in common with their authors, who, in my view, were people born blessed, their talents unattainable for me.

"Sometimes it doesn't help to believe that about yourself,"

I said. "If you're not lucky or not good enough, or if things happen that get in the way, what happens to the dreams? You might be worse off in the end."

I was thinking of Charlie, and a sudden chill descended on me. But it was only the Zamboni that had chugged through the opening in the rink while pushing a pile of ice.

"Still," Bryan said, "think of all the others who *do* succeed. It doesn't just happen, you know, you have to carry it along. *You* have to believe in it."

I patted his arm to let him know I appreciated his words. Being eighteen and a National Merit scholar had exacerbated his predilection for giving priestly advice. Bryan was into prophecy and I'd had enough Kahlil Gibran to last me a lifetime. Besides, Carline had just emerged from the locker room, and those oversized black eyes were stampeding in our direction. I tried to summon the right compliment that wouldn't betray my previous ignorance of her talent. Of course, she knew, but she accepted my praise graciously; then she suggested that we head home for a midnight ride in the Chris-Craft.

It wasn't really midnight but the moon was three-quarters full, and I could tell as we tiptoed down the stairs past our house that the couples inside were riding high. My mother's loud laughter was conspicuously absent, as it had been at their bridge parties ever since the Kellys had stopped coming up. She and Nini phoned each other often, and May drove to Staten Island for lunch once every few months. But it wasn't the same. You couldn't help noticing in Terese how well things were going: Tim was still sober, Nini was taking adult education courses, and the two of them had just returned from their first trip to Ireland. Marriage counseling, Terese said, had taught them how to communicate. Sometimes when Terese and I talked at our kitchen table, my mother would turn in the doorway to the porch and watch us, her face wistful and young. I didn't want to peer in a window on that night and see the circles rimming both eyes and her fluttery hands

166

exchanging a full bowl of cheese doodles for a tray full of empty glasses.

The inboard motor purred as Bryan steered the boat away from the dock and under the bridge. He didn't flip on his light until we'd cruised past the clubhouse and were approaching the five-mile-per-hour buoy. I lay my head back against the seat and watched the winking lights in all the Chinese lanterns strung across lakeside patios. Carline had slided next to Bryan and was sitting on her curled-up legs with one arm looped around his neck.

Bryan pushed the engine full tilt and turned to the right, starting the wide circuit of Rainy's middle. As we passed Rock Island he changed course, steering into a smaller, tighter circle. I knelt up on my seat, trying to figure out what he was doing. Carline waved a bottle of Coca-Cola over her head and screamed "Oooo-o-o-o-o-o-o." My brother's skin was white against the darkness of Cranberry Island. Round and round and faster and faster we went. The interior of the sphere we were orbiting was choppy now with colliding waves that sped out from the boat's wake.

"What are you *doing*?" I called.

Bryan laughed and pointed with his left arm at the waves while his right hand held the wheel in position. The water around us resembled the ocean now, billows churning and crashing and spitting spray high into the air. As the boat continued to circle, the smoother path we were riding on the circumference of the fray grew rougher as the swells lapped toward the boat. Bryan's skin was glistening wet, and his white unbuttoned shirt flapped behind him. We were all bouncing now, jiggling up and down as if we were rolling down a boulder-strewn hill in a wagon gone out of control. When I bit my tongue for the second time, I pushed between Carline and Bryan and yelled into my brother's jouncing ear.

"STOP!"

He blinked once and then cut through the boat's angry wake and moved out into calm, open water. I was soaked through and cold and in no mood to heed Carline's disappointed "aw-w-w-w."

"Didn't you like it?" she asked.

"No!" I could taste the blood in my mouth. "What were you trying to do, swamp the boat?"

"It'd take more than a few waves to swamp *this* boat, right Carl?"

The excitement between them hummed. Maybe it's just me, I thought. The bubbling circle looked pretty tame now that the waves were receding. Yet I can still recall the passage of those waves through my body and the jiggling, fragile movement of my brother's chin, his lips parted with the thrill of it.

Bryan tied up to Carline's dock and walked her to the house, keeping me waiting a whole fifteen minutes while they said good-bye on the unlit porch. Crickets buzzed and the lake sucked the edge of the hull. I slapped my hand in the water, restless with jealousy, with the sticky night, with the knowledge that my father would be snoring fitfully in the army cot tucked into the far corner of the living room.

*

That was the second year the Casey girls had climbed in the five-girl pyramid, and while I grudgingly acknowledged their skill on skis, their proclivity to annoy me knew no limits. Each one had kicked me in the chin more times than I could count, and they left annoying scratches on my legs and shoulders from their long red toenails. Twice, Ellen Casey had knocked the ski bar out of my hand and into the path of Terese's right ski, sending the five of us toppling into the water. Yet on that first Wednesday in July it was Bud Doonan, and not the Casey girls, whose recklessness has become Rainy Lake history.

When I woke that Wednesday the sky was overcast, but by noon the clouds had broken and Terese was stretched out on our dock increasing the injury to her peeling shoulders and singing "Happy Together" in tune with the Turtles on my transistor radio. I was grateful for those lazy times together during the day. After she'd quit the swim team and was living at Carline's all the way over in Weaver House Cove, I didn't see her as much as I used to, and it was hard. Bryan was working at the boat works, and May wasn't due up until after supper, so we'd used the opportunity of an empty house to read aloud sections of *The Group* by Mary McCarthy and to touch up the peroxide streak Carline had put in Terese's hair. She was hoping the streak would be solid platinum by the time Jimmy arrived to pick us up for practice.

We heard the Casey girls arguing before the boat appeared under the bridge. Ellen and Suzie Casey had thirteen- and fourteen-year-old bodies and brains the size of Milk Duds. As I reached out to grab the rope Jimmy threw me, Suzie whacked Ellen on the side of the head, arousing a blood-curdling scream that echoed all along the face of French's Grove.

"What the hell's the matter with you?" I asked Suzie. My own hand was itching to connect with the pleased sneer on her face.

"She called me a name. I told her if she said that one more time, I'd let her have it."

Ellen's blue eyes were moving rapidly. "CRISCO!" she screamed.

Jimmy intercepted Suzie's fist as I glanced happily at her butt, not big enough to draw attention but definitely rounder than Ellen's.

"Bud's already at the public dock waiting for us. If you two don't quit it, I'm gonna scratch this act. You got it?" Jimmy said.

"You can't do that," Ellen said. "My father . . ."

Jimmy leaned over her menacingly. "I don't give a shit about your father. You cause any more trouble and you're O-U-T."

Terese rubbed his shoulder affectionately as we jumped into the boat.

"Billy there yet?" I asked.

"Yep," Jimmy said.

I could tell something was wrong when I saw the soundless clench in Billy's body as he sat in Ty's boat watching Bud zigzag along the shoreline. Bud must have said something, for the veins swelled in Billy's neck as he worked the muscles in his jaw.

"Hi," I said.

When he finally turned in my direction, his face softened and he nodded with that thin, lopsided grin. Jimmy threw him the ski ropes, and the two worked at untangling them. Mike Cooper climbed out of his boat, tied to the other side of the public dock, and helped them. Mike was a freshman at City College in New York and wore his muddy blonde hair in a ponytail tied back with a leather string. The fact that he held the league record for the two-hundred-yard individual medley cut down the cracks from the men about his haircut and the peace signs he'd painted on the side of the family's motorboat.

I waved to Ginny Conroy, paddling toward us in her canoe with the Hogan girls—Patti, Eileen, and Mary—who'd volunteered for spotting duty. By the time Bud had quit clowning around and joined us, we five were belted up and ready: Terese, Ginny, and I in Jimmy's boat, Suzie in Mike Cooper's boat, and Ellen in Ty Malone's, the one Billy was driving.

"So how long is Ty gonna be gone?" Bud asked.

Jimmy frowned. "All week. I told you that before."

"Maybe I better drive Ty's boat." He cocked his head toward Billy. "It's a pretty big engine. He's never handled one this big before."

Billy's eyes slid like silk up and down Bud's body. Bud faced him, the scorn thick as syrup in his expression.

"Shut up, Bud. Everybody ready?" Jimmy said.

When we nodded, he called over to Billy. "Stay even with us—Mike to my left, you to my right." He turned to the Hogan girls. "Keep your eyes on the skier in back of your boat. If anybody falls, tell the driver right away. Remember, nobody moves in until every skier is accounted for."

Bud was watching Ginny, who was making a big deal out

170

of rubbing suntan lotion over her shoulders and down her arms. She wasn't very pretty but she had a great body, and even though she wasn't conceited about it, I could see from her coy manner that she'd been waiting for Billy as eagerly as I'd been and wasn't above wiggling her chest at him. When Billy shot her that killer smile, Ginny's face bloomed. Bud sped off full speed, rocking Billy in his wake. I slumped down in the seat as Jimmy steered the boat toward the middle of the lake.

The sequence of events remains blurry to me now, but we must have proceeded as usual: the two boats were out to the side flanking us while Ginny, Terese, and I held onto the long ski bar, our ski tips pointed up and ready. Ellen bobbed in the water about fifteen yards to our right, and Suzie was to the left. All five of us stood up smoothly, and Ellen moved in first to climb between me and Terese. Usually she skied up slalom beside me, rode her ski over the tops of mine, threw her own rope away as she lifted one foot after the other out of her ski, and started climbing across me. But today she moved in too fast, and the tip of her ski rammed into mine. I don't know how she kept her balance but she did, whereas I tumbled head-first into the water.

The shock of hitting so fast comes back to me: the sting in my eyes when I entered the water, the silence and increased coolness as I dove. I can recall a wall of honeyed light above me and then suddenly, the boiling spoke of an engine, its propeller a pinwheel of bubbling white. My heart heaved and jerked, its rhythm so audible I looked dizzily around, expecting to see it floating inches in front of my face. I had this instant, suffocating sense of danger. I wanted to stay down there in the dark, but I couldn't. As I paddled up, I searched fearfully for an engine, quickening my pace as I neared the surface.

Maybe I heard it first, a roar through acres of cotton. I didn't actually see the engine, but I knew he was over me again, that black sharklike shadow, and I dove, whipping my left arm over my head. I felt something hit me sudden and

171

sharp, like I'd bumped my arm on something, and I flailed in a panic with my right hand, kicking wildly upward. As my head broke the surface, I gulped in long and shuddery and then spun around, looking for the retrieval boat.

The three bigger boats were off in the distance. When he saw me, Billy headed in my direction. That's when I noticed the water around me darkening like a puddle of oil. My left arm hung awkward and heavy and when I lifted it, a spasm of such live pain gripped me that I screamed. Under the water the skin of my arm gaped white through a cloud of beet red.

Billy cut the engine and coasted up next to me. By this time I was having a hard time holding my head up. Suddenly he was in the water, and it was he who raised my arm to the surface. I heard the sharp whistle of his breath and saw the two ends of splintered bone, the thick lips of skin and blood spurting onto the side of his face. I wasn't feeling anything, just a cold numbness, and I had the sensation of my own death fluttering beside me, a warm physical presence studded with light.

I don't remember much after that, only that numbness and Billy's olive-green eyes. Terese said when Billy hoisted me over the side of Jimmy's boat, she threw up at the sight of my arm. She'd never seen bone before, she explained, and the blood was shooting like a pump. Those are the words she used, "like a pump."

Mike Cooper raced to the beach to call an ambulance while Billy worked on me. For the longest time afterwards, Terese apologized for being so squeamish. She gave Billy a T-shirt to wrap around the wound but he did the rest, she said. Ellen screamed at him to put a tourniquet on it, since everybody could see the artery had been cut, but he ignored her. Later, the doctor said he'd done all the right things: keeping a steady pressure on the arm, elevating it against his knee, covering me with a blanket, and propping my legs up.

He and Terese rode with me in the ambulance and stayed until Bryan and then my parents arrived later that night. My mother said the nurses found Billy and Terese a couple of gowns to put on over their bathing suits, which were stiff with blood. I was in surgery first to reconnect the artery, and then they set the bone. I didn't even wake up until the next day. May was asleep in the chair beside me, and Charlie and Bryan were sitting side by side on a bench in front of the window. Carline had come and stayed awhile, before driving Billy and Terese home.

The only good feeling I had right away was that my family was all together; the three of them hurried over to the side of my bed. My father was ashen but sober, and he ran his fingers lightly across the side of my face the way he used to do when I was little. They kept talking about Billy—how calm he'd been, how he'd probably saved my arm, how they'd never be able to thank him enough.

It was Bud Doonan's fault, Terese had said. He went in for the ski without checking to see if anyone had fallen.

"I could kill him," Bryan said, "for being so stupid."

"He wasn't just being stupid," I said.

They looked at me surprised, knowing I couldn't have seen him.

"He was trying to show up Billy."

"Why would he do that?" my mother asked.

"Because Billy's half black, that's why."

My mother's mouth opened slightly and she tipped her head in sympathy. I could tell she didn't believe it but didn't want to upset me by saying so. Charlie and Bryan were clearly puzzled.

I sighed. "Bud thinks kids like Billy can't do certain things. He wanted to show him how fast he could pick up the ski. It doesn't make sense, it's just the way it is."

It would have been simpler to have believed it was mere testosterone, or that it was Bud's jealousy over Ginny that had made him approach me in so careless a fashion. Yet the images that chafed beneath the surface of my sleep—the honeyed light, the roar of the engine, the spectral hull—included as well the clear sight of Bud Doonan's face as he leaned forward in the boat, one hand on the throttle, his voice echoing through clotted water: *nigger, nigger.* I can see the back of his head and the radius of blood encircling my own. I can see the whole thing happening and it's not like a dream at all, but as if I'm looking through the lens of a movie camera.

Of course, I wasn't really there, not on the surface anyway, so perhaps I've done Bud Doonan a disservice, although I doubt it. Reflecting on Bud always leads me straight to Paddy, his father, who'd been sounding off in the Pink Elephant for weeks about the rioting in Newark and Cleveland. "Whaddaya expect," he'd said to Charlie, "with that nigger Stokes as mayor." Paddy's name floated through my sedated head that day, but I didn't speak it. In my heart I believed that Paddy was also responsible. He'd passed along his prejudices to his son, who might regret the damage done to me but most likely learned nothing about his own hatred and the danger it posed to himself and others.

As I looked at Charlie and May standing forlornly beside the hospital bed, a well of pain opened in my chest. Maybe it was the Percodan starting to wear off. At that moment my need for their protection seemed almost staggering, so I reached for their hands and refused to look at the dark bottom of the boat swimming inches over my head.

*

Billy visited the hospital the day after the accident. When I first saw him, I was locked in battle between a dizzy, drugged stupor and the screaming ache in my arm the instant the Percodan wore off. He left behind a small package and the lingering smell of lake water. Bryan unwrapped the package for me, gazing confusedly at the cover of Emily Brontë's *Wuthering Heights*.

"Why would he give you this?" he asked.

I turned the book over in my hands. "Because Charlotte Brontë wrote *Jane Eyre*."

"How would he know that?"

"Because I told him I liked *Jane Eyre*."

"No, how would he know about *this* one?"

I studied my brother's face. "How would anybody? Maybe a teacher told him or he went to the library. Maybe he's got the book at home like we do."

He laughed. "I doubt it."

My brother would have been shocked if I'd called him on the prejudice inherent in his assumptions. But there it was, transparent as the window glass overlooking downtown Sparta. Transparent *now*, at least. Then, I laughed nervously, unable to explain the sharper edge to the nausea that accompanied my shifting regimen of narcotics and pain. Bryan sat on the chair next to my bed and read the opening chapter. His steady voice buoyed me up until the nurse arrived with my afternoon shot.

I'd been home almost two weeks when Billy came the second time. I didn't look up from *Wuthering Heights* until he was halfway across the bridge, and then a tiny ice cube of shock tumbled through me. My mother had driven back to Westfield for the day to put in a few hours at the shop and Bryan had just left for work, so I was alone. When Billy's face appeared at the screen, I stood up, feeling the weight of the bandage against my abdomen. It seemed so unreal that he'd be standing there on our porch, and it took me a minute to be able to actually face him.

When I tried to thank him, he waved his hand at me, and a rosy flush fanned across his honey-colored cheeks. So I held up the book to show him how much I'd read.

"I was afraid maybe you'd read it before," he said.

"I have, but I've been meaning to read it again."

He tipped his head and studied me, wearing that lopsided half-smile. "Why would you read it twice?"

"Because there's so much you miss the first time around. Not in every book, only some. Plus you get to have all those feelings again."

"What feelings?"

"Well, in this book there are two characters, Heathcliff and Cathy, who love each other from the time they're children, only he's an orphan taken in by her family so he's never considered good enough for her. She marries someone else and dies very young. Heathcliff never has her. It's a *tragic* story."

"You think they would have been happier if they'd married each other?"

"Yes, I do."

"Maybe they wouldn't. Maybe the two of them weren't meant to be happy."

"I don't believe that."

He leaned forward from the folding chair where he was sitting. "I think it's possible to be in a situation where whichever thing you choose, you end up getting hurt."

"Guess you have to be brave then."

I felt the weight of his eyes. He pulled two flies out of his pocket.

"What are they for?" I asked.

"They're yours; nobody else I know fly-fishes in the channel."

"Want to see my collection?" I asked eagerly.

I must have genuinely amused him. As I look at it from here, I think it might have been the initial thing that attracted him to me. He told me later that I was the first girl who really made him laugh, but I took offense, wanting to be the first girl who did other things for him. I'd seen the way my father and Tim laughed at May and Nini sometimes, and it wasn't flattering. I soon realized that Billy's amusement was different. It wasn't about him being smarter or older or male. Instead, it seemed to relieve him and to open up a bridge between us. Besides, each time he smiled I felt the way I did when they shot me full of Percodan: weightless and free from pain.

With my good arm I handed him the shoe box full of handmade flies. There were smaller boxes inside, each one labelled in black ink. Billy picked up a Royal Wulff and turned it over in his fingers.

"It's amazing. No one would ever know you made this."

"That's nothing. Take a look at these."

I picked up another box containing my glitziest flies. Most of them were bass flies, since bass generally preferred more color and pizazz in the water. He whistled as he examined the array of furred, feathered, and deer-haired flies.

"What'd you make this out of?" He held up a hair bug.

"A little sponge and some antelope hair," I said.

"Who taught you how to do this?"

I handed him my dragonfly, one of my personal favorites. "My father and brother have been tying flies for years; they mostly do bass flies, though. Books'll tell you anything you need to know. For instance, bass flies need a lot of action. That's why I use these rubber legs, plus I'm pretty careful with my hackle. The fish'll spit them out if they're too hard, so you should use soft rubbers and plastics, not metal or wood. And they're very sensitive to color and sound. Stick to natural food colors and add these little metal spinners and rattly things. Bass will hear it, especially in dark or muddy water."

"I'll strike a bargain with you," he said. "You teach me how to tie flies like this, and I'll take you trout fishing. We'll start with the stream and then go over to the Virgin. Bass are nothing compared with hooking a trout."

I shifted in my seat. "But, Billy, with my arm like this I don't think I can fish."

"You're right-handed, aren't you?"

I nodded.

"You should be able to cast all right. Can you use your fingers?"

"If I don't move my arm too much."

"I'll help you. As long as the other arm doesn't get wet, you should be all right. What'd the doctor say?"

"Just to take it easy is all. I'm off my pain medication, but I'm taking codeine with aspirin. It still hurts."

He stood up. "Let's give it another week, then. I work from

6 A.M. to 2 P.M., so I'm free in the afternoons. I'll come get you next Monday around three. That OK with you?"

The question *Why are you doing this?* floated by, but I let it pass without a sound. I climbed the stairs to the living room and wandered through the rooms. My arm itched beneath the cast, which I rubbed absent-mindedly on the back of the rocking chair. I was standing in my mother's bedroom when I heard the noise. May said it was Charlie's snoring that had made them decide to create a makeshift room for him in the little alcove behind the wood-burning stove. His snoring had nothing to do with it.

I couldn't help but smile as I looked around. Before, when my father had reigned over decorating decisions, the room had been tasteful and plain: white blinds and bedspreads, the creamy yellow walls bare except for a few abstract paintings. Since Charlie had stopped sleeping there, May had bought lilac-flowered matching curtains, bedskirts, bedspreads, and an army of small pink and lilac pillows trimmed with eyelet. On the walls she'd hung old photographs of me and Bryan when we were babies, grainy pictures of my grandparents on Jones Beach in the thirties, one wedding shot of her and Charlie, and her favorite picture of her and Nini standing on the dock wearing their green-fringed bathing caps. There were other things as well: a color picture of Jack Kennedy with excerpts from his inaugural address, a black-framed photograph of Robert Kennedy, Irish poems, a postcard picture of a woman upside down kissing the Blarney Stone, and two of the mushy anniversary cards my father used to send her.

At first, the noise was just a faint scratching over my head. Then I heard one high-pitched squeak. Sweat dribbled from my armpits as the room erupted with sudden, dark-winged life. *They're back!* The knowledge brought apprehension as well as an immediate, startled pleasure. I knew that once my parents heard them, Charlie would haul out the ladder and chemicals. Still, there was something hopeful about the bats' return, which corroborated the fact that their natures were stronger than circumstances.

*

I told Bryan matter-of-factly that Billy was taking me trout fishing. He was still feeling beholden to Billy and thought it was nice of him to spend time with me. It relieved him, too, since May had resumed work at the shop and he'd been hovering over me, playing endless games of chess while he listened to Bob Dylan on the radio and read aloud from the newspaper the latest troop movements and election polls. He hadn't a clue as to my feelings for Billy and assumed it was only a brotherly interest. How could it be otherwise? A boy like Billy could go down the tracks with any girl he wanted.

When Billy arrived at the dock in his old wooden boat, I tried not to look like I'd been ready for seven days. He loaded my fly-tying gear and tackle equipment next to his and smiled when I handed him a six-pack of root beer and the Entenmann's coffee cake I'd bought that morning at Sal and Joey's.

"You going to *eat* all this?" he asked.

"I thought we'd share it."

"Good thing you're skinny. I don't eat this stuff."

"Suit yourself."

I slid the box under my fishing vest so the icing wouldn't melt and took the only other seat in the front of the boat.

"What happened to the middle seat?" I asked.

"I took it out."

"Why'd you do that?"

"So I could lie down in it better. Sometimes I sleep in the boat."

"Don't the bugs get you?"

"Insects don't bother me—my skin's too dark."

I smiled tentatively at him and faced forward. It was hot without being humid, and the sun turned the surface of the water a shimmering aquamarine. I heard the familiar babble of laughter and shouts from the beach, glimpsed sand and fence and green dock, saw the bobbing five-mile-per-hour buoy, and then Billy opened throttle and we entered the big blue heart of Rainy Lake. At night, just when my eyes closed, I could feel the cool, carnelian dark, the engine splicing the amber surface, the bump as if I'd knocked my arm on the headboard of the bed. Yet I felt no fear as the wet spray misted my blouse, only relief that it was cooling the hot point in the center of my back where Billy's eyes must have landed.

When we neared the channel, he cut the engine and coasted through, pulling up at the same spot where he'd stopped the first time he'd showed me the stream. Smoothly he gathered up our gear and walked off into the trees. I carried my rod and vest and the melting coffee cake and hurried to keep up. By this time my arm was no longer the volcano of pain it had been after I'd been taken off narcotics and left to fend for myself on aspirin. There were periods of the day when the pain flared again, but for the most part it was bearable. The experience of physical suffering had given me a new and sometimes overpowering connection to my own body. At times, my whole life was reduced to the acute throbbing by which I gauged the passing of time.

Following Billy along the banks of the stream, I took care not to slip or bump my arm. He talked as we proceeded, instructing me on how to read the current, how to identify riffles and pools, and how to find the different lies where the fish hid and fed. I knew a fair amount about flies but couldn't match Billy for eloquence in explaining the life cycle of aquatic insects. The deluge of words made me dizzy: nymphs, duns, spinners, eggs, larva, pupa, gill filaments, antennae, thorax, midges, crustaceans, and invertebrates.

"Where'd you *learn* all this?" I asked him.

"My grandfather used to take me fly-fishing, more times even than my father, although he's the one who taught me about insects. They used to argue about it, because my father thought you should know the facts, and my grandfather said it didn't matter as long as you had good instincts about what the fish were biting."

"How'd your father learn?"

Billy shrugged. "My uncles knew things, and he read about it—you know, like you and your flies."

He said the fish were eating off the bottom, so he tied a nymph onto my leader. I could work the line loosely with the fingers of my left hand, but any nimble maneuvering was impossible. It didn't take me long to lose patience, as my line caught constantly and the clumsy movement of my fingers soon announced to every trout in the area that it was a fake fly and not a real one jerking across the surface of the stream. Billy intervened frequently, showing me how to retrieve the line more smoothly and helping me recover the flies that snagged. When we realized I was about done in, he fished by himself for a while. I leaned against a birch and licked the sweet icing off a hunk of coffee cake.

Billy stood in the middle of the stream. Water darkened his blue cutoffs, and his bare chest rose and fell in rhythm with the whistling loops over his head. There was something beautiful and yet contradictory in the picture he made. He more closely resembled a dark-skinned Huckleberry Finn than any of the richly outfitted men in the catalogues. Tennis shoes took the place of boots, and he had no use for waders, fancy caps, or the myriad instruments that dangled from other men's vests. A tiny pair of scissors, a thermometer for reading water temperature, extra leader line, and a few boxes of flies were all he carried.

It's easy now to identify the qualities in Billy that drew me. Besides the way he looked, with a smile that was pure magic, he had this stillness about him that was as deep and mysterious as the cool pockets near the bottom of the lake. Some boys are all up there on the surface, everything laid out neatly for you to examine. With Billy much of it was underground. Of course, some of what he held in was a confused and angry tangle that made him mistrustful and added an edge to his reserve. But the rest made me feel the way I did swimming laps at the end of the day: the beach empty, the water deep and dark, my mind cleansed so that each stimulus was as fine and sharp as a grain of sand.

After he'd finished and joined me on the bank, I displayed my fly-tying equipment and guided him through the construction of a stone fly. I couldn't use all my fingers the way I wanted, but it didn't matter, for he was able to translate my directions immediately. Billy had that same spatial and mechanical aptitude I'd grown accustomed to in the rest of my family, and I was grateful for it.

The silence ebbed and flowed without any pressure to make small talk or to fill in the gaps between sentences. Several times I caught him studying me, and it made me happy as well as nervous. I couldn't help wondering what he was looking for, whether he was drawing conclusions that would place me in the same ballpark as Marilyn Gland, or whether I'd be stuck on that unappetizing pedestal of being the girl too young, too nice, too skinny to screw around with.

*

I told Terese what I'd told Bryan, that Billy was teaching me how to fish for trout. People saw him pick me up and bring me home every day, and even Carline was quiet about it. My injury had given me a privileged status, and everyone must have thought that since Billy had practically saved my arm it was natural for us to become friends. I'm surprised I wasn't more hurt that nobody suspected that we might actually desire each other, that I was biding my time until Billy put his hands on me. Terese was the only one who knew how I felt.

Although he hated the little Spam sandwiches I made, Billy became a grudging convert to macaroni salad.

"If you throw some fresh tomatoes and green peppers into that macaroni salad, it'd be even better," he said.

I didn't consider suggesting it to May, who would not have taken lightly any criticism of her salad.

"Does your whole family eat like this?" he asked one day. We were spread out on a rock not far from where the currents of the stream and Virgin River joined, at a spot we'd fished with great success. I was eating my double-decker favorite: half peanut butter and jelly, half bologna. I held both halves together and ate them simultaneously so the flavors mingled.

"My mother doesn't really like to cook. I don't mind, but it bothers my father, although these days I wouldn't vouch for his taste buds."

"Why not?"

I bit my lip, unaccustomed to making confessions about my family.

"Is he sick?" he asked. He'd stopped eating his tomato and had fixed his olive-brown eyes on me.

I shrugged. "My dad drinks too much."

"How much?"

"It started out as too much at a party now and then and kind of grew from there. Now you can't even talk to him after eight o'clock at night."

"He drinks every day?"

I nodded. "I think it was the disappointment over his business. He went bankrupt and believes in his heart that he's a failure. My brother Bryan believes it, too, try as I do to make him understand we can't all be so perfect. Bryan used to really respect my father; that's why it's so hard for him now. You'd never have guessed it if you knew us before."

I was not about to cry in front of him, but talking about it was like opening a secret room where all your disappointments were stored, so I picked up my rod and walked along the bank of the river. It was wider than the stream and tumbled through woods and little clearings thick with wild columbine. The water was absolutely clear, revealing the spotted backs of trout feeding near the nut-brown bottom. Billy didn't follow me. He knew enough about family trouble to leave me alone.

Later, as we hiked back toward Disappointment, he inclined his head and asked casually, "You busy tonight?"

He was walking a few paces ahead of me, and if I had reached out my hand I could have touched the moist film coating the small of his back.

"No, why?"

"I thought maybe you'd like to ride into Sparta with me."

I knew he hung out with a whole pack of kids, some of them from Rainy, some from Disappointment; they were mostly kids he went to school with in Sparta. A lot of the boys had cars and drove the miles of meandering back roads between the lakes, either racing each other or necking with girls in secluded hideaways. Terese had said she'd met Billy and his friends several times at O.J.'s, a store in Sparta similar to Sal and Joey's.

"How come?" It was a dumb question but I had to ask it. If he was going to ask me to go with him at night, I wanted to know if it was a real date or not.

He turned around so suddenly I almost plowed into him. Not once in all the afternoons we'd spent together had he looked at me the way I wanted him to, not curious or friendly but heavy with desire. But there it was, a quickening that flushed across his cheeks. I felt it travel clear down to the soles of my feet. We stood there a long minute, our eyes wide open and not a sound anywhere.

"I like being with you, that's all."

I nodded.

The lake sped by in a blur—houses, trees, clubhouse, bridge. I heard the creak and boom of the diving board, splashing water, laughter. When we docked, my mother smiled and waved at us from a chaise lounge on the patio where she'd been reading.

"What time?" I asked him as he lay my gear on the dock.

"Eight. Pick you up at the circle."

After taking a folding chair off the deck, I settled myself beside her.

"You going out?" she asked.

"I just got home."

"I mean later." Her friendly face made me nervous.

"Billy asked me to drive into Sparta. The kids go to this place called O.J.'s. Bryan's been there."

"Mmm. You're spending an awful lot of time with him, aren't you?"

"Not especially."

"I don't see you with anyone else these days."

"That's 'cause Terese is doing ski club stuff every afternoon, and Carline is either skating or trying on a new hair color."

"Do you like him?"

" 'Course I like him. He saved my arm, didn't he?"

"That's not what I meant."

I wondered if somebody had said something to her. What would they say? Nothing had happened, nothing visible to anyone but Billy and me. If he'd been one of the summer boys, a Piper or Malone or Dolan, it would have been easy to tell her. But Billy Dove? Some knowledge deeper than marrow told me I couldn't trust my parents', or even Bryan's, liberalism on this one.

"You mean like a boyfriend? Are you kidding? I'm not his type, Mom. If I were prettier or built like Marilyn, that'd be a different story." I sighed.

"What do you mean if you were prettier? You don't think you're pretty?"

"Well, not in the classic sense, not the way you are."

She smiled and plucked from my mouth the ends of hair I was nibbling. "You're a beautiful girl, Danny, and you don't even know it."

I shrugged. "When's Dad coming up?"

Her face dropped and I wished I hadn't asked. "Friday, same as always. Have you heard anything upstairs?"

My face skidded into neutral. "Like what?"

"A scratching noise . . . I think it's bats."

"Look, Mom, I'm here every single afternoon and I haven't heard a thing. They couldn't get in anyway."

"When you go upstairs, listen. I'm sure I heard it when I came in earlier." She leaned down and picked up the newspaper under her chair. "Did you read the news?"

"What news?"

Seeing the serious look on her face I thought for a moment that someone else had been assassinated.

"Dr. Spock was sentenced today for two years. It says here, 'for conspiring to aid, abet and counsel men to avoid the draft.' Isn't that ridiculous, putting a man like that in prison? I still have his book at home; I potty-trained each one of you just the way he said."

I was starting up the steps when she said, "It's OK to be grateful to Billy, but don't let it go anywhere. He's not the right kind of boy for you."

My hand closed on the railing. "How do you know?"

"He's a Negro, Danny. And this thing with his father . . . "

"His father's white, Mom."

"That won't matter in the long run. Love is hard enough to sustain even in the strongest relationships. There are too many differences between you."

"All we're doing is driving into Sparta. You want something to worry about, why not Bryan and Carline? Now there's a pair ordained in heaven."

She smiled. "I like Carline, she has style and spunk. You ought to give her a break."

"Why not give me a break?"

"I meant what I said, Danny."

It shouldn't have surprised me. What did it matter, anyway? Better for them to think it was all gratitude, an innocent friendship brought about by circumstance and Billy's good will. My mother would have self-destructed if she'd smelled the true odor of my intentions. The irreconcilable nature of my image and Billy's provided us a certain safety, and I wasn't stupid enough to toss it away by telling the truth.

At dinner Bryan didn't ask what my plans were, and May was preoccupied with prying the meat loaf out of the roasting pan and serving up a bowl of baked potatoes. You're supposed to be able to eat the skins, Bryan told her as we gazed glumly at the blackened shells. I've often wondered if you inherit a taste for burned food or simply develop a tolerance for it. Some days I push the toaster knob all the way to DARK so the bread pops up crisp and charred; the taste brings tears to my eyes faster than an old photograph.

I'd showered and changed my clothes, but otherwise I left my face and erupting hair alone. It wouldn't be smart to draw attention to myself. I felt a little sorry leaving my mother, for most nights since I'd been hurt we played cards at the kitchen table or read by the yellow bug lights on the screened porch. It relieved me when she said *The Razor's Edge* was on TV with Tyrone Power and Gene Tierney. Other than the Kennedys, the only other famous person she'd wept over was Tyrone Power when he died of a heart attack during a fencing scene with George Sanders. He was older and not as handsome then, but she was devastated nonetheless.

It had been three weeks since I'd walked over the bridge at night, so the teenagers milling along the railings treated me like a celebrity. The word had gone out about the exposed bone and severed artery, and my arm had become one of the top ten hits of the summer. Jimmy said kids were still coming to his boat expecting to find blood on the bottom. They were disappointed I didn't have a cast they could sign, so they offered me cigarettes and sips of Coca-Cola instead.

Billy was sitting on the stone wall in the parking lot, in the same spot where he'd been the night of the King and Queen Dance last summer. He was wearing black jeans and a white T-shirt with the sleeves rolled up tight on his biceps; his feet were propped on the open window of the royal blue T-bird he'd inherited from his brother Douglass. Ginny Conroy had her elbows on the wall, talking to him. Without Bud shadowing her (he hadn't shown his face on the beach since my accident happened), she was doing a first-class job flirting with Billy. In that one second when he smiled down at her, cleavage flying right out of her halter top, I stalled on the tracks like a spooked deer.

If Billy hadn't raised his head just then, I don't know what I would have done. The look on his face gave me what I wanted, so I continued walking, heading for his unoccupied side. Ginny leaped up, her expression surprised but genuinely pleased to see me. You couldn't stay angry with Ginny for long, even for having a body like that. She was kind and generous, and it if weren't for my own stubborn passion, I would have steered her toward Billy.

"How's the five-girl coming?" I asked, knowing Fern Daniels had agreed to take my place.

She made a face. "Fern makes a big deal out of her wrist still being sprained, but after what happened to you we don't pay any attention to her."

"We'll see you later, Ginny." When Billy put his hand on my shoulder to steer me toward the car, Ginny's face folded with disappointment.

"She likes you," I said, considering how far I should slide over on the seat.

"She'd be a lot of fun, *if* I were interested. You can move over closer if you want."

I inched over, keeping my eyes on the road. Billy leaned down under the seat and pulled out a bottle of Ripple. "Want one?"

The thick-leafed trees closed overhead as we passed the Tamarack Bar and left the noise of the highway behind. Driving down Tamarack Road was like entering the Hansel and Gretel forest: sudden twilight and silence. The road was a blue-black ribbon unravelling through miles of woods. After I'd finished one bottle, Billy handed me another. I could understand what the liquor did for my father: that fluid bubble floating between your eyes, your limbs softening and growing lighter, any nervousness or sorrow evaporating as fast as the road behind you.

By the time we reached Sparta it was almost dark. Billy parked next to the boardwalk. There were lots of people walking around, sitting by the lake, or licking ice cream cones while they perched on the backs of benches set along the boardwalk. Guys called out to Billy and gave me the once-over.

In O.J.'s Billy played a game of pool with a boy named Skipper while I watched, holding a warm bag of french fries on my lap. When "Mrs. Robinson" by Simon and Garfunkle came on the jukebox, I moved my lips with the words. The teenagers here, like Billy, resided in the area all year long and went to school in Sparta. He had more in common with them, I supposed, than he did with the Rainy Lake kids. From what I observed they didn't treat him any differently for being mixed, although later he told me otherwise. He introduced a few boys by saying they ran track or pole-vaulted with him. One boy worked in the tool and dye shop; the lines on his fingertips were etched as black as Billy's.

When he started showing off for me with the cue stick, I realized he might be nervous, too. I was glad when he took his last shot and sauntered over to my chair.

"Salt," he said, running his finger across my lips. "Are you *always* hungry?"

"I must have a tapeworm," I said seriously. "I've thought so for years but nobody believes me."

He laughed, swung his arm around my good shoulder, and guided me toward the door.

"Let's drive," he said.

His face wasn't transformed by the speed the way my brother's was, but it excited him. The car hugged the turns and had no trouble exceeding seventy miles an hour. After downing another bottle of Ripple, we tossed the empties over our shoulder to the back seat, where they clinked and jingled on the floor. The trees rushed by in a tunnel of inky green. The shapes were no longer distinguishable but the smells were separate and strong: earth, bark, asphalt, and lake water.

Ten minutes later we turned onto one of the many side roads that intersected Tamarack. The car moved more slowly now, and the trees returned to focus with dust-colored branches and leaves trolling like a mossy sea. Suddenly, Billy swerved onto a dirt road so camouflaged by shrubbery I thought we'd simply driven into the woods.

The chirp of crickets right after Billy turned off the engine startled me, a whole army of living sound at a place where you thought you were totally alone. Billy had leaned against his window and faced me, his face wide-open and soft. I wasn't used to a boy's eyes on me like that—dark and unblinking, full of an almost palpable demand. With one hand he cupped the back of my head and pulled me toward him. My bandaged arm set me off balance so he moved forward, closing the distance between us.

Decorum has never been my strong suit and before I knew it, my lips were passing over his face, landing in all the caves and crevices I'd daydreamed about. I felt the tawny weight of his eyes as he sat there, quiet and waiting. Some boys can't enjoy it without being busy themselves, but Billy was patient, giving me freedom to explore.

We were there a long time. His hands covered every inch of skin between my neck and underpants, where, to my disappointment, he stopped. My bandaged arm didn't impede us; he was always aware of it, never pressing too hard against me, supporting my back with his hand as we twisted and rolled across the seat. By the time Billy's fingers reached the waistband of my shorts, I was conscious of each wave coursing through my body, the pleasure as pitched and sharp as the hills of pain right after my surgery. If I could have willed it, we'd have been naked, sealed to the ocean-blue seat of the T-bird for as long as it took.

Billy sat up first, then helped me up and started rebuttoning my blouse.

"Why'd you stop?" I asked, my breath quavery and loud.

"Because a few minutes more and I might not have. Don't you have any modesty at all?"

"What for?"

He laughed. "You're only sixteen for one thing. Your father'd probably have me arrested."

"That's ridiculous. How's he gonna know?"

He tucked in his shirt. When he looked at me again, his face was serious. "I don't want to ruin things."

"How could you do that?"

"By fucking you, that's how, before you're ready."

"Shouldn't I be the one to know that?"

He sighed. "It changes things—it's never the same afterwards . . . "

"Isn't it better?"

"Sometimes it is, sometimes it isn't."

"That doesn't make sense."

"I don't want you to get hurt."

"I won't. I just want it to be you, that's all."

When he ran his finger along my cheek, another stab launched through me. "Let's keep this simple, OK?"

I didn't want it simple. Nothing in my life was simple anymore, so why should this be? And why, when he'd gone down the tracks with at least a dozen girls, did he turn into a gentleman when it came my turn? All those things I was supposed to think about—that I'd be losing my virginity, that boys wouldn't respect me afterwards, that it might even be *wrong* —none of it meant a nickel. I'm not sure why, since I'd certainly been brought up right and had the nuns to thank for my first lessons on human reproduction. I'm grateful now for the respect Billy showed. But that night it meant only one thing, just as it did the night of the King and Queen Dance: he didn't want me. Not the way I wanted him, the way Bryan wanted Carline, the way my father used to desire my mother when they sat at the summer table drinking Pink Ladies. As we drove home I sank into the seat, marking the slow descent of my soaring dreams.

*

When Billy showed up at our dock at three o'clock the next afternoon, I wasn't expecting him. I was so intent on my observation of the soffits on the south side of the house that I didn't see him until he was standing right over me, blocking the sun with his bare chest.

"What are you doing?" he asked.

I stumbled to my feet, wondering if he smelled like lake water to other girls.

"Seeing where the hole is."

He peered up at the pitched corner of the roof. "What hole?"

"Where the bats are coming in and out. There used to be a nest but my father got rid of it. Now they're coming in again. I told my mother not to worry 'cause of the Sheetrock, but just the thought of them in there is driving her nuts. She's going to have them exterminated again if I don't do something."

"What can you do?" I never failed to amuse him, no matter how serious the situation seemed to me.

"I can plug it up, that's what, after they fly out."

"I'll do it now if you want. Where's the ladder?"

"You can't do it now. First, I'm not sure where the hole is, and second, they'll die in there. It's a maternity colony; the book says they have their babies at the end of the summer so if I wait too long only the mothers will have flown out. They don't come out till nighttime."

"You've got a book on bats, too?"

I glared at him. "What are you doing here?"

"I came to pick you up, same as always."

"I thought you wanted to keep things simple."

"What's more simple than fishing? You want to go or not?"

"I suppose. Nothing's happening *here*, that's for sure."

He knew better than to laugh and followed me down to the

192

dock, where he gathered my tackle from under the lower deck. "You need something to eat?" he asked.

"No!"

The ride cooled me down some, and the long walk along the stream to the Virgin River restored the happiness I felt whenever I was knee-deep in water limpid as that and bright as a new dime. Letting Billy hike out of sight, I found a spot I liked and stayed there. Usually he stayed nearby so he could help me untangle my line or retrieve the fish I caught. That time he didn't look back; his accurate reading of my mood was an uncanny gift he had.

Fly-fishing and sex were the closest I came to God that summer. I could make a chorus of perfect loops then, landing the line right where I aimed. My choice of fly and surface movement were so convincing that I got a hit within ten minutes. Tiring the fish wasn't too hard, as long as I didn't trip on any rocks, but unhooking him was a problem with only one arm and no Billy to help me. Upon studying the shoreline, I chose a gentle slope and worked the fish toward the shoals. When he finally surfaced, listing on his side, I relaxed my line and knelt down, searching for the hook.

It was lodged deep in the throat. Even with two hands I'd probably have caused too much bleeding and would have had to kill him. The best thing to do, Billy had told me, was to cut the leader at the hook eye and let him go. If the fish were lucky, the hook would dissolve and the wound would heal by itself. There's always that moment just after you've landed a smart and elusive fish, his eyes alien and glassy, his gills fluttering tiny forbearing sighs, when you feel the ironic power of your own inconsequential life. Much as I loved to catch them, I was inevitably humbled by their intelligence and beauty. With my good hand I snipped the leader, turned the fish around, and nudged it toward deeper water. Undulating sluggishly, he hesitated momentarily before darting off.

I sat down on the bank and dropped my head onto my right knee. I did not cry easily, and when I did it was usually inexplicable, a release of long-sequestered sadness. When I'd woken that morning my mother was downstairs in the kitchen talking to my brother. Charlie must have lost a client, and Larry, one of the partners in the firm, had phoned her to discuss Charlie's drinking. Everybody knew he had a problem, he said, but until recently Charlie had confined the drinking to home. Now you could smell it on his breath after lunch. And his behavior was becoming erratic. Days of relative calm were followed by days when he displayed a belligerent attitude in the office, when he pushed his own ideas at meetings as if no one else had anything worthwhile to say. Afterwards he'd be completely uncommunicative, depressed even. "It's not like Charlie," Larry said. "He's always been so easy to work with."

What could she do? my mother asked Bryan. He saw what happened every time she tried to talk to Charlie. In Charlie's eyes she'd let him down. It went back to the Hawkman house; if she had it to do over again, she'd support his desire to take the man to court.

Leave him, my brother said coldly. Leave him and maybe he'll stop.

I can't, she said. What if it made no difference? What would happen to him?

The timbre of my mother's voice had pushed me deeper into the void where I'd been swimming ever since I'd left Billy at the circle the night before. I'd taken all my fears about my family, all the trauma of the accident, and hidden them behind this big anticipation about Billy and me. I was crying hard when I felt Billy's arm around me. He ran his fingers through my hair, snagging on the tangles.

"What's the matter?" he asked.

I shook my head. "I can't explain it."

He looked off through the trees, and I felt grateful again for the way in which he understood my despair without needing an explanation.

"Can I do anything?"

"It's too late."

Working his fingers free, he traced a path to my ear. "How so?"

"Why don't you go find one of your other girls? What are you spending your time with me for?"

"I told you, I like being with you."

"Well, I want something you're not about to give." I twisted my head away from his hand.

"What are you in such a hurry for?"

"Weren't *you* in a hurry when you wanted it?"

He smiled. "I guess, but you're so young."

"How old were you?"

"Fifteen . . . . OK, so it's not fair. I don't make the rules. Every girl from Rainy I've gone out with has had a father ready to kick my ass. Yours isn't going to be any different, sure as hell not if he's drinking."

"So what if I didn't have a father, would you want me then?"

"Every summer girl has a father. The whole goddamn Community Club's a father. Why do you think I don't want you?"

I wiped my face on my bandaged arm. "You wouldn't have sex with me."

"Jesus, Danny, you *do* have rocks in your head. It was only the first time we've gone out. I've told you several times how much I like you."

"I didn't ask if you liked me. I said *want,* as in you want it so bad you can't hold back."

"You read too many books."

"This has nothing to do with books."

"If it makes you feel better, I *do* want you. I'd like to fuck you right here, now."

As I glimpsed the pink tip of his tongue through his parted lips, a cinder of happiness flared in my chest. "What's stopping you?"

"Don't have a rubber for one. Two . . . you think it's all going to be so perfect. Nobody'll find out, or if they do, they won't mind, we'll go on fishing every day. I'm telling you, Danny, life isn't that smooth."

"You are such a worrywart. You think the sky's going to fall on you and nobody else. Think about what'll happen to *me* if we don't sleep together. That's what I worry about."

Despite his amusement, he was curious. "What?"

I knelt up on my knees and faced him. "I'll graduate from high school a virgin; there isn't a single boy in my whole school I'd even consider. Then I'll go off to college where I'll meet a slew of Milquetoast boys without any magic or backbone whatsover. None of the other girls will be virgins. I'll be the only one, not because I believe in it, but because the only boy worth having wouldn't have sex with me. Pretty soon it will be a stigma, you know, and even though there's nobody I really want, I'll have to do it just to hold my head up. So I'll look around for a candidate. He'll be some pre-med student chopping cheese in a food co-op. When he invites me to come back to his room with him, I won't hesitate. By this time I'll be totally repressed and dying to get it over with, not caring about love at all. We'll make out for a while and then he'll take his pants off. I'll see that his penis is the size of a city block, no way's it going to fit in. It'll hurt so much I'll count the minutes until it's over. Then I'll walk home alone to my dorm. I'll be so disgusted I won't want to have sex again ever. Not for years anyway and then, if I'm lucky, I'll find someone I *really* want, someone who won't mind how old or inexperienced I am or whether I have a father. Or, I'll simply shrivel up like a prune, dreaming about love without ever getting any."

"Did you think that up just now, or have you been planning it a while?" he asked.

"Just now."

"What's a food co-op?"

"All the neighborhoods around colleges have them. You become a member and work several hours a week, and then you get a discount on the food you buy."

"Penis as big as a city block, huh? How do you know mine isn't that big?"

"If it is, it's the best-kept secret on the lake."

He laughed. "Listen, Saturday night's another BYOL Dance—are your parents going?"

"I suppose so."

"Good. I'll pick you up at your dock at eight o'clock."

"What for?"

"You'll see. Trust me."

*

My mother nagged Charlie right up until they left for the dance to do something about the bats. I wasn't worried. The last thing Charlie wanted was to flush out another nest, and I knew he couldn't hear them. How was he going to hear them now, when five years ago, stone sober, he hadn't? It made me happy to hear their voices rising and falling in the bedroom. He was humoring her by climbing up on a chair to listen with his ear pressed against the Sheetrock, and she was nervously pacing, her hands fluttering like twin birds. I knew it was one of my father's better days and that it wouldn't last, but the drama had restored their old equilibrium. He was in charge again: "Don't worry, May. It's all in your imagination. I know all about these things." She actually believed him as she gazed up at the few strands of blonde hair that had fallen onto his forehead.

When they left through the living-room door, he held her left elbow cupped in his right hand. I hoped the band would play "Begin the Beguine" early on so they could dance while my father was still graceful on his feet. Ever since we'd bought our house at Rainy Lake, all the women had commented on Charlie's agile dancing. "He makes me look good," May used to say. "Before I met Charlie I had two left feet."

I was hanging over the edge of the dock running figure eights with my finger in the rainbow-colored gasoline when Terese sat down beside me.

197

"You going to the party?"

The party was on Cranberry Island after dark. Somebody had even bought a keg. Bryan had been invited to Carline's for dinner, a treat he rarely passed up, especially when Gerry wasn't there. Frieda was an exceptional cook; she prepared meals with spices Bryan and I had never even tasted, like tarragon, rosemary, cumin, marjoram, and coriander. After dinner he and Carline were planning on joining the party, the biggest of the summer so far.

"I don't know. Billy's picking me up," I said.

Her look was wary. She must have suspected something. I'd been so evasive about my afternoons with Billy, and I guessed that it was easier for her not to know. She wouldn't approve, and then we'd have to argue over it. Still, I wanted to tell her. It was no secret that she and Jimmy had been having sex in the front seat of his car, and she might have offered some advice.

My silence came from fear and not shame. Some girls more rebellious than I would have flaunted it to show up their parents or other kids. Some might have waved the relationship like a flag to let people know just what they thought of the club's prejudice toward the Doves. I wasn't an activist like my brother or a rebel like Carline. The truth is I still don't like conflict and try to avoid it whenever I can—a cowardly trait, I suppose.

All I knew was that once people found out, I'd have to stop seeing him, and being with Billy was the one thing that mattered. Sooner or later my heart was going to get broken, probably when he left for boot camp, and I wasn't about to hurry the process along.

Watching Terese saunter across the bridge, I had an empty feeling. We both knew I was holding back, although I could swear part of her was grateful. You could smell the marijuana in the air, a bold move on the part of the teenagers sitting on the end of the bridge, since the beach was full of parents heading for the dance. The kids must have thought that with all the gin and whisky floating by, the adults weren't likely to make a fuss over a few puffs of marijuana.

"Jesus," Billy said when he docked alongside me, "you smell that reefer?"

I nodded.

"You ever smoke?" he asked.

"Couple of times with Terese and Jimmy. How about you?"

"Nah. Give me a beer anytime. Kids at school who smoke are potheads. They're so full of peace and love and reefer, they can't even spell their own names right. What's that look for?"

"Everybody who smokes grass isn't necessarily a pothead, Billy. My brother smokes it and he can spell words you and I have never even heard of."

"I suppose he's going to one of those war-protester schools in September, isn't he?"

"He's going to Columbia. Do you have to be so prejudiced?"

He laughed. "That's a switch, *me* prejudiced. I suppose I deserve a chance at it every now and then, don't I?"

I felt the heat in my cheeks.

"Well, hop in," he said.

"Wait. I have a favor to ask you." I reminded him about my plan for plugging up the hole where the bats were flying in and out. "We have to watch for a while so we know where it is."

As we sat on the rock beneath my parents' bedroom window, the dusk fell like ash through the leafy branches of the trees. The creaking bridge eventually quieted after the last couple had walked across to the dance, and the teenagers took turns ferrying out to Cranberry Island in the available boats tied up at the clubhouse. I loved this space between light and dark—the cool breeze and the silvery black lake, where skater bugs tracked the surface like a page of braille.

Billy rested his arm on my good shoulder and wove his fingers through my hair. Patiently, he worked his way through the tangles.

"Did you ever want something so bad you could hardly stand it?" I asked. "I sit here most nights thinking about my life. Bryan's usually out with Carline and my mother's alone upstairs. My father's usually home in his chair watching TV, only he can't even see the screen. He just keeps it on for company."

"What do you want?"

"Oh, you know. What does anybody want . . . . I think about *you* a lot."

"You do?" His hand dropped onto the rock.

"Yeah. I have for years if you really want to know."

"Years?"

"Ever since that day on the bridge when you got my book for me."

"Ever since *then*?"

"No need to worry about it. Some things just happen; you don't have any control over them."

I heard the compressed whistle of his breath.

"I didn't tell you that to scare you, Billy, just so you'd know I'm prepared for this. My wanting to sleep with you, it isn't some trifle. You'll be in the Navy soon and that'll probably be the end of it. But for right now, this is what I've been waiting for. That's all I meant."

He touched one of my curls with his finger. "You sure are something, Danny. What goes on in your mind . . . I can't ever figure what's going to happen next."

"That's good. It's what Carline has with Bryan—that and her skating—she keeps him off course. He's so programmed for perfection that you know just where he's headed, and then she comes along and stops him dead in his tracks. My parents used to surprise each other but they don't anymore. They no longer pay *attention*. A lot of parents are like that . . . . It makes you wonder."

"Look at how many there are." Billy nodded toward the bats skipping along the surface of the lake like planes on a runway. Their crepuscular wings made me think of V-shaped birds, the kind children draw.

I pointed to a spot about six inches from the pitched corner of the roof. "Whaddya think? About there?"

"Yeah, where's the ladder?"

We dragged it out from the storage area underneath the house, and I handed Billy an old flannel shirt of Bryan's, a flashlight, a square of screen I'd cut that afternoon, a hammer, and nails. After he'd stuffed the shirt into the hole, he nailed the screen neatly into place.

"Why do you care so much?" he asked as we replaced the tools.

"Bats do all kinds of things we should be grateful for. They eat mosquitoes, for one. This thing about them getting in your hair is pure hogwash, although try telling *that* to my mother. Besides, they were here first. I get tired of people thinking they *own* everything."

"But bats are so ugly," he said.

I followed him down my father's carefully crafted stairs to the boat. "Some people think fish are ugly."

"Come on, get in." He shook his head, wondering, I supposed, what he'd let himself in for.

When we passed the five-mile-per-hour buoy, we could see the bonfire blazing on Cranberry Island. Some kids were swimming off the rocks along the shoreline while others sat on the ridge just above, and waved greetings with bottles of beer. The bonfire made a lambent silhouette on the water, staining my cast and the visible half of my hand a dull ocher. I smelled smoke, roasting marshmallows, Coppertone, and beer. They were all there: Bryan and Carline, Marilyn, Terese and Jimmy, Ty Malone and Mike Cooper, Lou and Ed Sullivan, the Casey girls, Ginny Conroy and Fern Daniels, the Hogan girls. As we coasted by, laughter raining down, I felt like up there was the world, whereas in this boat it was just Billy and me. By the time we reached the narrow channel into Strawberry Point, the voices and music had diminished, and the bonfire was a shivering, solitary flame.

We putted past Gull Island, the tall green house where we used to rent, and the floating dock I'd played under while my parents argued over whether or not to buy. Now and then a voice called from inside one of the houses, where windows appeared like tiny hearths amidst the trees. When Billy steered toward the tall reeds that hemmed the old lake, I felt the first clutch of nerves in my abdomen.

As soon as he reached the middle, Billy cut the engine and the boat drifted. The silence took me by surprise, although after a few minutes there were other noises: the steady buzz of crickets, the rumble of frogs, cattails rustling amidst the constant current of lapping water. Billy unzipped his sleeping bag and spread it across the bottom of the boat. He threw me one of the seat cushions and motioned me down beside him, where he handed me a bottle of beer.

"Look." He pointed at the stars.

Occasionally I'd lain at night on our dock and stared up at the sky while ticking off the constellations or planets I knew: Orion, Sirius, Venus, the Pleiades, the Big and Little Dippers. On that night the sky was bigger than I was used to, the stars so numerous I had to turn my eyes away. The muscle in Billy's arm pillowed my neck, and I felt his hair brush my forehead. I could smell him—lake water and woods, a tinge of smoke, and something else . . . spicy and dark. The hull rose on both sides of us, and beyond it all you could see were stars.

I tipped my face toward his. As I saw his taut, shadowy cheek, the vein pulsing in his throat, my body was bombarded with tiny sizzling detonations as if I'd swallowed a live Fourth of July sparkler. His lips were as hungry as mine. I couldn't tell if the soft, sucking noise was the sound of our kissing or the lake nibbling at the boat.

After a while I sat up and began to undress. I was still scared he might chicken out again, and I wanted to be naked under that lucent sky. It was as though your whole life you had been covered up so no one would recognize you, and then that chance . . . your naked bodies, bone and muscle, every organ awake, skin and more luminous skin.

It took a long time, which is surprising considering how excited and young we were. His hands moved like beads of water, firm and then feathery light, fast and slow, guiding my awkward bumping cast as we rolled back and forth. Once I held his head in my hands and asked him to stop, unnerved by his lips, the pitch so keen I could hardly bear it. It hurt when he came inside me. Still, I wanted him to stay there forever, even when it kept hurting, when nothing more was happening for me and his own climb was finished. He smiled at me then and ran his tongue across my stomach This time I didn't stop him, not until he'd brought me past pleasure to another place, a peak sharp and splendid. Afterwards, I lay quietly against his chest as he wadded up his condom and stuffed it in the neck of my empty beer bottle.

"No," I said. "Give it to me."

"What for?"

I pulled it, withered and damp, out of the bottle and closed my hand around it. "So I can save it."

"You gotta be kidding."

"I save all my important things. I have a box full of stuff: ticket stubs, invitations, dried flowers. Like when I crowned the Blessed Mother on May Day, I pressed the crown and saved it. Or my ticket from *Spartacus*. My mother took me into New York on my birthday and we saw it. Kirk Douglas, I just loved him, more than Tyrone Power or Cornel Wilde even. I have my first nylons, all my swimming medals, my hair from when it fell out, all the birthday cards anyone ever sent me. Now I have this, too."

I felt the wet in my hand, heard the squeaky balloon sound.

"You're going to put my rubber in the box?"

"I'll press it first, like a corsage. Will it stay soft like this?"

"I think you're a little cracked, Danny."

"I suppose." I leaned up on my good elbow and kissed him.

203

"You feel better now?" he asked.

"Hell yes, a hundred pounds lighter."

He laughed. "When your father comes to arrest me I'll tell him about that college guy, the one with the big dick."

"My father won't find out. Nobody believes I'm capable of this."

"Wait'll I take you to the Byram Motel. The towels there are so thin you could fit one in your box."

Happiness coursed through me and I bowed my head to hide it. We drifted awhile. Billy may have slept, for I could hear his breathing change, his expirations almost noiseless against my forehead. I drank in his smell, the sound of insects and creaking wood, the night air on my naked back. After a while, when we'd dressed and passed once more into the big circle of the lake, I could see the bonfire still burning, the kids dancing on the ridge, their gyrating shadows larger than life.

*

August was hot and rife with tension in the larger world. Rioting spread to Miami, heavy fighting erupted on the Mekong Delta, Russia invaded Czechoslovakia, and seven hundred protesters were injured in Chicago during the Democratic National Convention. Bryan started wearing his hair in a ponytail; my father drove our Dodge station wagon right through the garage door in Westfield. He stepped on the brake, not the accelerator, he insisted. My mother filled the two refrigerators with flowers and made arrangements all day Saturday and into the wee hours of the morning. Her supple hands couldn't camouflage the lonesome edge to her eyes, the way she fondled the tall, spiny stems with undisguised yearning. *Touch me,* she seemed to say. I hugged her several times a day, guilty over my double life, the gap between her solitary nights and the wild, insatiable times I was having.

I don't know why nobody ever found out. The sessions in Billy's boat or the needle-thick ground along the Virgin were private enough, as was the blue seat of his T-bird parked under an awning of fretted trees along Tamarack Road. But we used no discretion at all when we rented room number fourteen in the Byram Motel on those muggy afternoons after Billy got off work. True, we didn't give the man our real names, but the motel was smack next to the highway, no place to hide, and neither one of us acted at all discreetly as we tumbled through the door, our lips sealed and my legs belted around his middle.

The room was painted chartreuse with brown shag carpeting. It gave our skin a jaundiced tone, which I have since associated with covert sexual activity. The dun-colored bottom sheet didn't fit and started sliding as soon as my back made contact. I have never been able to stand wrinkles in a sheet, so I spent our first afternoon at the Byram hopping up every few minutes to fix it. Soon Billy ripped the sheet off and tossed it toward a corner of the room. The mattress buttons on my bare back weren't much better so I made it a point to put one of my mother's lilac-flowered sheets in Billy's trunk. Each time we checked into the motel, Billy waited patiently while I stripped the bed and remade it, methodically tucking in each corner.

The padded headboard was covered in shiny gold vinyl, which left a metallic stain on the backs of my hands. At a certain angle as I lay limply on the bed, the dust dropped like snow through the sunlight and landed silently on Billy's inert back. I rested my face against his shoulder, drinking in the lake-water smell that nothing could dispel—not sex or sweat or shampoo, not even the baby oil that was turning my skin to pure velvet.

I felt almost reverent about these moments after sex. Billy always fell into a brief sleep while I lay propped on pillows, memorizing each curve of his face and body.

"Water," I said to him one afternoon, licking the sweat from his temple. "That's what you smell like."

He rolled over, smiling as he always did when I told him things. "Water, huh?"

"Do I have a smell?"

205

"Lots of them." He kissed a path from my belly button to the dampness between my legs.

"No. I mean my skin, all of me. Is there one smell more than any other?"

Sensing that I needed something from him, he lifted his head and eyed me.

"It's not a smell."

"No?"

"It's a . . . " he inched closer, "a feeling, I suppose."

"What kind of feeling?"

He thought a minute. "When I'm running the mile after school there are people around—other guys, the coach, girls in the stands—and noise. You can hear voices, your own feet against the ground, your breathing. You can hear the air rushing by. Then, just as you hit your stride, when you know you're going to win, there's a sudden weightlessness. It's like leaping off a cliff, only you don't fall. You go on and on into this huge silence. *That's* the way I feel when I'm with you."

It was the closest he'd ever come to saying "I love you," and I took it, holding the words in my cupped hands.

"I'm leaving, you know, at the end of next week," he said.

"I know."

"Great Lakes, Illinois, that's where I go for boot camp."

"You'll write me, won't you?"

"Sure. I can just imagine the kind of letter you'll write."

"I write very good letters."

"That's what I meant."

He rose from the bed and walked to the rust-colored chair where he'd dropped his pants. He slipped a small paper bag out from underneath and handed it to me.

"Here."

A black girl stared back at me from the cover of the book: *The Street* by Ann Petry.

"I told my mother how much you like books and asked her if she knew one you might like. The girls I know don't read the kind of books you read. She said this was her favorite, so I bought it."

I ran my hands over the cover. "I'll keep this forever," I said.

It would have been natural then to talk about me being white and Billy mixed, but we didn't. I'd inherited the problem faced by most adults who can't talk easily about race, not when one's white and the other isn't. White liberals get the words stuck in our throats, as if to say them—*black, Negro*—will betray something bad about us. We'll say them the wrong way maybe, exposing our ignorance, or we'll say too much, pretending to know things we can't possibly know. So we skirt the issue entirely, pretending it doesn't exist. For me it didn't. Neither did his father being in prison, him being a townie boy or enlisting in the Navy.

There is no difference between us, I said to myself over and over.

I wish I'd known more. Not that the direction we took would have changed much, but I'd have been prepared. I would have seen the gulf to be bridged, the laborious journey we'd each have to make to understand who we were in the world: a white, middle-class girl bound for college in love with a half-black townie boy, whose biggest dream was to see the world from the deck of an aircraft carrier.

Neither one of us knew what to do next, so we got dressed and left. It was our last time in the Bryam Motel, although we hadn't planned it that way. Had I known I would have left a candle burning on the bathroom sink or snipped a corner of the shag carpeting to put in my box along with the BM monogrammed towel.

On Billy's last evening we fished until dark in the channel and made love while the boat drifted along the shoreline of Disappointment. It was dark and buggy, and the next morning I woke with a swarm of bites all over me. Sitting there in bed I felt as if I'd been hollowed out like a pumpkin. It seemed impossible that my heart continued to beat inside my vacant chest. Cheesecloth swaddled my head so I could could barely see or hear the kids at the beach. I climbed back underneath the sheets, closed my eyes, and tried to blot out the dull echo inside my chest, the loss of light and color. I tried to blot out too the empty house, the boiling spoke of an engine, my father's fold-up bed in the corner of the living room.

Years later I told my mother what had happened that summer between Billy and me.

"I can't believe we didn't know," she said. "Such a big thing and no one even suspected."

Marcella Dove told Billy that she knew what he and I were doing every afternoon. Maybe she read between the lines of his letters, those spare missals that started arriving the very next week. Or maybe he'd changed, too, and she could see it— the world with all its rules and sadness held at bay while the two of us drifted alone and happy on the lake.

ACCIDENT (1969)

I WAS SEVENTEEN AND LEADING A DOUBLE LIFE. Something must have showed, for boys started calling me the first week of school and didn't let up no matter how many invitations I turned down. Not all of them, of course. Much as I loved sitting on the high green seat in Palone's Florist watching May arrange flowers, it wasn't my idea of a thrilling Saturday night. Home was worse. The TV droned on long after Charlie had fallen asleep in his chair with the slide viewer and a pile of old slides in his lap.

Boys are uncanny in the way they sense things. I didn't dress provocatively and hadn't even French-kissed a boy at school. I had lots of girlfriends, wrote the usual poems about dying and the Atlantic Ocean for the literary magazine, and read Russian novels all the way home on the bus. I was small-breasted and interesting-looking rather than pretty. There was no outward sign at all of those feverish afternoons with Billy or of what I dreamed about doing the next time we met. I told myself it was my ability to keep a conversation going with the dullest boy. Maybe it was my lack of fear or the genuine affection I felt for most of them. Maybe it was the *not available* sign in the recesses of my eyes.

I went to the junior prom with Larry Salinger. Besides having a literary last name, he wrote passing poetry in our creative-writing group and was the top-seeded wrestler in his weight class in the county. I liked the contradictions in him, plus the fact that he had brown curly hair and was the same height as Billy, so that when he kissed me good night I could close my eyes and pretend.

Things were changing fast for Billy. He wrote about the

gulf he felt between him and the white men in his unit. It was confusing, and I tried to pay attention whenever he mentioned it. On one hand, he said, he liked the feeling of unity among the men, a bond that could keep you alive when the time came. He'd made many friends, white as well as black. Yet the lines were more sharply drawn than he'd experienced before. He felt forced to identify who he was, to align himself with one side against the other. "How do I do that," he asked, "when half of me is white, the other black? How do I choose?"

In the end the choice was easy. When you look black you *are* black, he wrote, whether or not you're light-skinned or half-white. The white men considered him black; the blacks waited for him to declare himself. When he did, part of it was knowing what was expected, and part was what he was learning about himself. He talked about black power and the ideas of men like Malcolm X, H. Rap Brown, and Stokely Carmichael. He described how heated the men got over whose channel was on the radio, rock or soul. He asked if I knew the writers he was reading: James Baldwin, Eldridge Cleaver, Langston Hughes.

"Black men," he wrote, "are not as innocent as white men. Blacks are more cautious. It's not about the war, either. It's the way we think and how we live in the world."

Well, I mused, he'd certainly been cautious enough with *me*. I can see now that the letters gave him an opportunity to talk about the difference between us, and that he wanted me to understand it, too. But I couldn't. In my mind it was just Billy and me the way it had been on the lake. I knew that he still cared, even if he never said the words. Not the way I did, over and over, framing my letters with lipstick kisses and locks of hair sprinkled with Shalimar. It was a risk falling overboard like that, especially with him so far away and nothing promised between us. He was seeing the world just the way he'd wanted, spending his ninety-six dollars a month on R and R in Subic Bay and Hong Kong. Without him actually saying so, I suspected that he'd been with other girls, too, *women* probably, which is why I let Larry Salinger slip his hand under my shirt, thinking about Billy the whole time.

The winter stretched long and empty with Bryan away at school. Often May worked overtime at the shop. I would find cut-up chicken thawing in the pan with a can of tomato sauce and an onion sitting alongside. "Slip it in at five o'clock," she wrote. "Boil some potatoes and a package of frozen peas." Sometimes I wondered what the business offered her, besides the touch and smell of flowers. She was reticent to talk about her own life independent of my father and us, and I didn't ask. When I visited her at the shop, I was struck by how fast she worked and how often she smiled. Once she handed me her paycheck and pointed to the money set aside for her pension. "It's mine," she said proudly.

My mother had the ability to be completely there one minute, her caring visible and known, and the next to vanish without leaving the room. Her eyes would grow blank and distant, and if I tried to talk to her, she'd answer mechanically or cut me off in mid-sentence. She'd done this as far back as I can remember, but she perfected it during the years when my father was drinking so heavily. It enabled her to cope with her disappointments, of course, to travel inside herself and cultivate that landscape, but it made the rest of us feel invisible.

When the Dodge station wagon crunched up our gravel driveway, I turned on the radio and the back-porch light. I wanted the house to be cheerful and welcoming for my father. He liked it when I asked him questions about the latest Ada Louise Huxtable review on architecture in the *New York Times*. Sometimes he'd talk with his old spark about the building in question, and point out flaws in the design that Huxtable had missed.

On bad days, or if my mother was home and chatted too brightly about the shop, he'd grouse about clients or the other architects in the firm. So-and-so had trimmed the budget again, so-and-so got a bigger bonus than he did, so-and-so couldn't design anything that wasn't on a forty-five-degree angle. My mother nodded her head and kept quiet. We pretended, she and I, that this was a normal life. On Saturdays she took me shopping to the new mall in Menlo Park or out to lunch at Margie's Ice Cream Parlour for hamburgers and hot fudge sundaes. She asked me about school and Larry Salinger, whose father had a standing order of white roses delivered to their home once a week. "Mark my words," she said, "with a father like that he's bound to make a good husband."

In June, Bryan came home from Columbia with hair longer than mine and eyes fiery with politics. He'd sent me a cartonload of SDS literature and a fuzzy newspaper photograph of him standing on the steps of the student union with five hundred other androgynous-looking kids protesting military recruitment on campus. It didn't help his case with Charlie that Columbia students had joined the majority of students across America in sticking it to college administrations. Avowed liberal or not, Charlie was a vehement believer in boys looking like boys and in students not biting the hand that fed them.

Like my brother, I did not support the war in Vietnam. I believed that the dissension in the country was not a lack of will or patriotism but a sign that people did not understand or agree with the reasons for such a war. In the face of death, that is, the bloody face of which stared at us every night on the six o'clock news. It made me angry each time I saw a red-,white-, and blue-bumper sticker declaring AMERICA, LOVE IT OR LEAVE IT. Still, Billy was on an aircraft carrier in the Tonkin Gulf risking his life for his country. It made all the other boys visible. It also made it easier to understand my father, who'd been lost in the jungle himself and found his heart still there, despite his conviction that Richard Nixon had no more sense than his dog Checkers.

A weight lifted for me with Bryan home, as if a balance had been restored in the family. Charlie complained about his long hair and the fact that Grace Slick was singing about LSD and not some white rabbit. But I enjoyed their renewed arguments over Vietnam, which were not as heated as before and made for good dinner-table discussions. Not even Charlie could dispute Bryan's command of the facts, since Bryan had just completed a course on the history of Southeast Asia. My frequent questions about the servicemen and the actual day-to-day life over there allowed Charlie to tell some of his combat stories and to voice his concern for the fighting men. Even he saw the ludicrousness of Nixon's decision to intensify the bombing over Cambodia and Laos when he was supposed to be withdrawing troops from Vietnam. "Either get out and admit defeat," he said, "or give the men the wherewithal to finish it."

Summer resumed at Rainy as if nothing had changed in the larger world. Linda Hailey blew her whistle for swim-team practice at 8 A.M. the same as usual; Sal and Joey's opened with a fresh coat of paint and a new pinball machine. Men lounged in the open windows of the Pink Elephant, and we checked our clocks by the six-o'clock train that stopped every evening at the bridge. Townie boys raked the red clay on the tennis courts; teenagers gathered on the north end of the beach; and boats docked alongside the community club. The schedule of events was posted in its customary place on the bulletin board: Hawaiian Luau, BYOL Dance, Scavenger Hunt, King and Queen Dance, Ski Club Show, Sadie Hawkins Dance, Labor Day Boat Races, Swim Team Banquet. The Protestants held their service at 9:00 A.M. on Sundays, the Catholics at 11:00 A.M. The graffiti bloomed in the girls' bathroom, as did the pile of empty beer bottles and cigarette butts at the bottom of Lovers' Slope.

In the evenings after dinner I dropped anchor in the old lake and cast into the channel. As I sailed our small boat within calling distance of Billy's house, I felt full of hope and renewal. Now, I can only imagine such innocence, the way Billy says he imagines his life before Vietnam, before he knew who he was and how much suffering was possible.

*

213

When I woke that first Saturday in July, I looked out the window and saw Angie Fanelli, Angie Fowler now, strolling across the empty beach toward the dock. The sun was winking on the surface of the water and on the white sand around the lifeguard's chair. Having stayed out past 1:00 A.M. the night before with Mike Cooper, Bryan was lightly snoring on his side of the sleeping porch. The snoring grew louder at the end of the living room where my father lay sleeping on his folding bed. I tiptoed past the closed door of my mother's room, grabbed a towel from the laundry pile in the bathroom, and slipped out the back door.

The bridge swung gently as I ran across, slapping my hand on the wooden railing. After my injury last summer I hadn't rejoined the swim team, although Linda continued to ask. My arm had healed well, the doctors said, but I couldn't recapture my former speed. If I stressed it, my arm ached, and there was residual stiffness in the fingers of my left hand. Even so, I continued to swim my twenty-five laps every morning, the steady movement back and forth as soothing as a prayer.

I dove in a few lanes from where Angie was swimming and gave myself over to the constant rhythm and the cool, silky water. When I finished, she was sitting in the shallow water, leaning against the retaining wall. She'd taken off her bathing cap, and her long hair lay damp and tousled on her shoulders.

"How's your arm?" she asked.

"It's OK. I won't win any races but at least I can use it."

"You're not on the team anymore?"

I shook my head.

"That's too bad. Sometimes I wish I could go back—just swim my laps everyday and keep the times for Linda." She looked at me sadly and stood up. "It seems like somebody else's life."

"How's Wade?" I asked, not wanting her to leave.

The sun shone on her shoulders as she peered down at me. "You're going to college, aren't you?"

"Sure . . . I mean, I plan to. I have another year yet."

"You make sure you go. If some guy breaks your heart, you just pick up and move on. And don't be in any hurry to get married. You have your whole life for that."

I wondered for a minute if she knew about me and Billy, but then I realized she was talking about herself and Wade.

"See ya." She climbed up the ladder, picked up her towel, and walked down the beach. I watched her long-legged stride across the highway until she disappeared behind the shrubbery along Tamarack Road.

From the bridge I could hear the pinball machine in Sal and Joey's and Sal's sharp voice hollering at one of the boys. Joey, who was standing in front of the window, waved absently when I called out a hello to her. Her hair was pulled back in a ponytail, and she was wearing one of those sleeveless, flowered tent dresses. Without makeup, her face was very white and puffier than usual. Usually it was hard to see the resemblance between her and Angie. It was apparent only when Joey was well rested and smiling, when she had her makeup on, and the light was just right. On that day I recognized the same sad expression on their faces, as if they were staring out on a vast, endless plain.

As I climbed the steps to our house, past the potting shed and May's bountiful rock garden, up through the weather-stained, half-finished pergola, I noticed the deterioration in the porch logs. Reaching my hand into one spongy indentation, I came away with a fistful of rotted wood. My mother was frying up a skillet full of bacon, singing "Unforgettable" in her sweet, stoic voice. When she saw me, she smiled and touched me lightly on the shoulder with her small hand.

"Tell Bryan and your father we're almost ready to eat."

I leaned close to the mirror in my room and rubbed the moisture from my forehead. My hair, the longest it had ever been, tumbled past my shoulders. Absently I brushed the dust from the yellow and orange leis hanging from the mirror and felt a needle of longing for Terese. How I wished we were back in that summer when I was thirteen, reading Charlie's dirty books or lounging on Nini's plaid blanket on the beach, watching my parents' heads intersect like the limbs of a single tree as they studied Charlie's latest design for the potting shed.

Terese wasn't coming up that summer. She'd gotten a job in the hospitality department at La Guardia Airport, uniform and all, and she didn't want to spend the extra money commuting from New York to Rainy. Besides which, she'd broken up with Jimmy over the winter and was dating a boy who was a mechanic for United Airlines. I couldn't blame her for liking a boy who worked that close to planes. She'd promised to bring him with her to the next teenage dance so Carline and I and Frieda could meet him.

Frieda and Gerry Gland had split up in January. What was surprising was that he'd renounced other women altogether; he said he wanted Frieda and nobody else. It's too late, she told him. She'd been traveling with her Sweet Adelines all over the East Coast and had been offered a second job singing weekends in Moriarty's Bar and Grill on Staten Island. Sometimes Marilyn joined her, Terese said, and the two of them together would melt the coldest heart. Frieda's women friends and the singing must have filled up the hole in her life, because she didn't yield even when Gerry suckered the minister into pleading his case for him.

In the divorce settlement Frieda gave up the house on the Island and kept the cottage at Rainy. She and the girls rented an apartment near Moriarty's, not far from the ice rink where Carline was skating, working with a new coach Frieda had hired. On some week nights and weekends, Carline waited tables and drove up to Rainy whenever she could. She'd graduated from high school in June, but had decided to put off college for a year to concentrate all her energies on her skating. My mother worried that there were no adults at the Glands' house, which meant trouble for Bryan and Carline alone there. "The trouble you're talking about is old news by this time," I told her. "Don't lose sleep over it."

The paper rattled on the top bunk in Bryan's room, and I

called out that breakfast was almost ready. My father stood up from the edge of his cot where he'd been smoking a cigarette and shuffled into the bathroom. I winced at the gagging sound he made as he coughed up his morning sputum into the toilet. Chronic bronchitis, the doctor had said, aggravated by smoking and alcohol. "He needs to drop the booze and cigarettes and get back into shape," the doctor told May. I pushed aside the striped curtain into Bryan's room and stepped over piles of clothing, sneakers, and newspapers.

"Don't you ever clean in here?" I picked up his pillow from the floor and hugged it to my chest. The familiar smell made me smile: balsam wood, hair oil, and dusty flannel.

Bryan continued to write in a spiral notebook propped up against his knees.

"What are you writing?" I asked.

When I climbed onto the lower mattress and poked my elbows against his hip, he tucked the pencil behind his ear and frowned.

"Do you *mind?*"

I leaped down and rummaged among the debris on top of his dresser: an empty bottle of Canoe, a brush I wouldn't touch a dog with, pennies, charred matches, a dripped candle in a green wine bottle, Carline's sultry senior picture, his ticket stub from *Hair*, five stubby pencils, a folded-up album poster of Michelle Phillips, two roach clips, and a half-smoked reefer.

"Geez, Bryan, I can't believe you leave this lying around." I held up the joint and sniffed it.

"Put that back." He lay the notebook down beside him.

"What if they find it?"

"Right. Dad'd be lucky to find his own car keys. Mom never comes in here. Some people believe in respecting other people's privacy."

"Some people aren't as dumb as others are either."

"Oh yeah?" His blue eyes flickered with curiosity.

"Like I know there's a whole box of rubbers in *that* drawer, and in *that* one's a block wrapped up in a handkerchief that looks like hamster food, but I bet you can smoke it, and in *that* one's a stack of letters written to you by that girl from school whom you say is just a friend but I don't buy it, not with her writing you every other day . . . "

"You don't know what you're talking about. She doesn't write me every other day, and she *is* just a friend. I have a lot of friends who happen to be girls."

"Bet Carline's wild about *that.*"

"Carline and I trust each other."

"Look, if you're thinking of dropping her, you'd better be decent about it . . . "

"What *is* this? Carline and I are fine, no thanks to Peeping Toms like you. Since when did you turn into Carline's protector?"

"I don't have to be best friends with her to care whether she gets hurt or not."

"Well, I'm not planning on hurting her, so butt out." One long leg rolled over the side of the bed, and he dropped down beside me. "Talking about letters, Mom said you get them regularly from Billy Dove. I hope you're not falling for *him.*"

"What'd be the crime in that?"

His expression was serious. "You're kidding, aren't you?"

"We're just friends, same as you and what's-her-name. He's got girlfriends in every port he visits. If I *did* like him, it wouldn't be any of *your* business."

"Getting drafted is bad enough, but he *enlisted.* I can't understand how any guy could enlist in the fucking military."

"You're pretty narrow-minded, Bryan. The Navy's giving Billy something he could never have otherwise."

"What, the chance to kill Vietcong?"

"He hasn't killed anybody. He's an air mechanic; he works on F4s and A6s. He's not running patrols in the jungle like the Marines."

"No, he just sends pilots up there to bomb the shit out of the countryside."

"*He* doesn't do that, knucklehead, the U.S. government does. Besides, his squadron flies mostly reconnaissance missions, or else they're searching for men who've been shot down. He has three friends missing in North Vietnam—nobody knows if they're alive or dead. Billy says there's no chance we're going to win this war fighting the way we are."

"No shit. I didn't have to go to Vietnam to find that out."

"You're a real snob, you know that, Bryan? You think anybody who thinks differently than you is lower down on the food chain."

"That's ridiculous. I just don't want you getting involved with somebody like Billy Dove."

"I could do a lot worse than Billy Dove."

"You're not saying you *like* him, are you?"

I gazed at him, weighing my secrets. "And what if I did? Are you saying he's not good enough, Mr. Big-Man-on-Campus-Liberal?"

"It has nothing to do with that. I know his reputation with girls, that's all. And this thing with his father, it sticks with you, whether you like it or not. He has too many strikes against him. You don't know what you'd be letting yourself in for."

He trailed me into the living room.

"Look, Danny, there's lots of things I don't know, what you do with boys, for instance. I figure that's your business. Mom told me you've been seeing Larry Salinger, who I happen to think is an OK guy. I know it's been a hard year for you, I wouldn't have wanted to be home alone with Dad the way you have. I worry about you sometimes, that's all. You always settle for less than what I think you're worth."

"I do not."

"Yeah, so what colleges are you applying to next year?"

I rearranged the damp towel hanging over the stair railing. "I'm not sure yet. Jesus, Bryan, it's only July."

"Why don't you apply to Columbia?"

219

"That's where *you* go. Besides, it's too expensive. You're on a National Merit Scholarship."

"So, you could get a student loan. If you don't want Columbia, why not Boston University? Shit, Danny, you could apply to Berkeley if you wanted."

"I won't get into those places, Bryan. My scores aren't as high as yours. My grades . . . "

"Your grades are good and you know it."

"Not that good."

"So, just work harder in the fall, work as hard as you can."

I sighed. "Even if I did, they won't let me get a student loan."

"Don't accept it then. *Fight* them. I'll help if you want."

"I don't want any more fighting, Bryan."

He gripped my shoulders the way Father Burns did when he talked about the dangers of premarital sex.

"You've got to get away from here, Danny." He cocked his head to include the upstairs of our house. "They can't see how bad things are. *You* have to. You have to take care of yourself."

"I do, Bryan. I just don't get why you're so steamed up over colleges for me. How about Carline? She's not even going to college next year."

"Carline's trying to qualify for the Nationals. You know how much time and money it takes to be the kind of skater Carline is? *A lot.* She's practicing six or more hours a day. She'll go to college when she's ready."

His face softened then. "You try so hard to keep everything running smoothly. I understand why you do it, but it's useless. You can't change the way things are, Danny. You need to pay more attention to your own life."

"You worry too much." As I patted him affectionately on the cheek, I felt the stubble underneath my hand. He'd become taller than my father.

When we clambered down the stairs, my mother was pouring Charlie a cup of coffee and gestured at us to sit down. I glanced through the screens toward Sal and Joey's, from whose open windows still rang the bells of the pinball machine.

"How do you want your eggs?" May headed toward the stove.

"Sunny-side up," I said.

"Over lightly," Bryan added.

Charlie covered his smile with his napkin. My mother's eggs looked the same no matter what you asked for. Carefully she scooped one yellowy mass from the right side of the pan for Bryan and another, identical mass for me, and then plumped herself down with a satisfied sigh at her own place, where she spread a spoonful of grape jelly onto a piece of darkened toast.

"Help yourself to the bacon." She pointed to the full platter.

"You've already been to the beach this morning, Danny?" my father asked.

"Yeah. Angie was there swimming laps. I don't think she's too happy with old Wade."

"Nobody's surprised about that," Bryan said. "She only went for him on the rebound."

Charlie shook his head. "Ed Casey said Wade got into a fight last week at the Tamarack. They had to put him out."

"I wonder how much of it was Angie feeling hurt over Joe Malone and how much was her desire to get away from Sal and Joey," I said.

"She should have moved out on her own," Bryan said.

"That Sal's a tough character. Although you can't put all the blame on him—Joey doesn't exactly look like Maureen O'Hara." Charlie rolled his eyes dramatically.

My mother shifted in her seat. "That's not fair, Charlie. Joey's real pretty when she fixes herself up."

"Well, they're sure as hell not a model couple. I feel sorry for those kids they've got over there." Charlie reached for another piece of bacon.

We sat for a moment in silence, listening to the water lapping against the dock and Eddie Holman singing "Hey There Lonely Girl" on the radio. Just then Charlie slapped his hand on the table, rattling the silverware. "Let's have a party! This afternoon. You kids can ask your friends. Carline's not up, is she? Well, round up Ty and Jimmy and the others. May, you call the Caseys and the Pipers. I'll run over to the Sullivans. . . . He's playing golf later with Paddy and Tom Conroy and he can tell them."

"But Charlie, I don't have food for . . . "

"I'll take care of it. *Hey,* why don't you call Nini, ask her and Tim to come up. Terese, too. It'll be just like old times."

My mother's smile sent a shiver down my back. Bryan started piling dishes on one curved arm. "I'll drive into Sparta and pick up whatever you need."

"I'll go with you," Charlie said.

It was only later, when my father and Bryan had gone and May was talking happily to Nini on the phone, that I stopped long enough to take it all in. I could tell by my mother's buoyant tone, by the way her hands sailed on and off her lap, that the Kellys were coming. I remember the light on the floor and how close I came to crying. It had been so long since the four of us had done anything together.

As I rounded the railing at the top of the stairs, I was lost in those early summers after we'd bought the house. Something skittered by and I ducked, shielding my head with my hands. My first thought was that a bird had gotten into the house, or a large moth. I didn't want to connect the wheeling shadow I thought I'd seen with the sudden whirring squeak near the top of the fireplace. I searched the ceiling and beams thoroughly, but found nothing. My investigation of the soffits on the south side of the house didn't turn up any obvious holes or cracks, only more deteriorating logs like the ones under the porch.

Better to say nothing, I decided, at least until after the party. Charlie would have to treat the logs again to kill whatever insect was consuming them. *This* time if I found out where the bats were entering, I could plug up the hole myself. Bryan and Charlie carried in bags full of food and ice, a case of beer, and enough liquor to keep the party flowing past midnight. Charlie replaced a few planks of rotted railing and fixed the ladder on the dock. While May arranged cut flowers in her Waterford vases, I scrubbed the kitchen floor. Bryan rigged up his stereo on the porch and danced around to "Jumping Jack Flash" with an imaginary guitar.

By lunchtime the sun was radiating off the roof, and our faces shone with a fine coating of sweat. Bryan was the first one in the lake. The rest of us followed like ants, groaning with pleasure as we broke the surface of the cool, slate-colored water. As I swam back and forth between the bridge and the dock, my brother flipped off one of the cables, and my parents paddled side by side in the black inner tubes. We didn't speak, Bryan or I, when we rested finally on the bridge's concrete ledge. I could feel the muscle in his upper arm against my shoulder, and I watched his long feet and my shorter ones swiveling like pale fish under the surface.

Later, when Terese strolled into my bedroom without her new boyfriend, I was relieved. Jimmy still looked crushed every time I mentioned her name, and he was definitely coming to the party. I loved the thick, loose knot of hair at the back of her head, the way she lit up the dull logs behind her.

"You look great," she said admiringly. I was wearing a pair of denim cutoffs and a sleeveless white cotton blouse that showed off my brown shoulders. I was thin and lanky and no longer hid my wild hair or oversized eyes. "Flaunt it," Carline had told me. "With the right makeup you could look just like Sophia Loren." "Not quite," I'd responded, flattered by the compliment.

We paid no attention to the party gathering steam downstairs as we lay across my bed flipping through the photographs she'd brought. She had pictures of her in her hospitality uniform, pictures of airplanes, pictures of her new boyfriend Mick in his United Airlines shirt, pictures of Tim and Nini on vacation in Puerto Rico last spring. It was hard to believe that the lean, smiling man in the snapshot was Tim Kelly.

"They look good," I said.

"They'd just been snorkeling. Can't you picture it, Nini in that little green bathing cap?"

I laughed, thinking of the two women sailing under the bridge.

"Dad's just been promoted to Lieutenant. Sometimes, if Nini's working late, he picks me up at the airport and takes me out to the Ground Round for dinner."

She hopped off the bed and walked over to the bureau. With the proprietary confidence of the old days, she opened the bottom drawer where I kept my special box.

"You still have it!" she squealed, bending down and removing the lid.

I was too stunned to stop her. All my mementos from last summer—our first condom, the towel from the Byram Motel, Billy's best handmade fly. She hadn't yet noticed *The Street* by Ann Petry or the tied-up bundle of airmail letters stacked neatly beside the box. On top was the corsage May had made for Larry Salinger to give me the night of the junior prom.

"Is this him? God, Danny, he looks just like Paul Newman." She picked up the photograph of the two of us standing hand in hand under a white arbor bedecked with plastic roses. Just as I leaned down to shut the box, she spied the used condom.

"What's *this*?"

"It's a rubber, what do you think it is?"

"Well, I can see that, but whose?"

Billy's name hovered on the tip of my tongue. I swallowed to relieve the ache in my throat.

"You slept together after the prom, didn't you?"

I glanced at the photo of Larry and me, and noted how awkward we looked: me in that dumb dotted-swiss dress and him in the ill-fitting white dinner jacket that belonged to his father.

"You should see him in his varsity jacket . . . . He's really cute in that." I meant it, too, wanting to give Larry Salinger credit where it was due.

Terese's eyes, inches from mine, glittered like the wet back of a rainbow trout. "*Tell* me . . . did you like it?"

I leaned my head back against the log wall and closed my eyes. I could feel the lap of water underneath the boat, the silky path of Billy's tongue across my skin.

"Yes. After the first time we did it over and over, every afternoon almost."

"Where?" she whispered.

"We went to a motel out on the highway, the same one every time. It had a pukey-colored shag carpet. It was the most wonderful thing that's ever happened to me. I could hardly *bear* it."

"You must miss him—you know, when you're up here."

"I *do* miss him."

She stroked the corsage with her finger. "I'm glad you told me. I was afraid that last summer . . . "

Her words disappeared as she set the corsage back in the box and shut the drawer. I didn't think of it as a lie, only that she had one boy's face in mind while I had the other's.

Before I'd even reached the kitchen, I could hear Nini's giggle rising from the lower deck. Bottles of liquor were lined up like bowling pins on the counter, next to the silver cocktail shaker lying on its side in a puddle of butter-colored foam and half-empty jars of maraschino cherries and olives. The table was spread with open bags of potato chips, cheese doodles and Fritos, two cans of Planters' peanuts, and containers full of Wispride cheese spread and onion dip.

"Want a Coke?" Terese asked, taking one from the cooler sitting next to the sink.

I nodded, peering down on the group scattered across the patio and two levels of the deck. As often as I viewed it, I was still struck by the contrast between the unadorned, discolored frame of the half-built pergola and upper deck and the lush, meticulous bottom half. The fiery lilies, the intricate, tessellated patio, the potting shed, the rock garden covering the unbuilt landscape like an ancient tapestry: sedum and flowering hosta, spikey-blue bugleweed and white evening primroses, poppies and goldenrod and snow-in-summer, creeping mint and pink-flowered thyme.

Nini's giggle looped upwards like the flight of a bird. She was standing next to my mother, who was waving her hands and talking. The Caseys were there, Lois and Dan Sullivan, the Doonans, Jay and Betty Piper, Tom and Mary Conroy, the Hogans. Bryan was cradling a beer in one hand and gesturing to Jimmy Piper with the other. He'd inherited the drama of my mother's hands, the way they traveled like a baton to punctuate his words.

"Jimmy's here," Terese said, coming up beside me.

The younger group had taken over the dock: Mike Cooper had one long arm slung around Fern Daniels' shoulder; Jimmy and Bryan were conversing head to head; Ty was flirting with Ginny Conroy and Eileen Hogan; and Lou Sullivan was sitting in the back seat of the Chris-Craft with Suzie Casey.

"He's still stuck on you, you know," I said.

Terese shrugged and started down the stairs. I followed the flag of her poppy-colored hair and her tall, lithe body as she loped through the chattering adults to the dock, where she positioned herself next to Bryan and smiled up at him with her creamy, freckled face. *She still likes him.* I didn't need to linger over Jimmy's bobbing Adam's apple to know what he was feeling.

I hovered at the periphery of the party, more watchful than usual. I recall feeling sick early on and believe now it was a presentiment, like the one my grandfather had the summer before he died, when he embarked on a driving trip to see all of his grandchildren, giving each one of us two Kennedy half-dollars.

By late afternoon my father's cheerfulness had become disjointed and reckless—the result of too many martinis, perhaps, or the strain of swimming against the tide of the darkness he'd been battling for so long. Tim Kelly seemed genuinely happy to see him, and the two men talked for almost an hour, interrupted only by Charlie's trips up to the kitchen to replenish people's drinks. He made a point of keeping Tim's glass full of tonic water. Maybe that contributed to my father's disequilibrium. His old friend seemed to be in such control of himself; his face looked youthful and healthy, not the bloated, veiny visage of five years before. It was the first time I could recall Tim talking with such fervor about his job.

When Charlie plunged into one of his monologues about the office, I ran an ice cube across my hot forehead, and wondered if I had a fever. I'd heard the routine so many times: how ordinary his partners were, how unenlightened his clients and all those greedy developers were, how many carpenters just wanted to get the job done. "There are so many buildings going up," he said, "and not a single one you can be proud of. Nobody of any substance is going to want to go into architecture."

"Well, you've left your mark here, Charlie," Tim said. "I haven't seen a single deck on Staten Island that can compare with the ones you've built at Rainy."

He'd meant to turn the conversation in a more positive direction, but in waving his arm around to emphasize his point, he touched one more raw nerve in the fragile facade my father had constructed. Charlie gazed through the pergola toward the porch and scowled at the discordant music of Richie Havens's guitar.

When May and Nini joined them, Nini slipped up next to Tim and hooked her arm through his. They weren't conscious of how different they were from most of the other couples, who, for all their high spirits, were more separate than together, none of them even touching. I was standing just a few feet away with my trayful of Ritz crackers and dogs-in-a-blanket, mindful of the smoky clouds rolling in, when May dropped her half-smoked cigarette on the deck and squashed it with her red sneaker. I caught her face head-on and recognized that lost, lonely look.

Charlie saw it, too, and kicked the cigarette off the deck into the lake.

"Geez, May, you're marking up the wood."

She swung her head up toward the pergola and laughed. It wasn't the trilling, infectious sound we were used to, but a tight little knot that wiped all remaining pleasure from my father's face. "Like it's really going to matter, Charlie."

I felt the beat of a hoof between my eyes and brushed a sweaty hand across my shorts. A little later Charlie dropped the drink he was handing to Paddy Doonan and shrugged off with a surly quiet Paddy's attempts to pick up the glass. He and May avoided each other after that; they avoided Tim and Nini too, although there was so much noise and movement that I don't think anybody but the Kellys really noticed. Bryan was helping me load up a tray of sodas and beer when Charlie tripped over the threshold between the porch and the kitchen, and rapped his forehead on one of the glass panes of the door.

"You OK?" Bryan put out a hand to steady him.

Charlie veered out of reach. "Of course I'm OK, no thanks to this bloody door. What the hell do you have on? You call that music?"

A blind dropped over Bryan's face.

"Christ, Bryan, put on something we can at least *listen* to."

I moved swiftly forward, pulling the Beatles' *Magical Mystery Tour* album from the pile. "I'll play this," I said.

Bryan waited until Charlie had left with a new batch of drinks before stopping the stereo.

"Why do you do that?" he asked, dropping the Beatles' album on the table.

"Do what?"

"Try to smooth things over. Why don't you play what *you* want to hear?"

"So he can get madder than he already is? What are you doing?"

"I'm putting something else on, that's what."

When he clenched his jaw like that, the angles in his face resembled the brittle edges of the china figurines my mother collected. "It's gonna rain," he said, slamming the door behind him.

"Great," I muttered, recognizing Country Joe McDonald. I stacked the turntable with Tommy Dorsey, Simon and Garfunkle, Mitch Miller, and Carmel Quinn.

"One, two, three, what are we fightin for,
Don't ask me I don't give a damn
Next stop is Vietnam.
And it's five, six, seven open up the pearly gates
Well, ain't no time to wonder why
Whoopee, we're all gonna die."

Bryan's voice hovered above the crowd, and I wondered how many joints he'd smoked before the party. Some of the adults tapped their feet in rhythm and continued to talk, paying no attention to the lyrics. Ed Casey headed down toward the dock. When I realized that he'd engaged Bryan in conversation and that Dan Sullivan and Paddy Doonan were gathering to listen, I dumped the bowl of potato chips on the picnic table and hurried down the stairs.

"And what do you think's gonna happen in *Saigon* when we pull out?" Ed asked. "I don't believe even Nixon's got all his cards straight on that one. This peace with honor is pure bullshit. The Vietcong are gonna sweep right in and set up shop. Then what? All those other countries'll fall just like a string of dominoes."

"And what exactly happens when they fall, Mr. Casey?" I wasn't fooled by Bryan's polite voice. I'd watched him debate enough times to know he'd plunge like a shark through the first opening in Ed Casey's argument.

"They become communist, that's what. Don't they teach you anything in the Ivy Leagues?" His condescending gaze included Ty Malone as well, who'd finished his first year at Yale. Other than Jay Piper and my father, the men there were not college graduates and harbored undisguised resentment for those children who were attending prestigious colleges. Lou Sullivan was a freshman at Staten Island Community College, Bud Doonan had been accepted at the police academy, and Ginny Conroy was going to nursing school. Suzie Casey had applied to Katie Gibbs; Ellen would be lucky to graduate from high school.

Bryan swirled his beer in a slow, calculated gesture. "What they *teach*, sir, is the truth about what the majority of Vietnamese people have been fighting for ever since the Indochina War began in 1946. Freedom from foreigners and puppet governments dependent upon other countries—the Japanese, the French, the Chinese, and now the United States."

"You got it all wrong, son. The South Vietnamese people asked for our help to fight communist aggression. We all know the Russians and Castro are supplying the Vietcong."

"The Vietcong are not all communists, Mr. Casey. Many of them are nationalists, many are Buddhists, or members of other oppressed religious groups. They take help wherever they can get it, just like the regime in South Vietnam."

Dan Sullivan leaned a freckled arm against the railing and pointed his highball glass at Bryan. "Doesn't sound to me, Bryan, as if you know who the enemy *is* over there."

I recognized my father's labored breathing as he padded up beside me. The vein in his neck was pumping noticeably, and his eyes had that vacant, floating cast that always made me think of poor Gregor Samsa waking up with a shell on his back.

Mike Cooper moved away from Fern and joined the ring of men closing in around Bryan. "This isn't a war like the one you fought over in Europe, Mr. Sullivan. I'm surprised not more of you are speaking out against it, those of you who've seen the horror of war yourselves."

I sighed as Charlie moved forward, stepping carefully down the stairs to the dock. Mike Cooper, a sophomore now at City College, was an even bigger pacifist than Bryan, and the two of them liked to cruise at night in the Chris-Craft, smoking pot and talking about the war.

"Horror?" Charlie asked. "What would you know about horror, sitting safe in your dormitory rooms while boys your own age are out there in the jungle trying to win a war that *nobody*—not the government, not you, not even the South Vietnamese—wants them to fight properly? You ask those men and women at Auschwitz and Dachau about horror. Ask the men who died at Pearl Harbor. Ask the boys who died in Da Nang last winter."

As the hoof tunneled deeper into my head, I bargained on Bryan's ability to see how plowed Charlie was. Then I noticed the bloodshot membranes in my brother's eyes and the tensile grip he had on the neck of his beer bottle. Charlie cut him off just as he opened his mouth to speak.

"You don't know a blessed thing about what it's like over there. You scoff at anybody in a uniform like it's some kind of disease. Demonstrating for Nixon to pull the plug on them. Oughtta send *him* into the jungle, send you *all* in, then you'll see what the Vietcong are like."

My mother slipped past me and up to Charlie, whose shirt she tugged gently. "Would you come upstairs, Charlie? We're all out of ice."

"What are they dying for, could you tell me that? You at least knew why you were there." Bryan's voice softened a notch in deference to my mother's anxious face.

Charlie shook his head. "It's not true. You go in there thinking you know, but you don't. In those moments when you're most certain you're going to die, you're only sure of two things: you've been given your orders and if you run they'll call you a coward."

"In our day," Dan Sullivan said, "you got the call and you went. None of this turning tail and running off to Canada. I lost a brother in the Coral Sea and a cousin in Korea. They were proud of serving in the military."

Lou Sullivan climbed out of the Chris-Craft and stood next to his father. "Well, if they call my number you better believe I'm going. You won't catch me burning my draft card."

"I'd serve only as a conscientious objector," Mike said. "I won't kill anybody, I can tell you that much."

"I don't know what I'd do," Jimmy said glumly.

"You mean you wouldn't go?" Terese asked.

"Of course he'd go," Jay Piper said. "No son of mine is going to burn his draft card or hightail it off to Canada."

Bryan sighed. "You talk as if it's so black and white, as if there's only one way to love my country."

Paddy Doonan elbowed past Dan Sullivan and waved one hand in front of Bryan's face. "I don't need a college education to know what it means to love my country. And I say some boys are cowards, no matter how well they talk."

"Hey," I said, moving onto the stairs, "that's not fair."

Bryan didn't flinch; his flinty gaze was locked on Paddy. My father gazed absently out at the lake, his arms hanging forlornly by his sides.

"That'll do, Paddy." I was glad for my mother's anger. She'd never liked Paddy Doonan or his son, but since my injury last summer, she had only contempt for them.

It wasn't Charlie's quiet voice that startled me; it was the eerie way his gaze floated over our heads. "It's hot in the jungle, hotter than you can imagine. And dark, things growing so close no sunlight gets through. Before you know it, you're knee-deep in mud, the water's climbing past your knees, your nuts are wet and cold, and that's when you forget where you are and imagine yourself back home. Then you hear this sound, a dull, quiet thud, not much really but you know exactly what it is. You try to move your legs faster, only there's so much sludge it's like slow motion. You can hear your breath rattling, the guy behind you moaning in terror because you don't know where it landed or how many there are and you can't move fast enough. There's this popping sound then, not as loud as you'd expect, and the man a few yards behind you is blasted onto the coiled black roots of some tree that grows there and he's jerking like a fish on a hook, his eyes rolled back, one leg gone, *dead* in a matter of seconds."

Nobody moved. Charlie blinked a few times, visibly trying to steady himself. My mother fumbled with her hands. Tim Kelly appeared between my father and brother and took Charlie's arm.

"Let's go upstairs, Charlie, and see about that ice."

Maybe it was the gentle way he spoke to my father, as you'd talk to a child or to someone who was really sick, but it snapped him back from wherever he'd been traveling. Charlie pulled his arm away, knocking my mother in the chin with his elbow.

"*You* see about the ice. Turn off that damn music while you're up there."

I don't remember who said what next, but Bryan was in the thick of it still. Mike nodded his head in assent, while beside him Jimmy hunkered in mute indecision under the disapproving eyes of his father. Tim Kelly had backed away from Charlie but remained on the steps, so I was relieved when Tommy Dorsey drifted down from the porch.

"I'd go to Canada before I'd go to Vietnam," Bryan said. "A guy on my floor at school has a brother who left last spring for Vancouver."

"That's the most yellow-bellied thing I've heard yet," Paddy Doonan snarled. "But what else can you expect coming from a school like that? Nothing but a bunch of drugged-up hippie nigger-lovers spitting on the flag. I don't know how your father puts up with it."

When the beer bottle bounced off the dock and my brother lunged forward, I pushed to the front of the circle. My mother and I were poised protectively, unsure where the biggest danger lay. I didn't think Bryan would hit Paddy Doonan, but he had raised his fist, and his jaw was locked.

"You're a *pig*, you know that? I don't know why my father invited you. Why don't you just take your fucking ass out of here?"

"Bryan!" Charlie's face flushed red. "You have no right to talk to Paddy that way. He's a friend of mine and a guest. I want you to apologize."

My brother's nostrils flared and he worked his mouth back and forth.

"*Apologize*! You gotta be kidding me. Apologize to *him*?"

Feet shuffled. Whispers disappeared in the ocean roaring around us. Charlie flung off my mother's fingers and gripped Bryan around the upper arm. His knuckles were white.

"*Yes*! Apologize to him."

No one knew what to say or where to look. My brother's face was riddled with contempt. I don't think he saw the glass breaking in my father's eyes, the plea louder than his rage. Bryan yanked his arm free and turned his back on Charlie. Dazedly I rubbed my forehead as my brother pressed through the crowd gathered at the railing and climbed the stairs to the house. The first drops of rain had fallen without notice, but now the rain swung like a curtain across the water and blurred the lines of the bridge. My first thought was to cover the Chris-Craft, but when I knelt down to lift the tarp out of the back, I heard the shouting from the house. I moaned, not at their voices, but at the pain inside my head.

Some of the women spoke to me as I stumbled up the stairs. I don't remember. They might have been saying good-bye or asking if I was all right. My father and brother had never yelled at each other like that, not even at the worst of times. The rain was falling hard now, and the tone of their voices made me think of water rising, swamping the garden and pushing through the screens. My mother stood beside them in the kitchen. I was aware of her fitful voice, her hands fluttering in the air.

234

"I don't care what your disagreements are!" Charlie shouted. "You don't talk to a friend of mine like that . . . " He was interrupted by a spasm of coughing.

"But he can talk to *me* anyway he wants, is that it? Why? Because he's old? That makes it OK for him to insult me?" Bryan laughed harshly. "You're a piece of work, you know that? You ever think that maybe you should be defending *me?*"

"Not when you talk like that to a guest in my house."

"What is this *guest* thing? What if he pulled a gun on me? I'm supposed to let him shoot just because he's a *guest* of yours?"

"Don't be ridiculous."

"Oh yeah, *who's* being ridiculous?"

It was the sneer in my brother's voice that made Charlie fairly boil with rage. "Dammit, Bryan! I told you to apologize."

"He doesn't deserve an apology. None of you do."

"I am your father, not some piece of *garbage!*" Charlie slammed his balled fist into the wall. "I'm sick of you treating me as if I'm some kind of criminal. What have I *done?* I don't mistreat you, do I? I don't ignore you. I don't put you down or treat you with disrespect, *do I?* So what the hell is your problem?"

"You don't get it, do you? I don't think you even remember it's been so long. Nothing matters to you anymore. That's why you keep drinking. How do you think that makes *us* feel?" His slow aspirations whistled as he struggled for control. "I used to really admire you. I used to think you knew *everything.* Even after you went back to the firm, you could have kept fighting. You had so much going for you. But you didn't, you just gave up. Take a look at yourself, Dad. Look at what you've become. I won't bring my friends from school here. I don't want them to know who you are now."

Bryan's face was splotched and wretched. My father's body sagged. Weakly he put up his hand, as if to defend himself.

Bryan whirled past me onto the porch and out the door. I heard his feet on the stairs, the rain falling, my mother's frightened "Bryan!" trailing after him.

I remember it now as a bolt of light, like the flashbulb of a camera exploding in my face, and then immediate, stupefying darkness. I shuffled onto the porch, where I smelled the rain, the stirred scent of the lake, the blast of gasoline as the Chris-Craft lurched backwards from the dock. By this time the hoof was beating with such frenzy against the inside of my skull that I looked down at the floor, convinced I'd see it there, the two halves of my head rocking like the split shell of a coconut.

But it was only the dock billowing on my brother's wake. I paced back and forth, drawn irresistibly to the north end of the porch where I pressed against the screen, unable to see any farther than the bridge. The pattering rain echoed the beating in my head and I knew, suddenly and with acute clarity, that something terrible was about to happen. I went back into the kitchen, where my father stood rooted to the linoleum. His face resembled the pumice my brother kept on a shelf underneath the house.

My mother extended a hand to me. "What's the matter? Look at me, Danny."

I couldn't. Only at him, although hard as I tried the words wouldn't come. I clung to his arms and squeezed, struggling so to speak that he focused, finally, blinking twice and furrowing his eyebrows.

"What is it?"

"Go after him," I said. "He's in trouble. I know he is. Something's going to happen."

"He'll be all right." My father sighed.

"You don't understand. Something's going to happen to him. I *feel* it. You have to go after him, right now, before it's too late."

Something in my tone or face touched him, for he glanced uncertainly toward the porch. Then he shrugged it off.

"You're imagining things. He needs to blow off steam, that's all."

It was like a sudden detonation erupting inside my head. "Go after him, *now*! He's going to hurt himself. I know it, I can feel it, something bad is going to happen. Please, Daddy, go. Go after him. *Go now!* Get in the boat. Now, Daddy, *now!*"

My father hesitated, gnawing his lip, then moved past me. Tim Kelly appeared by the railing of the deck and called out to him. Charlie climbed into the small fishing boat without answering, pull-started the engine, and steered toward the bridge. Nini and Terese stepped out from the side of the potting shed where they'd been standing under the underhang of the roof and watched the boat until it disappeared from sight. May placed one hand against the screen. The sight of her hand occasionally comes back to me now, her papery skin the same ashen color as the water.

Terese told me later how she followed me onto the bridge. "I stood right next to you," she said, "but you didn't see me. You kept staring out at the water, not saying a word. Your face was all tight and pale, just like it was after the accident. It was raining so hard and we could hear the sound of a motor. You knew, didn't you?"

No, I didn't. I only knew the danger he was in, the image of his relentless face above the wheel. It took forever before I could make out the little boat beside the five-mile-per-hour buoy. It was moving so slowly. The wood was cold beneath my hands. When he was closer, I saw my father's head sunk slightly forward, one hand on the throttle. Then I saw what looked like a dark blanket on the bottom of the boat, only it wasn't a blanket at all, it was my brother's blue-jeaned legs. Terese cried out suddenly, for she saw the top part of his body at the same time I did. *He's sleeping. He looks like he does in the morning.*

My mother was rushing down the stairs when I landed on my knees at the edge of the dock. Bryan was curled up, one arm over his head, the other resting by his side. His ponytail had come loose and I reached involuntarily to pull the blonde hair out of the water.

"Don't," my father said.

His eyes fell on me, and my whole body went suddenly still.

"Charlie." My mother's eyes were huge, perfectly round. Nini put an arm around her waist.

"He's gone, May."

Gone. Not a drop of blood on him. His lashes made tiny brushstrokes on his cheeks. There was no bone showing, nothing broken or twisted. *No wound anywhere.* I touched the palest part of his cheek just below the lashes and it was warm. *He's right here . . . sleeping.*

Nini prodded me back from the edge, as Tim and my father lifted Bryan and laid him gently on the dock. His head flopped sideways. My mother shook her head. Then she knelt beside him and put her two hands on either side of his face, studying him as you do a newborn child. Nini sobbed when my mother pitched forward, draping herself across his chest. My father flinched at the unearthly, keening sound she made and turned his head toward the wall of gray rain between us and the beach. *He isn't out there. He's here, right here. Sleeping.*

Time passed. An ambulance came. Charlie helped the two attendants raise my mother, and she sat slumped against Nini. The older man examined Bryan's body. "What was he doing?" he asked gravely.

When my father started to speak, I saw it—the only wound visible—there in the dark cone of his eyes. He spoke slowly. "The Chris-Craft was up on the rocks at Rock Island. He'd been thrown onto the bottom of the boat. There wasn't . . . " His hand shook as he passed it in front of his eyes. "There wasn't any pulse when I checked him."

"Was he taking drugs?" the attendant asked.

"Only marijuana," I said, "a couple of reefers is all."

"Did he crash?" Tim asked doubtfully. *No blood, no bruise, no wound anywhere.*

Charlie shook his head. "A man came over in a boat. He lives right on the lake near Rose's Beach. He saw Bryan from his front porch. He said Bryan was driving around and around in a circle making big waves. One minute Bryan was standing up, the next he disappeared from sight. Soon after that the Chris-Craft went right into the island."

"Was he hit by lightning?" Nini asked.

The attendant shook his head. "It's possible that he popped up and down so fast, so forcefully, that he severed the spinal cord. It's a freak thing of course, but when you mentioned the waves . . . . They'll have to X-ray him to know for sure."

I peered over his shoulder at the distorted angle of my brother's head. His lower lip was the color of a ripe plum. The wind rustled his hair, and I could see his face and the whipping white sail of his shirt. I could see the boat hurtling through the waves, and his chin jiggling up and down. The second attendant pulled a sheet over him. My father and Tim followed the stretcher across the rocks to the steps by Maudie McDonough's house, the shortest route to the road.

Terese and her parents stayed and tried to help. Other people came, but I didn't see them. Nini and Terese cleaned up the kitchen and offered us food. No one wanted to eat. My mother lay on her bed with her face to the wall. Tim went with my father to make certain arrangements. Someone from O'Leary's Home for Funerals in Westfield would drive to Sparta General and take the body. Father Burns wanted to come up, but my father said no. Terese phoned and spoke to Frieda Gland.

I remember standing on the threshold of my brother's room. There were mounds of clothes on the floor, books and newspapers, sneakers. I could catch the faint smell of marijuana. I pulled his pillow from the bed and held it to my chest: balsam wood, hair oil, and dusty flannel. Still holding the pillow, I climbed onto the top bunk and searched through the bedclothes. I wasn't doing this for a reason. It was more automatic than that, like the way Bryan used to sleepwalk straight to the toilet and pee without opening his eyes.

The notebook was a journal, dated at the top left-hand corner of each page. I went right to the last entry, the one he'd been writing this morning. He'd held the pen just so, in his right hand. I ran my palm across the paper, awash in the incomprehensible lessons of that day. His smell was still in the room, he'd written *this* just hours ago. He'd been standing at the wheel of the boat, and then a few minutes later he was gone, not a mark on him. *I am never going to see him again.*

Each time I woke during the night Terese leaped up from the other bed. Her hair smelled like strawberries. Nini slept in my father's bed next to my mother. The ever-present sound of weeping emanated from all corners of the house. Once I wandered into the living room, Terese behind me, and saw Tim sitting next to my father on his cot. His shoulders were hunched and his head hung level with his knees. Tim's hand was in the hollow of my father's back, and he was talking softly.

In the gray morning, when Terese was finally too deep in sleep to hear, I got up again. My mother stood beside the bunkbed, her forehead against Bryan's mattress. She was weeping, deep, breathless heaves that tore me to the quick. When I lay my hand across hers, she gripped my fingers and wept even harder. There is no bottom to this kind of pain. You think you'll wake up and something will have changed, but it doesn't.

*

When I left the room at O'Leary's Home for Funerals where Bryan was, I headed toward the back door. I noticed crabapple trees through the window, fresh air, sunlight. From a room to the left of the door came a long shuddery sob. Inching round the doorframe, I peered in. The walls and carpet were a deep maroon color. *Thank God he has the blue one.* Carline was folded over at the far end of the room, her long arms crisscrossing her chest.

When she'd arrived earlier that afternoon with her mother and Marilyn, I'd bolted for the ladies' room, unable to watch.

240

That first viewing—the waxy profile, the hands, the groomed husk of a face—it's another of those passages that change you forever. You have no choice but to navigate the crossing as sanely as you can, but something inside you has been extinguished.

Carline was wearing a short, navy blue sheath with navy textured stockings. At the sound of my voice, she glanced up. I was surprised at the swift response of my own tears. *The wounds are everywhere.* In the blue room my brother lay in his body, unrecognizable to me. The rest of us had been transformed, this new knowledge imprinted on our faces like a tattoo. I plucked a Kleenex from the ever-ready box next to the red couch and swiped at the ink blots under her eyes.

"You shouldn't have worn makeup," I said.

She was a good two inches taller than I, and she had to bend down to rest her forehead against mine. We lay our hands on the other's shoulders, forming a bridge with our arms. It was the first time since that night at the fireworks that I could remember touching Carline. It felt good, knowing how much my brother had loved her. I don't know when exactly Terese entered the room or what she thought when she saw us, but she piled in with her freckled arms, making muted, catlike sounds in answer to Carline's weeping.

We were bound together for life, the three of us, like it or not, these girls who had loved my brother no less powerfully than I had. I let go my arms when my mother marched into the room, her face hidden behind an armful of plastic ferns.

"Mom, what are you doing?"

She tossed them onto the couch. "I specifically told Jack O'Leary there were to be no artificial flowers. They had them hanging right over the coffin."

I brushed the dust from the ferns off her black jacket. She sighed deeply and left. Later, when visiting hours were over and Charlie had driven off with Jack O'Leary to see about a cemetery plot, I followed my mother as she made a circuit of the room, examining the little cards on each arrangement. I thought she was simply noting, like I was, who had sent flowers.

"You'd think they'd send something better than that," she said, her mouth pursed.

"What's the matter with it?" It was a big arrangement, lots of yellow and blue.

"Look at it, it's all carnations. Paradise Floral gets the commission every year to plant the island in front of City Hall, too. Shaffnit's isn't much better. Look at that red one over there, *anybody* could have done it. Now, *here's* a nice one. It must have come from somebody's garden." She held up the card. "Marcella Dove. That's odd . . . was she here?"

"I didn't see her. Maybe Marilyn brought them."

She looked at me quizzically. "They know each other," I said, "Marilyn and Marcella Dove. She must have sent them because I'm friends with Billy . . . you know."

She nodded and walked over to the coffin. We stood for a few minutes looking down at him. "It's solid mahogany." She ran a finger along the dark wood. She had to take hold of her hand then, balling one trembling fist into the other.

"If I could only change places with him," she whispered. "I'd give my whole life just to have him back for a few minutes."

I felt the same way. I was angry at him for leaving, angry that I was the one left behind. I wondered what I could have done differently, searching my memory for every word I said to him on that final day. My parents' guilt was unbearable. It colored the rest of their lives, although I don't think Bryan would have wanted it to be so. It was my brother's hand, after all, on the wheel. He was the one who stirred up that wavepool, who loved the bucking wet thrill it gave him.

Carline cried all through the funeral service and would not come to the grave. I was not surprised at the number of people in the church: former teachers, coaches, Boy Scout leaders, the high-school librarian, men he'd worked with at the boat works, students from Columbia I'd never met, the men and women from my father's office, the staff at the florist's, friends from as far back as I can remember. Jimmy and Mike Cooper helped me choose the music, which the priest allowed and my father didn't seem to hear. He was numb with grief and the debilitating pangs of alcohol withdrawal.

Once the headstone was in place, I went with my mother every morning to plant the grave. Mostly I watched as she turned over the soil and dug holes for the multitude of bulbs and flowering shrubs. It was a pretty, grassy spot on a knoll by a small pond. I was comforted that he was near water. When it filled out, the garden was spectacular and became quite an attraction in the cemetery. My mother tended it daily, stopping at the cemetery on her way home from work. She kept an extra set of gardening tools and gloves in the trunk of her car.

My parents did not return to Rainy that summer. The lake didn't frighten me; I had no interest in apportioning blame. Yet there was something about my father's mute misery and my mother's bouts of weeping that crushed me. I could do nothing for them and felt even lonelier in their presence. They sensed my discomfort, and in their bewilderment and grief took it as a judgement upon them, which is why they let me go back to Rainy by myself.

I packed my brother's things into boxes, and spent long afternoons fly-fishing in the channel or on the Virgin River. I did my laps every morning and occasionally swam out to the bridge to sit on the ledge. Sometimes I lay on the lower deck and contemplated the splintered prow of the Chris-Craft, which bobbed serenely alongside the dock. The chrome-plated hardware along the front was badly dented, and in several places in the hull, planks had been split by the impact and pro-truded like broken bones.

I thought about Bud Doonan's boat circling over my head, the blood spurting from my arm, my brother standing at the wheel one minute and dead the next, not a mark on him. He'd severed his spinal cord, the coroner said. What were the odds of such a thing happening, one in a million maybe? I read through his journal page by page, committing the words to memory. I took his pajamas and bundled them inside a plastic bag, placing it in the drawer next to Billy's letters. Whenever I unrolled the bag and shook them out, I could smell him: balsam wood, hair oil, and dusty flannel.

Terese drove up regularly to visit, carrying books and containers full of macaroni salad. "I can't concentrate," I told her. "I can't taste anything, either. Tell your mother not to bother." She sat beside me on the porch swing and read aloud chapters from *To Kill a Mockingbird*. Her steady voice was the only shelter from the darkness that periodically swept over me. Harper Lee must have had a brother to be able to write about Scout and Gem that way, and if so, I've wondered often how he coped with Harper Lee's untimely death. Terese chided me about how thin and tired I looked. "This better be gone the next time I come," she said, spooning the macaroni salad onto a plate. I had to throw most of it away to honor my promise.

On one of those afternoons, when she'd tired of reading and had rested the book on her bare knees, I turned to her, surprising both of us with the suddenness with which I blurted out the words:

"The condom in the box you saw?"

She gaped at me, confused.

"The day of the party when we were in my room, you opened my special box . . . "

"Yes?"

"It doesn't belong to Larry Salinger. It's Billy's. And the motel I told you about was the Byram. It was Billy Dove I was with, not Larry."

Terese blinked. *The thing about death is that it makes everything else inconsequential.*

"You slept with him?"

I nodded.

She made an odd, whistling sound. "Do you love him?"

"Yes, I do."

"Does he love you?"

"I'm not sure. It's been a long time. I don't think he's going to come home from Vietnam the same person."

Terese smiled sadly. "Well, you won't be either. Small comfort, huh?"

*

Word went round that Angie had left Wade and was working part-time in the store, so I decided to pay a visit. It was a shock when I saw her behind the counter, for she'd cut off her long brown hair. The boyish hairstyle made her seem different, alien and slightly unformed, as if she'd just arrived from a foreign country.

"A chocolate malt," I said.

I was still uncomfortable with the way people avoided the subject or stuttered through a lengthy condolence, so it was a relief when Angie handed me the malt and said soberly, without dropping her eyes, "I'm real sorry about your brother, Danny."

She told me, after I asked, that she'd filed for divorce from Wade.

"It's my own fault," she said. "I never should have married him."

"Are you still working at the nursing home?"

She nodded. "They cut my hours, though. I just got an apartment in Neptune, so I'm working here to earn some extra money. My mother can use the help."

I gazed at her long, slender fingers as she wiped the countertop with a checkered dish towel. "You think you'll stay here long?"

"I'd like to go back to college and get my degree, maybe go to med school. I don't know how I'd afford it, though."

"Couldn't you apply for a scholarship?"

"Maybe." She hesitated a minute. "How are your parents doing? I haven't seen them up since . . . "

"It's easier on them if they stay at home. They blame themselves for it." I sighed. "Everything's different now."

245

"I can understand." She looked at me kindly. "You be good to yourself, Danny."

The malt tasted like rubber, but I drank it anyway. Sighing again, I wondered whether her real father, Vincent Fanelli, had died of a disfiguring wound or some single gunshot that no one could see. I left a dollar tip on the counter and walked across the parking lot and into the darkened kitchen of the lodge, where I asked Arlene, the girl working there, for a bag of french fries. They were forty cents a bag now. When I bit into one and couldn't taste anything, I started to cry. I stumbled across the tracks to the clubhouse and leaned against the window ledge of the girls' bathroom. Carline had carved her name and Bryan's in the web of hearts and initials on the log wall. Once I'd made it past the spillway, I curled up in the shade and listened to the buzz of motors on the lake.

Larry Salinger drove up to see me but I sent him away. Maybe later, I told him, when I can talk about what happened. Carline appeared unannounced some nights and took me with her for long, meandering drives along Tamarack Road. She didn't say much when I told her about Billy, although I caught her studying me at times, as if she thought there might be something else she'd missed.

"What are you going to do now?" she asked one night as we sat on my dock and counted the swooping bats, flaring infrared as they bisected the blinking red Ballantine sign.

"What do you mean?"

"Are you thinking about college?"

"You sound just like Bryan."

"He wanted you to go away to a good school."

"You talked about it with him?"

"We talked about everything."

"I haven't even thought about it."

"Can I say something?"

"No."

She smiled. "I never had a brother, and my father's an asshole. I always figured that if somebody in my family was going to make it, it might as well be me. I didn't actually consider Marilyn . . . you know, that she'd make it first or she'd make it instead."

"I don't know what you're talking about, Carline."

She sighed. "Bryan would have become something really wonderful, everybody knew that. He was afraid that your family pinned too many of their hopes on *him,* and that you didn't seem to mind."

"I didn't."

"Well, that worried him. He thought you and your parents should pin some on you."

"That's ridiculous."

"All I'm saying, Danny, is that you could be . . . well, you could go right to the top, with your brains and the way you *see* things. Bryan never wanted to stand in your way . . . "

"He didn't!"

"I know. It's just that he's gone now. There's only you. You have to become something, for both your sakes."

It took a long time before I stopped crying. She stayed with me, and before she left I showed her where the bats were flying in.

"You want to sleep at my house?" she asked.

"I don't mind them," I said. "They've been here longer than I have."

*

The afternoons and early evenings in the channel passed like quicksilver through my fingers. After my laps I'd go back to bed and sleep through the sunniest part of the day. I drew the curtains and buried my sore eyes in the pillow, not minding the heat. I preferred the waning brightness of this interlude between afternoon and twilight. The lake became noisier and more agitated around dinnertime as boats returned home. Voices carried across the water; I heard the hum of cars on the road. Then, gradually, the water settled smooth and gray.

247

Silence fell, except for the sough of weeds and cattails, the plink of fish feeding on the surface.

My loops unfurled like transparent wings, and when a fish took my fly and dove, I worked him patiently back to the boat. It always took me by surprise when I caught a fish—his tenacious weight and cryptic eyes, the final acquiescence after he'd ceased thrashing and sagged helplessly in the net. I breathed easier once I'd let him go, lingering over the slow slithering-away of his tail.

One night, as the shadows loomed thick and furry along the shoreline, I putted through the channel into Disappointment and tied up to Billy's dock. Many nights I'd drifted in the boat waiting for the lights to blink on and her silhouette to appear behind the curtains.

Marcella Dove's forehead crinkled as she peered at me. "Come in!" she said.

She dropped sprigs of fresh mint into a pot of tea and sat across from me, folding her coffee-colored arms on the oak table. I thanked her for the flowers.

She nodded. "I'm sorry I couldn't come myself. I phoned Billy, you know, and we talked about me going. Louis, that's my brother, was worried about my car. The transmission's been giving me trouble."

"You actually talked to Billy?"

"There's a number they give you for family emergencies. I had to wait for him to call me back."

I shook my head. "I had no idea you could talk to him over there."

"It isn't easy, I'll say that. He said he's going to write you." She put her hand over mine. "I'm real sorry, Danny, for your family. I know what it's like to lose someone."

I sighed. "My parents blame themselves, I'm sure of it."

"That's the way of it and it makes no sense. The Lord gives and the Lord takes away. It's the sad truth."

"My father hasn't had a drink since it happened. I don't know that it's going to matter all that much."

"Sure it will. It's a start, isn't it? You just got to get through the days any way you can. Sooner or later things will get lighter . . . it's the way life is. Nature abhors a vacuum, you know? You won't ever forget but you'll get beyond it." She poured tea into yellow-petaled china cups.

"I'm not sure I understand what's happening with Billy."

"What do you want to know?"

I hesitated. "He talks a lot about being black or white. I keep thinking he's trying to tell me something but I'm not sure what it is. I just don't think that way about Billy."

"What way?"

"About what color he is."

"Maybe he wants you to think about it."

"Why?"

She lay her hands out flat on the oak table and studied them; her fingers were long and tapered like Billy's. "Being white you don't *have* to think about it. That's a privilege most white folks don't understand. Billy doesn't have a choice. I think he wants you to see that."

She paused a minute, considering. "I came here with my family from Mississippi. My people are all Negroes; I grew up that way. But Billy and his brother, they've lived their whole lives in a white community. They see themselves as different, but not necessarily as *black*. Me being lighter-skinned and their daddy white, it was easy. In the Navy Billy's meeting lots of other black men, even mixed boys like him. It's important for him to understand who he *is*."

"Does it mean he won't want to be with me anymore because I'm white?"

She looked at me kindly. "I can honestly say that you're the first girl Billy ever cared that strongly for. I could tell by the end of last summer. It's just that you're both so young, you're not really formed yet. He's not going to be the same person when he comes home. He won't see the two of you the way he did before he left."

"I wish he would. I don't want it to be different."

249

"But you *are* different; it doesn't mean you can't care about each other."

"I still don't . . . "

"Look, Danny, you have parents who own two homes and intend for you to go to college. You live on a lake where they don't even allow black people in the club."

"But *I* don't agree with that."

"It's your background, whether you agree with it or not. I think what Billy's asking is that you think about what it means to be white in this country, that's all. Then try to imagine what it means to be someone who's *not* white."

What it means to be white. Gone, not a wound anywhere.

I sighed, feeling the heat from the tea on my forehead. We sat for a while in silence. The boat knocked against the dock; insects whined. I fought the urge to lay my head against her shoulder.

"The sun hurts my eyes, so I sleep during the day. It's not that awful then, waking up. During the night if I get tired I'll nap on the couch. The worst thing is waking up in the morning." I shook my head. "Everything is so empty, like you're falling through outer space with no hope of ever landing."

She pushed up from the table, walked into the kitchen, and returned with a dried flower which she lay beside my cup. "It's a passionflower. See the crown in the center? It represents the crown of thorns worn by Jesus, and these five stamens refer to his five wounds. I've always found it a comfort that when they rolled back the rock, He was *gone.*" She handed me a small burlap bag. "Take this. Add one teaspoon to a cup of tea, and make sure the water's boiling. It'll help you to sleep."

"Come any time," she called after me as I climbed into the boat.

The moon was so bright I didn't need a flashlight. I trolled lazily, gazing up at the purple edges of trees and the innumerable stars. I searched the sky for a sign—a shooting comet, a falling star, a constellation in the shape of his face. As I reached the big middle of the lake, I cut the engine and coasted. This was where I felt closest to him, not in his room, his life stacked up in boxes against the wall, not at his grave or in the Chris-Craft or with Carline or Terese or my parents, but here where he'd passed over. It had taken one swift moment for him to disappear, and nothing afterwards would ever be the same.

I understood then that if it could happen to my brother, it could happen to anyone—my parents and friends, *me*. It was terrible knowing this, and yet I took comfort in my brother's solo journey, which paved the way so to speak, leaving behind the faint glow of his passage.

RECOVERY (1970)

I HEARD THAT BILLY WAS BACK FROM SUZIE CASEY, who cruised into Dottie's Cake Box in Neptune right before closing. She pleaded in her whiny voice for a dozen day-old jelly doughnuts, although she knew full well that the Sisters from Our Lady of Perpetual Hope were due any minute to pick up the leftovers. I might have missed the name *Billy Dove* altogether if she hadn't hesitated half a second and then raised her voice slightly when she said it, in the same way kids had been doing for years whenever they mentioned the Doves.

"Ninety-six cents," I said, plopping the bag on the glass counter.

"You got any damaged layer cakes in the back?" she asked.

I put my hands on my hips, blocking the doorway. "You know as well as I do, Suzie, that we donate the damaged food on Friday night to the Sisters so they can distribute it . . . "

"And *you* know there's a note from Frank hanging right there that says employees can take food that hasn't or can't be sold. I work the Friday shift same as you, Danny, so don't pretend you know something I don't. I'd like a chocolate one."

I stomped into the back and mashed the cake into the side of the box before tying it up.

"That'll be another $1.89 for the cake."

"Half price, Danny."

"OK, $1.91 total."

"Coming to the Tamarack later?"

"Maybe."

"Well, see ya then." She picked up the bag and headed for the door.

"How'd you know about Billy?" I asked.

253

"Ginny saw him this afternoon in Sal and Joey's. He was in his uniform. Aside from the fact that he's wearing his hair in an Afro, he looks really good. That's what Ginny said, but then she's *always* liked him."

I refigured the totals in my cash drawer and wiped the countertops with ammonia one last time. The Sisters chattered softly as they packed loaves of bread into paper bags. Sister Regina beamed when I handed her a box of miniature Danish pastries and a lopsided marble layer cake.

"Sister Anne Eucharia has a hankering for the lemon cheesecake if you could manage that next week."

"I'll do what I can, Sister," I said.

After they'd driven off in the convent's beige station wagon, I retrieved my bag from behind the cash register, locked both doors, and left. I yearned for a pastrami sandwich or a dill pickle to counteract the smell of dried chocolate, raspberry jelly, and sugared icing smeared across my white uniform. When I came to the Byram Motel, I sped by without a glance. I hadn't written Billy in over four months. Why should I? *He* was the one who'd re-enlisted for another three years, after trying to convince me it was safe out there. He'd been promoted to airman mechanic second class, he said, he was just furthering his education, like me, and seeing the world the way he wanted. What was the problem?

The *problem* was that Billy was sure to end up a casualty, or sure to marry someone else, someone who was part black or all black or part some other color, a woman who'd understand him better than I ever could. He'd be right about that, too, which didn't make it any easier. With Larry Salinger I was at least standing on solid ground. He was fun to be with and trustworthy and the most accomplished boy poet I knew. Plus, we had things in common—both of us white and middle class, bound for college in September. So what if I went through the motions with a numb disinterest whenever he parked his father's Mustang behind the bleachers in Woolsey Park? Each time he touched me it was as if it were happening to somebody else. I was wrapped in a caul-like membrane that muted color and made all sensations seem flat and faraway. I didn't mind. It was an improvement over the tunnel I'd been pitched into the day Bryan died. After dating Larry Salinger for six months, I was sure of two things: he was the best I could hope for, and there'd be no falling through empty space when it was over.

"You're a coward," Terese told me, "and it isn't fair to Larry. The guy's nuts about you."

"Oh yeah? What about Jimmy Piper?"

"At least I had the decency to break up with Jimmy when I didn't love him anymore."

"Well, that's what I'm doing with Billy."

"That's pure horseshit and you know it. You're breaking up with him because you're scared, plain and simple. And you're taking Larry Salinger for a ride."

"Well, he's not complaining. Besides, he's going to Syracuse in the fall. He'll forget all about me."

"Right, just like you've forgotten about Billy."

When I reflected on it, I could admit I wasn't being fair to Larry, even if I believed he'd known all along and wanted me anyway. Thinking about September eased my conscience. We'd all be going our separate ways then: Larry to Syracuse, me to the University of Michigan, Billy to Barcelona and Athens and a hundred other exotic places.

As the Rainy Lake Lodge approached on my left, I slowed down for a better view of the parking lot. There across the lake was my mother perched on the edge of the dock in her pink bathing suit. Charlie had sold the Chris-Craft last winter, and I still buckled with sadness each time I saw the stacked-up sawhorses on Maudie McDonough's patio.

I parked the Fiat next to the Palone's Florist van, which had SAY IT WITH FLOWERS written in pink swirly letters on the side. The living room smelled of the chemicals my mother and I had been painting on the logs to slow the insect infestation. The bare bookshelves gave me a jolt, even though I'd been the one packing the books. I'd chosen the few I wanted and was boxing up the rest. My mother had taken two of the rocking chairs and the big braided rug into the shop. The rest of the furniture would stay with the house. "Why not?" May said. "It's in good condition and we certainly don't want it."

I took the plateful of tuna casserole warming in the oven, threw on a handful of potato chips, and headed down toward the dock. Mike Cooper lifted his burly shoulders from the band saw and smiled broadly when I handed him two poppy-seed Danish pastries.

"What do you think?" he motioned toward the slatted roof on the pergola.

"Looks good," I said. "What are you going to do about the color?"

The lower deck, which my father had bleached and sealed after he'd finished it years ago, was a light sandy gray. The wood on the top deck had weathered irregularly, creating streaks of light and dark.

"Your mother said I should go ahead and bleach and seal this part. It's not a very good match, but she said it won't matter."

As carefully and efficiently as he worked, Mike was no carpenter. He simply couldn't do the detailing and expert finishing my father had done on the lower deck. Since my mother was trying to finish the deck with minimal expense, she'd asked Mike to buy a cheaper cedar than the number three my father had used for the lower deck. The knots were everywhere, as were the dents Mike had made hammering in the galvanized headed nails. "They'll rust," I told May, remembering my father's lecture on the virtue of aluminum nails. "You wouldn't plant your rock garden with all marigolds, would you?"

"They won't rust right away," she said. "By then we won't have to worry about it."

Mike leaned against the picnic table and eyed me curiously.

"What?" I said.

"Guess who was here looking for you a while ago?"

"Who?" I felt a sudden lurch, as if a trap door had opened and dropped me into open air.

"Billy Dove, all dressed up in his Navy uniform."

"Is that a sneer on your face or did something die inside the Danish I just gave you?"

"It pisses me off, seeing him parading around in that uniform, that's all."

"I don't guess he was parading around, Mike. He probably just got home."

"So what's he doing *here* if he just got home?"

"He's a friend of mine. He might have wanted to say hello."

"I just don't like these guys acting like they own the world . . . "

"Cut it out. How many returning vets do you know, anyway? Seems to me they're doing a lot more hiding out than showing off with all the crap they have to swallow from people like you."

"Listen, anybody who'd enlist for Vietnam's got his head screwed on backwards."

"What a narrow little world you live in, Mike."

"Look who's talking, Miss Bakery Queen."

He plucked a globule of chocolate from the front of my uniform and flicked it over the railing. I poked him in the ribs with my elbow as my mother swam slowly toward the ladder. "I swear, Mike, sometimes you sound just like Bryan."

When he sighed, I was sorry I'd said it. Those moments were not so frequent then, moments when the present stalled and you hurtled back to your former life. I wondered if my brother would be as tall as Mike, if he'd have a ponytail tied back with a piece of leather, or hair sprouting like new grass on his tanned chest.

"Hand me the towel, would you, Danny?" The lavender dome of my mother's bathing cap appeared at the ladder, and she puffed lightly as she pulled herself up and stood dripping on the dock.

257

I followed her to the patio where we sat on folding chairs alongside a sheaf of purple iris. She peeled off the bathing cap and shook her short curly hair. It was peppered with gray, and without makeup the skin beneath her eyes resembled the fine sheets of filo dough the baker used for strudel.

"Mike's almost done," she said.

"I know." I handed her the bakery bag with two cinnamon crullers. "Is Dad coming up?"

She closed her eyes as she bit into one. "We'll see. I think we ought to paint the kitchen, spruce it up a bit."

My father had only come up a few weekends this summer. In June my mother had met with the realtors, had the house appraised, and hired Mike Cooper, who could hammer two pieces of wood together and was looking for work. She spent her weekends painting and packing; she was determined to get a good price for the house.

"I'm done for the day, Mrs. Fillian. You want me to work tomorrow?"

"Sure, Mike . . . you should pick up more stain in Neptune."

"Coming over to the Tamarack, Danny?"

"I don't think so."

"We'll all be there if you change your mind."

As he walked across the bridge, my mother's gaze lingered on his departing back, his shoulders broad as Bryan's. "Why don't you go, Danny? It'll do you good to get out."

"I get out every day, Mom."

"I'm talking about fun, not work."

I shrugged. "Maybe later."

"I hear she's going back to college." My mother pointed toward the back of Sal and Joey's, where Angie was leaning against a windowsill smoking a cigarette. A few yards away her brother Nick hung onto the pier while Joseph swung back and forth from a black cable.

I nodded. "She's been working all year, saving her money. She wants to become a doctor."

258

"Joey'll sure miss her."

"She taught me how to do a flip turn," I said.

"She did? I never knew that."

"She never should have married Wade."

My mother chipped away at the red fingernail polish on her thumbnail. "There's so much to consider when you marry someone. It shouldn't be done in haste."

"I don't put much store in marriage . . . " I shook my head.

"What are you talking about? What's better, living with someone? That's not commitment, Danny. What if you have children?"

"I see so many unhappy people."

"No one said being married was easy. If you have problems, you have to . . . "

"Work them out? So what about you, why can't you and Dad do that?"

She sighed.

"You could get help, like Mr. and Mrs. Kelly did. Terese said the counselor did wonders for her parents."

When my mother looked at me, I read her regret on my account and something else brimming beyond words—fear, I suppose. What was she afraid of? What could she possibly reveal to a counselor that would be harder on my father than what he'd carried with him since Bryan died?

"Do you still love him?" I asked.

She blinked, startled at the question. "Of course I do. It's not that simple, Danny. I just have to be patient."

"What are you waiting for?"

"You make a promise when you get married—for better or for worse, in sickness and in health, until death do us part. Your father's . . . well, it's like he's lost somewhere. I am too, I guess. But we'll get through it—we just need time."

"How much time?"

"I don't know." She said it simply, with resignation.

I intended to lie down for a few minutes, but when I woke, it was almost dark. I showered and changed, deciding to go

259

out after all. My mother was rocking gently on the porch swing, absorbed in her sorrowful gaze at the silica surface of the lake. Voices ehoed off the water, and cigarettes flared like fireflies from the end of the bridge. I could smell the paint and newly sawed cedar.

I touched her lightly on the shoulder. "I won't be late."

She nodded absently. Those long, flat months after I'd returned home from the lake, she'd drifted into my room several times a night. Since she couldn't talk about her feelings regarding my brother, I assumed she was making sure I was still there. I understood her fear, the same fear I had that no one I loved was safe: every time the phone rang after ten o'clock at night, every time my mother was late coming home from work, every time my father rubbed his left arm or put his hand on his chest. "The pain isn't physical," the doctor told him. "Your heart's fine." My father disagreed and I believed him, understanding the fine line between mental and physical suffering.

One night late in the winter, I'd reared up from the dinner table and pitched my plate across the kitchen. It shattered against the toaster oven. My parents jerked simultaneously, pulled like fish out of water, and stared at me with alarm.

"OK," I said, trying not to sound too shrill. "He's gone. He's never coming back. But guess what? *I'm still here.* I'm not invisible and I'm not dead. I've got a pile of college applications sitting on my desk. I have important decisions to make. So I'd appreciate it if you'd snap out of it and give me some help."

They sat down after dinner and read through the New Jersey applications. My mother's salary would pay most of the costs at a state college; I could have my pick, and live on campus at any of them.

The second folder I handed them held the *other* applications: Penn State, Boston University, the University of Michigan, Berkeley, the University of Oregon.

"I want to go to one of these," I said, "if I get in."

"We can't afford these, Danny," my mother said.

"I'll apply for financial aid, and I'll get a job on campus. I'll work every summer."

"They're so far away . . ."

"It's *what I want*."

She bit her lip and leafed through the financial aid forms. My father scrutinized me for a long minute.

"I don't think you should borrow too much. You'll probably want to go on to graduate school," he said.

"Graduate school?" my mother looked up, surprised.

"She may decide to become a lawyer."

"I don't want to be a lawyer," I said.

"Or politics, you might run for office someday."

"I don't . . ."

"I'm just saying *what if* . . . you don't want to burn all your bridges at once, do you?" He turned to my mother. "We'll sell the house at the lake. That way Danny can go where she wants, and you can buy your share of the business from Frank Palone when he retires next winter."

My mother's eyes flickered toward him and then retreated. She was looking for an excuse, just like he was. They'd already decided that they could not live there again. Rainy Lake threatened the fragile control they'd achieved, threatened their ability to concentrate, to work, to get through the day without falling into that bottomless well again.

I was the only one who had resisted selling the house. I'd made peace with the tragedy without it impinging upon the place itself. I still drew sustenance from the lake, although I understood why my parents couldn't. There were moments, no matter where I was, when all noise and motion ceased, and I was on the water. I could smell fish and bark and gasoline, hear metal clinking against wood and feet batting across the bridge, see my brother's blonde head bent over the Chris-Craft. I could see Billy's hands extricating a hook from deep inside a fish, the light dying over the middle of the lake, the patient stars.

"We won't sell unless you agree," my mother said.

I applied to ten schools. The acceptance letters surprised me, although the counselor said my class rank had shot up and my essay was the finest she'd ever read. Sometimes, as the three of us sat around the kitchen table, their earnest faces inches away, I was overwhelmed by the complexity of our lives. I was just beginning to understand the flip side of tragedy, the gifts available for those capable of taking them. My father was sober for the first time in years; he'd even quit smoking. He'd resigned himself to staying at the firm and no longer complained about his clients or his partners' inferior design skills. My mother and he had united in their acute desire to see me happy. Yet, when left on their own, they sleepwalked through the days without more than a few sentences passing between them. The rancor had dissipated and so, too, had any spark remaining of the two people who'd wandered the gardens of the Alhambra together or who'd stood head to head over my father's drafting table, when their dreams were as real as the common language they shared.

I decided on the University of Michigan and told my parents matter-of-factly that they could put the house on the market. Some instinct claiming the future over the past had bubbled up out of a deep, hitherto unknown part of me. I'd realized that I needed to set myself free from my parents and the allure of trying to save them. Shortly afterward, Billy's letter arrived with the news that he'd re-enlisted. His next tour of duty would be the French Riviera. It was possible that he'd be sent back to Vietnam after that, but by then he was sure the war would be over. As I fingered the tissue-thin airmail letter, I thought it must be a sign. *These pieces of you, when they're taken, do they ever grow back? Are they replaced with something else?*

A new pack of kids had claimed the end of the bridge near the railroad tracks. They were mostly fourteen and fifteen with familiar last names: Hogan, Smith, Sullivan, Conroy, Casey. On Saturday mornings I sat on the clubhouse railing as the swimmers, long-legged and nervous, stepped to the edge of the dock and leaned into their starting positions. The sun-burned, freckled faces differed little from those of their older brothers and sisters who'd swum with me and Bryan. On my occasional visits to Rainy Lake now, I still see those faces poised on the lip of the dock. The children and teenagers I once knew stand in cheering clusters on the beach amidst a sea of strollers, pails, and shovels.

A dart whizzed by my right shoulder as I approached the horseshoe-shaped bar in the Tamarack.

"Watch out," Suzie Casey cried, brandishing a fistful of darts over her head.

Through the racks of beer mugs, I recognized Wade Fowler on the other side of the bar. He was talking to Val Johnson, whose father, Ned, owned the Tamarack. Val worked as a waitress in the Rainy Lake Lodge during the week and bar-tended there on weekends. She was tall and big-shouldered with ample breasts and hair bleached white as a toilet seat. She told great stories and had a foul mouth, which served her well when a boy copped a feel or spilled beer on one of the pool tables. Wade was scowling and I guessed Val was trying to talk him into going home.

The jukebox was playing "Nights in White Satin" by the Moody Blues. Ty Malone, wearing a green Polo shirt and bell-bottom jeans, was slow-dancing on the scuffed wooden floor with Ellen Casey, who had on a white halter top and tight black cutoffs.

An arm looped around my neck and I smelled the familiar combination of sawdust and marijuana.

"You came," Mike said, smiling down on me.

I wasn't sure whether Mike's keen interest in me this summer was brotherly or otherwise. He was still soft on Fern Daniels, who was playing as wide a field as usual, and he'd met Larry Salinger a few times. I preferred to think that Mike had simply extended his friendship from my brother to me.

"Give me a Bud, would you, Val?" I said.

Jimmy Piper motioned me over to a wooden booth next to the jukebox. Listening to his cynical, quick wit always made me laugh. Tonight he was laying it on thick about a professor at Villanova who'd given him a D in freshman English. That's why he was only up on weekends; he was taking a makeup class at Rutgers' Camden campus and working part-time at Sam Goody's near his home in Cherry Hill.

"Where's Terese this week?" he asked, as he always did.

"Cincinnati."

He swirled the beer at the bottom of the bottle. "She still seeing that same guy?"

I shook my head. "He transferred to Kennedy; she was kinda bored with him anyway. She's dating somebody she met on a flight home from Seattle. He's into pharmaceuticals."

Terese was a stewardess for TWA. She crisscrossed the United States daily and was studying French and Spanish in her spare time. At the rate she was progressing, she said, she'd have no trouble being accepted for the international routes as soon as there was an opening. When Carline had competed in the Nationals in Seattle last February, Terese maneuvered a free ticket for me on one of her flights. Terese didn't even blink when I spilled my 7-Up onto the lap of the man sitting next to me. She sopped it up with a white towel and replaced his magazine and my drink in minutes. She read the safety instructions in a suave, radio voice, deftly dispatched sixty lunches, and courteously rebuffed a thirtyish man in a steel-gray suit who wanted to buy her a drink in the airport. I was almost as proud of her as I was of Carline, who placed ninth in the Nationals, drawing the attention of the commentators with her maverick style.

Carline pulled off three triple jumps and two flawless double axels in her first performance, which she skated to "Lara's Theme" from *Dr. Zhivago*. But it was her sexy, raucous rendition of Chubby Checker's "The Twist," in which she wore a sequin-studded black body stocking, that earned her the highest marks and roused the audience with her footwork and odd-angled spins. As she bowed to the cheering crowd, Frieda and Marilyn tossed armfuls of red roses onto the ice.

Wishing Carline would breeze through in her fringed suede jacket and cowboy boots, I looked longingly toward the front door of the Tamarack. She'd been given a morning coaching job at the ice rink and was taking five credits in summer session at Staten Island Community College. She was thinking about a major in structural engineering. I no longer doubted Carline's ability to realize the goals she'd set for herself, especially with a 696 in math on her SATs.

I danced with Mike and then with Ty Malone, whose fine blonde hair smelled like Prell shampoo. Ty had maintained the family tradition by going to Yale, but he was majoring in sociology instead of pre-med. His brother Joe had been accepted at Georgetown for med school. Jimmy liked to razz Ty about Joe's thinning hair. Since Doc Malone had been bald ever since we could remember, we figured it was just a matter of time for Ty as well.

After slaying Suzie Casey at darts, I flipped through the selections in the jukebox. I was hunched over the glass, rolling a quarter between my thumb and forefinger, when I saw the blue T-bird through the window. I concentrated on the red letters, the way the needle descended on the black disc just before the music started. My head was swaddled in cotton batting, and I felt a painful compression in my chest.

Ginny Conroy called out his name in a high, happy voice and hollered to Val for another beer. I inclined my head just enough to see her arm resting on his shoulder. He was wearing jeans and a white T-shirt that set off the coppery dark skin of his arms and face. When Jimmy walked over to say hello, he blocked my view. I gripped the edge of the jukebox, trying to steady myself, and, when I turned to look again, Jimmy had moved and Billy was gazing straight at me. You rehearse this moment a hundred times, thinking you're ready. The face you knew better than anybody else's, that you've lain awake trying to remember. My legs were knee-deep in cement, and I couldn't take my eyes off him. I was stunned by how familiar he was and yet how changed.

He was bigger than I remembered, taller and more muscular. Age is a hard thing to describe: the skin stretched more tightly across the bones in his face, something speculative and watchful in the eyes. His hair was cut in a short Afro and that, plus his sun-darkened skin, made me notice how fair Ginny was in comparison. I slipped my quarter in the slot, punching "Judy Blue Eyes" by Crosby, Stills & Nash. Their voices spun a cocoon around me, and made it hard to move.

"Hi," he said.

He leaned one hip against the jukebox. An expression resembling surprise unfurled on his face, followed by a kind of immobilized excitement, as if he'd just seen a rainbow trout rise to the surface. I was unnerved by how intensely I wanted to reach out and touch him. It seemed impossible that all this time had passed, and yet it felt like it was yesterday.

"Can we sit down?" He steered me toward a booth. I was aware of the group gathered around Ginny at the bar. Their eyes were tracking Billy's purposeful movements and my naked face.

"I heard you were back," I said, surprised at how dry my throat was.

"I wrote you I was coming home. Didn't you get my letter?"

I ran my fingernail across the scarred wood tabletop. "I didn't read it."

His eyes narrowed slightly. "When did you stop reading my letters?"

"About four months ago, when I told you not to write anymore."

He kept me pinned against the booth with his eyes—big and determined, the color of evening sun on a patch of cattails.

"You look different," he said.

I braided my hands together, startled at how cold they were.

"How?"

He leaned forward. "Grown up, I guess. Takes my breath away just looking at you."

My eyes filled so fast I hadn't time to wink it back. This wasn't the way it was supposed to go. It was settled, four months back when I received his letter and decided, driving home from a movie with Larry Salinger, to end it there and then. We were two different people moving in separate directions. Sooner or later, one way or the other, it would end. Why pretend it wasn't so?

"I can't," I whispered.

"Can't what?"

"Can't do this . . . be with you, talk about us, anything. I gotta go."

"Danny."

He was too close. Grazing my hip on the corner of the table, I bolted past the bar and out the door. I was halfway across the parking lot when he caught up with me, gripping my elbow hard.

"*Stop*, Danny . . . please. Talk to me."

"You don't get it, do you? I don't want to talk to you. Look, I'd like to be friends but I can't, that's what I told you in my letter. It's bound to end eventually, you said as much in your letters, and I'd as soon it be now as later."

"I never said that. How do I know what's going to happen? You're eighteen years old, Danny, you're going to college in September. Are you saying you want to get *married*?"

"Of course not. You'd never marry me anyway. We're too different, remember?"

He sighed. "I was talking about the present, about understanding each other right now. There are things we need to face, that's all, if we're going to be in a relationship, if we're going to be friends even."

I glanced across the metal roofs of cars to the pale lines of the tennis court, where the nets resembled a web spun across the dark.

"I have another boyfriend."

"Larry, I know. How important is he?"

I scuffed my sandal across the loose gravel. "Kind of important."

"Are you in love with him?"

I formed the *yes* in my head but couldn't get past the painful squeeze in my throat. The door to the Tamarack slammed, and Mike's City College T-shirt appeared behind Billy's left shoulder.

"You OK, Danny?"

I shook my head to clear the blur his body made. "God, Mike, of course I'm OK."

"You owe me a game of pool," he said, keeping his eyes on Billy.

"Since when?" I asked.

He shifted his feet. Billy turned around so their two foreheads were inches apart. The bones were lining up in his jaw. "You got a problem, Mike?"

"Me? I don't have a problem, but Danny here . . . well, I'd like to see her safe inside."

"Look, Mike, I don't need you following me around. Billy is a friend of mine, like I told you. Now go back inside."

They sized each other up. The air was sharp as a knife between them. Studying their bodies, I knew that if they fought, Mike'd get the worst of it. He must have known it, too, although that wasn't why he shifted suddenly and ambled toward the highway. He'd focused on me finally, blinking in surprise at the implacable message on my face.

"Guys like that," Billy said, following Mike's path across the field, "are dangerous. At least with people like Bud Doonan you've got all your cards on the table."

"Mike's nothing like Bud Doonan. It's not about color, or your father either. He doesn't like the fact that you enlisted to go to Vietnam."

"Oh yeah?" His head swung round and I saw in the slow, slightly lopsided smile something new: not toughness exactly, nor bitterness either, more a sense of resignation about what he knew.

"You think it has nothing to do with color, or where you come from? You think because Mike joined a civil rights march on campus, or votes Democratic, that he's innocent? Let me tell you something, Danny. If the men in white sheets showed up at the Tamarack looking for me, Mike wouldn't lift a finger to stop them."

You're blowing things out of proportion, I wanted to say. *Just ignore it.* But then I remembered Marcella Dove's counsel that night in her kitchen, about why it was possible for me to ignore it when Billy couldn't. So I remained silent. I didn't agree with Billy's assessment of Mike Cooper's character. What was important was that *he* believed it, and that I try to see it through his eyes.

"Are you in love with him?" he asked again.

When I didn't answer he took my hand and led me toward the T-bird. I sat stiffly against the door as he drove into the blue-black wilderness beyond Tamarack Road. Neither one of us spoke. Billy didn't touch me again, and I don't remember even looking at him, although after a while I felt a stirring in that deep, unremembered place that had been blocked off since my brother died, and I could see clearly the brindled ridges on the trunks of trees, leaves the color of myrtle, the road daisies blooming white and yellow.

We didn't make love that night, or the next, or the night after that. When he arrived at the house to pick me up, my mother mentioned the flowers Marcella had sent to Bryan's funeral, how beautiful they were and that she regretted never having thanked her in person. They chatted politely and in general terms about his tour of duty in Vietnam. Did he ever get seasick, what was the food like, was he very homesick? On the few occasions on which my father was present, he quizzed Billy about the planes and the morale of the pilots who were actually seeing action. Billy was generous and detailed in his answers, which pleased Charlie and prompted him to share some of his own combat stories.

When we walked across the bridge, Billy's hand resting lightly on the waistband of my shorts, I could feel my parents' scrutiny. Any protest they might have made had been silenced by the decisive way in which I'd explained our friendship. I'm sure they were reassured by the fact that he was only on leave, after all, and that come September we'd be thousands of miles apart.

When I worked the late shift, Billy showed up at Dottie's Cake Box at closing and helped me carry trays of cakes and pastries into the back. I saved hard rolls and pumpernickle bread for him. I taught him how to decorate a birthday cake, and laughed at the awkward, heart-shaped leaves he drew from a cone filled with green butter cream. It was nice in the back room, empty and peaceful, surrounded as we were by the sweet, yeasty remnants of an industrious day. The employees had made a small lounge area against the back wall: two easy chairs and a sagging couch covered in a cheerful, poppy-strewn print.

It was here that Billy told me about Les Baylor, who'd returned from a mission drooling out of the corner of his mouth, unable to see anything but the balls of flame running across the cratered ground and the bottom of the chopper stippled with blood. Or Bo Angel, who was rescued from the smouldering fuselage of his plane with the charred stumps of his legs oozing like melted butter. Billy described long days on the ship, the thousand small ways you passed the time, the men and their stories: Cy Wheaton from Wilmington, Delaware, whose grandparents were buried with their pink Cadillac in the backyard; Caesar Spoon from Louisville, Kentucky, whose sister had given birth to Siamese twins joined at the shoulder; Bobby Davis from Milwaukee, who burned two vigil lights each night to ward off the ghosts of dead Vietcong.

He gave me books to read: *Cane* by Jean Toomer, *Invisible*

Man by Ralph Ellison, poems by Langston Hughes. I was glad the routine of Navy life had provided him with the time and impetus to read. He gladly wrote down books I recommended: *The Old Man and the Sea* by Hemingway, *Catcher in the Rye* by J. D. Salinger, *The Heart Is a Lonely Hunter* by Carson McCullers.

It took him a while to finish *Jane Eyre,* he said; he'd started and stopped three times. He thought Rochester was a bore. Jane would have been better off belting him on the side of the head. And what about Bertha? They had her in a *cage*! Didn't anybody understand the woman was insane, that she couldn't help what she did?

"There are men in prison with my father who are sick like that, or caught up by circumstances beyond their control. Then there are men who are just plain evil. There's a difference, you know, my father says you can almost smell it."

He'd visited his father before returning home. He'd appeared at the prison in his uniform with a photograph of Douglass standing on the deck of the U.S.S. Saratoga.

"How much longer does he have?" I asked.

He shook his head. "A long time. I think about Lloyd Sloane sometimes, and his family. I'm sorry for what my father did, although I understand how it can happen. I see the way these fights break out. A guy changes the station on the radio, makes a crack about your hair, your mother, the girls whose pictures you have pinned inside your locker. You're sitting around with time on your hands, things escalate. My father's temper . . . it's gotten him into plenty of trouble. Lloyd and some of the other men rode him all the time. 'Come on, tell us, what's it like sleeping with a black woman?' Shit like that. If he hadn't been carrying that knife . . . " He patted his back pocket. "Hell, I carry a pocketknife all the time. You don't want to be caught in some bar overseas with a Marine who sees you dancing with a white woman."

He laughed. "We've always been considered trash by the people at Rainy, since my mother's black and we live on Spirit

271

Road, but when my father stabbed Lloyd Sloane it was as if we were suddenly subhuman. People treated us like we were all criminals. My mother still feels it. The guys on the ship, though, they don't hold it against me. Some of them have stories worse than mine."

It was on one of those occasions, as the two of us sat shoulder to shoulder on the couch, that I took him through Bryan's final day. Things were coming back to me. You protect yourself by forgetting, taking in as much as you can bear and blotting out the rest. Even now when I recall that day—the first glimpse of my brother in the bottom of the boat, the ragdoll flop of his head, my father's eyes, and May's keening cry—I wonder how I stood it. You don't process the details at the time; they get stored away until you're ready for them to surface one by one. Every day another moment had returned: the creak of Bryan's bunkbed, the bells of the pinball machine, the smell of bacon, their hateful voices, the music—Jim Morrison, Country Joe McDonald, Joan Baez singing "Joe Hill." I can see my brother's chalky skin, the black rosary beads wound around his fingers, his hair stiff with hairspray.

I hadn't cried that hard the day Bryan died or after the funeral or on all those tearful nights alone in the house. It's as though you've traveled down and down looking for answers, wishing your life back, wanting him to walk through the door just one more time, wanting to speak to him, to *stop* it somehow, and you can't. You want to believe what the nuns taught you, that there is a place where you'll meet again in some fashion, but it won't be for years and years and by then you may not even remember. That's the thing you can't come to terms with, that you'll *never* see him again. It can obliterate you, this knowledge. You turn inside out, unable to stop the painful heave your weeping makes.

Billy didn't say anything. It was his silence and the reassuring motion of his hand on the small of my back that enabled me to journey back into that well, to see it all again or maybe for the first time, no longer shielded by the shock. I was touched, as I had been in the past, by Billy's kindness, a quality that has led me then and now to my truest friends.

*

When he kissed me, we were sitting on his front steps eating the rhubarb pie his mother had baked, two weeks after he'd come home and halfway through his leave. There'd been many moments before this when I'd have gambled on either one of us making a move, but it hadn't happened. Marcella had cooked us dinner: fried chicken, kale and collard greens, candied yams, and biscuits. She sat across from me in a saffron-colored dress that pulled the gold from her skin. When she left for choir practice, she handed us two slices of steaming pie.

"You're too skinny—eat!" Her nylons grazed my arm as she hurried down the steps.

I tasted the tart rhubarb on Billy's tongue, smelled the honeyed fragrance of his hair and water lapping against my face and into my open mouth. I'd never been in his room before, never seen the green plaid blanket on his iron bed, the wooden lamp, the snowflake-shaped water stain in the corner of the ceiling. His pillow was hard and flat, the kind you mold to your chest. Our bodies were different; two years had added flesh to mine and hard muscle to his.

There was one instant, when Billy was deep inside me, his back arched and the bones in his face almost visible, that I wanted to run from the room, leaving behind the malted light and sudden vault of pleasure. I knew that on the other side of this thin wall lay the encroaching dark and slow, endless falling. As if he read my thoughts, Billy covered my hands with his. So I gave myself over, sailing with open eyes into that white ether where you can fall as far as you climb, where there's no safety from suffering, where you're as full and real as you're ever going to be.

*

273

The yearning to have said good-bye never goes away. It intrudes upon all the simple, mundane acts of your life: cleaning the bathroom, finishing the last line of a letter, dropping your child off at school. It may be just the fraction of an instant but you weigh it, each departure meaning something.

The day before Billy was to fly out I called in sick at the bakery so we could go fishing on the Virgin. He caught three rainbows with the dry flies I'd made him. It was sunny and by midafternoon so hot that we stripped off our gear and lay down in the river to cool off. That's the moment that stays with me, not the next morning in Newark Airport as he strolled toward the runway, his duffel bag slung over his shoulder. I remember the water and glossy, furred stones, the painful glow of goldenrod on the bank. My head was rolled back between my shoulders, my eyes closed, when he started talking.

"I didn't want to love you, not that summer after you hurt your arm, not when we slept together, not on the boat when I'd get your letters, not even that night at the Tamarack when I saw you standing by the jukebox."

He sighed. "But there's something that happens when I'm with you, just seeing your face or hearing your voice . . . everything else disappears for me." He rolled over so that I had to look at him. "I love you, Danny, and I'm not going to let you go easily. Nobody else has come close, not even once."

I ran my thumb across his cheekbone. "There's a price for everything, isn't there? You pay if you have it and you let it go, you pay if you try to hold on. Maybe that's what we're supposed to learn, which one will offer us the better life."

*

I set up a dinner with Carline and Terese on my last weekend. We agreed to make dinner together at Carline's, where we could use Frieda's spices, her jelly roll and soufflé pans, the little tools for mashing garlic cloves and slicing eggs into perfect slices. Terese arranged cloth napkins into fans and poured

Sangria into pink-tinted glasses. In her apple-green sundress and lace-up sandals, with her bobbed hair and flawless make-up, she matched the coiffed table setting. Carline made me laugh, as she stood at the counter with her white hair pinned carelessly back, skin-tight denim shorts barely covering her small ass.

"What's so funny?" she asked.

"Nothing." I watched her long fingers as they plucked cilantro leaves for the salad.

"Beer for me, Terese," Carline called.

We talked about Ann Arbor, about Terese's latest attempts to master Italian, about whether Carline should start her engineering courses now or skate competitively for another year.

"It takes so much time and money," she said, "and I don't think I'll go much higher. Some of the girls coming up are as good as I am, and they're only *fourteen*."

"Is it hard to think of giving it up?" Terese asked.

"Sometimes. If I devoted my whole life to it next year, I might do better, but I keep asking myself, what would that *mean?* For some girls it would mean *everything*, which is the way it should be, but not for me, not anymore. Coaching's all right, I can always do that. I think maybe it's time to focus on something else."

"Well, it'll take you a while to get through an engineering program, so you might as well start." I said. "God, engineering . . . it'd be like studying Chinese for me."

"I'd like to study Chinese," Terese said.

Carline laughed. "I don't know how you do it, Terese. I have a hard enough time with English." She refilled my wine glass. "What do *you* want to study?"

I gazed through the screen door at the floating dock in the middle of the cove.

"Everything, I guess: history, psychology, literature. Sometimes I think about becoming a writer. I'd like to bring my family back again the way we were in the beginning. If I wrote about our life since coming to Rainy, maybe I'd understand what happened."

Later, after we'd cleaned up and gone out to the dock, I passed around chocolate chip cookies from the bakery. "You think Billy will go to college?" Carline asked.

"I doubt it. He wants to work on planes," I said.

"He could get a degree in mechanical engineering, then he could design planes at Boeing or someplace like that," Carline said.

I shook my head. "He likes being a mechanic. I might be wrong—anything can happen—but he'll probably get a job working for an airline. Of course, he and Douglass still talk about running their own business, you know, repairing engines and stuff."

"You're going to see other guys, aren't you, when you go away to school?" Terese asked.

"I suppose so."

"That's good. You shouldn't settle on one boy too early." I noted the careful way she'd phrased her words.

"What if I stayed with Billy, would that bother you?" I rolled the bakery bag back and forth between my knees.

Her eyes darted from Carline to me. "It's just, well, I can't quite picture you *married* to him."

"Why not?"

"Come on, Danny, living in one of those houses on Spirit Road? What if you had a child, have you thought about that?"

I laughed. "Who says we'd live on Spirit Road?"

"I think she's talking about what your life would be like if you stayed with Billy Dove," Carline said quietly.

"I know exactly what she's talking about. Look, I understand it a lot better than either of you do, and I've just scratched the surface. If Billy and I stay together, you two will have to come along with me or you'll get left behind, simple as that. As for now, I'm too young to make any plans. I'm trying to concentrate on the present, on going away to college."

276

"We're just thinking about your best interests, Danny," Carline said.

I smiled ruefully. "I can tell you this much, if I ever do get married, I'd want to be sure I had the real thing, like I have with Billy, and I'd want it to last. You have to be vigilant, you know, because it slips away."

"I'll say," said Carline, "but then sometimes it's better, 'specially if you're married to some bonehead."

"That's what I meant by starting out with the real thing," I said.

"How do you know if you even have it?" Terese asked.

Carline's gaze was locked on the western rim of Weaver House Cove, where the smudge of trees on the shore formed a doorway into the big middle of the lake. "You just do," she said softly.

"Some people get it back," Terese said.

"Some people are given everything they could ever want, and they don't take care of it. That's the worst, having had something really priceless and losing it." I pointed to the first star. "Look."

Carline rested her head on my shoulder. "I don't know that I'll get a second chance with loving someone. I had my number the first time round."

I touched the ball of hair on her neck. "Sure you will, Carl. Your capacity is boundless."

Once dark had fallen, and spindles of light had formed a ring around the cove, we piled our clothes in Gerry Gland's old rowboat and dove into the lake. Our bodies stole through the greenish-black water like glowworms, recoiling when we touched the mushy bottom or the algae-covered sides of the boat.

"Race you!" Carline headed toward the floating dock.

We took turns diving, laughing at our naked breasts and the pale moons our buttocks made as we stood with our legs straight and arms outstretched at the edge of the dock. I remember the lambent surfaces of our bodies and the basslike echo we made as we bobbed between the barrels. Eventually, we lay side by side on our backs and called out the names of constellations. We lay for a long time, mesmerized by the torrent of stars and the riffled sound of water.

*

I wonder often what I would have done with my life if my brother had lived. Certainly I would not have written this book. Would I have written at all? That's the scary part. The irony is that Bryan, more than anybody else, believed in me. He'd have been so disappointed if I'd continued to coast along, exerting minimum pressure on myself, and yet his absence made me visible. It's been one of the most painful truths I've had to learn.

When I visit Rainy Lake now, it amazes me how little things have changed. The Cyclone fence, the sand, the lifeguard chair tipped on its side like the husk of a primeval animal. The water is sibilant and constant, the smell so raw that I can close my eyes and there I am—twelve years old again, straining to finish my twenty-five laps. I walk across the clubhouse porch and stand at the far end, looking out on the biggest part of the lake.

It is raining. The scene is as loud and black as the memory of my father's face as he passes alongside me in the boat. I lift my hand to stop him but I can't. Just as I can't erase the smell of my brother's skin or the shadow he made, inches higher than mine. Or the dark, sweet face of Billy Dove standing waist-high in the reeds of Disappointment Lake.

About the Author

Mary François Rockcastle has a B.A. in English from Douglass College (Rutgers University, New Jersey) and an M.A. in Creative Writing from the University of Minnesota. She currently teaches in the Master's of Liberal Studies program at Hamline University and lives in Minneapolis with her husband and two daughters.